A BRIGHTNESS LONG AGO

GUY GAVRIEL KAY

HODDER &
STOUGHTON

First published in Great Britain in 2019 by Hodder & Stoughton
An Hachette UK company

1

Copyright © Guy Gavriel Kay 2019
Map © Martin Springett 2019

A CIP catalogue record for this title is available from the British Library

Hardback ISBN 978 1 473 69233 6
Trade Paperback ISBN 978 1 473 69234 3
eBook ISBN 978 1 473 69235 0

Printed and bound in Great Britain by Clays Ltd, Elcograf S.p.A.

Hodder & Stoughton policy is to use papers that are natural, renewable and recyclable products and made from wood grown in sustainable forests. The logging and manufacturing processes are expected to conform to the environmental regulations of the country of origin.

Hodder & Stoughton Ltd
Carmelite House
50 Victoria Embankment
London EC4Y 0DZ

www.hodder.co.uk

The celestial spheres endlessly resound.
But an instant is invincible in memory.
It comes back in the middle of the night. Who are those holding torches,
So that what is long past occurs in full light?

—CZESŁAW MIŁOSZ

VARENA•

BARIGNAN•

FIRENTA•

DONDI• ACORSI•

BISCHIO•

AVEGNA•

ROSSO•

MYLASIA•

REMIGIO•

RHODIAS•

SARANTIUM◎

SAURADIA

•SENJAN

•MEGARIUM

•DUBRAVA

SERESSINI
SEA

PRINCIPAL CHARACTERS

(Characters are generally situated in their city of origin, not necessarily where they are when first encountered in the text.)

In Seressa

Guidanio Cerra, also called Danio, and sometimes Danino
Alviso, his cousin, a bookseller in Seressa
Brunetto Duso, a guard
Duke Lucino Conti, afflicted by a stroke
Ricci, acting as duke

Petronella ⎫
Dario ⎬ neighbours of Guidanio
Maurizio ⎭

In Macera

Duke Arimanno Ripoli
Corinna, his wife
Adria, their youngest daughter

In Acorsi

Folco Cino d'Acorsi, lord of Acorsi, a mercenary commander
Caterina Ripoli d'Acorsi, his wife, sister to Duke Arimanno
    of Macera

Folco's men:
Aldo, his cousin and second-in-command
Gian
Coppo Peralta
Leone

Vanetta, Folco's sister (deceased)

In Remigio

Teobaldo Monticola di Remigio, lord of Remigio, a mercenary
    commander
Ginevra della Valle, his mistress, mother of his two young sons
Trussio, his oldest son by his late wife
Gherardo Monticola, brother to Teobaldo, chancellor of Remigio

Monticola's men:
Gaetan, his second-in-command, from Ferrieres
Collucio, a captain in his company

In Avegna

Guarino Peselli, founder of the celebrated school there
Erizzio and Evardo Ricciardiano, brothers ruling in Avegna

In Mylasia

Count Uberto of Mylasia, called "the Beast"
Novarro, his chancellor
Morani di Rosso, chief steward of the palace
Opicino Valeri, a merchant
Erigio, his eldest son

In Firenta

Piero Sardi, a banker, ruling Firenta
Versano, his older son
Antenami, his younger son
Ariberti Boriforte, a military leader

In Rhodias

High Patriarch Scarsone Sardi, nephew to Piero

In Bischio

Carderio Sacchetti, a shoemaker
Mina Sacchetti, his aunt
Leora, his daughter
Carlo Serrana, a rider in Bischio's race

Also

Jelena, an itinerant healer
Brother Nardo Sarzerola, a cleric
Goro Calmetta, a merchant of the city of Rosso
Matteo Mercati, a celebrated artist
Gurçu, khalif of the Asharites, besieging Sarantium

PART ONE

CHAPTER I

A man no longer young in a large room at night. There are lanterns
and lamps, torches in brackets, a handsome table, tall, shuttered win-
dows, paintings in shadow on the walls. He is not alone. Even so, he finds
his mind turning back to when he was, indeed, still young. We all do
that. A scent carries us, a voice, a name, a person who reminds us of
someone we knew . . .

There are events going forward in this moment, but there is also a
delay, a pause in the rush of people coming and going, and the past is
closer at night.

He is thinking of a story from when he was learning the world and
his place in it. He cannot tell all the tale, and he won't. We see only
glimpses of history, even our own. It is not entirely ours—in memory,
in writing it down, in hearing or in reading it. We can reclaim only
part of the past. Sometimes it is enough . . .

The sailors say the rain misses the cloud even as it falls through light
or dark into the sea. I miss her like that as I fall through my life,
through time, the chaos of our time. I dream of her some nights,

3

still, but there is nothing to give weight or value to that, it is only me, and what I want to be true. It is only longing.

I REMEMBER THAT autumn night very well. It would be odd if I didn't, since it set me on a different path from the one I'd thought I was on. It changed the arc of my days, as Guarino might have put it. I could easily have died. No arc at all, if so. I had images of knives come into my mind for a long time after. The one I carried, the one that had been used before my own.

I owe my life to Morani di Rosso. I light candles to his memory. He was a good man; I think it is fair to say any friend of Guarino's had to be. Morani was chief steward of the palace in Mylasia. He had accepted me on Guarino's recommendation. Which is why I was in the palace on the night Uberto the count, also named the Beast, was killed by the girl.

It seems necessary to say that though I was a pupil in Guarino's school it was not because my father had any rank at all. Guarino, the best man of our time I believe, when invited to open a school at the court in Avegna made it a condition that he be allowed to admit a number of lesser-born children—clever ones, showing signs of promise—to be educated with the sons and some of the daughters of nobility.

I was admitted that way. My father was a tailor in Seressa. I feel no shame in saying that. I know what he was, I know what I was, and am. The cleric in our neighbourhood sanctuary by the great canal was the one who noticed me. I had quickness, he declared, was a well-formed, well-mannered young man, had taken easily to my letters and numbers.

Tailors in Seressa (and elsewhere) do have a little status. They enter the homes and intimate chambers of the great, conversing with them at fittings, learning their needs (not just in clothing), sometimes guiding those needs. Ours is a time when public display matters. Most times are, I suppose.

At our cleric's urging, my father mentioned me to one of his patrons, a member of the Council of Twelve, then the cleric wrote a letter to that same man, and . . . matters were set in motion. I have a memory of my mother the morning I left—she saved a yellow bird from the cat. She chased the cat away, then turned and hugged me goodbye. I don't know if she cried; if she did, it was after I had gone.

I spent seven years with Guarino in Avegna. There is a bust of him now in a palace courtyard there, outside the rooms where the school used to be. The school has been closed for years. Guarino is gone, my father (Jad defend his soul) is gone, many of those who mattered in my life are. It happens if you live long enough.

In that school in Avegna I lived through and left my childhood. I learned to write with skill, not merely competence. To speak gracefully in good company and debate with clarity. To deal with weapons and the new form of accounting. To sing (with less grace, in truth), and to ride and handle horses—which became my joy in life.

I learned to address my betters properly and my equals and inferiors also properly, and to do so with at least an illusion of ease. I was taught something of the history of Batiara and of events in our own time—though we were spoken to carefully as to that last, because certain things were not said, even at the school. Towards the end, I was helping with the younger students. I was in no great hurry to leave that sheltered place.

Some of us learned to read texts of the Ancients. We learned of Sarantium in the east, the City of Cities, what it had been a thousand years ago, what it was now, and how the Asharites, the star-worshippers, threatened it in our time. We heard tales of emperors and charioteers.

Those languages and stories of the past, along with access to Avegna's palace horses, were a good part of why I stayed with my teacher longer than most. Those things, and loving him.

I had begun to think I might become a bookseller and bookbinder at home in Seressa where the trade was growing, but Guarino said I was suited to serve at a court, to use and share what he'd taught me. He regarded that as part of his task, sending men and sometimes women into the world to have an influence, guide others towards a better way to be, during a time when violent men were ruling and warring through Batiara and beyond.

Time enough to make and sell books later, he said—if you decide you want that. But first, take a position where you can give back some of what you have been given here.

He'd written a letter to an old friend, which is how Morani di Rosso and Mylasia came into my life. Morani offered me a position at the court there. The Beast's court.

We make our own choices sometimes, sometimes they are made for us.

I've thought often about what my life might have been had I gone home to Seressa instead and opened or joined in running a bookshop. My cousin Alviso had just started one, alongside one of the smaller canals. But Alviso hadn't been to the celebrated school in Avegna. He hadn't had that gift in his life. Opportunities given are responsibilities. They taught us that.

So, I went to Mylasia. There were and there are bad men ruling some of the larger and smaller city-states of Batiara, but I don't think many would dispute that Uberto of Mylasia was among the very worst in those days.

It was interesting, I suppose it still is, how vicious men can take power and be accepted, supported by those they govern, if they bring with them a measure of peace. If granaries are full and citizens fed. If war doesn't bring starvation to the walls. Uberto was a man who had sealed an enemy in a cask to see if he might observe the soul escaping when his prisoner died.

If men and women are to be killed we want that to happen somewhere else. We are like that, even as we pray. In these years, as hired armies go up and down the hills and river valleys, fighting for a city-state that's hired them or raiding for themselves, as High

Patriarchs war with half the nobility and conspire with the other half, some have seen the conflicts of the great as sweet, seductive chances to expand their own power.

Villages and towns are destroyed by angry, hungry soldiers, then sacked again a year later. Famine comes, and disease with it. In times of hard peril, a leader strong enough—and feared enough—to keep his city safe will be permitted a great deal in terms of viciousness, what he does within his palace.

There was no secret to it. Uberto of Mylasia was well known for what happened in his chambers at night when the mood was upon him. There were stories of youthful bodies carried out through the smaller palace gates in the dark, dead and marred. And good men still served him—making their peace with our god as best they could.

Balancing acts of the soul. Acquiescence happens more than its opposite—a rising up in anger and rejection. There are wolves in the world, inside elegant palaces as well as in the dark woods and the wild.

People sent their daughters away from Mylasia and the nearby farms in those years because Uberto was what he was. When young girls sufficiently appealing were not readily found, he had boys brought to him.

It was known, as I say. We'd heard the tales in Avegna. Some of the others at school, better born than I, had even joked that having women brought to them (no one joked about the boys, it would have been a risky jest) was one of the appealing aspects of power. They didn't talk—to be fair—about *killing* them, just the pleasures of a night, or more than one.

Uberto never had anyone brought for more than one night. Most of his guests survived, went home, were even rewarded with coins—given that marriage would be difficult for the girls, after, and the boys were shamed.

Not all left his palace alive, however. Not all of them did.

THE FIRST WAY I might have died that windy autumn night was if
Morani had not sent me for wine by way of the servants' stairs
when word came that the girl had arrived.

When someone was brought to the count at night, Morani took
the post outside Uberto's chambers himself. As if he would not burden
another soul with what this was. He had done so for years, apparently.

That summer and fall he liked me to stay with him before and
after the arrival—but not when the girl or boy came up the stairs.
This had happened three times already. That night was the fourth.
I do not believe in sacred numbers, I am just telling my story as I
remember it.

Outside the count's rooms Morani and I would converse of the
wisdom of the past. I'd recite poetry for him, on request, while behind
the door Uberto did what he did. We would hear things sometimes.
Morani's face would be sorrowful, and I thought I saw other things in
him, too. Mostly he would keep me talking—about philosophers,
precepts of restraint, learned indifference to fortune's wheel. He'd
drink the wine I'd brought up, but never too much.

He couldn't protect me from knowing what was happening, only
from being part of sending someone in. He did have me stay with
him after. Perhaps he found it hard to be there alone. Perhaps he
thought I needed to learn some of the dark things about the world,
alongside the bright ones. In certain ways, I have since thought, that
is the condition of Batiara in our time: art and philosophy, and beasts.

Had I been standing beside him when the girl was led up the
staircase between torches, had the guards who brought her seen me
with him there, I'd have been held equally responsible, without any
least doubt, for what ensued.

But they did not see me. Only Morani was there to greet her
gently, usher her through the door after searching her, carefully, for
any weapon she might have. The guards would have done so downstairs already, but as the palace's chief steward, Morani was formally
responsible outside that door.

I *was* there, however. I did see her.

I had come back up with the wine flask already, was standing in the shadows on the back stairs, out of sight of the guards and the girl, but with a view of them. And so I saw who she was.

I didn't believe she'd have remembered me at all, had I been visible, but I knew her on sight. It hadn't been so long. And I realized, immediately, that something was wrong.

I did nothing, I said nothing. I let it happen.

Morani di Rosso's death is on me, you may fairly say. I owed him a great deal, I liked him a great deal. He was a kind man, and had small children, and I recognized the woman and still let things proceed to where they went, which included his execution and dismemberment in the square not long after.

I have often thought that the world the god has made—in our time, at least—is not generally kind to good men. I do not know what that says about me and my own life.

We accumulate sins and guilt, just by moving through our days, making choices, doing, not doing. His is a death for which I will be judged. There are others.

⊙̶⊙

She saw the outline of a servant in the shadows of the second stairway. He held something, probably wine. He didn't matter. What mattered was appearing anxious for the steward, but not fearful to a degree that might suggest something to hide. She remembered to seem awkward in the good clothing they'd sent from the palace for her.

They had discussed this when the plan was conceived, when she'd agreed to do this, though Folco had made clear it was only a thought, an idea. He couldn't command her. Of course not. He'd said he was fairly certain this could work.

She'd believed him. He wouldn't send her to her death, not for Mylasia. Not for anything, really. Death would be something she could avoid while achieving what he wanted. She was a weapon for him, and no good commander wasted weapons. She was also his niece.

She'd said yes, no hesitation. She wasn't, by nature, inclined to hesitation. There were many reasons to agree. Uberto of Mylasia summoned children and killed them, for one thing. She wasn't a soft person, not given her own family, but Uberto . . . offended her. She had never killed anyone, so there was that, an awareness within her tonight. It wasn't hard to let the steward see her as anxious. She was. She smiled at him, tremulously. She was a good actress, it was a part of why she was useful.

The steward introduced himself, gently. He searched her for weapons, as the guards had. They'd enjoyed themselves; he did so with dignity, but he was thorough.

"What is your name, girl?" he asked.

She used the name they'd made up when she'd moved to the farm outside the walls four months ago.

The couple who'd been paid to pretend she was their relative, coming to them after the death of her mother, would be leaving tonight. They should be moving now, in fact, as fast as they could in the autumn darkness. Their hope would be chaos in the palace and city, delaying investigation and pursuit—no one with the power and clarity to order it.

Part of the transaction had been a horse and cart that would be waiting for them, and more silver than they'd ever seen in hard lives. They'd leave their farm with almost no belongings, a fire left on the hearth, smoke rising, so as not to arouse suspicions. They had taken a great risk, but you did that to get ahead in life. Folco's captains were good at judging people and they'd chosen well. Adria wished that couple luck, but she didn't spend time thinking about them. Fortune was capricious, and faith was challenging for her, for various reasons.

"He is in a quiet mood tonight," the steward said.

She had no idea if that was true, or just meant to ease her own observed fear. She nodded. She said, softly, "Is that good, my lord?"

He sighed. He was grieving for her, she saw it. She didn't care. He was still sending her in to that man, wasn't he?

It didn't matter. One way or another—whether she did what she'd come to do, or she failed inside that room—this man, di Rosso, was now in mortal danger. Unless, right now, searching her . . .

He turned up nothing. It was possible a woman might have noticed, but unlikely, and there wouldn't be a woman here.

Folco had someone from Esperaña in his service now and the man had skills not widely known in Batiara. She'd been afraid, preparing herself, after the summons came to the farmhouse—but fear was something you mastered, not a thing that defined you. Folco told all of them that, often. You didn't deny you felt it, you ruled it.

She was older than the very young girls Uberto preferred, and probably too tall, but she was a handsome woman, and there weren't many of those left in or around Mylasia. She had never come to market, that would have been too obvious, too much an invitation, but she'd not hidden herself from those on nearby farms, and there were always people who would tell the palace guards of a likely girl, for coins. They'd counted on that happening. People were usually predictable if you thought about things enough. Folco also said that all the time.

She wished a bad death to the man who'd told the guards, however.

It might have been a woman, of course. She preferred not to think so, but how could you ever know? People were ferociously poor. Farmers were abused everywhere, taxed mercilessly to keep the artisans and merchants in the cities happier with their lords—and so less dangerous. Even Folco did that in Acorsi. A few extra coins on a farm as winter came might mean firewood, food, could keep someone alive, with their children.

Everyone wanted something they didn't have; it might be as simple as bread or warmth. Gurçu, leader of the Asharites in the east, wanted to take Sarantium, the City of Cities. She herself wanted more freedom than the world wished to give a woman. Some people wanted love.

Folco wanted Mylasia. It was a move in a long game against an old enemy, and not Uberto, either.

It was unlikely he'd be able to claim the city immediately, but there was a chance of it, in the disruption she could cause tonight. And even the threat of Folco moving nearer would unsettle Teobaldo Monticola, whose city and lands lay south of here—and a reckless, violent man like Monticola might make mistakes when unsettled.

She had learned some time ago that the hatred between Folco Cino d'Acorsi and Monticola di Remigio was a large thing in the world, this part of it at least.

It had brought her here tonight, hadn't it? To this palace. Her own choice. She told herself that. It was almost true.

"If he's quieter it almost always means a calmer night," the steward said, answering her question. *Calmer*, she thought. "Be . . . agreeable, but not eager. He likes . . . the count likes a sense that a girl knows nothing of . . . these matters."

"I am a maiden still," she said. It happened to be the truth.

"Of course, of course!" he said quickly. She saw him blush by lamplight. He cleared his throat. "I will be waiting. Right here."

"Why, my lord?" she asked. A little reckless.

"Well, to call the guards to take you home, after."

"Oh," she said. "There's that, then. I thank you." She spoke with a country accent. "Will he hurt me?" she asked. It seemed the sort of thing a girl might ask, with the tales told.

He looked away. "Just . . . be agreeable. As I said, he's quiet tonight."

"Yes, my lord," she said.

She could still see the outline of that figure on the servants' stairway. The two guards had gone back down the main staircase.

"Come now," said the steward. He led her to a heavy door. He knocked, softly.

"Send her in to me," came a voice, immediately. Hearing it, she did feel a great fear. The steward opened the door.

Adria walked in. The steward shut the door behind her.

A handsome room. She had been raised in a larger, wealthier palace or she'd have been overawed. She needed to appear so, she reminded herself.

There were windows on either side of a built-up fire on the far wall. Another door to her left, ajar. That would lead to inner chambers. A patterned carpet on the floor to one side of the room, in front of a second fireplace. Lamps on tables for more light, wine on one table. A mostly finished flask, she saw.

To her left, on the wall with the partly open door, was a bed. There was no carpeting there, and the wooden floor was stained darker in places. She knew what that would be. She would not yield to fear, she told herself. Two tapestries were on the wall to her right. Firelight illuminated them. Both were hunting scenes. He thought he was hunting her.

She was here to make that not be so. He was a wild beast and she was the hunter tonight. She had hunted animals all her life, in the woods outside their own palace. The thought gave her courage. She smiled, tremulously again, and sank to the carpet on her knees in an awkward salute. She lowered her head, clasped her hands, did not speak. It would be a grave presumption for a farm girl to speak to the count of Mylasia before she was instructed to do so.

"Stand," was what he said, a rich, smooth voice. "I will look at you."

She stood up quickly. Kept her head lowered. He ordered her to lift it. She did. She was careful not to meet his eyes. He wore a blue silk robe, loosely tied. There was nothing under it. He was a big man, not young, but with dark hair still. He had been a war leader, commanded armies, won himself a city with a sword. It happened that way, often. Folco was a mercenary too.

But Folco was not like this man. This one was a monster, and she had come into his den. Firelight wavered. *My choice*, Adria told herself again.

"You are so old," the count of Mylasia said. "Goods left on a merchant's table in the sun. Fading, as all bright things fade." It sounded like poetry. She hadn't had time in her life to learn much poetry. "Unfasten your buttons," he said. "Do that. Show yourself."

She stared at him, eyes widening. She almost bit her lip, remembered in time. He smiled, came nearer. He laid a hand on her arm, not harshly, just to move her towards one fire. For light, she realized. He wanted to see her. She was trembling. It wasn't an act. You didn't deny fear, you mastered it. She brought her hands to the buttons of the gown they'd brought to the farm for her. The bodice was green. The sleeves detached, they were a russet colour, as was the fall of the long gown towards her ankles.

He watched. His eyes were on her fingers. The buttons were stiff, it wasn't hard to make it seem as though such items were new to her, a tall, awkward farm girl used to wearing a knee-length tunic pulled on over her head. If he checked her hands they would be rough. She'd been here for months, and had been doing outdoor work in Acorsi before coming south. Folco had suggested that. He was a man who prepared.

The count stepped back a little, watching narrowly. She finished with the buttons and the upper part of the gown fell open.

"Old," Uberto said again. He was looking at her breasts, not her hands. "Too tall, too old. Overripe fruit and flesh. And a thin mouth."

She needed him to kiss her. Or she had to kiss his hand. She needed him not to know she wanted that. Everyone wanted something, she thought. He came nearer again. She twisted her head away.

"No," said Count Uberto of Mylasia. "No. You do not turn away. Not from me."

She kept silent. He laid two fingers of his left hand on her cheek and forced her head back to face his. She shivered. He smiled, seeing that. *He enjoys when they are afraid*, she thought.

Then he moved that hand from her cheek to the back of her head, clutching her hair, and he pulled her to him, his mouth covering hers, hard, heavy.

And in the same moment he stabbed her in the thigh with a blade in his right hand.

Adria screamed. Pain in a swift, hard wave, and she knew this man might have poison on his blade.

As she had poison on her mouth.

Second coating of what she wore on her lips, the under-layer protecting her from killing herself with it. Or so the man from Esperaña had promised back in Acorsi.

Uberto twisted his knife then pulled it out. Pain ripped right through Adria, and despair. She staggered. He let her fall back, watching avidly.

"My lord!" she cried. "Why . . . ?"

"It hurts, does it? There is pain in the deeper pleasures," said the man who ruled here. "You will discover that tonight." He still held the blade. Adria looked down. There was blood on her torn gown, and on the carpet. She was badly hurt. She wasn't sure if she could walk. Which would mean her death, if it was true.

But . . .

She let herself stumble towards the fire, as if the wound in her leg had unbalanced her. He watched. His eyes were dark. You could call them hungry.

"We are born in blood," Uberto of Mylasia said. "A girl your age has known that for years."

Adria placed a hand on the wall beside the fire.

"My lord," she said again, whimpering. Her leg felt as though it was going to give out on her. She really wasn't sure it would bear her. She wanted to cry. Everyone wanted something.

"Disrobe," he said. "Let us see your wound. We must tend to it."

"You stabbed me, my lord," she said. She was letting time run. The Esperañan had told her it would not take long.

"I did. I will possibly do so again, and certain other—"

The Esperañan had not lied. Uberto of Mylasia began that sentence but never finished it, or any other.

She saw the knife drop from his hand. There was, amid all else, a fierce, cold pleasure, seeing that. Not just relief. She might die here, if she couldn't move properly, but the man in front of her brought a hand to his throat and opened his mouth to scream, and no sound emerged. Another part of what the Esperañan had promised them. The victim would not be able to cry out, summon aid. He would fall without speaking, though that might make a noise.

It did, not a loud one. He threw out an arm, reaching for support, but there was nothing where he stood. The soft thump when he hit the floor might be understood outside as many possible things, some a part of what they thought was happening here, just as her scream would have been. She would not be the first person, Adria thought, to have screamed in this room with Uberto of Mylasia.

She will be the last, however. There is that.

His eyes were wide, she saw terror in them. Both hands at his throat now as he struggled for breath. The pleasure she felt was possibly unworthy. She wasn't about to consider if that was so. She moved from by the fire, the wall. Her leg almost gave way and she gasped. His knife had not gone all the way in, though, not to the hilt. He'd just wanted her afraid. Probably the blood excited him, but there would be no poison in her. Not in her.

She looked at the man on the carpet. He was still trying to call out—to the steward outside, to holy Jad, or to ward off the demons he might now be seeing as his life ended.

But he wasn't dead yet. Adria bent down, gasping with the motion, and took his fallen knife. She stood above him. Calmly, speaking in her own voice now, she said, "Folco Cino d'Acorsi has decided you are a waste of Jad's gift of life. I am sent to end that waste. My name is Adria Ripoli. You will know my lineage. Die in pain, and never see light."

The blue robe had fallen open. Her weight on her good leg, she leaned down and plunged the knife into his genitals. Then did it again, to be sure, and for the children who had died here.

She wasn't a kind-hearted woman, no one in her family was kind, but you could picture children brought to this room in terror to be savagely abused and sometimes killed, and that could cause you to use a knife this way, over and above the poison on your lips.

She watched him die. More blood—a great deal, in fact—on that beautiful eastern carpet. His maimed nakedness was a proper end, she thought. If there were worse men in their world, she didn't want to ever be in a room with one of them. He belonged to Jad now, for judgment. She had sent him there.

And there were things yet to do—if she could—if she wanted to live. She did want that, urgently; she wasn't ready to be judged herself.

"*My lord, please!*" she said loudly, in the farm girl voice.

She dropped the knife and crossed, limping, trying not to cry out, towards the windows. The new style of fixed glass on one of them, old-fashioned shutters on the other. This, too, had been noted before she came. Folco prepared. His men did so, as well, or they did not remain his men.

She opened the shutters. They creaked, but only a little. It wouldn't be heard. She leaned out and looked.

The rope was there, tied to a spike in the stone wall, dropping into darkness. They'd placed a man in Mylasia some time ago, one who knew how to climb. He would have wedged the spike on an earlier night, then attached the rope this evening after they'd learned she'd been summoned. She was to leave the shutters open, let the guards rush in, look out, see the rope . . .

Draw the wrong conclusion. Because there was no actual escape down this wall of the palace, not for her. They were three floors above the ground, and though she had skills that were useful to herself and to Folco, climbing hand over hand down a rope was not one of them, and there were always guards in the square below.

Those coming into this room here would not know what she couldn't do, however. Nor would they be aware that Folco had

bribed a one-time servant in this palace to describe the inner rooms
of the count's chambers, and tell him of the hidden stairway. There
was always a hidden staircase from the lord's private rooms, Folco
had said. Adria had known that from her family's palace, too.

She needed to get to that stair, then down and out to where there
would be men waiting to help her away. There would be a horse to
ride, freedom, life.

But she could barely move.

She was afraid she was going to pass out from the pain. She
cursed. If the whoreson hadn't stabbed her . . .

The whoreson had intended to do worse. He was dead. She
was not.

No one had ever promised her easy paths in life. Certainly her
father had not. He wasn't that sort of man. Wealth was hers, as the
daughter of a duke, but nothing easy. Not for a woman, especially.

She crossed back to the dead man. She bent down, gasping with
the effort, and took up the knife again. She used it to cut a piece of
his robe free and she packed her wound with it. She took the belt
from the robe of the man she'd killed, pulling it out from under
him. She tied it around the packed wound. Her need was to try not
to drip blood as she went. She almost screamed again, doing all
this. Then she remembered, and did scream, softly, for them to hear
her outside.

She looked around, trying to think if she'd forgotten anything.
The wound, for the moment, wasn't bleeding through the cloth. It
would soon, she thought.

She limped, breathing hard, to the half-open inner door and
went through. Third room, they had told her: a panel on the left-
hand wall, far side of a fireplace. A latch in the mouth of a lion
carved in the wood there.

It would be weak to collapse, she told herself, dragging her
body forward. It would also be death. She kept herself moving,
leaning on tables or with a hand on the walls, grasping at the posts

of a bed in the second room. She was weeping with the pain now. She wiped at her eyes.

She got there, the third room. She found the lion and pressed the latch that opened a panel. There was a staircase within. She had been promised there would be, hadn't she?

It was utterly black inside. Adria turned, swearing, and made her way across this room to claim a lamp from a table. She put the blood-ied knife in the belt of her robe. Only then did she realize her buttons were still undone. She did them up. It could be amusing, a desire for modesty at the edge of death, but she remembered the ruined naked-ness of Uberto, behind her, and she wasn't amused.

She went back to the open panel and through it, stooping, crying out softly as she bent. She pushed the panel closed behind her. There would probably be blood on the floor and carpets on the way, she knew. There was nothing more she could do about that. She'd need to hope—pray?—that no one noticed it, at least not tonight. That they'd be too dismayed and afraid, would have rushed to the open window, seen the rope, raced down to the square, shouting for guards.

After a few steps, however, Adria realized that was not going to matter. She had two levels to descend on these narrow, slippery, stone stairs, holding a lamp, and she wasn't going to be able to do it.

❦

It wasn't an encounter I was likely to have forgotten.

A little over a year before, Folco Cino, famed among the military leaders of Batiara and, since his father's death some years past, the lord of Acorsi, had come on a visit to the ruling Ricciardiano family in Avegna, and stopped by, on the morning of his second day, to greet Guarino, our teacher. Folco was possibly the most celebrated graduate of our school.

Everyone called him by that name, familiar as it might be for the ruler of a city. Guarino had told some of us it was deliberate. "He makes himself seem kind that way. He can be, but don't be fooled," he'd said.

We were unlikely to be, he was one of the most feared mercenary commanders of the day. Preferring his given name was unlikely to erase that from anyone's awareness, I thought.

He had brought two people with him that day. One of them was the tall woman I would later see being led into a room where Uberto of Mylasia awaited her.

I would recognize her in Mylasia because I was one of those in the garden of the school the day Folco came to us a year before, along with half a dozen of the older students and two of our youngest ones, twins. The young brothers sang a song of greeting as our famous guest entered, their voices sweet in the late-summer morning light.

Guarino nodded brisk approval when they were done. Folco d'Acorsi, grinning, said, "I remember singing that song!"

He gave each of the boys a coin, then stepped forward to embrace our teacher fiercely, almost lifting him off the ground. We were startled. Shocked, in fact. Guarino, released, straightened his grey robe, and said, "Dignity is to be treasured, perhaps above all else."

Folco laughed. I could see, from where we stood, the notorious hollow socket of his right eye. He refused to wear an eye patch. Everyone knew about that wound. There were conflicting stories of how it had happened. One was that it had been caused by Teobaldo Monticola, which might explain some things.

Folco said, "Quoting Azzopardi, Teacher? You don't even agree with Azzopardi! What about 'None deserves your love so much as he who teaches you wisdom'?"

"That's him as well, yes," said Guarino with equanimity. "A better thought, I agree. I am pleased you have not forgotten. But love can be shown in many ways." He did smile, I remember. His wispy hair was chaotic in the wind.

"It can," agreed the lord of Acorsi. "Will you dine with us, Teacher, after we hunt? Erizzio has said I should invite you."

I had thought he would be a bigger man, his fame as a soldier was so great. Folco Cino's hair was a light brown under a soft red cap, some grey in it. He had a fiercely beaked nose and a scar on the same cheek as the missing eye. He was strongly built, muscular. You wouldn't want to wrestle him, I thought.

"I will do so with pleasure," Guarino said. "Convey my thanks to the count. But before you go, I have brought some of our pupils this morning to show their skills, if it is agreeable."

"It would be entirely agreeable, if time permitted. But I am riding out with Erizzio and Evardo, with matters to discuss before we hunt, pertaining to Rhodias and Firenta and developments there."

"Indeed," our teacher said. "The Sardis grow powerful."

"They do," said Folco d'Acorsi. "Piero wishes to hire me again. My army."

"Of course he does," said Guarino.

The lord of Acorsi favoured us with a glance. "I have no doubt you are exemplary, all of you. Your teacher would not have brought you this morning otherwise. Accept my regrets and my good wishes. Carry on, always honour him, he is the best of us. Come, Coppo, Adria, they'll be waiting for us." He bowed to Guarino, turned, and strode out of our small garden, a man of violence and culture and power, one eye bright, one empty and dark. The tall young woman and the man followed him, dressed for riding.

We know he is the best, I wanted to say, but knew better than to speak. So, I never did ride a horse that morning for Folco d'Acorsi, to show him what I could do. It is even possible certain things might have unfolded differently if I had. The thought has occurred to me. I've never shared it.

I did see the woman that morning, however. Tall, auburn-haired, thin. And I heard her name and saw her looking about the garden, bored. We talked about her after. How could we not talk about her, young men seeing Adria, the youngest daughter of Duke Arimanno

Ripoli of Macera, niece of Caterina Ripoli d'Acorsi, and so of Folco, by marriage? She'd walked with him into our garden and walked out with him.

But that was not the name I heard her give Morani, in Mylasia, when she was brought up the palace stairway as a girl from a nearby farm, summoned for the count's pleasure.

I stood in shadow on the back stair and I did nothing. I watched Morani search her and take her to the door and knock and usher her through when the count said to do so.

Which is why I still feel, to this day, Morani's soul, his death, marked to my account with the god.

When I am summoned, when my life ends and I'm to be judged, I will plead that Uberto's death that night, the innocent lives saved and avenged, be offered in the balance. I didn't kill Uberto, of course, just as I didn't kill Morani, but I knew, watching the woman go in, that she was there for Folco, and to kill.

Not for justice, but for power, the savage game of it, the dance of pride and enmity in our time. I had been a pupil of Guarino's, hadn't I? I knew the geography of this corner of the world. I knew where Teobaldo Monticola's city of Remigio was. And Folco's Acorsi, where that was. With Mylasia lying between them here.

And I decided, watching, clutching the wine flask Morani had sent me to bring, that *why* didn't matter to me if the Beast died that night. I had been in that palace long enough, I had seen what he was, and I was young, justice meant something to me.

It never occurred to me the woman might fail. Which is astonishing, as I look back.

I waited a few moments then came into the antechamber. It was more an open landing than anything else. There was a long, low chest against the wall of the room where the count and the woman were. Morani was sitting on that. I brought him the flask and a cup. He unstoppered the wine and drank, not bothering with the cup, then passed it back to me.

I shook my head. He raised his eyebrows. I usually did drink with him on those nights. With a shrug, he took another drink. I remained standing, which was normal for me. I was frightened, I remember, and knew I must not show it. We listened for sounds while pretending we weren't doing that. We could hear voices, but not the words spoken, unless they were loud.

Morani said, softly (because we could also be heard within), "No wine?"

I shrugged in turn, and lied to him. "I had too much last night."

"The young should be able to do that," he said, trying for a smile.

I managed a wry face. In truth, I'd felt, from the moment I saw the woman, that I might need my wits about me.

"Have you any poetry about gardens, Guidanio?" Morani said. "Gardens in springtime?" He almost always used my full name. I was Danio, usually, and sometimes another form of my name I didn't much like, from childhood.

"I think I do," I said. We heard the count's voice through the wall, from the side of the room nearer to us, away from the bed and the table where he kept the things he played with.

Morani drank again.

I said, perhaps foolishly, "Is this worth it? For either of us?"

He looked at me. "Our souls, you mean?"

"Yes." Though that wasn't precisely what I'd meant.

"No, it isn't," he said. "I am going to write letters for you this winter, Guidanio. Find you a better post."

"You know I am honoured to serve you, signore. You know—"

"It isn't serving me!" he said. He sighed. "I'm getting old, and so many depend on me. And I try, by staying, to . . . make things better?" He looked up at me, his expression almost pleading. "I have *seen* famine, Guidanio. Sieges, cities sacked and burned. Terrible things, I've seen. Mylasia is safe from these right now, the people here are safe, because he is—"

The count's voice, sharply. Then the woman screamed.

It seemed to come from directly behind Morani. I flinched. He half stood, then sank back down onto the chest. We looked at each other. *He is quiet tonight*, he had said to her.

"*My lord . . . why?*" we heard her cry.

"A garden," Morani said quickly. "A poem about a garden, Guidanio. Or anything. About anything! Sunlight."

The count's voice: low, smooth as olive oil, warm as wine mulled in winter. Nothing more from the girl. I was supposed to say a poem. I reached for the flask, after all, and took a drink. They served good wine in Mylasia under Count Uberto in those days. My heart was pounding, I remember.

"It is difficult to think of one," I said.

Morani's eyes on mine. He said, "The difficult is what we rise to!"

I lowered my gaze. Guarino had said the same thing. In the school. Which had a garden. And existed to teach men and women to be graceful and capable in the world. And perhaps kind, if they could manage it, especially if they held power. Most of those in the school came from power and would go back to it.

I said:

> *There is a place I remember on summer nights,*
> *Though it is lost to me and all men now.*
> *Fountains splashing between orange trees,*
> *And the scent of jasmine drifting at night.*
> *I was—*

We heard a struggle on the other side of the wall, then something different, muffled.

Morani turned his head, listening.

What I did next didn't change anything, because Uberto was already dead. I know that now. He had already kissed the girl brought to him—or sent after him. But I didn't know it then, and

I did intervene to keep Morani di Rosso where he was, after we both heard what sounded like someone falling.

I said, "Do you know the verse, signore? It is a translation from the Asharite tongue, from the west, long ago, when they ruled in Esperaña, before the infidels fell to the swords of holy Jad."

"Why would you offer a poem by an unbeliever?" He turned back to me.

"Guarino says there can be wisdom and beauty in unexpected places. We owe much of our knowledge of the Ancients to the Asharites, translated."

"I know that," he said. He took another drink. He was looking at me. "I also know they wish to destroy Sarantium right now. The golden city . . ." He trailed off.

"You asked for a garden," I said.

We heard the girl's voice again. Too quiet to make out her words. But then: "*My lord, please!*"

And it is a terrible thing to tell, but Morani leaned back, reassured there was nothing amiss. Because a woman had just sounded terrified in the room behind him, and we had heard that before.

I know, I know . . . I have said he was a good man. You will accept my saying that, or refuse to believe it to be so. We will all face judgment at the end.

I continued with the poem. I didn't know the poet's name, names are often lost as time runs. Mine will be, I have done little to be remembered. Uberto might be recalled—as a foul monster or as the lord who kept Mylasia safe for twenty years. Perhaps both?

I believe Folco d'Acorsi and Teobaldo Monticola di Remigio will both be remembered for a long time. I could be wrong. We can always be wrong about time. I also have no idea *what* will be said of them when centuries have passed and the stories are false or distorted, when perhaps even the palaces they built or expanded lie in ruins, and no one knows how beautiful a man or woman was, except, perhaps, because of a portrait made.

Maybe it is the art that will outlive us all. Although I know at least one portrait by the great Mercati that, though brilliant as a work of art, looks nothing at all like the person, because I did know the subject of that fresco.

On the other hand, as to artists outliving us all, I had been reciting a verse I loved just then, and I had no idea who had written it.

A quieter scream. Not so much pain this time as distress. Still from the wrong side of the room, towards the tapestries.

"Should I call to him?" Morani asked.

He never asked me a question like that. He always did, on instructions, call out to the count through the door at intervals. Uberto knew he was hated. He was careful.

"Isn't it too soon?" I asked, as though indifferent.

Jad forgive me for that, too. I *knew* something might be happening in there that was not as it was supposed to be.

"Too soon," he agreed.

I finished the verse from the west. I offered another poem, a newer one, a favourite of Morani's, by Matteo Mercati, in fact, widely judged to be not only the best sculptor and painter of our day but also an accomplished poet, and forgiven, because of these things, for his many sins. He died not long ago. I met him once.

I have also thought, often, through the years, about why some people are forgiven and some are not. I kept Morani sitting there, drinking the good wine, for an interval. Not a long time; he was clearly unsettled. Suddenly, he stood up.

"I am going to call," he said.

He walked to the door. My heart began pounding.

"My lord!" Morani said loudly. "Is it well with you?"

This is what he had been ordered to do through nights like this, until the girl or boy was sent back out to us. Or until men were summoned to remove a dead child. Uberto would have gone through to his inner rooms by the time they arrived. He didn't linger to watch Morani supervise that task.

When Morani called through the door, the count of Mylasia would reply, "It is well, steward," and Morani would nod his head shortly, though there was only me to see him, and return to his seat on the chest.

That night there was no answering voice.

Morani repeated his call. Silence came heavily through the door. I shivered.

One more call, then Morani took a steadying breath and opened the door. I saw that his hand was shaking. He went in. I followed him.

"Dearest Jad, who loves his children," said Morani di Rosso.

I still remember his voice, saying those words. I think he knew in that moment that he, too, was dead.

◦✦◦

Courage and will weren't always enough, it seemed. That was a hard thing, Adria thought.

It was proving difficult to remain alert, even conscious, through the pain. It was numbingly cold in the damp stone stairwell. She heard rats, possibly other things. She had a lamp, she could see the slippery steps, but her left leg would not act the way she needed it to. She couldn't step down properly. She'd managed to sit and was bumping her way down, the wounded leg outstretched, because she couldn't bend it without crying out, and she didn't know who might be on the other side to hear.

Not that it mattered, if she couldn't get to the ground level and the small door—hidden by bushes, they'd told her—that would open into an autumn night outside the city walls, to Coppo and the others, and horses, and escape.

She was on a landing now, trying to summon strength. This would be the second floor of the palace. If she looked she'd likely find a door here, too. She needed to rest, knew it was dangerous, but . . . she needed to rest, if only for a little.

She woke to a sound and a surge of pain. She saw light from another lamp hit the wall above her on the stairs, from beyond that bend. The lamp and whoever was carrying it weren't visible yet. Her own light had gone out. Not that it mattered.

They would do terrible things to her, she thought. She did have Uberto's knife in her belt. You could control some things, even at the end. Could she kill someone before she had to kill herself? Or was that asking too much of the god?

ఇం

We saw the blood first.

It was pooled, thick and dark, at the count's maimed genitals. I stared, then looked away, swallowing hard. I had never seen anything like this. I had been a child, then in Avegna as I entered manhood, never in war. We had heard of babies thrown in the air after cities were taken, then spitted on pikes as they fell, for sport. But those were just stories for us at school, however horrifying. We studied the philosophy of the Ancients and music and proper conduct at a court. We fought each other with wooden swords, then carefully with real ones, under supervision. There had been some broken bones, some wounds, a stabbing involving boys from families that hated each other, not . . . this.

But when I looked at the count's face I saw something. His hands were at his throat, clutching it, as if he had been struggling for breath. I did that myself: made myself breathe. And I made myself think.

Guarino had always said the true courtier came patiently to a conclusion when confronted with the unexpected. I wasn't a courtier, but he'd been my teacher, and I was trying to live my life as he'd taught.

I stared down at Uberto, at where his hands were. The woman, Adria Ripoli, could *not* have entered this room with a blade. She'd been searched twice. But she might have—

"*Look!*" Morani said.

He crossed quickly to the open shutters. They should not have been open on an autumn night. I followed, stepping around the blood. I felt unwell. The cold air helped as I leaned out beside him. He pointed down, and I saw the spike in the wall, just below—and a rope descending from it.

"*Guards!*" shouted Morani. "Guards below! *Assassin!* A woman is escaping among you! *Find her!*" He looked at me, his expression aghast. "Did she take his knife? And overpower him? How?"

I turned back into the room and made myself look again at the count's body on the carpet. His robe open, he was obscenely exposed in death. His eyes were wide and staring. Those hands at his throat. I saw no knife by the body.

Morani was still at the shutters, shouting again to the guards in the square. I heard faint replies from below. He'd be heard in the palace, too. Men would come rushing into this room, would find what was here.

I looked around again. Trying to *see*, to understand. And this time I noticed something else, possibly because I was trying not to look at the dead man. I had no pity for Uberto of Mylasia but I was disturbed by the sight of him. And so, looking away, I saw three dark spots of blood on the wooden floor by the inner doorway leading to the count's other chambers.

Morani suddenly turned, looking over his shoulder. "Guidanio," he said—and I will never forget the kindness, the care for another's life, he showed in that moment—"*get out of here!* You fetched my wine, you gave it to me, you went back down. Now leave, quickly! To your bed, or wherever you'd be now if not here!"

He didn't wait to see if I obeyed. He turned back to leaning out the window where the assassin had escaped. There were more men shouting from below now, there would be torches.

Except, she hadn't. She hadn't escaped that way. It was a deception. There had been planning here. But they hadn't counted on blood, I thought.

I did what I did. I didn't have to. I could have gone to my room as instructed, down the servants' stairway, come rushing back up with everyone else as the palace tumult grew. I would have had a different life.

I checked that Morani wasn't looking and I crossed to the inner door instead. But first, I bent quickly and wiped the droplets of blood from the floor with a cloth from the sideboard there. I took the cloth with me through the half-open door and I followed the trail I saw, cleaning the red drops as I went.

So you can call me a part of that assassination if you wish. I will not deny it. I had known who she was when she came up with the guards. I knew it was a deception. That Folco d'Acorsi was part of it. And then I followed her, concealing the signs of blood.

First room, second. She'd been wounded, but she'd done something to mostly stay the bleeding. There was enough for me to see, however. And others later if I'd left it there. I didn't, though.

Entering the third room I saw that the trail led to an inner wall by a fireplace. I went and looked. Nothing to see, but there wouldn't be. I had lived for years in a palace complex in Avegna. Young people, curious, bored, we would wander, explore. We learned things. I used my hands, feeling. I reached into the mouth of a carved lion on the wall panel and I pulled at the latch I found there, and a part of the wall disengaged with a click.

A stairway, black as a moonless night. Blacker than that. I walked away and claimed a lamp from a round table in the centre of the room. I saw another drop of blood by the table. I wiped it up and went back to the opening in the wall and before I could think too much about what I was doing, the folly of it, I went into that space, ducking down, and I closed the door behind me—as she must have done.

I stood still for a moment and I did feel terror then, and the awareness that I was betraying the lord of Mylasia, and the good man who had accepted me here, and treated me well.

But with Uberto dead, where was the treachery to him? (Not the most honest thought of my life.) And if I went down these hidden stairs and captured the girl . . . ?

But that wasn't what I was there to do, was it? Or I'd not have covered the evidence of her passage, would I?

I stuffed the cloth into my belt opposite my knife in its sheath and I started down. Even with a lamp it was treacherous. I almost fell right away on a narrower, slippery stair. I couldn't see any light below. It was possible she was already outside, wherever this stairway led.

But as I went down, the light I carried showed more blood, not just droplets now, and I didn't think she would be moving very fast. I worried about the absence of light below me. She'd be able to see the glow of mine if she looked back.

I heard sounds through the wall. The palace would be rousing to the horror of what had happened. Not all would be horrified, of course, but there was no way to predict what would come now. If I captured the girl, or killed her, I might be a hero in Mylasia—or not, depending on who followed Uberto here. His only son was a child, his wife lived most of the time in their country home. That boy, I thought, was likely to be killed.

I came around another curve of the stairs and I saw her below me in the cast light of my lamp. I stopped.

She was sitting on the landing where a doorway to the second floor would be. She'd only made it that far. Her light had gone out beside her, or she'd put it out. She lifted her head and looked up at me.

She said, softly, because we could hear people moving in the room outside, "Kill me, if you have any soul at all. Make yourself brave enough."

Her voice wasn't just quiet, it was weak, deathly weary.

"You are in pain," I said. "He stabbed you, then you used his knife on him. But he was already dead before then, wasn't he?"

Her manner changed. She shifted her shoulders but didn't try to stand. I didn't think she could.

"He was nearly dead. Not quite. I took some pleasure in that."

"With the knife?" *Pleasure*, I thought. "It was poison, then?"

I came down a few steps. We needed to be quiet.

"You are the man who was on the back stairs," she said, not answering me. "I saw you."

I hadn't known that. "Yes," I said. "I know who you are."

"*What?*"

I shrugged casually, but I wasn't feeling a courtier's calm at all. "You are Adria Ripoli of Macera, daughter of the duke, niece to Caterina Ripoli d'Acorsi. You came to Avegna with Folco once."

She swore savagely, like a soldier. "Jad rot your soul!" she said. "You are the foulest fortune of all!"

More than dying here? I almost said.

"Because I know you?" I saw her reach for her belt. "You won't be able to stab me," I said. "I can stay right here. I can raise my voice and summon men to come through the entrance beside you."

Her hand stopped, she stared up at me. She had red hair, I remembered from the garden. Her eyes were wide, I couldn't tell their colour, I hadn't noted it that first time. We'd all been watching every movement Folco made.

She closed her eyes, and I understood that as pain. Of course it was, why else would she be sitting on this landing in the dark? Then I grasped something else.

"I am bad fortune because I can link you to Folco and undermine his intentions here."

"If it is ever known who I am, I cannot *do* any of these things any more. Even if I live, somehow."

"What things? Killing men for Folco d'Acorsi?"

She looked up at me again. After a moment she said, "Living a life I choose."

"You . . . chose this? This stairwell? Murder?"

She didn't answer at first. She shook her head. Then, in a different voice, "You were in the garden when we went to his school. You were one of those they paraded out to perform for him. That is how you . . . Oh, Jad curse fortune's wheel for this."

I was surprised again. It had been so brief, that encounter, before d'Acorsi had called her and his other attendant away. To hunt, I remembered.

I was thinking hard. But not to very clear effect. I didn't like the feeling. I said, "If I were here to kill or expose you I'd have shouted by now, wouldn't I?"

She needed a few breaths before she could speak again. She said, "Why are you here, then?"

"I'd feel happier if I knew," I said.

She laughed, softly. She did laugh, in that cold, fearful place, wounded, expecting to die.

She said, "We must somehow make you happier, then. Shall I kiss you?"

That wasn't what it appeared to be, I thought.

"You poisoned him that way?"

She nodded, after a moment. "That is clever of you. Folco said Guarino was the best teacher in Batiara."

I said, "The best man, we tend to say."

Her turn to shrug. "He does, too. So . . . why *haven't* you called for others? What are you doing, besides wanting to be happy?"

I didn't answer. It was quiet on the other side of the wall now, the room beyond had probably emptied.

I said, "This stairway leads outside the city?" The palace had been built into Mylasia's city wall, and if the staircase's last turn was west . . .

"I was told so," she said.

"They have a horse for you? You are being met?"

"Yes," she said. She drew a breath. "That was the plan. Before the foul thing up there stabbed me and twisted the knife."

"You can't walk?"

"I can caper and dance," she said bitterly. "I was sitting here to admire the view and share witty conversation with whoever came to capture me."

"Let's go," I said. Said it just like that. Lives turn on a moment. "If you lean on me, can you get down these stairs?"

She stared up, in the flickering of my lamp. "Why would you do that?" she asked.

A perfectly good question.

I said, "I'm not sure. I hated Uberto, it didn't take long. The man I honoured here is almost certainly dead now—because of you. You made it past him with poison and you killed. And . . . I have no strong feelings about Folco d'Acorsi taking control in Mylasia."

"A very precise answer," she said, after a moment. "Also, clever."

"Generous of you to say so. But answer me. Can you stand? Can you move?"

"With help, maybe."

"The knife, put it away," I said.

"I could always pull it out again." But she did put it away.

I went down to her. It was her left leg that was wounded. She'd tied something over it, high up. I went on that side of her, shifted the lamp, pulled her upright, with an effort, by the arm. She gasped, swayed. I draped her arm over my shoulders.

"We don't have to hurry," I said.

"Not a possibility," she muttered through teeth clenched on pain.

"I step down, you hop on your good leg."

"Ah. They teach this dance in Avegna?"

My turn to be surprised by laughter. And another feeling, in that moment.

"And at the end we kiss each other on each cheek," I grunted, bearing as much of her weight as I could.

"That would kill you," she said quietly.

I'd forgotten. For a moment, I had.

"In which case we can certainly defer the kiss," I said, taking the first step down. I held the lamp in my left hand. We needed it. My right arm was around her waist, supporting her as best I could.

"Defer, signore? Defer our first kiss?" Adria Ripoli said, and I was lost.

I can place it. That moment, six words lightly spoken as I helped her escape. The recollection is so clear. I sometimes think I will live endlessly in the memory of the two of us on that stair.

I didn't see her after that for some time.

CHAPTER II

The tale in Jelena's family was that their farmhouse and orchard outside Varena had existed for a thousand years and had been in their family for almost all that time. With allowance for pride and exaggeration, there was evidence it was extremely old. The house even had an ancient, mostly worn-away mosaic—of birds, many different kinds—on the floor of a room that had once been a study, they'd decided, but had been used for different purposes over the years.

Their stone wall running alongside the road to and from Varena had been repaired frequently. They'd done it twice in this generation. Apple trees had been planted and replanted in the orchard. The house itself had so many additions it sprawled confusingly and one needed a builder's eye to tell where the original rooms and walls were.

Varena had expanded as well in some periods, then retreated again if wars or plague years depopulated it. Right now it was small again, so that their house and land were farther from the city walls. Her grandfather's sense was that this was as it had been when the house was first built. He was one who believed it was exceptionally old, or parts of it, at least. He pointed to the floor mosaic as evidence. It was the same age as the mosaics in the old sanctuaries by the city, he would say. Just look.

Jelena had looked, of course. She had gone with him as a girl to see the works on those sanctuary walls, but it was hard, without understanding mosaic (and who did, these days?), to come to any conclusions about how old they were. Floor mosaics and those on a wall or dome were different, anyhow.

It *felt* extremely old, their property. She could say that. She also had a sense of presences, in some rooms.

She'd learned to trust such sensations when they came to her. They weren't the same as, say, feelings of hunger or desire. These were . . . more inward. Deeper? Sometimes she had an *awareness* of things not actually present, or not for anyone else. She thought of these as spirits, because she didn't have a better word. It was possible they were ghosts.

She had tried to talk about this to her mother once, but stopped when she met with incomprehension and some fear. That was disturbing. If your mother could be made fearful by you . . . ?

Some things, she'd eventually decided as she grew, were . . . well, they *were* inward, they were your own. If you felt, with certainty, that you knew someone was a good person, or not so at all, at first meeting, or if you knew they had an illness, or you sensed something hovering near them . . .

Her awareness, sometimes, as to someone's health was a thing that could get the clerics coming to talk to you, or worse, and their family was already erratic in attendance at sanctuaries of the sun god. Best not do more to draw attention to themselves in this old farmhouse outside a city that had allegedly been royal all the way back to the barbarians, in the days when Jad's light first came to Batiara.

Jelena spoke sometimes, when certain she was alone, to the birds on their mosaic floor. She listened for replies. Sometimes she thought she heard voices, though not the words spoken.

That she hadn't shared, either.

She wasn't at home now, in any case. She'd left four years ago, still young, unmarried. She had decided she wasn't going to marry, and entering a Daughters of Jad retreat was out of the question given that her beliefs, and her mother's and grandmother's, were . . . well, the clerics would call them pagan.

She didn't use that word, but if pressed she'd have said Jad of the Sun was one god, one power, among many. That there were others in forests and rivers, overhead in the sky, deep in the earth.

This was heresy, of course. There were few unbelievers in Batiara. No Asharites other than slaves captured—and those were mostly sent to the galleys of Seressa, unless they were kept as a show of status by a wealthy family. There were some Kindath. Varena had a handful of them, worshipping their two moons. They were tolerated, as in most cities, for a tax paid to be allowed their faith, unless times turned bad, and then tolerance could turn dark and sometimes violent.

The Kindath were said to know a great deal about divination, foretelling, medicine. Jelena had thought—still did think, at times— of trying to study with one of them, but it was difficult for a woman. Most things were.

She'd lived in several places in the years since leaving home. A neat, small woman with alert eyes and light brown hair. She was a calm person, and people seemed to find her calming, as well.

There were challenges in this chosen life, of course. More than she'd even guessed there would be. She carried knives and had taught herself to throw them as well as stab. She'd never killed anyone, but there had been two occasions she'd had to use a blade. She'd considered learning how to handle a bow, but hadn't got around to that. A bow, she still thought, might be a good weapon for a woman.

The years after she first left Varena had seen many small mercenary armies and bands of lawless men criss-crossing Batiara. If there was a war between city-states, they'd take service with some leader and be paid for killing and looting. When a war ended they were unpaid and hungry, and they still killed.

So, you took considerable risks moving about as a woman—or even as a man, really. She'd tried not to be on the road too much. Her father had given her some money in exchange for surrendering her share of rights to the farm and orchard, yielding them to her brothers. The land title went down the woman's side (it always had, for longer than any of them could remember), but Jelena didn't want to stay, and they made the change.

She kept away from Firenta, that growing, aggressive city, because it also had an aggressive set of clerics. She lived first near Avegna, then outside Acorsi for two years. Folco Cino, the celebrated mercenary who ruled it (his grandfather had claimed the city), was aggressive too, but it was a milder place in terms of faith. Folco was an educated man, not just a war leader. There were a few of those. You could quote philosophers, Jelena thought, and still burn a family in their farmhouse.

When she'd last moved, south towards Remigio, it was because of a lover dying. Jelena hadn't been able to save her. A fever that came and never left. The memory still hurt at night. She'd always felt that some moments in your life could tell you to make a change.

She never did much to let people know she was living somewhere and could offer services for those unwell—but word of healers tended to spread in the countryside, because even the poor needed them. It was generally kept from the clerics. There was a view among the more extreme that the very act of healing was a flouting of Jad's will, an interference with the decreed course of a life.

But in that small town near Remigio—Teobaldo Monticola's city—she'd treated an Eldest Son of Jad from a retreat outside the walls. She'd been frightened about that (she was hardly immune to fear)—both because of what he was and because he had been wounded by Monticola himself—but the man had proved to be grateful and generous, and she'd felt protected by him, after.

She still wasn't sure why she'd moved from there. Perhaps she didn't like the idea of someone protecting her, of being seen as owing a debt, even if it really wasn't. Her lover, a man that time, had gone to Firenta, as it happened. He was a master mason and they were building and building there, even more than Monticola was in Remigio. Ambitious Firenta paid craftsmen extremely well under the Sardi bankers who ruled it in all but name. He had invited her to come with him and she'd thought about it, but decided she would not.

So that became another time when life was telling her to make a change, Jelena had decided.

For safety on the road she joined a group of pilgrims returning north to Ferrieres from Rhodias, then left them quietly, and sooner than she'd planned, when an unsettling certainty came to her as they passed a hamlet not far from Mylasia.

For all her moving about, she was still in one corner of Batiara mostly. You could make changes regularly, pull up your life like a plant by the root, and still be quite near to where you'd been born. She could be home by the orchard, walking the mosaic floor, seeing her family, in a week or two if she wanted.

She didn't do it. She would not go home. She would make her own life, with or without love or friendship, though she'd prefer both, given a choice. She didn't understand where her stubbornness came from, just as she didn't understand the spirits she saw, or the certainties that came to her. She was still young, coming to terms with all of this. She did believe hers would not be a traditional life, whatever it turned out to be.

One day, she thought, she *would* go farther. Perhaps across the narrow sea to Sauradia, even beyond. Sarantium appealed to her, seeing the City of Cities, that place of ancient wisdom, gravely imperilled in their time. The eastern emperor kept sending urgent calls for aid. Some said the encroaching Asharites under their khalif might even take it one day.

That was impossible, of course. Sarantium's walls were the most massive in the world, and the sea guarded it as well.

She'd moved into an empty house in that hamlet near Mylasia. She scorned a man who tried to claim he owned it and that she'd have to pay him, but then she offered to help his young son who suffered from an affliction of the chest she'd dealt with before, and she did heal the boy.

After that it was all right. People paid her in food and firewood, which was perfectly good for her. She'd taught herself not to feel loneliness, most of the time. The woods nearby and the river and the night held powers she needed to try to understand, and she was learning these. She noticed, brushing her hair, that some of it was turning white. She was young for that, but it ran in her family.

She had known she might have to keep moving from the day she left home, choosing this life. Moving was a part of what that choice meant. Safety could have a different meaning for different people, and might be impossible.

For some, there was a calling, however. A voice in the soul, you could say. She seemed to be one of those. No point denying it by now. She was on this road, it was hers. She had laughter within her, wryness. Passion, too, though that could unsettle her, and she tried not to engage with it too much. She would never have said her decisions had been the most prudent, but she also knew her gift was real, however hard to define it might be.

She'd have said she was content, and learning things, if asked by someone she was willing to answer.

THE GIRL WAS in a bad way when they brought her. Jelena told them that immediately. From her first experiences as a healer she'd realized that saying this was important. People might need to prepare, and they might also need a reason not to blame you if someone died. Anger and loss could make some men violent, and she lived alone most of the time, with little in the way of protection.

They were only in her house because one of the men with the girl was from Mylasia and had heard of her. She reminded herself to ask how he'd learned where she lived. These things mattered. If people were coming to her because it was dangerous to go to a physician, for example, then she was at risk.

The hamlet—a dozen houses—lay about two days' hard ride north-west of Mylasia. Two days had been too much for the girl, but they'd evidently felt a need to put distance between themselves and the city. She didn't know why. If there was news, they'd outraced it.

They'd come to her small fence—three men and a woman who could barely ride—after sunset. They'd probably waited in the trees for darkfall. Her dogs barked by the gate to warn her.

It was night now. Her new patient was asleep in the treatment room. (She'd divided the small house into living and working quarters.) There was a slight fever, a little unexpected, and Jelena's fingers at the woman's throat found a too-quick pulse—but those things didn't feel grave, not yet. She'd given her a willow bark infusion, and betony when the woman said that her head ached.

The next days would tell if the wound was going to go bad. There was little Jelena could do if that happened. It was too high on her leg for even a skilled surgeon to amputate, and she wasn't a surgeon. The injury had looked all right to her, however. A knife, twisted, not as deep as it could have gone. She'd cleaned the wound with vinegar and coated it with honey and it was bandaged now. The initial cleaning would have been painful, but the woman had stayed silent, hands clenched.

Using honey on wounds was new for Jelena. She didn't know why it worked to help healing, but it did. Sweetness against bitter death? A pretty thought, but too simple. The father of Carlito—the boy she'd helped—had beehives and was generous now in supplying her. People could be grateful, kind. The world wasn't always harsh.

With a wound like this, a healer could mostly just watch after doing what she'd done. She'd give one of her infusions each time the patient woke, keep an eye on the fever and the colour and thickness of the urine. Blood loss was a concern, especially after two days on horseback. She'd change the dressing often. A scar would follow, possibly a limp—one could at least hope not. She'd tell the three men to pray. She'd already told them to sleep somewhere else. If they'd come this far, and to a woman healer, they were afraid to take her anywhere else, and Jelena didn't need more danger brought to her door. One of them at a time, she'd said, could come check on the girl, taking care to be unseen.

They'd given her silver right away, at the gate, even before bringing her in. Their expressions had been urgent, frightened. Perhaps frightened for themselves. Jelena had called back the dogs and let them enter.

She mattered, this girl—to these three, to someone else.

Two of them, not the one from Mylasia, were soldiers by their look. The girl—woman, really, though she was young—was harder to place. A peasant's roughened hands, but . . .

There'd be time to sort that out. Or there wouldn't be.

The silver had startled her. It was exceptional to be offered so much, it carried a message. She'd been given silver only once before, that Eldest Son from the retreat outside Remigio. He'd been wounded in the shoulder and slashed on the cheek by Teobaldo Monticola—for urging him to surrender a violent life and his mistress and seek reconciliation with Jad before it was too late.

Not wise, that exchange. Not with that man. What sort of person, abandoned by wisdom, provoked the lord of Remigio like that? Monticola's temper was . . . you could say it was legendary. And it was said that he loved his mistress a great deal. A beautiful woman. Jelena had seen her once.

The cleric had been brought to her because no doctor in Remigio would treat him, so afraid were they of their lord. She still thought the wounded man had been a fool, however brave in his faith. Teobaldo Monticola might have virtues, but he was known to be vicious when crossed. There were many stories. He'd ridden past her once, while she was in the city at the market. A tall, unsettlingly handsome man. Best military commander in Batiara was the general belief. Wealthy because of it. Even had estates across the narrow sea, outside Dubrava. Vineyards and olive groves, it was said. Led his army out in springtime, serving whoever paid him most that year, to support his city and citizens.

Not a man you challenged in a public place as to how he lived his life.

You could respect a holy man's piety and still think him a fool. The world allowed both things to be true.

And her own folly? The freely chosen risks of this edge-of-the-world life? That was different she always told herself when the thought came, but she did find the evasion amusing. You needed to be able to laugh at yourself, especially if you were mostly alone.

⚬❦⚬

"Which of the two of them do we hate more?" the High Patriarch of Jad asked. He raised the question lightly. He was in a pleased state of mind. He often was. Currently, he was in a sumptuously decorated bathing room inside the main palace in Rhodias on an autumn morning. He was fondling a newly favoured courtesan with one hand while holding a ripe orange from Candaria in the other. He was enjoying the variant textures and firmness of breast and fruit.

The holiest cleric in the Jaddite world was immersed in a deep and very hot bath. Hot baths were frowned upon by his physicians; they opened the pores to contagion, apparently. He had elected to ignore this observation. He would take his chances with pores and contagion.

The woman was in the water with him, turning pink, pleasingly, and giggling at his touch. Two of his councillors sat on a stone bench above, to his left. He had offered them oranges, they had declined. It was extremely warm in the room. A large fireplace blazed, with a frescoed image of Jad above it, done by someone apparently important once. There was a ridiculous amount of art in these palaces.

He saw that his advisers were sweating, wiping at their faces. It amused him. He was exceptionally content this morning, in fact. He had an erection under the water, and those didn't come so readily in the morning.

He'd dismiss the two men soon, let the woman do the things she did. But first there was this vexing matter of Folco d'Acorsi and Monticola di Remigio that needed attending to. It seemed to High Patriarch Scarsone Sardi that those two men needed attending to rather too frequently. He'd been in his lofty position less than a year, and their names kept recurring—and they weren't even lords of important cities.

His Uncle Piero in Firenta, who had turned a banking fortune into control of a city that *was* important (and then used more of that money to make Scarsone the Patriarch), had been urging him to do something about the feud between the two men. It was, Piero Sardi had written just last week—again—a matter of stability in the middle reaches of Batiara.

Unhappily, his uncle, a man of undoubted acuity, had not actually said *what* Scarsone should do. One answer, of course, was to have one of the men killed. Or both, he thought, looking fondly at the woman's plump ripeness beside him in the water. It was somewhat hard to focus on affairs of city-states while aroused, but he did have his burdens. One made sacrifices for the god, delaying pleasure (briefly) for duty.

And this matter was rendered more complex, and urgent, his advisers had just made clear, by the assassination five days ago of Uberto of Mylasia.

No one, Jad knew, would mourn Uberto, but Mylasia lay midway between the cities of the two men who worried everyone so much, and it was . . . possible, one of his councillors had delicately put it (men were *so* delicate here, Scarsone often thought), that one or the other of them had acted to end Uberto's life.

It was not permitted to celebrate this, evidently.

Uberto, vicious as he was, had played a role in balancing politics and power in that part of the world, the advisers had been saying as he bathed and they perspired. Who knew what would follow in Mylasia and the lands around it now? Who might come to rule there? What their allegiances would be? Circumstances, in short, were now unpredictable. And holy power was, it was emerging more clearly all the time, best protected by earthly power.

In the view of Scarsone Sardi, circumstances in the world were always unpredictable, if not outright dangerous. It was the condition of life in their time. For example, he kept being told that the Jad-cursed Asharites and their appalling khalif, Gurçu, might possibly capture Sarantium. *That* was a man worth killing, he thought. Not that they had a way to do it.

He had no great affection for the Sarantines. The arrogant Eastern Patriarch, who was about a hundred years old, was constantly lecturing him—in letter after letter—on his duties, demanding armies and money. But Scarsone wasn't going to deny it would be a bad thing if Gurçu took the city everyone called the most glorious in the world. Sarantium the Golden.

At the same time, it wasn't as if he could actually command a force to sail or march to its defence! What sort of power did that Eastern Patriarch think Scarsone had over the city-states here, or the kings of Ferrieres and Esperaña, or the Holy Jaddite Emperor in Obravic—who was *supposed* to defer to him and defend the god but was a major threat instead?

Threats, danger, balance awry. One could be grim and doom-haunted, or enjoy what there was to enjoy in the world, which was not inconsiderable, for some.

The matter of the moment was Folco Cino and Teobaldo Monticola. Maybe they'd kill each other, he thought.

They were genuinely formidable mercenary leaders, those two, with genuinely formidable armies, and he, the High Patriarch, needed armies. Each of them might serve him—or be bought by his enemies, depending on whose coffers were deepest in a given year. Wherever one of them served, the other would likely go the other way. The two of them, he was told, were also a part of the balance of the times.

He could grow to hate that word, Scarsone thought.

There was much to learn. He accepted that. He wasn't a fool, though he suspected some here thought he was. They'd learn soon enough. And he had his uncle behind him. Uncle Piero was someone no one alive considered foolish. Or wished to cross.

"Shall we not wait and see what follows in Mylasia?"

He'd asked that a moment ago. It was why they were silent now, sweating, clothes darkening with it, trying to frame an answer to what he thought was a good question.

Waiting was often the best solution, to his mind. A problem might go away by itself. That had happened for him in various circumstances over the years, as a moderately (in his own view) unruly young man in Firenta, then a cleric, placed in the service of Jad by his uncle, who saw it as a path for his advancement—and that of the Sardis.

That had worked out well. He didn't know what his uncle had spent to buy this highest of offices for him, for their family. He couldn't imagine wanting to know.

In the silence that had followed his first question, he'd continued by asking the one about which man they hated more here in Rhodias. He was curious, mostly.

Two good questions, he thought. Neither was receiving a reply. The woman had begun moving a foot up along the inside of his leg under the water, unseen. She'd keep going up, then drift it back down, as if suddenly shy. She was quite lithe, he'd discovered.

One of his advisers—the northerner—cleared his throat. The other, noting this, opened his mouth but then closed it. He'd wanted to speak first, but didn't know what to say. Scarsone had had that happen to him, too, in his family.

It was enough. He was tired of them.

"We will wait," he said. "Do nothing yet. Send to Mylasia to find out what we can about how the Beast was killed. We still don't know."

He enjoyed saying "the Beast" instead of Uberto.

Men called Teobaldo Monticola the Wolf of Remigio, but that was different. It spoke to prowess in battle, not vicious ugliness. His uncle had warned him to be cautious with the lords of Acorsi and Remigio, while working to curb them. They didn't have significant power, their cities were too small—not like Seressa or Macera (which was a threat under the Ripoli), or the emerging greatness of his own beloved Firenta—but the two men had large and loyal armies. They also hated each other, for reasons no one seemed especially precise in explaining. Something in the past.

You could hate someone for reasons you'd forgotten, the High Patriarch thought. Out of habit, as much as anything.

In fact, he *still* believed it might well be best if they were allowed to fight each other. One would win, or they both might die . . . ? There were other capable leaders of armies in Batiara, surely. A younger generation, as he was of a younger generation. Perhaps he could even claim control of one of their cities for Rhodias. Or both!

This was a game, Scarsone thought. Yes, people died in the playing, but that always happened, didn't it—and didn't it tend to be the unimportant? He thought he might enjoy this game. In due course. For the moment, there were other amusements.

"That is my decision," he said. "We wait. You are dismissed."

The two of them stood. Kindly enough, he added, "We will speak again on this."

They bowed and walked out, damply.

"Am I also dismissed?" the woman beside him asked, affecting an aggrieved tone. The High Patriarch of Jad laughed aloud. He splashed her. She splashed him back, which was startling and delightful.

◈

Sometime before this, back in the heat of summer in Acorsi, which was inland and lacked a port and the moderating influence of the sea, Folco Cino, lord of that city, had been in the chambers of his lady wife Caterina at day's end, admiring her, which he often did.

Her maid was brushing the lady of Acorsi's unbound hair, which was still reddish and lustrous, despite her being no longer young and with four children birthed alive. It would be scented after brushing, with musk and clove powder. Red hair was a trait in the Ripoli, men and women. So was the arrogance that came with a dukedom in Macera now, even if it *had* been bought by her brother at staggering cost from the Holy Jaddite Emperor, who always needed money and claimed the power to dispense titles.

Caterina, gazing at herself in a mirror set in a frame studded with pearls, said to her husband, whom she loved, "If anything happens to her, I shall leave you for a retreat. You are warned."

An old conversation, this one. Folco, who was notorious for his fidelity to his wife, cleared his throat, nodded towards the servant (his wife saw this in the mirror), and said, "I live in a state of being warned by you for something or other."

They did not name the person being referred to. It wasn't necessary.

"I don't like it," said Caterina.

"I know. She knows. Her parents don't like it either, and no cleric in Batiara would. Should she be given in marriage, then? Or choose a retreat? Your brother can buy her a First Daughter position anywhere he wants, and perhaps save his soul in the process."

"She wouldn't be likely to stay, and Arimanno's soul needs more than that."

"Exactly so," said the lord of Acorsi. "So why are we discussing this again?"

"Because she doesn't have to live in so much danger," said his wife.

She still hadn't turned around. There were earrings, rings, and a necklace on the table before her. She would put them on before rising, she never went out of these rooms unadorned. She was charitable, brilliantly clever, and loved jewellery.

"The same danger as my cousin Aldo, or Coppo, or anyone serving me," her husband said.

"Folco, she isn't your cousin Aldo, nor is she Coppo Peralta!"

"No. But she's as good. My love, I'm not just saying this. She can't wield a sword or go to war with me, but in almost every other way Adria is one of the best weapons I have."

"A weapon," said his wife. She noted that he'd said the name now.

"She wants to be a weapon," he said. It really was an old debate.

"She wants your approval. Your love, in fact. Indeed, if I died she would—"

"*Stop*," he said, a different tone.

Caterina looked at her husband in the mirror. She saw him look away, wincing. She did stop.

"You are not," said Folco d'Acorsi quietly, "permitted to die before me. I have told you this."

"Permitted," she mocked—or tried to, but failed.

He said, after a silence, "Caterina, there are men and women who are marked or who mark themselves for different lives. Adria is one of those. We know it. Her father also does, even if against his will. It is why she's here, not in Macera, not entering a marriage that could affect Batiara. I am trying—with your permission—to give her that different life for a time, before it *will* have to change. To respect what she's shown us all that she wants. My love, on some of those paths, at moments along them, it might become dangerous. But it is still her choice, and she's not a child."

She looked at him in the mirror, which was extremely expensive, gold, those pearls on its border.

"Very well, but promise me—"

"I cannot," he said.

THREE MONTHS LATER, the dry heat broken, autumn upon them, grapes being harvested outside the city walls, he came to his wife again in her rooms. A morning this time, the sun just risen, the hills through an open-shuttered window vivid with colour—russet and red and gold.

She was in a robe, reading a letter from her sister-in-law. The maid was laying out the first of the day's clothes.

He said, briskly, "Good morning. I must leave, my love. Six men with me. There are matters that need my attention. We will hunt and . . . deal with what emerges."

"Only six?"

"No more required. This is not war. I will send messages, as ever."

She looked at him from her chair. Her eyes were a pale green, memorably so. Caterina Ripoli was one of the aristocratic beauties of their time. It was a marriage that had honoured him greatly, for services done Macera as its mercenary commander for years. She had—unusually—been given the opportunity by her father to decline. She had not done so.

"Come back to me," she said. "Do not die."

She always said that.

"I can't die yet. I have too many sins unexpiated to be allowed Jad's light."

"Indeed. And what will you do about those sins?"

"Am I not doing? The sanctuary we are building?"

"Ah. That. The noise destroys my mornings."

"We all make sacrifices for faith," he said, grinning.

He was an ugly man, in truth—a missing eye, a scar, a hooked, raptor's nose—but his smile was a life-enhancing thing. Men and women loved him. She, first among all, responding to his own love for her, from the start and to this day.

He bent and kissed his wife, and left.

This happened ten days before Adria Ripoli, posing as a farm girl outside Mylasia, received a visitor from the palace there, bearing clothing, and instructions that on the next night she would be taken to attend upon the count. There would be, she was informed, a generous reward. Should she not be present when the escort came, the farmhouse would be set on fire and she and her aunt and uncle would be found and killed, wherever they went.

Coppo Peralta, who had been watching over her for Folco since the summer, also under an assumed identity inside Mylasia, had known a summons was coming.

The neighbours by that farmhouse were being observed by others who had come south with him. The younger son from the nearest farm had been followed into the city several days before. He'd been alone—and without goods for market. It wasn't a market day.

He'd gone to the palace guard by the main entrance, unusual for a farmer. He had been seen speaking to a captain there. Then he'd turned around and left the city, without doing anything else at all.

Folco had told Coppo, back in Acorsi, that someone was likely to do this. It was at the heart of their plan. Coppo had asked if he could kill whichever man this turned out to be, but it had been made clear to him that this was not permitted. Not until after, at any rate.

It might take time for the next steps to commence within Uberto's palace, but not *that* much time, and Folco's men were always told by him to be ahead of events, not chasing them. A message to Acorsi took at least four days at this time of year. Coppo sent a man north that same day. Then he went to the sanctuary he preferred in Mylasia, to pray.

If this was beginning, finally, they surely needed someone to beseech holy Jad for safety and success, and Coppo was the likeliest among them. He spoke his prayers at least twice a day every day of his life, in a sanctuary whenever possible, to honour his mother and his god.

Coppo had two men with him, plus the one from Mylasia who had agreed to assist them here, for a price. One of these he stationed by the western gate, and so they did know when courtiers from the palace rode out towards the farm. They would want a look at Adria. Folco had told him this would happen—and her, of course. She was old for Uberto, and too tall, but she was lithe, with splendid auburn hair. Folco had had no doubt she'd be invited to come to the Beast at night.

Coppo had his own thoughts on Adria's appeal: modest, he'd have called it himself, but he'd admit if pressed that his resistance to her was partly his response to how unnatural it was for a woman of high birth (for any woman!) to live the life she was living with them.

It was not *proper*, in his view, either in the world or in the sight of Jad. Still, she was as unyielding as any soldier Folco had, and Coppo had never heard her complain, or refuse a task, or do it less well than . . . well, than Coppo himself, if you excepted feats of strength and weaponry. She also rode better than any of them. It was irritating but undeniable.

And, truthfully, Coppo doubted he'd have been brave enough to take on a role such as the one she was to play: alone at night in the chambers of the count of Mylasia, intending to kill him and escape.

Coppo was responsible for that escape once she got outside the palace. In fact, after a deeply unsettling interview with the lady Caterina back in Acorsi, the afternoon before he and Adria and the others had set out in early summer, he understood that his responsibilities extended to his own survival.

"If my niece does not come back," that lady had said, receiving him in her chambers, "I will arrange for our new Esperañan to poison you. I thought, in fairness, you'd want to be aware of this."

Fairness? It was *entirely* unfair, Coppo had thought, given that this scheme to lay claim to Mylasia was Folco's, with Adria's agreement and approval, and Coppo was merely there to assist—and he didn't even like it!

What made it even more unfair was that whatever his personal judgment with respect to the desirability of Adria Ripoli, there were no limits—at all—as to how beautiful he thought her aunt, his commander's wife.

He was embarrassed in her presence, only a maidservant in the room with them, to find himself remembering certain night thoughts he'd recently had concerning the lady of Acorsi.

And now she was threatening him with death! At the hands of a scented Esperañan who clearly preferred men to women. Coppo would never, ever say a word against anything his commander did—he loved Folco, he would die for him—but in his own view of the world and the proper actions of brave men, you fought on a battle-field with swords so you could meet the gaze of anyone you killed. He even disliked bows and guns, and he hated the new field cannons.

Still, and always, there was no one like Folco in the world, and if he was employing these tactics—including this never-a-soldier poisoner from the west—then Coppo Peralta would do everything he could to assist. He'd risk his soul.

To the woman that summer day, the elegant, green-eyed figure who slipped into his dreams, he said only, in a rush of words, "If I fail my lord—or you, my lady—I will deserve any punishment you visit upon me, including death."

He was a soldier, a big man, unhappy in rooms like this, not a courtier, never that. He had no ease in him, he was fidgety and awkward speaking to her. *Being* with her in this room, her room. But he meant every word.

She looked at him, seemed to look right into him. She said gravely, "How perfect you are. How does he find and hold you all? Go. Go do whatever your lord requires. Bring her back."

HE WAS *TRYING* to bring her back—but she'd been knifed in the thigh, and was bleeding heavily. They didn't dare stop, however, not before achieving some distance from Mylasia. That had been made clear to him by Folco before they'd come south.

Actually, one stop she'd insisted upon, before they'd gone far enough at all. She'd made him hand her the small pouch he'd carried here, given by the Esperañan back in Acorsi. She did something to her mouth, still on horseback, with the contents of a vial she took from the pouch. Coppo didn't ask questions. Some things you didn't need to know.

What he did know was that Adria had done what they'd come here to do. Chaos would descend on Mylasia in the morning, even tonight, and that meant people were going to be killed. It might or might not impede any search for the girl who'd assassinated the count and escaped through a window into the square, somehow eluding the guards there. Those guards would be interrogated about that. How had she avoided them? Had they *assisted* her? Coppo suspected they were all dead men.

The large question was, who would take control now in the city? Folco had designs in that regard, but it would take time to see if they could be realized. Their own Acorsi, lovely as it was, had no port. Mylasia did. Ports were good things to have. That was the reason for all of this. And Coppo and Adria had been given orders not to linger anywhere near Mylasia.

They were going to have to stop fairly close, however, because the first night's riding had made it clear to him that he'd be killing Adria Ripoli if they didn't find her treatment soon.

He'd caught her once sliding off her horse. He'd ordered a halt then, in an olive grove, much too exposed this time of year, even at night. He looked at her leg in the dark (no torches) and he felt as much as he saw how it was bleeding. He put a fresh cloth in the wound, and tied it, but that would only do so much. She needed it cleaned and salved and wrapped, she was losing too much blood. She was also shivering now.

Leone, who had elected to leave Mylasia and come with them, after being the one to scale the palace wall and plant the spike and rope, said he had heard of a healer in a hamlet ahead of them. Coppo was frightened and unhappy but he didn't see a choice. He told Leone to take them there. Sometimes all you could do was pick the least bad thing. It took the rest of the night and all the next day, they didn't get there till sundown.

It was a terrible ride. They had to stay off any decent roads in the daytime, could not allow themselves to be seen too readily.

Four people on good horses? Of course that would be talked about! But neither could they wait for another nightfall. Adria wouldn't last so long.

On the way, riding beside her whenever the paths or trails were wide enough, Coppo thought about the moment he'd seen her come out from the palace, through that low doorway behind bushes and a thorn tree. There had been a man with her. Not part of the plan. He'd thought he'd have to kill that one, until he saw that she was being supported by him.

He moved towards the two of them, cautiously, and realized how badly she was hurt. He swore. He tried not to do that, generally. It was impious.

He heard her say, to this other one, "You did not have to do this."

"I know," the man said. "Call me a fool. I'll accept it."

"I can do that," Adria said. He knew that tone from her, though her voice was weak. Then she said, "Do you want to come? With us?"

Coppo blinked. *What?* What was she—

"I'd be very happy to stay with you," this man said quietly. It was too dark to see him clearly. A pause, then the man went on, "But honour demands I remain here."

"Why?" Adria asked.

"Morani. I have to try to protect him."

"You are not likely to be able to do that," Adria said.

"There's no way he could have been aware of the poison."

This man knew *much* too much, Coppo thought, really alarmed now.

"Doesn't matter," Adria said flatly. "He let me in."

Enough, Coppo Peralta decided. He strode up to them. They both startled, then Adria saw it was him.

"Coppo!" she said. "Jad is good, after all."

"He is," Coppo agreed, making the sign of the sun disk. "You did it?"

"I did," she said. "But I am . . . I will have trouble riding, I fear."

"I doubt she can," the other man said. "Have you another plan? A boat?"

They didn't have another plan. And who was this to be talking that way?

"Nothing for you here," Coppo said brusquely. "I thank you for helping her. We'll deal with this now."

Adria hadn't yet moved away from this man. She still had an arm around his neck. Now she removed it, awkwardly. She said, "You saved my life. I will not forget this encounter."

"Nor I," he said. "Pray for me."

"I'm not good at that. I'll get Coppo to do it."

A mistake, Coppo thought, she should *never* have named him! What if this one was tortured?

"He is good at prayer?"

"Very." A pause. Coppo waited impatiently, frantic to start moving. Adria said, to the other man, "I would kiss you in thanks, but—"

"It would kill me. You said before. And for the moment you don't want to do that."

Coppo heard her laugh, softly.

"For the moment," she said. Then finally—finally!—she came, limping badly, to Coppo's side. "You'll have to bear my weight on the left side, and lift me onto the horse," she said. "I'll do the best I can."

She'd looked back then, but said nothing. Neither did the man. To Coppo he was no more than a shape in the dark, a voice. The stranger turned and went past the tree and bushes and back through the door. He closed it. They heard a bolt slide.

If he'd helped her escape, Coppo thought, he ought to have come with them. Going back into the palace, chances were good he was a dead man.

Not his concern. Except for the fact that he might be tortured, and he'd heard Coppo's name, which could link tonight to Folco.

He was about to point this out to Adria, but decided not to. He pretty much carried her, being an extremely big man, to where the horses were. He lifted her with both arms around her waist and got her onto one of them. She cried out when she had to swing a leg to the other side of the saddle.

She looked down at him, drew a ragged breath. "He knew who I was, and that I was with Folco. It didn't matter that I said your name. Never assume I am being careless."

A Ripoli she was, always would be. Born to arrogance and power, however she might run from it.

Coppo grunted, nodded his head. Questions and answers would come later.

They rode, Leone guiding, Coppo beside Adria, Gian at the rear, silent and capable. They went north first, then took a path west along the river in the chill of an autumn night, vineyards on their left, as the blue moon rose behind them over the sea.

ৡ৵ঌ

Jelena would live a long life and call herself blessed when she died, though she would not be without griefs and losses, for whose life is without those? She would end her days some distance away, across the sea to the east, dangerously.

She would meet men of strength and courage, and one woman perhaps even more brave, more reckless, than the one in her treatment room this night—though the one in there, recovering from a knife wound, had a vivid force to her.

One giant of a man she would love, and he would father her only child, though she never told him he'd done that and they would never live together. It would never occur to her to tell him of the child—or her love. They could have placed a burden on him, and she would not be indebted or a burden to any man—or woman—in the world. Nor was he a man to be bound.

He would die with Jelena beside him, however, and neither of them had ever expected that he'd die old, in a bed. She would weep that night. She was never without passion or longing, only determined not to be claimed by anything or anyone but her craft and calling. She'd wanted her daughter to go away, shape her own existence, but that didn't happen. Not everyone had the same nature, and there were worse things than a clever child who stayed with you and learned, to the degree she could, the skills you could teach. There were worse lives for such a child, too.

But even with all of this, through the long arc of her days, Jelena never forgot that autumn night near Mylasia.

IT STARTED WITH Carlito, then the dogs barking at the gate after night had fallen. Jelena was always watchful of those in her care as darkness came, and then in the time before dawn, when souls could too easily slip away. She was with the woman in the treatment room, changing her wound dressing again, several lamps burning, and the fireplace. Light was important for what she was doing.

The wound was still bleeding. It had been because of the riding, she said to her patient. She had been given a name when she'd asked for one; she was certain it was false. Same with the three men—they were hiding their identities, to protect someone else, she thought. She hadn't been told how the injury happened, how a young woman had been stabbed in the leg then had to seek treatment away from anywhere it might be reported. She didn't need to know. Her task was healing, and she'd been given silver.

The men had slept elsewhere the previous night and stayed away through the daylight hours. The people in this hamlet were good to Jelena because she was good for them, but you didn't invite speculation, and if someone with coins were to arrive on horseback, in uniform or livery, asking if there had been riders passing by, or staying . . .

One of the three men had slipped back in quietly, the leader, just now, to ask after the woman, then speak to her in whispers when he found her awake, and Jelena permitted it.

He badly desired to ride on. Jelena had made it clear that she could forbid them nothing, wouldn't even try, but if he wanted his companion to keep her leg and live they could go away themselves if they had to, but would need to leave her to be treated.

The woman said, "Would he come here?"

The man looked nervously at Jelena. "I sent . . . um, Marco last night, to say where we are, but I doubt it. We are too close to . . . the city."

He wasn't a good liar. *Marco* was another invented name. There were mysteries here, and Jelena wasn't lacking in curiosity. It was just that you couldn't make someone trust you, and sometimes it really was better not to know things.

Carlito whistled as she'd taught him, from outside, and the dogs stayed quiet, knowing him. The big man, at her nod, hid himself behind the door to the treatment room. Carlito came up the walk and through the front door, carrying a stone jar of honey.

"I thought you'd need more," he said, importantly.

He was clever and quick. Probably doomed to have these do him little good in the life he'd be allowed. Jelena had begun thinking about such things, how much having a *chance* to do what you were good at mattered. This boy would stay here all his days, most likely, or go off to be a soldier—and likely die that way, not find a better, freer life.

"Thank you," Jelena said. "I did need more." She didn't, but why tell him that?

"I saw something on the way," Carlito said. "One man on a horse."

The dogs started barking in that moment.

Jelena looked at the boy. "One only, you are sure?"

"Of course I am," he said.

"Good. Thank you. Off you go then, right now, side yard and home. No delay, Carlito, I am very serious."

He looked at her, saw that she was. He nodded. It was possible he'd disobey, but she didn't think so. He liked that she let him help and called him her friend, he didn't want to lose that. He went back out, cut left through the yard to a gap in her fence. She followed to the doorway and called off her dogs. One man was all right.

It was just one. She saw him dismount by the gate.

"Put the horse in the trees," she called softly.

"Of course," he said, whoever he was. She saw him lead his mount towards the copse west of her yard. She waited. He came back on foot. She kept the dogs beside her. It was cold out. She became aware of the big man behind her now in the doorway. He'd moved quietly.

"I didn't think you'd come," he said to the one by the gate. "We were just talking about it."

"She is all right?" the other one asked. He was a voice in the night, the light didn't reach so far.

"She seems to be," the big man said.

The one outside said, politely, to Jelena, "May I enter through your gate?" The courtesy was unexpected.

"Yes," she said.

He came into her yard and up the path and saluted her and named himself. His true name. Not a man who hid his identity. And so, for the first time Jelena encountered Folco Cino d'Acorsi, who was famed through Batiara, and was standing on the path before her door, at night.

She bowed. Her heart had begun racing.

"I am honoured," she said. "Will I now be killed?"

"Not by me," he said.

He gestured, and she stepped aside for him to enter, but he didn't. He stood in front of her. A smaller man than she'd expected, strongly built, remarkably ugly, in truth, with the eye, a scar, a broken nose. He didn't wear a patch over the eye. The bigger, younger man came out, nodded to him, and at a gesture of Folco's head, went up the walk to stand by the gate. He'd keep watch now, Jelena realized. The night had changed with this arrival.

"She is in the treatment room to your left," she said. "This is someone who serves you?"

"This is Adria Ripoli, youngest daughter of the duke of Macera," he said.

Jelena felt, abruptly, as if she needed to sit down. He looked at her. "It is, you might thereby understand, important that you heal her."

He went into the treatment room before she could say anything to this.

"In Jad's holy name, Adria, what have you done to yourself?" she heard him say, through the door.

She didn't hear the reply. She went to the fireplace and began boiling water for her patient's next infusion. She was thinking hard, using routine to keep herself steady. What was this woman doing here? A *Ripoli*? In this house?

But, aristocrat or not, visitors notwithstanding—she'd make the man leave soon if she could—the processes of treatment were not to be altered. They were talking quietly in the other room. She hoped, even more urgently, that Carlito had gone straight home. This was too large a thing, these people were far too important, there was real danger now.

She let the habits of work, movement of hands, slow her heart. You were better at what you did when you were calm.

But then whatever calm she'd worked to achieve was shattered like a thrown drinking glass hitting a wall, because the dogs started up again, frantically this time.

She crossed quickly to the door and opened it. She heard the big man on watch speak a challenge from beyond the gate. Folco d'Acorsi hurried out of the treatment room and stood beside her.

"*Coppo! Don't fight him!*" he shouted into the night.

Too late, because there came sharp, quick, hard words—then a clashing of swords and then—almost immediately, it seemed to Jelena—the sound of someone falling, with a cry.

The dogs were still barking, wildly.

"Jad rot his soul in darkness!" the man beside her snarled. "I am going to kill him this time. I am."

Jelena saw a shape at her gate, another very big man, and heard a deep, soothing voice, not that of the one named Coppo—and her dogs fell silent.

Something that never happened with a stranger.

The gate was opened. Someone paused to greet the two dogs, and then approached, a long stride. She saw him sheathe a sword.

He stopped on the path, a few steps from the doorway and the light.

"He challenged me, d'Acorsi. I may have killed him. Why did you send him out alone?"

Folco, beside her, was breathing hard. "A mistake. I didn't expect you yet."

"Yet? You thought I was coming?"

"Of course I did. You are terribly predictable." Contempt, rage, something else. Jelena put her hands together, so they wouldn't tremble.

Folco turned to her. "This is an unquiet night for you. I am sorry for it. Here now comes Teobaldo Monticola, called the Wolf of Remigio by some. I think he likes the name. He's come here to trap me. If he has killed a man I value, that will displease me greatly."

"He challenged me," the other man repeated mildly, coming nearer. "Foolish, if he knew who I was. I'll have to risk your displeasure."

He was, Jelena saw as the light reached him now, memorably handsome. He was also just as well known as the man beside her, and perhaps even more dangerous. She had seen him the one time in Remigio. Not someone you forgot. It was, Jelena thought, surely impossible that these two were here. The world did not *do* things like this.

"I'll boil more water," she said.

Both men laughed in the same moment. There was no mirth in either, though. The air felt rigid, as if it might crack. She didn't see ghosts. She did feel fear.

"I'll have your man brought in," the handsome one said. He walked a little way back towards her gate and called orders to men Jelena couldn't see. He turned back. "Your six will have been disarmed, d'Acorsi. I said they weren't to be hurt, yet. I can't promise, of course."

"How did you know there were six?" The voice was soft.

Monticola looked at him. "We watched you coming."

"No you didn't," said Folco d'Acorsi, so quietly this time he could barely be heard. "That's a bad lie."

Jelena expected, from that moment, that she'd die before morning came.

CHAPTER III

Prayers in a sanctuary were believed to have more weight but the liturgy taught that you could invoke Jad anywhere at any time, that the god was always present, even at night when he drove the chariot of the sun under the world to battle demons in darkness to defend mankind.

Coppo had been told once that in the east Jad was depicted not in luminous, bright-haired glory, but as dark, bearded, anguished: suffering for his children and labouring under the burden of protecting them. It was heresy, but sometimes Coppo thought that this way of picturing the god made sense. The duty of care, the responsibility of protection, these *weighed* on you. And in the world Jad had made for his children there was more than enough suffering to go around.

He told himself his own sorrows were minor in the scheme of what there was, but he missed his father all the time, every day. That accident in the quarry had cut off a decent man too soon, left his only son, at ten, responsible for too much. *Responsibility*, that was Jad's great burden, wasn't it? Why should mortals escape it?

He was standing alone in the night, neither moon yet risen, outside the cottage of the healer Leone had found for them, for Adria.

And now Folco was here, more quickly than Coppo had expected. But he'd had to tell Gian to report that Adria had been hurt achieving what she'd come to do, although she'd done it. They all worried greatly about her—especially Folco—given who she was, and the lady Caterina's displeasure as to her role with them.

"If my niece does not come back, I will arrange for our new Esperañan to poison you." The lady of Acorsi had said that to him, to Coppo Peralta, who dreamed of her. She didn't mean it, he was *sure* she didn't mean it, but even so . . .

And now he had Folco to worry about, in this isolated cottage too close to Mylasia, where it was certain that violence and tumult had already begun. At least, Coppo thought, with Folco here he didn't have to make *decisions* any more.

A sound from his left. A horse, a man dismounting, not bothering to keep quiet. Coppo drew his sword.

"Identify yourself," he called into the night.

"Delighted to do so," came the reply. "I am Teobaldo Monticola di Remigio. You will know of me. Shall I kill you or will you stand aside?"

Coppo had never not been a brave man, and here was his own lord's fiercest enemy in a world with many of those. Pushing towards this man's Remigio was a reason they were here, why Adria had gone into Mylasia.

"I cannot stand aside," he said. "And you cannot enter this house, my lord, unless invited."

"Both, in fact, untrue," said the voice in the dark. Coppo saw the figure of a man as big as he was emerge from the night. "Save your life and move from the gate. I am alone, for what that is worth."

"You will wait here and I will go in and report."

"No," said the other man. "That isn't how this happens, soldier. I like surprising people. I haven't surprised Folco in too long." Coppo heard a sound he knew, a sword unsheathed. "I don't believe I'll permit a guard to deprive me of that pleasure. I dislike being deprived. But I truly have no desire to fight you."

"I said stop!" Coppo said, and levelled his blade.

"Oh, dear. I believe you have now threatened me," said Teobaldo Monticola. "Why would any man of sense do that?"

Coppo was good with a sword, which made it horrifying, even before extremes of pain arrived at his left shoulder and then that same side, how easily the other man mastered him. It took no time, none at all, really, it was scarcely even a fight. He heard himself cry out as he fell to the hard ground.

He could say that cry was intended as a warning, but in truth it was only pain—and the fear he was dead now, here in the night.

The other man, the lord of Remigio, didn't even look down at him. Coppo heard him step past and open the gate he'd been defending. He thought of his mother then, in the retreat where she served, washing laundry for the Daughters of Jad. Coppo was all she had. Well, no, she had her god.

Jad, from tonight, might be all there was for her. He put a hand to his side and felt the wet blood there. He seemed to be on his back, looking at the sky. Stars, so many of them, then a slow blackness growing. He felt shame, and pain, and an astonishing sorrow. He wondered if the god carried this much sorrow all the time. He hoped it wasn't so.

⚭

Two men in riding gear, no livery to identify them, carried the wounded man into Jelena's treatment room. Blood dripped where they walked.

They were decently careful of him. Jelena had the sense they had done this before. Of course they had, if they were soldiers of Remigio's lord. His father had won the city. Had been offered it by the citizens, in fact, as a leader who could protect them. Folco's grandfather had done the same in Acorsi. Strong men with an army? It was better they defend you than the opposite.

The carefulness didn't matter, she saw, after they set the wounded man down on the pallet she used when she slept in that room to be near a patient. Her heart sank, looking at this man. Not much past boyhood. Though boys died in war. And women and girls, and always the poor.

The soldiers went out, booted feet stepping through blood. Jelena knelt by the pallet and examined the wounds.

"Dear Jad. Can you save him?"

It was the woman on the bed, her patient. She was sitting up, a hand to her mouth.

Jelena stood. She had made a decision when she first began as a healer. She would tell truth about what she could and could not do.

"No," she said. "This one will leave us, I fear."

Years later she would change this practice, become skilled at dissembling, giving awareness of approaching death time to arrive— because those around a dying person, sometimes loving that person, had their own needs, and these were also to be addressed if you were in the world to heal. But you needed to be older to learn some things, and Jelena was still young that night.

She heard a noise behind her, looked in time to see Folco d'Acorsi turn in the inner doorway and go back to the living quarters. After a hesitation, she followed. There was some slightest chance, she thought, she could prevent violence in her own house. More likely she'd be part of the dying to come before the thin moons rose.

Monticola's two men had gone outside. She was alone with the lords of Acorsi and Remigio, who hated each other with an intensity that was known through Batiara.

Without speaking, she walked to the fireplace and the kettle. The water was boiling. She set about making her infusion for the woman in the other room.

"He will die?" said Teobaldo Monticola. Folco had evidently said something. "I am sorry for it. It was unnecessary. He shouldn't have drawn his blade."

"You could have disarmed him," Folco said.

Jelena, her back to the two of them, shivered at what she heard in his voice.

"Perhaps," said the bigger man. "It is dark out there, I couldn't be sure he was alone. It seemed reckless to concern myself over-much, once he levelled a sword. I had him brought in here, d'Acorsi. Give me that."

"Give me that," the other mocked.

"I think so, yes," said Monticola, mildly. "So, here you are. It has been a long time. You have aged. You are even uglier. Where is the rest of your hair?"

Jelena turned. Monticola had seated himself on a chest by one wall, legs outstretched, crossed at the ankles. Folco d'Acorsi was standing in the middle of the room.

A pause before a reply. "I misplaced some of it." Folco wasn't smiling.

"Was our last encounter at the Sardi wedding? Piero's older son, in Firenta?"

"Were you there? I forget."

The other man smiled. "No you don't," he said.

Jelena walked, head high, carrying the herbal infusion, past them both and through the inner doorway to the woman lying on the bed.

"Drink this," she said. She handed her the cup and went to the man on the cot. "He is unconscious, he is not feeling pain."

"You know that?"

"Yes."

"He would want prayers," the other woman said. "And to have a cleric. It matters to him."

"No cleric nearby. You do the prayers."

"I am the wrong person."

"You think? If he has family, you can tell them the words were said."

The other woman stared at her. But a moment later Jelena heard her begin to speak the familiar phrases of the liturgy of passing. She didn't believe in them, but she'd heard them all her life.

She knelt again by the pallet and looked at the two wounds. The shoulder she would have been able to deal with, but the wound in the side would kill. The man was breathing, but had no colour in his face, already, and blood had soaked, was still soaking, right through the thin pallet to the floor beneath.

"I would try to ease his pain, but I truly don't think he feels any," she said. She was talking to herself as much as to the other woman. She also realized that she was repeating herself. She was shaken and afraid. People had died in this room before, but not from violence. Combat, war, murderous hatred had not entered her yard. Only the accidents of childbirth and farm life, the courses of illness. She wondered if she should be feeling more anger. Perhaps that would come.

As she watched, kneeling beside the cot as if in prayer (she was not praying), Jelena saw the moment when this man died. When it ended for him, began, changed.

Life could be in you, its gift, burdens, opportunities, and then . . . it wasn't. A heartbeat, no heartbeat. You were a body on a pallet—gone, with nothing to share about what lay beyond.

She placed his arms on his chest. She looked back at the woman on the bed. "I am sorry," she said. She stood up again. "Do you know his family?"

"A mother only, at a retreat near Acorsi."

"She is a Daughter of Jad?"

"She works for them."

"Then prayers will be spoken for him."

"Do you care? Do you believe in any of it?"

That was a deal more than Jelena cared to share with a stranger. She'd heal them, or try, but her beliefs were her own. She was startled this woman had seen her clearly enough to ask—and felt bold enough.

"I believe in whatever offers comfort to the living. I am sorry for you, too, it seems you knew each other well."

"It seems," the woman said bitterly.

She went back to the other room. The two men were there, one standing, one sitting at his ease, or seemingly so. She didn't think they'd spoken since she'd left, which was extraordinary. As soon as she reappeared, Folco said—as if they'd been awaiting her, an audience, someone to attend a performance, "Is he dead?"

She looked at him. "I regret to say he is." She turned to the other man, where he sat on her linens chest. "Can you have your men carry him on the pallet from my treatment room? There is a shed to the right of the door as you go out, in the yard. It is unlocked, he can be put on the chests there for now."

"Why does it matter?" said the big man. "He's dead."

She looked at him. "I have a woman I am treating. I do not want a dead body there with her. Will you be good enough to help or shall I send for men from the village?"

"That's not a good idea," he said.

"Then call your men."

Both of them wore swords, had knives in their belts. There was hatred in the room, like a presence. It made her dizzy, almost faint. She wondered suddenly if Monticola knew who the woman in the other room was. He might not. He hadn't seen her.

From outside came a muffled cry, and another, then a series of scuffling sounds. A crack, as of a branch underfoot, or something else.

Both men looked to the door, which had been closed against the cold night. They were listening. Neither moved.

"Your six men," said Monticola. "As I said before, if they are wise they will have been disarmed only, not seriously injured. Are they wise?"

We watched you coming, he had said. And the other had called it a lie.

Folco didn't answer. Instead, he walked to the door. He opened it.

"Cousin?" he called out.

"It is done," they heard.

"How many?" Folco asked, not loudly.

"Twelve, as you said."

Jelena, instinctively, looked at Teobaldo Monticola. He was carefully expressionless, but his posture had altered.

"Thank you, cousin," Folco said calmly. "Please now select three of them, Aldo, men without wives or children if you can, and kill them. Coppo Peralta is dead in here, I am sorry to say."

Someone—the cousin—swore violently in the night. "Only three, my lord?"

"Three. But attend to it."

"Yes, lord."

Monticola stood up. He seemed to fill the small room.

"Acorsi, if they do that, I will kill you here, and then the healer, and then the Ripoli girl who went to kill Uberto for you. Choose quickly."

He did know who the woman was, Jelena thought.

In the doorway Folco turned to him, and Jelena actually saw him smile. "No you won't. There are twenty of my men surrounding this cottage, not six, and you love your life too much to die just to try killing me and two women, one of them the duke of Macera's daughter. Don't bluster. It doesn't become you."

He closed the door, stood facing the other man.

Jelena retreated towards the fire. She was terribly afraid. She saw no spirits hovering near either man, but she did feel death in this room, or nearing it.

"You might have me killed regardless. If you have twenty men."

"I do. I might."

"It will be known who murdered me. It isn't a thing you can do in secret."

"I agree," Folco said.

"I told people where I was going."

"I have no doubt. Simple prudence."

"You'd die first, and both women."

"I could run out the door."

Monticola laughed aloud. "You'd kill yourself first."

The other smiled thinly. "You know me so well."

"Well enough. But . . . it seems I cannot kill you here. Because you lied about how many men you'd bring."

"Lucky for me I did that, then."

"But you can't kill me either."

"I'm still thinking about it."

"No. You aren't. You want to, but you aren't thinking about it. Desire is different."

Folco lifted both hands in mock admiration. "Such a subtle mind!"

"And I didn't even study with Guarino, to learn ancient speeches and new court dances."

"That still bothers you?"

Monticola shook his head. "Less than you think. Less than you've always thought. I'd have learned to sing there and fucked some girls, I suppose, but I've never lacked for girls, and I bring musicians to my court." His turn to smile. "And Mercati came to paint my dining room ceiling and my portrait before he came to you."

She could see it: the words, amazingly, were a thrust that went home.

"But then I lured him away," Folco said.

"You *did*! So much money. And lost him this year to Rhodias and the fat young Sardi High Patriarch. With your portrait not even complete, they say!"

"Ah. You follow the movements of artists now?"

"Of course. I am building in Remigio. I also have more than a maidservant in your palace, Folco."

"A foolish thing to tell me, if it is true."

"Perhaps. Perhaps I am lying, as you always do. As your father did. But you still can't kill me here, nor I you, since you are right, oh pupil of Guarino: I don't want to die in a pagan healer's house tonight."

Jelena thought of speaking, then decided it was a bad thought.

She must have reacted, though. Both men turned to her.

"Is there wine, by any chance?" Monticola asked. "We rode a long way to this hut."

It wasn't a hut, it was a house. She only nodded, however. She didn't trust herself to say anything.

She knew who the girl was, and her lineage, and what she'd been in this corner of Batiara to do. A Ripoli? Killing Uberto of Mylasia? This night was beginning to feel impossible.

She turned to the table by the fire. She took a flask and poured two cups of new wine, a gift from the vineyard this morning. Her hands were steady enough. Because she was angry she left the wine on the table, didn't carry it to the men, which a host should do.

These weren't guests, she told herself.

Turning, she saw Teobaldo Monticola smile again, seeing what she'd done. It made her gesture feel petty. A man aware of his beauty, she thought. He wore his dark hair long in back, short across the front, showing a high forehead above the straight nose usually called Rhodian, from the statues that remained of the Ancients. His eyes were lustrous, also dark. He frightened her, she was willing to admit that to herself. A sense that present courtesy, control, was a surface that could easily disappear. She moved away as he came over to claim a cup. He took the other, too, and handed it to d'Acorsi.

"Well done with the six men," he said. "A clever trap."

The other man nodded. "I have wondered about two or three things the past half year. Who is she?"

"My spy? No one who matters. Is she dead?"

"She will be, when word reaches my lady wife. After questioning, done before clerics, to record it."

"Questioning. I doubt that will be kind. The Ripoli don't like being deceived, do they?"

"None of us do. Not even the Monticola. Your father was displeased with your mother, after all."

The bigger man stiffened. That story Jelena knew. Everyone did. Monticola's uncle and his mother: murdered when discovered together.

She heard another noise from the night. A cry. Not an animal.

"Three," Folco d'Acorsi said, his voice hard now. "For someone I cared about."

"Ah," said the other. "You *cared* about him? Makes such a difference!"

"I can kill six," said Folco.

He meant it. She could see that. This one, too, she thought, was terrifying. In his ugliness, in his muscular force, the coldness of his will and intelligence. These were not men one would want to choose between, to say that the one was serving good in the world and the other not.

They were serving themselves, she thought.

"You won't kill six," said Monticola. "It goes against all you have been taught. What if Guarino hears of it?"

Folco d'Acorsi drank from his cup before answering. Jelena found herself holding her breath.

He said, finally, "Very well. This is where we are, what I propose. We both go from here tonight. I will have my men free yours."

"Very kind of you. But hear me first, and—oh—is the Beast dead, in Mylasia?"

A hesitation. "You'd know by morning, so . . . yes, he is."

"How sad. A pious man, beloved of the god. There will be much lamentation. And who knows what might happen there now?"

"Who, indeed? Only Jad."

"Ah. Well. As to that. Jad also knows this, Folco—you will not, you *will* not move this way, in *my* direction, into Mylasia. If you send so much as a dozen men south I will know it and will have word shared that it was Adria Ripoli who killed Uberto—on your instructions."

"Will you be believed? At all?"

"I think I will, once evidence is given before the High Patriarch and the Holy Jaddite Emperor of how he died, and the girl's description, and her link to you and your lady wife. And the fact of an Esperañan of certain repute having come into your employ."

"Ah. That one. Your spy spoke of him, also?"

He was trying to appear undisturbed, but Jelena thought that this was unexpected, and not pleasing.

"I detest poison, you know," said Monticola.

"You've used it."

"I have. I still detest it. And I can say I would never have sent a girl, *that* girl, into so much danger. Her life means so little to you? Is she just a hunting falcon? No more than that?"

"She is my niece. She is—"

"Does your wife even know what you sent her to do?" There was a silence. Monticola laughed. "Folco, you like to believe you are virtuous and I am not. It is a lie. Like your numbers here tonight."

"Not like that, no."

"Yes, like that! You lie to the world—*and* to yourself. You have done so for a long time, and we know the biggest one. Yours and your father's."

"Do not go—"

"I will go wherever my desire takes me, d'Acorsi. At least I am honest about what I will do, and will not do. Go home and reflect upon it deeply. Consult a philosopher. Or . . ." He smiled again, the good teeth. "Or we could have torches lit, our men to witness, and fight in this yard until one of us is dead. No one in power would have anything to say against it. I suspect they might be pleased."

"Really? What foolishness!"

Monticola laughed again. "What fear. I can beat you on a battle-field. I can beat you in combat. I have two eyes and a city on the coast for trade at sea, and my body doesn't pain me when I ride a horse too long. No wonder you hate me, d'Acorsi."

The other's turn to smile, Jelena saw.

"I have so many reasons to despise you and your family. Shall I start with your murdered aunt? Then your own poor, dead, inconvenient wife? The Monticola . . . sweet as summer wine."

Jelena saw the bigger man put his cup down, carefully. He spread his feet. He had gone pale.

"I wouldn't," he said. "I really wouldn't, d'Acorsi. You need to be more careful. I can propose a course of action here to a man I keep being told is intelligent, or I can kill that man tonight. I may be wrong about the intelligence. Show it. Two women depend on you."

"Two? Why would you possibly kill the healer?"

"I need a reason?" Teobaldo Monticola said, looking at her.

"Most men do," Jelena said, her voice steady enough.

"Ah, but if you believe this one, I kill to amuse myself. Very well, a reason: because you are healing a woman d'Acorsi has used to threaten me."

"And you think I *knew* that?"

"And you think I care what you knew?"

Silence in the room, and outside in the night.

"Your proposal?" Folco said finally. "I am listening."

Jelena realized she had been neglecting to breathe again.

"We both leave. I have no reason to report how Uberto died if you don't force me to. His death doesn't hurt me unless you come south, and I obviously don't want to make an enemy of the Ripoli in Macera. You married shrewdly, I give you that."

"Go on," said the other man.

"You would force me to act if you make the slightest move on Mylasia."

"And if I do not, you agree not to do so?"

"I don't have to agree. You have no way to compel me."

"But I do. The Ripoli, forgotten them already? My shrewd marriage? So powerful, so wealthy. A dukedom now! And there you were, spying on one of them in my palace. The duke's dear sister! You placed an assassin in her chambers."

"She wasn't an assassin."

"That tale can be told differently, my lord of Remigio. She will certainly admit to it under questioning. Recorded by clerics. You know how questioning goes. You aren't nearly strong enough to withstand the Ripoli, let alone the new Sardi patriarch—who might decide Remigio suits his *own* family's ambitions."

"Ah. The Sardis. Firenta again. The bankers."

"The very, very wealthy bankers. With a High Patriarch in the family now."

"Piero bought that."

"Of course he did! But they have it, don't they? We both need to take care. We are not powers like them, or the Ripoli, or Seressa. We are soldiers with small cities who look for space to survive among them. Of course," he smiled thinly again, "if you choose *not* to take care and are destroyed, my sorrow will be limited."

After a moment, the big man smiled back. He picked up his wine. He drained the cup, turned to Jelena. "This autumn's? From hereabouts? I like it. I will have some sent to me." He actually bowed to her, with grace. "Thank you, healer. We have intruded upon you in the worst possible manner. I would have been reluctant to kill you, by the way. Perhaps you will attend upon me one day in Remigio. We can be gracious, and I don't need my physicians to be devout."

He turned back to Folco before she could speak. "If you accept what I said about Mylasia I have what I came for and we can both go. A wager? Mylasia will *not* accept Uberto's son. The boy will be killed. He may be dead already. They'll aim to be a republic like Bischio or Seressa."

"No wager. I agree with you. They'll need an army. I wonder whose they'll hire."

Monticola looked wry. "Not mine, not yours."

"Not mine, not yours," the other echoed. He finished his own wine. "Go. I accept your proposal. You should not have killed that man out there."

Anger again, sudden, vivid. "He was a soldier on guard at a gate in the dark. He drew his sword on me. I have said it three times. Was he your lover? Is that it?"

"*Go!*" snapped Folco d'Acorsi.

And Jelena feared it would all come apart.

"You do not speak to me like that," said Teobaldo Monticola quietly. "Not ever. It is understood?"

Folco did not look away. The death of his man outside was burning in him, Jelena could see it. Something occurred to her: he might not lose in a fight with the other man after all.

She saw him turn abruptly and cross to the door. He opened it, cold air came in. Into the darkness he called, "Release them, cousin. They will be riding away with their dead. His lordship of Remigio will tell them they are to do so in peace. You will let them do that. It is understood?"

A long pause. "It is. If you command it."

"I do, Aldo."

Folco turned back to the other man. He said, "It has been a pleasure to take wine with you and discuss affairs of the world. We must do so again, Jad letting us live to such a day."

Monticola grinned. He had regained his self-control. And again, Jelena thought: *He knows he is beautiful.* He didn't look like a wolf, but the name had been given for other reasons. She also knew a story about a Daughters of Jad retreat and Folco d'Acorsi's sister. Vanetta, her name had been. The retreat was outside Varena, near her home. She'd grown up knowing that tale, the rumours.

"Come to us in Remigio!" Teobaldo Monticola said expansively, gesturing. "Perhaps in springtime when the sea breeze is fresh. You live so far from the sea! Bring this healer and your Ripoli girl, if she lives. Perhaps even your lady wife? We can sport in the sunshine there."

Folco d'Acorsi said nothing.

Monticola walked out past the other man by the door, brushing closer than he needed to.

Jelena thought, *Death was here when they were here, and is gone.*

Then she thought about the man slain by her gate. And three more out there now, and felt shame for that thought.

⚬✙⚬

Adria knew that soldiers normally buried their dead where they fell, if there was a burial; sometimes war precluded that. Among members of a mercenary force their homes might be widely scattered. Folco had men from Ferrieres, Karch, Sauradia, all over Batiara. One from Esperaña, with a knowledge of poisons.

Also, a daughter of Duke Arimanno of Macera, a woman who ought to have been married by now, ruling beside a husband somewhere, bearing heirs. Or being trained to rule in an important religious retreat. It wasn't as if she'd been destined for a terrible life. It just wasn't hers yet, she'd decided. And had been allowed to defer destiny—for a time. She needed to be grateful. She was, in fact.

It occurred to her that getting *her* back to Acorsi might be difficult. Macera and her parents were even farther north. She wondered if it was time to go home. She wasn't ready to do that. There was more she wanted—demanded—of the world.

She didn't think she was going to die here. The healer had said as much the last time she'd changed the dressing. She was clearly pagan, this surprisingly young woman. Many of the healers in the countryside were, where physicians were scarce and traditions lingered. There were no sun disks in the house that Adria had seen, and the woman had not made the sign of the disk when Coppo died. If you paid attention, you noticed things.

Doctors in cities and palaces were even Kindath sometimes, in their blue and silver clothing. There were treatments, remedies from long ago, and those not raised in the faith of Jad seemed to know more about them. Even the Asharites, Folco had told her once, had knowledge people here didn't. She'd never seen one of the followers of Ashar herself. They were greatly feared, of course. Unless captured and enslaved.

But it was not unusual for women of rank to have heretics of one sort or another treat them. You didn't *announce* it, though you might share someone among family or friends if they proved capable. Childbirth could kill, you sought help anywhere you could.

Most lords of cities or commanders of armies had an astrologer or some other reader of the future in their employ. This, too, was forbidden. Such men or women were supposed to be reported to the clerics and exiled from a city, or burned if the mood was dark. The world was precarious, however, deeply so. Prayer and sanctuary rituals mattered, but someone prudent would not want to be in the hands of clerics only, except at the end of life, perhaps, to ease the judgment that came when you went before the god.

She wasn't surprised when Folco said they'd be burying Coppo tonight, towards the woods west of this house. She understood the secrecy. There were twenty of them here, it turned out. A very large number to be in such a place, and it was not to be known that Folco d'Acorsi had been here, or a Ripoli woman—her.

She hadn't known about Monticola's spy in Acorsi. She had a good idea what her aunt would do to that woman, what her mother would have done if it had happened at home.

It was, in Adria's experience, untrue to think of women as softer than men, though she had never known any woman to be a monster like Uberto of Mylasia. Her sister, before she married and went away to Obravic, had told her that certain empresses of Sarantium had blinded and maimed their children, for various reasons. Alixana, long ago, had apparently done that, she said. But their mother had told Adria this was a legend only, that the Empress Alixana had never even had a child. Adria didn't know, either way.

Sarantium, great as it was, felt a mystery: gold-tinted, bejewelled, misty with the passage of time. Mosaics, dolphins, chariot races. Dazzling glory once. She didn't know much more, or even much about those things she *had* heard stories about. The past, she'd often thought, was hard to hold on to. She'd have liked to see the racing.

There was a small sanctuary in Varena with a mosaic of Alixana and the Emperor Valerius. She'd never seen it, but had been told by her father that the empress's face didn't look like a murderer's. Artists could lie, of course. There was that.

Folco's own portrait by Matteo Mercati was not yet finished. Apparently, that was common with Mercati: judged to be great, always in demand, no assurances he'd stay anywhere long enough to complete a work. Folco's likeness was being done in profile, his left side. It hid his blind eye and scar. You'd never know it was missing if you didn't know the man. Paintings were messages not truths, her aunt had said.

Truth could be hard, too. Coppo Peralta had died on a blood-soaked pallet in this room. It was a sorrow and an anger. People died, one sister and one of her brothers had, it was why people tried to have many children. But this felt different. Teobaldo Monticola had killed him. He had killed many men in his time. So had Folco, of course, but that was not the point. She'd kept looking across the room at the dead man she'd known since arriving in Acorsi. Coppo had brought her here, badly wounded, to a healer—else she might well have been the one lying dead somewhere.

Since Mylasia, Adria thought, she was also someone who had killed a man. Uberto had been vicious, she kept telling herself. Had deserved his death. She was aware, however, that Folco might have wanted the count of Mylasia killed even had he been pious and benign.

She knew her parents would be fiercely unhappy about all of this. Her father the duke would be icily angry with Folco for putting her in so much danger, although possibly not distressed that she knew how to kill. He would file it away as *useful*, because that was what he did, how he was. A shrewd, fearful man.

This was not the night to wrestle with these thoughts. She wondered if she was feverish again, all these jumbled ideas, like buttons in a bag.

"Get me up," was what she said to Folco. "I have to be there."

"No," he replied. And the healer, entering, said the same.

It was a matter of some satisfaction that she overcame both of them.

They carried Coppo outside after his grave had been dug in what would have been hard, cold earth. Folco's cousin Aldo, with Gian, helped Adria make her way out, wrapped in a woollen cloak of the healer's. Aldo was grim-faced. Her Aunt Caterina had told Adria that he hated Teobaldo Monticola even more than Folco did. Families, history.

It hurt if she put any weight at all on her wounded leg. She was afraid she might never walk normally again, or ride without pain— and riding mattered so much to her.

Too soon to know, the healer kept repeating when Adria had kept asking. The healer wasn't much older than her but already had the composure of someone who had lived a full life. Adria wondered if she'd ever present that way to people. She wondered if it was real in this woman, or just an appearance.

Too soon to know, she thought wryly.

They stopped by the grave, the two men supporting her. It was dark. No torches allowed.

Folco led the service. He'd have done this many times, she knew. No commander could keep the loyalty of men for as long as he had without their believing he would usher them towards the god, if need arose, with care.

Loyalty, Adria thought, looking up at the stars and both crescent moons now above the fields, had many different wellsprings. Shared blood, a cause, a faith? Love? A soldier would also be loyal to a leader who could *win* in the field, ensure they were paid well. Sometimes they looted a city or town that had not done the wise thing and surrendered. That happened, it was allowed. Three days of looting was the rule. She knew it, knew some of what happened.

And if you were a soldier and you died, you wanted to believe the rites might be chanted above you, as now for Coppo in chilly darkness by trees near a hamlet, with his companions gathered, two dogs circling quietly, and the moons in the autumn sky. With the others,

Adria offered the responses she'd known from her first memories, as they prayed for light for Coppo Peralta's soul, with Jad.

She discovered she was crying. Tried to tell herself it was the pain in her leg, on hard ground in the cold, but it wasn't. He was not a man she'd loved (there was no man she'd loved that way) but she'd known him well and he was gone. You could be loyal to a friend.

❦

He doesn't want to be dead. Doesn't have any wish to be looking down on this gathering in a night field, hearing his commander's voice ushering him to the god, though it would be worse if no one did, there was that.

It pains him to have lived a life without achievement. He had intended to have achievements! To serve faithfully and with skills that would lead him to rise in the esteem of Folco d'Acorsi. And perhaps his lady wife, of the Ripoli. He had wanted to earn money from service in war, invest it wisely, so he might have enough to offer the holy retreat where his mother laboured that she might live there as a guest when she grew older, praying and prayed for, not working at all hours to be permitted to stay.

He'd have truly liked to be able to do that.

Perhaps Folco . . . but he doesn't think Folco has any idea about Coppo's mother, where she is. Adria knows, they'd talked about it once. Maybe she will tell the lord. Maybe, if she . . .

The dead, he thinks, seem to be all about wishing things had been otherwise. At this beginning of the journey, at any rate. He isn't certain where he is, what he is. He hasn't gone far, yet it feels very far.

But he seems to be . . . lingering. He can still somehow see those gathered here, hear the chant and response. Adria is with them, wrapped in a cloak. He's aware the moons are shining, offering a blended light. There are stars. They seem brighter now, somehow. Light, he thinks, light is what he has always longed for.

And now the words below seem to be coming to an end, or, if they are continuing at the end of the burial rite, he can't properly hear them any more, or see the figures there as clearly. They are blurring, sight and sound.

He has no idea what comes next. He wishes he had not drawn a sword on Teobaldo Monticola. He wishes he were still alive, to love and fear.

He is not bitter. He is sorrowful.

Such a short life, he thinks again. No mark made upon the god's world. No ripples. Most lives are like that, he supposes. He imagines Jad must find that acceptable or he'd have made things differently.

But how should he know, Coppo Peralta, gone now?

❧

Folco went north before sunrise, he needed to be away from here, unseen. He left her with the healer, and Coppo in a grave.

Adria knew he had come south to lay a trap, but also to assess what was happening in Mylasia, judge whether it was possible to begin something bold there. He hadn't schemed to have Uberto killed out of any morality. He wasn't that sort of man. His dream was of a port. Acorsi had no access to the sea, Mylasia did.

That wouldn't happen now. Monticola had fallen for the trap— the story about six men—but he knew too much, and *would* share it to keep Folco out of Mylasia. And that would include exposing Adria's role—which meant her name, her family's name. Which couldn't be allowed to happen.

Not every plan or devising bore fruit. Some led to deaths. Leadership, governance, war, power all carried these risks. He'd said that to her in the treatment room after they'd buried Coppo. His men had been outside, already mounted, ready to ride. If Folco was grieving she couldn't see it, but he was good at hiding his thoughts and feelings.

It was dangerous for him to linger. Even without clothing to identify him, Folco d'Acorsi was a celebrated man with only one eye and a well-known scar. He could be recognized—former soldiers from one force or another were all over Batiara.

He had come south with a certain purpose and that was forestalled. You adapted, he said. Adria was in good hands here, and he'd leave Aldo and two others to bring her home when the healer

said she was all right. Adria wanted to leave with them. Neither he
nor the woman named Jelena even considered that to be an option.

"I won't take you," he said. "Find a horse and ride alone if you
feel like a fool, niece. Try not to die."

Not especially kind words to someone who had done what she'd just
done for him, but he was like this with all of them if they were foolish.

She would have to stay a week, even two, perhaps. There were
risks in that, if Mylasia became stable enough for someone to begin
searching for Uberto's assassin—a tall woman with reddish hair,
brought to him at night from a farm.

Folco said he didn't think that was going to happen in the city—
stability—and this was an obscure hamlet. His men would pay
attention to tidings, and react if they needed to. His cousin Aldo
was the best man Folco had, she knew, his second-in-command,
with him from the start, when they were young.

He saluted her briskly on both cheeks, and left.

He did say "Well done," before he walked out.

After, she realized she hadn't told him about the man who'd helped
her escape the palace. He might be useful, but she didn't know his
name. He'd been at the school in Avegna, had seen her there with
Folco. Clever, he'd been very clever, and had brought her out when
she'd been expecting to die on that stairway. She ought to have learned
the name. You wanted to be able to find such people again—if he
wasn't killed in what was coming in that palace and city. She supposed
she could trace him through the school if she decided it mattered.

The healer was changing her dressing again. There was blood
showing through the outer layers of bandaging. The woman was
still unhappy about Adria walking and standing. But you *did* these
things for a friend when he died. When he ought not to have died.

The healer's hands were quick, steady, sure. *Assured* was a better
word. She had long fingers, Adria saw.

"How long have you been doing this?" she asked. They were
alone in an empty house, some hours yet to sunrise.

"A while," the other replied, removing the blood-soaked wrappings, setting them aside. Adria looked down but couldn't see much.

"Where did you start?"

"My work? At home, a little."

"Where is home."

"North."

Adria laughed. "You don't like talking about yourself, do you?"

"No," said the other, though she looked up, and smiled briefly. She was small, neat, her hair was long, mostly a light brown, some white showing already.

Adria leaned back and, as the healer continued to deal with her wound, high up on her thigh, found herself unexpectedly slipping towards feelings that had not been present for some time.

She felt herself flushing, hoped the other woman wouldn't notice. But the sensations, or the aspiring towards sensation, did not go away. She'd been touched there before. Not often, but a Ripoli daughter did have access to assistance in this regard from the women of her chambers. Better than a man slipping into a room, into her, and the risk of a child. It was known and accepted. She hadn't done it often, but . . .

After a few moments of trying to remember the last time anyone had touched her, aware of a quickened heartbeat, Adria cleared her throat and said, "Would it be a breach of your duties as a healer if you were to ease me in other ways?"

The hands slowed for a beat, then continued as before. Adria's body treated as a problem to be addressed. But the healer said nothing.

Until she was done. She straightened the bed coverings over Adria, checked her pulse at her wrist, then looked levelly at her.

"I will make the evening drink for you now. But listen, first. If you had said that you desired me, that you wondered if I desired you, we might have had a different conversation. But not even a Ripoli can use me that way. Nor, if you truly are trying to *not* live such a life, doing what you seem to be doing, should you speak so to any woman—or man. Expecting service, claiming the right to it? I *think* you mean to live a different existence, my lady, but I might be wrong."

She left, with the bloodstained bandages.

Adria felt as if she had been stabbed again. Her cheeks were hot. She squeezed her eyes shut.

The healer came back with the drink a little later. Adria thanked her for it. Neither of them said anything else. She slept not long after—that was the point of the infusion, after all.

She fell asleep ashamed and woke the same way.

JELENA LAY AWAKE for what remained of the night, tangled as in a thicket by anger and stirred desire—and an unexpected compassion. Eventually she saw the sky begin to brighten through cracks in the shutters. The other woman was younger than she was, but had already done something Jelena would never have dreamed of doing, involving risks on a terrifying scale. And killing! But it seemed she remained what she'd been born to be, a daughter of Macera's lord, raised in the grandest city-state palace in Batiara.

Growing up in such a fashion, Jelena thought, took so much out of a person—if you wanted to change your life—it demanded so much.

⁊⟊⟊

The three men killed outside the healer's house that night, by order of Folco Cino d'Acorsi, were also young—because he had stipulated unmarried and no children. They were carried a distance south by their fellow soldiers, then buried towards sunrise when the light came back.

They each had a story that had taken them to that farmyard, but none that went from it, except to graves in strange ground.

PART TWO

CHAPTER IV

I haven't always found that it is our intentions, the decisions we make, that shape and guide our lives. The opposite, just as often, it seems to me. Impulse creates our stories, or chance, the entirely unforeseen. And what we remember of our own past can be unpredictable. I didn't learn this at school in Avegna, but I think Guarino would have agreed.

Beyond that, we are often borne where the winds of our time carry us. We might sail where we like in a ship—until a storm overtakes us, or pirates, boarding at sunrise. Calm waters and easy winds allow an illusion of mastery, control. But it is only ever that. The devout say we must trust in Jad. I have come to believe life is easier for them. Reversals are more easily dealt with when there is faith.

I have seen too much by now to be truly devout any more, though I still fear judgment for that sliding towards heresy, especially when I'm awake at night, and I often am. It is an uneasy world one walks through when there is no firm belief in what will come after, or that what happens to us as we live through our days is affected by the correctness of our faith.

I don't talk about this, of course.

I WATCHED ADRIA RIPOLI disappear into the night, supported now by another man. I was struggling for poise, or clarity at least. Neither came to me. I remember feeling an impulse to follow them, follow her: she *had* asked if I wanted to come. I could do that. There were far worse men to have as a leader than Folco d'Acorsi, and he'd be in my debt for saving his niece, who had killed for him that night.

It still shook me, that he'd used her in that way and that she had chosen such a task. *Task?* Weak word, I told myself: that a woman had elected to enter the palace of Mylasia and murder the count, taking that on her soul.

It was possible that the wealthy and powerful were simply not for people like me to understand. I didn't believe that, however. Not after years at a school among the children of power. I did think I understood them, or that I could. But the Ripoli of Macera were one of the wealthiest families of all. That had to mean something. Arimanno, this woman's father, had bought himself a duke's title for a rumoured sum so large it was deemed impossible by many.

I heard their horses beyond where I could see. I could still catch up to them. She had invited me. We had moved together in the dark and I had heard her laughter, elicited it, realized her courage.

And I didn't go.

I let her ride away. Why and how do we make choices at such times? Fear, caution, honour? I will say the heart of it was honour for me that night, though there will have been other things at work. But it seemed to me, *bone deep* as the poets say, that I owed it to Morani di Rosso to at least try to help him avert a fate that seemed inevitable—because of what Adria Ripoli had just done.

As to why a man taught philosophy would be thinking of averting the *inevitable*, I have no good answer. We don't always have answers when the road of our life forks and we have to choose a path, at speed, in the night.

There were decisions to make that might save or end my own life first. Did I re-enter the palace, bolt the door, go back up that same stairway? Or stay out here and go around, back towards the city gate, hoping it was open, that men were out searching for the assassin who had—clearly!—escaped down a rope to the square and somehow eluded the guards there?

Those guards, I thought again, under stars in a cold wind, would very likely die, depending on what followed in the palace now.

That thought—*what followed in the palace*—was what took me back inside. I'd left my lamp on the lowest step, and by Jad's mercy in small things, it still held its flame.

I started back up. There was nothing I could do about the blood on the stairs—I did wonder how well she could ride, how far, but I had made a choice and wouldn't be there to see. There would certainly be blood on my own leggings, and I'd be stepping through it as I went up. I'd need an answer for that when I stepped out, and I didn't have one.

I left the hidden stairway on the first floor of the palace. The third was where I'd entered, the second where I'd found Adria. The first floor was where we servants and guards and minor officials had our living quarters. If the god was kind, they'd all be roused by now in tumult and fear. Searching in the palace or outside, or gathered gawping in the antechamber by the dead count's rooms.

I listened for silence, prayed for it, admitted myself unworthy of Jad's help, then lifted the latch. Listened again, drew breath and opened the door.

Had there been guards, had there been *anyone* in that room when I stepped out, bloodied and furtive, my life would have ended in Mylasia, tortured and flayed. There is no doubt of this.

I'm alive, telling my story, my part of a larger story. There was no one there.

I closed the panel and went quickly through that large room, a refectory, and turned left and left to my own bedchamber. I shared it with two others—and neither was inside. I closed the door and checked my hose. Blood on the right leg, some on my boots. But I wasn't trailing blood where I walked, which was a gift of grace. I changed to my other leggings as quickly as I could, boots off to do it then back on, fearing all the while that the door would open, hard questions asked—and dying.

I stood up, trying to be calm, not doing well at it, then reminded myself that Adria Ripoli had gone into the chamber of the Beast alone, knowing he killed people there. It helped. It did.

I went out and up the stairs. I saw people now, hurrying up or down. We all eyed each other nervously. One man was crying, sitting on a step, no shoes. I didn't know him.

These were the servants' stairs I'd taken with Morani's wine. I made a show of speed, as if summoned. Two steps at a time, I went back to the third floor—because that was where Morani would be, if he hadn't been taken away already, or killed already.

And right then my life forked again on an autumn night.

There were twenty or thirty men in the antechamber, a tumult of voices, gesturing as we Batiarans are said by others to always be doing. (I don't do that myself, or I don't think I do.) I didn't see Morani, so I drew a breath and began pushing towards the door, still acting as if I'd been called there.

Half a dozen inside, including Morani. He was alive.

Someone was speaking loudly. The dead man was still on the carpeted floor. Uberto's body had been covered with another carpet, not especially well. I bent and straightened the covering, to hide his face better. His eyes still gaped. No one had closed them. I had a thought, and made a point of stepping in the blood pooled beside him. An explanation for blood on my boots, if I needed it.

When I looked, I realized that the speaker, a man I didn't know, was asserting control here—or trying to. He was big, broad-shouldered, well dressed.

"I want everyone in the palace searching! Here, below, all through the city! I want that woman found!" He was nearly shouting.

I want, I thought. Who was this?

"We are all aware of that need, Signore Valeri." This was Uberto's chancellor replying, a man I didn't yet know well. He had clearly dressed in haste. His thin hair was disordered; he wore no hat. "It is good of you to offer to assist the court. I believe matters will go more smoothly if you leave it to the palace guard and officials."

"Leave it to you? You blundered into this murderous calamity! No honourable man of Mylasia will leave *anything* to you now!"

I blinked in surprise. I probably wasn't the only one.

"Indeed? Your concern is for the count and his family, signore?"

The chancellor would be a man deeply versed in nuance and diplomacy, to have survived in his office. He'd been here for years.

The man named Valeri glared at him. He was red-faced, perhaps fifty years old. This time he did shout. "How dare you! What *else* would be my concern?"

"Ah. Well. As to that, there are," said the chancellor gravely, "many things a man might be thinking about tonight. You should know I have already sent a guard to the holy retreat where the countess is. And the count's child is guarded, safely with us."

"What? Who told you to do that?" Valeri snapped.

"Signore Valeri," said Morani, speaking for the first time, "with the greatest respect, why would officials of the palace have an obligation to tell a merchant what they are doing, or wait for his direction? As the chancellor has just said, it would be very much better if you were to return home. We are all frightened and angry tonight. Morning will show us more clearly how to proceed."

There was a silence. I looked from Morani to the chancellor—his name was Novarro—and then back at the big-shouldered merchant. It seemed obvious, even to someone young as I was that night, that Valeri had come here hoping to find chaos and weakness to exploit with assertiveness.

He levelled a finger at Morani. Something in the way he did it made me step nearer. No one had said anything about my being in the room yet; I think only Morani had noted me. Servants and minor officials come and go in a palace. They are like furniture, hardly seen. Something occurred to me and I looked around. The three other men in the room were also strangers to me, and they were dressed in livery. They had come with the merchant. And they were armed.

The man named Valeri said, "You dare even speak? *You* are the one whose treachery lies at the heart of this!" He wheeled back to the chancellor. "How is this man still alive?"

Chancellor Novarro said, softly, "Signore, that is a most terrible accusation. I say again, you would be better to—"

Valeri drew a sword. In the palace, in the count's room.

"*No!*" he cried. "It is not better for Mylasia to let foul conspiracy flourish! The people need leadership, not evil men in this palace killing their lord!"

He levelled his blade at Morani, who did not flinch. I remember that.

"*Signore!*" said the chancellor again. But he didn't move.

I did. Forks in the roads of our lives. Things done, without thought or conscious decision. A moment claiming us—and the rest of our days.

Valeri took a fighter's step towards Morani, sword extended. I took two towards him, very fast. I was young and quick, I had my knife out as I moved. And I stabbed him twice from behind, once in the lower back and then through the heart.

"You do not draw a blade in this room!" I shouted. "No one does!"

Valeri fell. He was dead, in fact, as he did. His eldest son was senior in his family from that instant, even if he couldn't know it yet. Various aspects of the future of Mylasia and other places flowed into and out of that moment, from what I did. The forks in our path are not only for ourselves.

"*Guards!*" the chancellor shouted. "*To me!*"

The three men who had come with Valeri, who had not reacted

quickly at all, now began to do so. They made to draw their swords. One did get his blade out—then sheathed it as five guards burst into the chamber.

"Gentlemen," said the chancellor to Valeri's three men, "you will lay your swords down, please."

They didn't hesitate. Their employer appeared to be dead, and they were surrounded by palace guards. Swords were laid down.

But a second man had now been killed here. By me.

I looked at the chancellor. "My lord, tell me I did right! He was going to kill Signore di Rosso. He drew his weapon on him! In this room! Who was he to give orders here?"

I didn't have to work to simulate panic and a plea. I had just killed my first man. The same night Adria did, though I didn't have that thought until later.

"Who, indeed," said the chancellor of Mylasia. "This," he added quietly, "is a terrible night."

Morani was looking at me. I couldn't read his expression.

Chancellor Novarro's brow knit. Then he said, "Guards, kill these three men, please. I begin to see whose conspiracy this was, who sent a woman to kill the count."

My jaw dropped.

"My lord chancellor—" Morani began.

But the palace guards of Uberto of Mylasia were well trained and not shy about killing. The three men of the merchant were easily dispatched. One, quicker than the others, turned and tried to get out the open window to the rope and down. He didn't make it. He died with his body half in and half out of the window. He stayed like that until morning, when he was taken down to the square and cut into pieces with the others.

"We do not yet have the woman," the chancellor said. His colour had risen, I saw, but he sounded more confident now. I understood something: *someone* needed to be blamed for tonight. The city would be in chaos, and chaos spawned violence.

Chancellor Novarro appeared to have made his decision. It seemed that the merchant, Valeri, had rolled dice boldly, and lost. If they didn't find the woman—and I was fairly certain that, unless she couldn't ride, they would not—there would now be a story to tell from the palace: of a conspiracy in the city, and its treacherous leader slain.

Valeri's family, I thought, would all be killed, down to the children. Their houses, land outside the walls, ships if they had any, all these would be destroyed or smoothly claimed by someone who paid bribes in the right places.

The chancellor, I had been told, was a wealthy man, bribes had been welcome. Also, the heir of Count Uberto was nine years of age. He'd need a steward to guide him, and Mylasia, for years.

I looked at Morani. He was staring at Novarro. He said nothing. This development might, I realized, save his life. Or not.

THE WORLD KNOWS what happened in Mylasia in the days that followed.

Or, Batiara does. Because we are important—our city-states are influential, wealthy, the High Patriarch is here, in Rhodias— we tend to assume that what happens among us must matter everywhere.

It isn't so. Events in a small city like Mylasia would scarcely have been noted in Karch or Esperaña, and Sarantium had its own dangers to attend to. Beyond that, the affairs of the powerful (or would-be powerful) are not the ones that matter most to most people living their lives, waiting for winter, for example, and what it would bring.

Mylasia stopped being my tale, though I had played a role, and would do another thing that mattered before I left. Uberto's death and what followed did become a much-told story of our times, though, and a caution to other leaders.

The chancellor had it put forth in the morning that the murder of Count Uberto had been devised by the Valeri family, that they had undoubtedly had accomplices among other merchant families, and these would be discovered.

Make no doubt of this, he had his criers proclaim in the palace square.

The girl had not been found, however. Looking back, that was the deadly flaw in what Chancellor Novarro tried to do.

Mylasia was a city of emerging merchants, controlled for a time by a dark and detested lord. They endured him because he could ensure safety for the farmlands and hunting lodges they were all acquiring outside the walls, and for their ships in the harbour (at sea, safety was not in his control).

The girl who'd killed Uberto had escaped past all the guards in the square. The count's heir was a child and would need a steward. The chancellor was known to be smooth, greedy, and cunning, but no leader of mercenary soldiers . . .

These things put together smelled of fish left over at the end of a market day, as the phrase went.

It smelled of dead bodies in the palace square over the coming days.

As it happened, the eldest son of Opicino Valeri, a man named Erigio, was both shrewd and aggressive. He had friends among the sons of other merchants, and they all had family guards—because merchant ships needed men-at-arms against raiders from Senjan across the narrow sea or Asharite corsairs from the southwest. Those merchants with ambition, and fighting men to command, saw a chance—and they took it.

It had happened in other cities, power changing from a lord—however his family had come to power—to a commune, however it was defined and led.

There wasn't normally so much killing as happened in Mylasia, but that wasn't unknown, either. Duke Arimanno of Macera, Adria's father, had more of his palace cannon aimed *into* his city, trained on his people, than he had facing out against possible attacks from elsewhere.

We were a violent people in a violent time. Few of us were strangers to watching men and women die.

What was unexpected in those first days in Mylasia—for me, at any rate—was that Novarro, the chancellor, survived. After publicly laying the blame for assassination on the elder Valeri and his friends, then seeing a younger Valeri take charge of the city with *his* friends, Novarro somehow persuaded them that an experienced man would be important to ensure continuity and safety. None of them had governed, he said, none of them knew the leaders of other cities as he did. He would serve them with all his heart, he said. They would *need* him, he said.

He surrendered the child to them on the second morning. Gave a nine-year-old boy to Erigio Valeri and the others to kill. That death was not a public execution, there was a worry it might agitate people. The dead body was displayed, however—no rumours of an heir alive somewhere in the world could be permitted.

The countess was allowed to remain in her religious retreat. She presented no obvious danger. Women of the aristocracy *could* rally soldiers and the people, but this was not such a woman. She had hated and feared her husband, and barely knew her child. They left her to Jad.

Morani di Rosso was killed two days after Uberto died, in the square before the palace.

It was not a formal execution. He was killed by a mob that had been caused to gather. Novarro gave him to them, as an offering. Morani, he declared, had been part of the conspiracy. He had slipped the assassin in to the count—with a knife. The tale of the bloodied groin was put forth. The savagery of it, Novarro declaimed, was unprecedented in their beloved Mylasia.

So Morani died that same way. Knives severed his genitals after he'd been stripped for all to see, exposed to that cruelty in a cold morning light. He cried his innocence to Jad, but it was difficult to hear him amid the roaring of the mob. Then they tore him apart. No burial to be allowed.

I watched from a palace window. I made myself do that. It will always be with me. I do not like large crowds even today. I fear them.

I knew something else back then. Chancellor Novarro had offered Morani the opportunity to be part of his plan. Morani could be the one to deliver the count's child to the leaders of the new commune. The chancellor had told Erigio Valeri already that it would be Morani di Rosso, a good man, who would do that.

I am not sure, even now, why Morani refused. He loved his family, he was not in any way tired of life, Jad's gift. Nor did he have—I *knew* this—any loyalty to Uberto at all.

I think, it is the best thought I have, that he was devoted to the idea of being loyal, in a world with little of that. That a man needed to drop an anchor somewhere, declare a truth, find a harbour.

He would not surrender a child to his death, though he knew that someone else would. Perhaps in the darkest times all we can do is refuse to be part of the darkness.

I am still not sure. Nor am I even certain he did right, looking back.

I am a different sort of man, I make different calculations, I suppose. His sons and his daughter were killed, and terrible things were done to his wife before she, too, died. How do we balance the account of a soul?

None of the merchants who formed the Mylasian commune cared that Uberto had been assassinated. His death was their gateway. But there needed to be villains in the story shaped for the world. Morani di Rosso was made one of those, part of the tale.

Some time later, I would go to Avegna and tell Guarino what had really happened, and what I myself had done. He wept, which caused me to do the same.

Tears might be a sign of having honoured someone, but they do not take away the truth that you watched him killed by a mob, from an upper window in a palace.

Nor can it be denied that Mylasia remained safe—and a less fearful city at night—under the rule of the commune that followed the Beast. The merchants, guided by their chancellor, made arrangements with men who had been Uberto's mercenary captains. A large initial payment ensured their leader's commitment, and this was followed by a city house, land outside the walls, and then a well-dowered bride. The merchants never fell short in payments to their mercenaries, after. They were too clever for that.

The chancellor, however, died in his bed half a year later.

I did that.

My second killing. But that one was different. It was planned, not impulsive. I had a horse waiting for me when I escaped—down the same hidden stairs and out the door I had taken Adria Ripoli through.

I woke Novarro before I killed him. I spoke Morani's name in his ear as my knife went in. I don't think of myself as a violent man, but I am surely a child of my time, as we all must be.

☙❧

There were conflicting and confusing stories from Mylasia, but one thing that seemed clear to Jelena was that the boy, Uberto's son, had been surrendered and murdered. The body had evidently been shown, though some said (of course) that it might have been any child's body.

There were reports of considerable violence. Two days on horse was not safely distant from that, she thought.

She let Adria Ripoli leave within the week. If she was honest with herself, part of the reason was her own increasing distraction, having the other woman in her house. *This is someone you are treating*, she kept telling herself. But that didn't help as much as it ought to have. At night she lay in bed with half-dreams of making the Ripoli girl please *her* by way of apology. Then, because she was such a kind person, Jelena would turn around and . . .

The other woman had apologized, the first morning after. "No need, but it is accepted," Jelena had said. But of course there was a need, and her acceptance was . . . complex. She didn't think her patient knew how much so. Which was good.

Better, all considered, for Adria Ripoli to head back north before trouble in the city might find her, and also better for this small house and the healer living here.

"I will instruct one of your escort as to changing the dressing, but it shouldn't need too much attention now."

"I've watched you do it many times. I can see my own leg and I am reasonably capable. I'll do it myself," the other woman said. "Though I'm sure they'd enjoy doing it, and looking." She was impatient, amused. Ready to be gone, Jelena thought.

She was walking well. It was a fair guess she'd not have a limp. A scar, yes, but only a lover or a servant or someone helping with childbirth would see it.

"I'll give you dressings and a bottle of what I clean it with."

"Wine won't do?"

"Not as well," Jelena said. She was being brisk herself. "You don't need the honey any more. If it opens up and starts bleeding find another healer, or a doctor farther north."

"I will. I am truly grateful," Adria Ripoli said. "I hope you know it."

"I was well paid," Jelena said.

"Not enough for what happened when the two of them were here."

"That's probably true."

"Nor enough for the insult I offered that night," said Adria.

Jelena felt herself colouring. "I said what I wanted to say, you apologized. It is all right."

"Not entirely so. I might have missed my chance to have nights with you beside me," said the other woman. "I did learn a lesson, if that means anything."

"Our lives are about learning lessons," Jelena said, turning away.

Rote words, they didn't even *sound* like her, but she was unsettled again and trying to hide it. Probably failing. The three men were outside, readying the horses. It was very early, a grey, cold morning, the autumn sun about to rise. She had both fires lit. Extravagant, but she would put one out when they rode away.

"But am I right? If I had asked as a respectful person ought to have, would you have stayed?"

A terrible question! *Respectful person.* There was a note in Adria Ripoli's voice Jelena couldn't define. It might just be the pleasure of feeling well again, being able to walk and ride and . . . do other things. This was not, Jelena decided, the time to teach another lesson to the child of the duke of Macera as to what should and should not be said casually aloud on a morning, with others just outside.

"Stop for rest more than you normally would," she said. "You will need to move the leg, change positions. It may cramp on you. And remember, keep it clean, watch for bleeding."

Change positions, she was thinking, looking at the other's tall, slim form. Adria Ripoli's eyes were grey or green, depending on the light. She had the long nose that was allegedly a mark of her family. And the family's hair. Jelena cursed herself inwardly, but she also wanted to laugh—at how the mind could work, or be guided. Both men and women could conjure desire in her, but she was normally *much* better than this at dealing with it.

"I'll do that," Adria said. But then, after a pause, she added, "I am certain Folco and my aunt would make an honoured place for you, if you were to come to Acorsi."

Jelena shook her head. This, at least, was easy to address. "If I had wanted to be at a court, I'd have been at one by now."

"Our desires can change," Adria Ripoli said.

She pulled on the man's fur-lined cloak and hat she'd be wearing. Better to not be seen as a woman riding with soldiers in the time just after a woman had killed the count of Mylasia.

"We should go, my lady." It was the one called Aldo, Folco's cousin, outside. "Best some distance before light. Better for the healer we were never here."

"Of course," Adria called back. "I'm ready."

She stopped beside Jelena on her way to the door and kissed her on one cheek. Not both, which would have been the formal thing to do.

She had killed Uberto of Mylasia with her mouth, Jelena thought, when she was alone again. She put out the fire in the treatment room. She had defined herself as a rebel all her life. Had chosen to try to find a different way a woman might live in the world. That one, who had just ridden off, was doing the same.

If you thought about it, she was doing so even more than Jelena was. There were many women healers; there were not so many women who had done what Adria Ripoli had done. The idea pleased Jelena, eased her disquiet. It was a *good* thing, she thought, that there were women working to widen the world in different ways. They could nod at each other in passing, in recognition, then carry on expanding what was allowed.

She decided she felt better. She did wish she had a lover here.

She took a walk with her dogs when the sun was higher, found some late herbs she'd been wanting. She saw a stag any hunter would have longed for. She watched it until it went back into the trees. She slept better that night.

SOME TIME BEFORE spring she decided it was time to move again. She woke one morning—it had happened before—with that certainty. A decision already made, the sun rising on the truth of it.

She gave the dogs to Carlito and went west, paying to join a party of merchants headed towards Firenta. They were pushing the season to get their goods there early, claim a better price. She wasn't going there—she still didn't want to be in a large city, not yet, at any rate—but it was a direction, and a larger party on the road was always safer.

She didn't have a destination in mind, though she thought a town might be better this time, less isolation. Solitude had its virtues, but it could also weary the soul.

It was already her thought that she might one day, if she lived, leave Batiara, at least for a time. Take ship east across the narrow sea, find more of what the world offered, in Dubrava, even in Sarantium itself. Perhaps go all the way there, yes, and see the city which had been the centre of the world for so long.

She never got that far, but she did go that way.

ᘒᗉᘒ

Brother Nardo Sarzerola, who lived, and honoured his god, in a large sanctuary and retreat near a road and a river and among fields, was young, not high in seniority at all. He was, however, deeply imbued with zeal and faith. He considered himself a warrior for Jad, and was also, perhaps, the slightest bit innocent.

He was standing in the roadway at the moment, in the middle of it, in fact, blocking the path of fifty horsemen Teobaldo Monticola di Remigio was leading on a springtime afternoon.

Wildflowers were in bloom on one side of the road, red and white and a very dark blue. Someone had once told Nardo his eyes were that shade of blue. The breeze swayed them pleasingly, and the young leaves on the trees on the far side of the river, beyond the field there, were rustling. There were bees among the flowers in the late-day light. In the far distance, southeast, a walled town could be seen, high up (as they tended to be). The sanctuary was north across the river, not on a hill.

Monticola, lifting a hand to halt his company, appeared amused—for the moment. Anyone who knew anything of the man was aware this could change quickly.

"Good morning, cleric," he said, sitting a large horse easily.

Brother Nardo, clad in sandals and his yellow robe, had a staff and a basket with him. He had waded across the river to gather herbs for the infirmary. He had already set down the basket. Addressed, he spread his legs and gripped his staff firmly with his right hand as if he were some prophet from the first days of the Jaddite faith in the time of the Ancients. He was fair-skinned, beardless. He said, loudly, "We know you by your banner, Wolf of Remigio!"

The use of *we* was, all things considered, an affectation. The only people nearby were farmhands spreading manure in the field to the south. They had, of course, stopped their work to watch horsemen approach and go by. The horsemen had also stopped. There was a man in the road in front of them.

"That one's dead," said a labourer to the one next to him.

"A cleric? Surely not so, in Jad's holy name!" The second man quickly made the sign of the disk with muddy hands.

"That's Monticola di Remigio, you slug-brained turd. Look at the banners!"

"I don't know banners."

"I do. The robed one's dead if he doesn't move aside."

"Then he'll move," the other said placidly. He was to live a long life, that one—and remain mostly placid through it.

Nardo Sarzerola had been reading, as it happened, in the *Lives of the Blessed Martyrs*. Their Eldest Brother was of the view that younger clerics should strive to improve themselves by reading if their tasks were done and it was not an hour of prayer. Tasks were almost never done, and there was a great deal of praying. The sanctuary was well endowed, from as far west as Bischio and Firenta, so they had many names of the dead to cite each time they prayed, candles to light, intercessions to invoke. This was always the arrangement. Endowment money on behalf of the soul of someone gone. It meant that prayers took longer, but what holy man could complain of that? And it also meant they had winter firewood and ample food . . .

Still, Nardo had taken to heart, from the reading he'd managed, the idea that if one's life belonged to Jad that might sometimes also mean the ending of one's life. A pious man's death, the *Lives* made clear, could be a mighty weapon in the service of the god.

And Teobaldo Monticola, here on a horse in front of Nardo, was a notorious defiler of piety and a lifelong wager of war. The stories about him, violence going back to his youth, were, frankly, horrifying in Nardo's view.

He had prayed, quickly, when the dust on the road gave way to a sight of banners—with a wolf emblazoned on them. The evil man *proclaimed* his identity, even as he wielded unjust power in the god's world.

Nardo did not engage in careful weighing of decisions, normally.

He had stepped into the roadway in front of the approaching party, and he decided, as he did so, that they'd have to end his life, because he would not move from their path. Who knew what evils the Wolf was planning where he went? What innocents would suffer?

He was greeted civilly, but the forces of darkness were known to deploy false courtesy to lure men from Jad's path. He was *on* that path, was Nardo Sarzerola, and not easily lured. Those who honoured the god to the doors of death were not only men and women of distant days, and one need not be a great man to be virtuous. Perhaps, indeed, courage in the service of Jad was what *made* a great man?

He said, hating the quaver in his voice, "I know you."

"I'd hope so," said the big man on the big horse. He still sounded diverted. "Else little point to banners or fame, wouldn't you say?"

"I would say infamy!" Nardo snapped.

He was still unhappy about his voice. He'd never liked his voice. It was thin and rather high, and there was that wobble—as now—when he was excited.

"Ah," said Teobaldo Monticola. "Is it infamy? Forever? It is decided? How that saddens me."

A man behind him laughed.

Nardo said, stoutly, "I enjoin you to follow me to our retreat, to kneel before the sun disk in the sanctuary and seek absolution for your many crimes. It is never too late!"

"In truth, I have often found it too late for many things," said Teobaldo Monticola. It was possible now to detect a note that was less amused. "For you, in this case, it will soon be too late to continue living and return home with your little basket."

Nardo found that his legs were shaking under his robe. But he said, "I have made my peace with dying here."

"Here? Dying *here*? To stop me from riding to watch the race in Bischio? You think Jad will honour such exhausting stupidity?"

When it was put that way . . .

But he would not *let* it be put that way!

"The god honours those who honour him!" Nardo liked the sound of that.

"Oh, Jad save my soul from misbegotten clerics dumped at birth by a sanctuary gate at night," said the man on the horse in front of him. It was unclear how he knew the details of Nardo's birth. Perhaps he was just . . .

One of the Blessed Victims, Boriforta, had been killed by twelve arrows. Some of the horsemen behind Monticola di Remigio carried short bows, Nardo saw. It *was* the time of the celebrated spring race in Bischio. It was likely true that this company was going there. Fifty men was not a warlike force, it was a proper guard for the lord of Remigio. Even so, this man's was a blackened soul that had served the dark all his days!

"You still need to come with me to the sanctuary. Our revered Eldest Son will lead us all in prayer and you can repent of your crimes."

"And add to your endowment?" Amusement again.

That would not be, Nardo thought, a bad consequence at all. And very good for him, too, should Nardo become the cause of substantial funds arriving.

"That will be for you and our Eldest to consider," he said primly. "I am but a cleric there."

"Then in Jad's holy name, and by his blood and chariot, what arrogant fucking presumption makes you think you can block my way? Jad scorns the arrogant, remember?"

"The god's name is defiled in your mouth!" Nardo said firmly. And knew, even as he spoke, that the words might kill him.

Monticola's face reddened. "I've had enough of this," he said. "It no longer amuses. My son is on his way to Sarantium, or on the walls already, to defend it with men and weapons I have provided him. How many of your sanctuary have heeded the summons, cleric?"

A troubling statement and question, no doubt about it.

Nardo suddenly felt out of his depth.

"His soul is his own," he said. "You are not him."

"Enough. You wish death, it is yours. Pray now. I grant you a moment."

Someone moved forward from behind Monticola, a man on a dark-brown horse. He was as young as Nardo, and not in Remigio livery.

He said, "My lord? Might I speak?"

"Do so quickly," said Teobaldo Monticola. "I have lost patience. Fools do that to me."

"Then let him look foolish, my lord. Don't make him a martyr, which is what he seems to want."

"Go on."

"But that's it. We go on. He can't *stop* us, my lord. He is a man in the road, and this road is well made and wide here. We go around him, on both sides, my lord. He *is* being a fool, and we can make it clear, if only to those in the fields there."

A silence. Then Teobaldo Monticola threw back his head and laughed.

"Jad's light! Why," he said, "did none of my own men say this?"

The young man shrugged. "Perhaps all soldiers see an untaken castle or town left behind as dangerous. This man with his basket is no castle, my lord."

A gust of wind swirled. The leaves in the wood were louder. The Wolf of Remigio said, "Guidanio Cerra, I am pleased I had you join us. You will lead the right-hand column, soldier or no. The left, follow me. Either side of our little cleric here. Harm him not, just pass him by!"

Which is what they proceeded to do. Nardo Sarzerola thought of striking upwards at Monticola with his staff as he went, but that wasn't how you acted, and the moment passed too quickly in any case. He just stood there, dust and grit rising to sting his eyes and obscure his view of the world, including the god's bright sun, as fifty horsemen went by him.

It felt . . . well, it did feel foolish.

After they'd gone, after the dust had settled, he coughed and wiped at his eyes and looked about him. The flowers and leaves were as they had been. The labourers in the field had returned to their tasks. The sun was a little lower. The wagons of Remigio, guarded, carrying supplies, bringing camp followers—whores and mistresses, no doubt—appeared ahead of him. He could block those, but it would be ridiculous.

He was alive! The thought was sudden, intense. Clearly, *clearly* Jad had duties for him in the world yet. That was it. That was the message to take into his heart!

Shortly afterwards, because of certain words spoken to him on that road, with the deep meaning he found embedded in them, Nardo Sarzerola received the blessing of his Eldest and set forth, alone, to the east.

He took ship at Mylasia (clerics were not charged for passage), crossed the narrow sea and joined a party heading overland from Megarium.

He reached Sarantium in the autumn. He was entirely overwhelmed by the gold and glory there, it was beyond what a soul could imagine. He was rendered speechless with awe for a time by the grandeur of that city named the glory of the world for centuries. Many other men and women had been. Sarantium was what it was, even when endangered.

The liturgies of Jad were very different east and west. People had been killed for those differences. There were two patriarchs, one in Rhodias (Jad defend him!) and the one here in Sarantium. But they were all children of the sun god, and the infidel Asharites were trying to claim the City of Cities. Pious men could not stand for that, and Nardo Sarzerola was such a man.

He would die holding a spear, having aged a great deal in a short time—standing next to the eldest son of Teobaldo Monticola, whom he had sought out when he arrived. They had become the unlikeliest of companions. Their lives ended on the same day, within the innermost of the great triple walls, when Sarantium fell.

Young Monticola wore his family colours, carried a shield with a wolf upon it. He was a trophy for the conquerors. His severed head was paraded on a pike, then placed with others above the once-mighty landward gates. Nardo was just another cleric in a yellow robe. His body remained where it fell, was partly devoured by hungry animals, then burned on one of many pyres. The fall of the city shook the foundations of the world.

CHAPTER V

I had no intention of joining the company of Teobaldo Monticola di Remigio. I didn't care one way or another about him. I knew his name and reputation, of course. He'd become the ruler of Remigio after his father had claimed it, and he was a celebrated commander of a mercenary force. He kept Remigio secure and the granaries full with the very large fees he made from cities like Seressa and Macera, or from whoever was High Patriarch, switching from one to another and back again, sometimes in mid-campaign, as all the mercenary leaders did. It was a turbulent, dangerous system but it was ours in Batiara then. It still is.

It had been discovered, long before, that it was less expensive for cities to hire mercenary companies in spring for several months than to equip and sustain their own militias year-round. In addition to which, an urban militia could easily turn on the leaders of a city. Much too easily.

Not that the mercenary system lacked weaknesses. A commander could become so strong he might take control of a smaller city. Or he might marry a daughter of a ruling family and inherit power in that way.

We live, it might be said, in unstable times. Dramatic, interesting, magnificent in many ways. But not stable. You would never say that.

Monticola di Remigio was often declared, in those years, to be the greatest of the mercenary leaders. It was possible that he was. He didn't have many rivals. Perhaps only one.

He was said to be both hot-tempered and arrogant. There were stories told of savage things he had done, but there were stories like that about *all* the commanders, including Folco d'Acorsi, his enemy. Monticola, like his rival, had married a woman of better birth than him. He'd had a son by her and a daughter, before she died. He'd also had a number of mistresses, one of whom had borne him two more sons, more recently, and was said to be the great beauty of the age. People said that about many women associated with power, mind you.

But . . . I had nothing to do with him, no *thought* of him as I made my way west that day. Had I not encountered his party on the road, had I not previously decided that, before going to my teacher in Avegna then home to Seressa and my family, I'd see the celebrated race in Bischio, I'd have had an entirely different life.

Such reflections can make us feel less in command of our lives than we like. Fortune is a wheel, some philosophers taught. It takes us up or down, randomly.

The clerics say it is *not* random, that Jad has devisings we cannot understand. Guarino, always devout, guided us to think that way, for all his love of the ancient teachers. Sometimes, over wine at night, he'd acknowledge a different view.

Who among us, man or woman, is without contradictions?

I HAD STOPPED FIRST, in my flight from Mylasia, at the farmhouse from which Adria had been brought on the night she killed Uberto, back in the autumn. That was easy enough, though perhaps foolish. A copper coin to a labourer in a field guided me there.

The people living on that farm now had moved in after the couple who'd tenanted it—and had pretended the girl was kin to them—had fled in the night. The land was owned by the Valeri family, it turned out. I didn't know whether to find that amusing or not.

Opicino Valeri's sons, led by the eldest, Erigio, were at the centre of the emerging commune and council now. It hadn't taken long.

I didn't linger. I was in some haste, having just committed my second murder in Mylasia. You might have thought I was a dangerous man.

There was no reason for me to have gone to that farm. It wouldn't tell me anything. I knew where Adria was going, if she survived. She'd invited me to come with them, to serve Folco, although she didn't even know my name.

That bothered me, I remember. The part about the name. I was young.

I wasn't going to Acorsi. It was time to go home. I still had that notion of a bookshop in Seressa, joining my cousin Alviso if he'd have me. I'd stop in Avegna. I had to tell Guarino about his friend, which would be hard.

In the meantime, it was spring. Flowers had returned, birdsong, the mornings were brighter. Hearts were brighter, including mine. I had survived a winter in a dangerous place, even though I was the one who had killed Opicino Valeri. I survived for the simple reason that no one knew it had been me. I'd been too unimportant, invisible, and I'd left the room right after.

Besides which, it had become evident almost immediately that Erigio wasn't especially grieved by his father's death. That happened in some families. The older man standing in the way of an ambitious son.

As a consequence, there was no great attention paid to who had killed Valeri. His actions, bringing armed men into the palace, stood to embarrass his children or place them at risk. He was removed from the palace quietly and buried quickly, body and perhaps memory.

You can say I was lucky. You'd be right.

I'd decided I would ride to Bischio before heading home, for no better reason than the season it was, flowers on hillsides, the famous race upcoming. And because I loved horses, loved them perhaps more than anything in the world.

I'd bought a good one with stolen money. The palace had been looted in the aftermath of Uberto's death, by people from the city, by those of us within. I'm not proud of that either. I prayed for forgiveness all winter, kept my head down amid disruption, then killed the chancellor in his bed: hand hard over his mouth, knife into his throat, Morani's name in his ear before he died.

I left that night under both moons, the stars dimmed by their light. A sense of freedom, the future ahead of me like the road I was on under blue and white light mingled, the sound of my horse's hooves drumming.

❧

Ginevra was being jolted about with almost every roll of the carriage's wheels on the spring roads. She was also bored. She was never going to regret coming with Teobaldo to Bischio to see their race. But still . . .

She'd have been happier on horseback, but she knew that being in a carriage, shielded from the sun and common eyes, was a symbol of respect. It was an announcement to the world that she was worthy of that—and in the great scheme of things, her long dream, such a declaration mattered more than comfort.

She was trying not to make too much of it. Teobaldo was a capricious man and things could change. But she was here, with him, on the road west.

She had been the principal mistress and—she believed this—the genuinely beloved of Teobaldo Monticola for ten years now, since she was fifteen. They had children, both of them were sons, and his wife had died years ago.

Her campaign was underway: to be wed, and have the children legitimized. A campaign as carefully thought out as any battle or siege by a good commander. A legacy in it. None, really, without. Men weren't the only ones who thought about legacies. And it mattered even more now with his eldest son in the east.

The east meant Sarantium, and there were some who thought that this might mean death. That the City of Cities was going to fall.

It was hard for her, surely for anyone, to imagine that the thunderous calamity of that might truly come to pass. The god would not allow it, even if his mortal children seemed to be doing little in the way of preventing it. But she was more than capable of imagining what Trussio Monticola's death might mean for her—and her children—given that there was no other son alive from his marriage. She would never, as a pious woman, wish Trussio ill, but . . .

So Ginevra della Valle rode in a carriage like a wife, even if she wasn't one, and was entirely happy to be going to Bischio and its festival and race. You could endure boredom for a time.

She carried her best jewellery and had two changes of expensive clothing for every day they'd be there. She was aware (of course she was) that she was beautiful, and that this mattered to him. Matteo Mercati was to paint her portrait after he returned to Remigio to finish Teobaldo's. That mattered, too. Another marker. He was unpredictable (artists were) but he was celebrated. Another big, handsome, vain man, although that one's interests did not lie with the women he painted. He'd want Teobaldo more than her. The thought diverted her.

But image, stature, wealth, the display of wealth. All of these signified. Status needed to be proclaimed, shown forth: in a jewelled necklace, a portrait by a well-known artist, the hugely expensive marriage of a daughter, the expanding of a palace or building of a sanctuary. People needed to *know* what you were—or declared yourself to be.

This might make it difficult for the lord of Remigio, probably the most renowned military leader of his day, to marry his longtime mistress when he might claim a bride from a distinguished family.

She had better lineage than Teo did, and he knew it, but the della Valle were not *powerful*, they added nothing for him, and power was the game they all played.

Her cards at the table were known to her: he did love her, she had two sons by him, she understood him extremely well, and it seemed that reassured and did not unsettle him. Some men, she often thought, could be like high-strung racehorses themselves, and not just when they were ridden in bed for pleasure.

Teobaldo had explained about the race they were travelling to see, what it was, how it was different from most, but it had been right after lovemaking and she was often vague in her thoughts at such a time. Not the best thing, but it was simply true that he pleased her deeply as a lover, always had, and she knew that pleased him, his vanity, which was good.

She heard voices outside. Men speaking lightly at first, then less so. This carriage in which she and a maidservant rode was covered, which would have been too hot in summer, but it sheltered her from wind and sun in this season, and she needed to protect her skin, which was fair. It did mean she couldn't see anything unless she leaned forward and lifted the side flap back. She did so.

Distractions were good.

Collucio, the leader of the five men assigned to her (and not happy about being back here with the carriage and wagons, she knew), was speaking to a rider who had evidently overtaken them and wished to pass. Collucio was capable, had been with Teobaldo a long time. He was also—in her view—another prickly, vain man who sometimes brought out the worst in Teobaldo.

"I said, I like your horse," he was saying.

"And I said thank you," said the other man. She leaned farther forward to bring him into view. He was very young, she saw, tall, slim, not formally handsome, but his carriage on his dark brown horse was excellent and his voice was pleasing.

"I don't believe you are understanding me," Collucio said.

"When I say that, it means you are to offer the horse to me, then we settle on a price. I will be fair."

"I have no doubt you would be," said the other rider. She guessed he might be Seressini from his accent, but there was something else there, too. "It would be unsuitable for an officer of the lord of Remigio not to be fair. It would reflect badly on his commander."

"I don't think I like your tone," said Collucio.

Ginevra had heard *his* tone before. It didn't presage a calm discussion.

"I apologize, if so," said the other man. He was keeping his poise, but he had to be afraid here, she thought. Unless he was a fool. "I meant no offence. I also need my horse, or I can't get to where I'm going."

"I am happy to offer one of ours," Collucio said, "as part of any payment."

"Thank you again. I like my horse. May I be permitted to pass?"

"Regrettably, no," said Collucio.

The discussion was public. In her experience this always affected men's ability to settle matters peacefully. Pride became part of the equation.

"You would steal a man's horse?"

That, she thought, was a mistake, even if it was true.

"What did you say?"

"I believe you heard me. You have asked if you can buy my horse. I have said no, with thanks. What else is there in this, other than theft?"

"Well, I could kill you, then the horse has no owner."

Too far, too fast, Ginevra thought. She could intervene, but this was undeniably diverting. She'd be a little sorry if the appealing young man was killed this morning, but it wasn't as if they *knew* him.

"You would do that? You would shame your lord and the woman in that carriage? Force her to bear witness to murder?"

He had seen her looking out.

He was observant. And good with words—she suspected a court in his background. He rode like a courtier, not a soldier. He also, she realized, looking more closely, didn't carry a sword. Which was foolish.

"It isn't murder if I challenge you."

"Ah. A challenge. For what cause?"

"You have . . . you have offended me."

"By not letting you buy my horse?"

"That . . . yes. For that reason!"

A silence. Ginevra changed her mind: she didn't believe the young man was afraid. She decided he was thinking.

He said, "Very well. I have no sword, I am not a soldier, it *would* be murder if we fought. This is about a horse, I propose a race. Use your horse or any in this party, even one of those up front with your lord. I ride my own. Winner takes the other's mount. I challenge *you*, captain."

Ginevra wasn't bored any more.

"That is not how this is going to—"

"Collucio," she said, pushing the curtain all the way back, letting herself be seen, "it is a fair challenge, and there is no honour in killing a man who has no weapon."

"I would give him a—"

"Race him," she said, knowing it would be heard as a command. "Do it for me. I wish to see this. But send a man to Teobaldo first. He will also want to watch."

He would. And his being here would change this again, ramp it up in importance. Collucio could lose face now, he was at risk. She didn't mind that. She liked brave young men. She now hoped this one wouldn't die.

"Contessa," said the young rider. She wasn't, of course, but it was a compliment, and he bowed in the saddle. He wasn't *so* unhandsome, she decided. A large nose and ears, but . . .

"Your name?" she said.

"I am honoured you wish to know it. I am Guidanio Cerra, riding to Bischio to see the spring race before returning home to Seressa. I am also honoured to salute grace and beauty, encountered unexpectedly." He bowed again. She had been right. There was a court in this one's past.

"Watch your presumption!" Collucio snapped.

"There is none. He has," Ginevra murmured, "said nothing displeasing. Send to Teobaldo and choose your horse, captain." She looked at the young man again. No smugness or triumph; a watchful look. He had to win a race now, against an experienced soldier. She said, "What course do you propose?"

He looked around, taking his time, then pointed. "Across the meadow to the pine tree on the hill, around it and back here. Though, of course," he nodded politely to Collucio, "the captain is at liberty to propose another."

The captain looked murderous. It was mostly her fault, Ginevra knew, making this even more public, bringing Teobaldo into it, but a woman had to do *something* to amuse herself on a long road, didn't she?

IT IS EASY TO say I made a mistake, but what should I have done? You encountered people—merchant parties, clerics, couriers—on the roads all the time. I had been doing it for days. It had made no sense to slow my pace to remain behind this carriage and three wagons and their escorts, until—when?—they pulled over at an inn for the night? Why would I do that?

I suppose one might argue I should have done it once I saw the wolf banner. Or, there *were* cart tracks I'd passed, there would be others soon enough. I might not know where they led, but there would be a way back to the main road. I could have tried to cut along one, or gone trampling through the fields on our left, to come out ahead of these people.

But even knowing they were Monticola's men, with the slight thrill of fear that came with that, there was no war that spring, no reason for there to be trouble. My guess was they were headed for Bischio too. I made a choice: to ride up to the carriage, politely pass by, then deal with the larger company when I caught up to them.

I had been told by Guarino—and other students at the school, to be honest—that I had more of a temper than was good for a man. It didn't feel that way to me. It wasn't *anger* so much as, perhaps, an exaggerated sense of dignity, not wanting to yield too much or too readily—which wasn't appropriate for someone of my circumstances, I'll admit to that. However well regarded my father might be in his trade, it was still a trade. He cut and shaped clothing for the wealthy, measuring them on his knees, bent over his table. Then hoping they'd pay what they owed him, because there was little he could do if they didn't.

Also, concerning the events of that morning, which were significant in my life, I loved the horse I had chosen in Mylasia. First horse I had ever owned, bought with my own money—leaving aside how I had obtained that money. I had named it Gil, and I was not inclined to let him go to a soldier for some coins and one of the pack horses with these wagons.

I didn't like this captain—his name turned out to be Collucio—but that couldn't be allowed to matter, since he could kill me too easily, with no fear of blame or consequence. That was the way the world was (the way it is). I was riding a horse a soldier wanted, I could die for that if I didn't let him take it. The only people watching us were workers in a field, and the god's sun would fall and die in darkness before they spoke against a soldier.

That was where it stood, until the astonishingly beautiful woman in the carriage moved a curtain back and looked out. I had no idea then who she was, but any halfway intelligent guess had to make her a mistress of Teobaldo Monticola, and any man alive might envy him that, I thought.

I was, of course, aware that Monticola himself would be with the larger group ahead. I hoped, suddenly, that he didn't much like this captain of his.

I watched a messenger gallop forward. The woman in the wagon had ordered that, not Collucio. He sat his horse and glowered at me. A look that probably could have ended my life right there if he'd been a pagan magic-wielder or someone with the power to summon Jad's might to his cause like the prophets of long ago.

My luck, he was neither.

I eyed his horse, trying to judge what it would be like in a race. I'd said he could ride any animal they had, but it was unlikely a soldier would pick anything but his own. His was a deep-chested grey that would have staying power, I thought. That would normally mean my getting out in front, but I already had an idea how I might deal with this course I'd proposed. We'd raced horses a great deal at school, and riding had been my joy. I was, in fact, fairly confident.

A mistake. I'd forgotten that I was going against a mercenary captain being watched by his company and commander. The woman might disapprove of violence, perhaps, but with the lord of Remigio present, her lord, she'd surely keep silent.

TEOBALDO, AS SHE'D EXPECTED, approved of this race. He was bored, too, she could see it, and they had a distance yet to go to Bischio. He might kill men when he needed distraction but this was adequate as a morning's entertainment.

"I'd give you Maretto to ride, Collucio, but if you lost him to this boy I'd lose both a horse and a captain, because I'd kill you for costing me my joy."

Collucio laughed, not convincingly.

The young man she'd decided was from Seressa offered a thin smile. He'd already bowed deeply, properly, to Teobaldo. He was young, yes, but wasn't a boy. Teobaldo was like that with men, pushing them downwards unless he built them up.

"I thought *I* was your joy," she said archly to the man she needed to marry. He laughed. He was suddenly, Ginevra saw, in a great good humour.

"Around the tree, then," he said. "Then back across this road on my left side. Everyone make room. Winner wins a horse; I kill the loser."

Teobaldo paused to eye both men, then he burst into laughter again at his own sally, the handsome head thrown back so far he almost lost his wide-brimmed hat.

It was, Ginevra thought, harder for others to laugh, because it was the sort of thing people thought he might do. It wasn't, not truly, but the world didn't need to know that. He had spoken to her about how *useful* fear could be. It did make men, even those who served you, a trifle unsure if you were jesting, of course.

He turned to her. "My lady, will you start them?"

He always spoke to her with extreme courtesy in public. Alone, their words for each other might be divertingly otherwise, but alone was different, and they excited each other, still.

She accepted a hand in stepping down from the carriage and adjusted her own hat brim in the sun and breeze. The two riders moved to the edge of the road a little past Teobaldo, facing the meadow, each looking back over a shoulder at her.

She thought the horses might be evenly matched, but she didn't believe the young stranger knew what he was getting into. Soldiers were an entirely different kind of man, she had come to understand. Sieges and sacks, marches in cold rain without food, burning farms, killing people fleeing from those fires. Killing, much killing. These things made a man different over time. Human life became shallower, had less weight when you had seen or caused so many deaths, left behind so much suffering. You could always go to a sanctuary and pray for Jad's forgiveness, whatever you'd done. Then go back to do it again.

She lifted a glove in one hand, and let it fall.

THE SOLDIER NAMED Collucio went to the front. I'd thought he might. I let him. His commander was watching, and his fellows. A race was a flashing of pride as much as skill, for some. Not for me. A race was about winning, but I wasn't a nobleman, or a soldier.

I was happy to have him lead. The meadow grass was high enough already to make the lead horse work harder. I let him push through for both of us. The tree was uphill from the road and a distance away. This would not be a flat-out race.

He realized that fairly soon and slowed his horse, so I did the same, staying behind. A slower pace was good for me if I was right about his big mount's stamina. I had never raced Gil, which might mean this was a terrible mistake, but I had confidence in my judgment as to horses, and I didn't think it was.

On the other hand, I wasn't ready for a knife to come out of the belt of the man ahead of me, when we were some distance from the watchers on the road.

I should have been. This was a veteran of war, a captain in a celebrated company, and he'd have no intention of losing a race and a horse to some boy in front of Monticola. What is there to say? I was still young. Not a boy, but not enough past it, perhaps, even with the two men I'd killed by then.

I had a knife of my own, but no great skill with it, not measured against this one. Collucio stayed in front, making sure I could see his blade. *Pass, or even try, and this greets you,* was his message in the sunlight.

"Coward!" I shouted. "You're a coward!"

"You think this is a *game?*" he shouted back over his shoulder.

I suppose he was right about that. It wasn't like those races we'd had outside Avegna. I had left that world.

He kept looking back to mark where I was. I stayed right behind him. We were climbing, nearing the solitary pine atop the hill. Gil was moving easily beneath me. I hadn't been wrong about him. The challenge was to get past, be quick enough to do it without being sliced or stabbed. I could die here as easily as anywhere else in the world, it occurred to me. Monticola would make his captain pray for forgiveness at the next sanctuary, perhaps offer a donation there. They'd tell the story of the race over their meal, praise Collucio's new horse.

I have admitted it, people said I was too quick to anger in those days. I could channel and control it most of the time, I had that in me. A half year of planning had preceded a knife in the throat of a man in Mylasia, cold vengeance for my friend.

I was cold in my thinking during that race up a sunlit hill, I remember. But I *was* angry, from the moment I saw the knife. Not afraid. When I search my memories, I don't find fear.

I dared not stab his horse, even though it was possible from where I was: I could pull close and slash his mount in the haunches then pass when it stumbled. But I was quite certain that though Collucio could freely cut me to pieces, leave me dead in that meadow, if I injured the horse of an officer of Remigio's lord, I would be killed that morning. Guarino had taught some of us about certain philosophers' reflections on justice among men.

Those ideas, justice, were nowhere near that race.

On the other hand, I could make the man in front of me *think* I might stab his horse, and we were a long way from the watchers on the road now, galloping up the hill towards the tree where we'd turn.

When you are cold in your anger it can be a useful thing.

I decided. I shouted at Gil, slapped him with my hand, and he responded, moving up on the other rider's left. I drew my own knife in my right hand, let Collucio see it as he looked quickly back.

"I'll fucking *kill* you if you even touch my—" he roared.

Or, he started to. He cut off that cry when I made my real move. He'd lurched left and slowed, so he could attack me if I came beside him.

I was ready, and I had a good horse. I pulled up, just a little, then I slapped Gil *hard* on the left side of his neck, and we went by the other horse—on the other side, the right side—while Collucio was still turning the wrong way, ready to knife me if I got too close.

I was by him before he could swing around.

I heard a curse, and glimpsed his knife slashing. I leaned all the way right in the saddle, holding on, then we were cleanly past, and then at the tree and coming around it, and being a little wide there was a *good* thing, it made the turn smoother, easier.

I was racing downhill as Collucio was still tight-reining his mount around the tree, too close to it.

I remember him screaming that he'd kill me, all the way back down to the road. I sheathed my knife well before we got there. I rode across the road on Monticola's left, as instructed. Slowing, I patted Gil, letting him walk. I told him, in his ear, that he was my own dearest love and it felt true just then. I straightened in my saddle and stopped near Teobaldo Monticola.

I said, "Do your soldiers kill those who defeat them in a race, my lord? With your approval?"

His expression was grave for a moment. Then he grinned. "Not normally," he said. "Though it has happened. Collucio, hold peace." Collucio was beside us by then.

"My lord!" his captain shouted. "He was going to—"

"Going to what?"

"Use a blade! On my horse!"

"Did he?"

"My lord!" The captain was red-faced, enraged. He would truly have murdered me that day, I do not doubt it. Not everyone's anger runs cold.

"I see you have your own knife out. In self-defence?"

Monticola's voice was mild, but you could fear that tone.

"To . . . to protect one of our horses," Collucio said. The *our* was clever, I thought.

It didn't help him. "Is it so? I believe I saw you swing at him as he went by you near the tree."

"For the insult, my lord! To all of us."

There was a silence. I felt the breeze.

"I do not," said Teobaldo Monticola di Remigio, "feel insulted."

The woman, whose name I would learn was Ginevra della Valle, and who would not long after be the subject of one of the most celebrated portraits of our time, laughed aloud in the morning light, exposing the long throat the artist would clearly love.

I let myself look at her only briefly. It was Monticola who mattered here. He was gazing at me thoughtfully. He said, "Collucio, dismount, the horse is his. Keep your saddle."

I said, "I have no desire to deprive your company of a war horse, my lord. I wanted only to pass by in peace."

"I understand, but a wager was made." He was still looking thoughtful.

He was also correct. There would be shame for his company now, and for him, if a debt was not paid.

I said, "I am happy to accept a fair payment, leave your captain his mount."

He glanced at Collucio, who had not, in fact, dismounted. The man looked stunned. That didn't distress me.

Monticola said, "He will not have money enough here to pay you the value of a good horse. I do. I will advance it for him. He will keep his horse and repay me when we are home. It is agreed." He looked at another rider back by the second wagon. "Take forty serales from the strongbox for this man."

Forty? I suddenly had a great deal of money.

Monticola smiled at me. "Where did you learn to ride like that?"

No reason not to tell. "I was fortunate enough to attend the school in Avegna for many years. Riding is a part of what they teach, and it was my passion."

"You went to Guarino's school?"

"Yes, lord."

"Why was it fortune?"

"I have no lineage, my lord. My father is a tradesman in Seressa."

"I see. He must know men who matter, then."

"Yes, lord. To my great good fortune. As I said."

He still looked reflective. Perhaps amused again, as well.

"Where are you riding?"

"To Bischio, my lord."

"To watch the race?"

"Yes, lord. Then home to Seressa."

"To do what? In Seressa."

"I have the intention of becoming a bookseller," I said.

I heard laughter. Not from him. Nor the woman, either. It crossed my mind, after, that she probably guessed, or even knew before he did, what was coming.

"An honourable trade, for a certain sort of man," he said.

The soldiers grew quiet.

"I do not believe you are such a man. Not yet. I have," Teobaldo Monticola said, causing my life to change, "a proposition for you."

Which is how, though it was only formally to be for the duration of the ride to Bischio and the time we stayed there, I became a part of the company of Remigio and its lord.

An encounter on a springtime road. The random spinning of fortune's wheel. It can sway us, change us, shape or end our days.

HE KEPT ME by him the rest of the way west. I was aware I was being evaluated, though by what measure I didn't know. Monticola was not what I had been led, by rumour and tale, to believe he would be. He still made me anxious. There *was* an undernote of violence, the possibility of it, even if he laughed easily. He rode better than I did, better than any of us, in fact.

His second-in-command was a man from Ferrieres named Gaetan. He was small, lean, bald-headed, smooth-shaven. He never smiled, never looked angry. He made me uneasy too. Men who reveal nothing can do that.

But later on that first day I was the one who sorted out the problem of a cleric in the middle of the road. Not Gaetan, not Collucio, not Monticola himself. It was, of course, because I was the only man in that company who was not in the habit of killing people who challenged or offended them. There was a real possibility that, had I not spoken, the cleric would have died. Fortune's wheel.

Then, some days after, at a place where a wide road from the north met the east-west road we were on, to go forward as one to Bischio, we encountered Piero Sardi of Firenta's second son, overdressed in gold and silver, riding in extravagant display, a hundred men escorting him, all richly garbed. He had trumpeters and a drummer, half a dozen carriages, and the finest horse I had ever seen in my life, being led, not ridden.

And someone else, as well.

⁂

The general agreement in Firenta was that Antenami Sardi was not the swiftest member of the powerful banking family ruling the city in all but name, but that he was an *amusing* man. Everyone used that word. They didn't use it about his father, or his brother Versano.

He had been given careful instructions by those two as to the wealth and power he was to project in Bischio—which Firenta intended to besiege and conquer the following year.

It was time, his father had decided. The cities were too near to each other, and though Bischio was smaller it was irritatingly arrogant, claiming taxation revenue from towns in between. Money mattered to the Sardis; they had started as bankers, and they still were. Firenta's growing strength—and pride—required submission, especially now that, splendidly, they were no longer in conflict with the High Patriarch.

The High Patriarch was one of them.

It had cost a staggering amount of money. Antenami knew

that. He didn't know exactly how much; he hadn't asked, they probably wouldn't have told him. But his cousin Scarsone had been elevated to the highest holy office in the world. It was remarkable. He wondered if Scarsone was still a lively companion. They'd had good evenings together.

And now the Sardis were to begin recouping the cost of placing Scarsone in Rhodias, Antenami did see that. They would start by gaining control of Bischio, one way or another, and claiming the taxes of its surrounding towns and cities. It made sense.

His brother and father tended to. Antenami knew that his father, Piero, was brilliant with money, and that his brother was shrewd and cold. He himself was (generally) content to be well liked and rich. It made for a pleasant life.

Bringing the horse had been his own idea. If he'd told his father and brother what he intended to do with it, his plan would likely have been forestalled, he'd decided. They were like that with his plans, so he didn't tell them.

Antenami Sardi had no thought of challenging his brother in succeeding their father (both of them terrified him), but he did believe he was entitled to small pleasures, and entering his new, magnificent stallion in Bischio's famous race—to show the world how glorious the horse was (and he was!)—seemed a *splendid* thing to do.

Wasn't the trip about display and assertion? He'd say that, after, to his father, or perhaps write it in a letter, which might be easier, and safer, in case Piero disagreed, which he tended to do, in Antenami's experience of life and his family.

Riding south on a spring day, pleased with the world and his place within it (under Jad, and by the god's grace, of course), he saw a man riding back from one of the scouting tasks their mercenary captain had required along the way. The rider was coming quickly. Antenami became aware of a possible unpleasantness.

It seemed unfair to him, *wrong* somehow, that unpleasantness kept intruding upon the world, even on a bright day in springtime.

They were, he learned (the report was made to their mercenary, but protocol was observed and it was done in Antenami's presence), approaching a junction at the same time as a party from the east.

Normally, this would not be cause for consternation. More than a hundred people from Firenta accompanying the son of Piero Sardi, banners flying to make this clear . . . no one in Batiara, with the exception of the High Patriarch, would expect to not give way, especially around here.

There were, he heard, fifty riders or so in the other party. Not inconsequential, then, and they appeared to be mostly soldiers. Antenami's company was primarily his friends, sons of other merchant families, with their own retainers. They did have twenty mercenaries. His father had insisted, though Antenami, to be honest, hadn't wanted them, because he was also afraid of the mercenaries' leader.

It was explained to him, by that leader, that the present difficulty arose because the other party was from Remigio.

That did bring clarity. Even Antenami understood that it might not go entirely smoothly if they met Teobaldo Monticola at a joining of roads. And he certainly could not give way to a smaller party from a lesser city, on lands Firenta claimed. The loss of prestige would be enormous. He could *imagine* what his father would say, picture the icy contempt on his brother's face.

In short, an unpleasantness was indeed at hand. He hated that.

"We can go faster!" he suggested.

This, it was explained, would be undignified in itself, a possible source of amusement, even derision, since people would come to know of it.

One of the problems with being powerful, Antenami Sardi had often thought, was that you were always being watched, judged, commented upon.

"Well, we can't fight them just to be first on the road!" he said, forcefully.

"No, of course not," said his commander. "It is a difficulty."

Antenami Sardi found the whole thing silly. He didn't say that (of course). What he said was, "I believe I am in need of refreshment, and I would enjoy a visit with the women. Why don't we call a halt? This is a pleasant place. We will eat. Perhaps we will hunt." He enjoyed hunting.

His commander looked at the scout. They both looked at Antenami.

"That," said Folco d'Acorsi, who had been hired by Firenta this spring, for his usual very large sum, "is a genuinely good idea!"

Antenami smiled happily. He liked being pleased, but he also liked pleasing people. He liked having good ideas. He said, "You will join me back at the wagons? The women *keep* talking about you, hoping you'll visit."

Folco smiled back. "That is gracious of them, and of you, my lord." (The Sardis were not lords, and his father was careful to ensure no one called them that—in Firenta. Out here, it seemed an acceptable, small enough thing.)

"Then come," he said.

Folco d'Acorsi shook his head. "Perhaps later? I believe someone should ride forward. I will enjoy greeting the lord of Remigio, and it is, perhaps, the . . . proper thing to do?"

Proper thing to do was a phrase that carried, in Antenami's experience, a message. People were always telling him what the proper things were.

He managed a shrug. "Probably right. I'll come forward with you, then."

"We'll stop our party here, as you so wisely suggest, and carry on, just a few of us, to express our pleasure," said d'Acorsi, "at this unexpected encounter."

His voice was not entirely aligned with pleasure, Antenami thought.

He did think he knew why. Acorsi and Remigio, the two great mercenaries. Their history. It was hardly a secret. Hadn't one of their early encounters happened around here, years ago? A few days east? One of his friends would know, if he remembered to ask. It occurred to Antenami that there might be a story to share over wine later about this meeting at a crossroads.

On impulse he dismounted and had his man change his saddle. He rode Fillaro to the merging of roads. He wouldn't be the one to ride him in the race, of course, but it was good for a stallion to be under saddle, and good for his own pride and pleasure to have people see his wonderful horse.

"I WILL VERY happily buy your horse," said Teobaldo Monticola di Remigio. "At any price you wish to name. He is magnificent, Signore Sardi."

He did not say *my lord*. Propriety dictated that Antenami call *him* that, as lord of Remigio.

In the circumstances, he was uncertain what his brother would have done. (He usually tried to make these decisions based on that.) Folco, their hired mercenary, was also a lord, his family ruling for three generations now in Acorsi. The Sardis were only rich bankers, not lords—but they controlled a city many times the size and wealth of either of theirs. It could make for complexity, these rituals of protocol.

But the truth was, these two men, however famed and fierce, did whatever they did at the sufferance of greater powers, and Firenta was one of those now. Firenta, Macera, Seressa, the Holy Jaddite Emperor in the northeast beyond the mountains, the High Patriarch in Rhodias (always).

The great mercenaries earned money with their armies to sustain power in their small cities. They might be lords in name but Antenami's brother called them lordlings. He had always been swift with mockery.

Antenami decided to avoid the issue, often the best thing with a dilemma, he'd found.

He spoke politely, without salutation. "Isn't he beautiful? But no, this isn't a war horse, and I enjoy him far too much. My thanks, however."

"No thanks needed. It is a pleasure to look upon him." Monticola was a big, remarkably handsome man. Antenami, who considered himself good-looking as well, was an appreciator of beauty: horses, women, men, art, a tavern song . . .

Of the two celebrated commanders with him now, Monticola was far more impressive to look at. On the other hand, it was Folco d'Acorsi, ugly as he was, that his father kept hiring for Firenta, and trusting with their campaigns.

Folco it was who had taken Barignan for them three years ago, though that wasn't an entirely happy recollection. As Antenami recalled it (his memory wasn't reliable), that city, wealthy from alabaster mines, had refused tribute one year, and claimed independence. They had then held out behind walls, forcing a siege, and the soldiers besieging had become ill in summer heat, many dying, so that in the end Folco d'Acorsi had apparently felt he had no choice but to allow them two days' freedom to pillage inside when the walls were finally breached by artillery.

War was never going to be pretty. A reason Antenami had never joined a campaign. He remembered his brother riding to Barignan in haste afterwards, and offering a considerable sum to placate the city, since they did intend to govern it and hatred was not useful. It must have been a bad sort of sacking.

He didn't know what a good sack would look like, mind you. Folco had been summoned back to explain. He had evidently done so adequately; he was still their commander. He was here. Another powerful symbol for Bischio to see. They'd know the story of Barignan, of course. Everyone did.

D'Acorsi was staring now at Teobaldo Monticola. It was not a genial look. Monticola appeared to be ignoring him, still gazing at Fillaro. And who could fault him for that?

There was much more tension than Antenami liked, however. He tried to break it. He said, stating what would surely be obvious, "I can't sell him, in any event. I'm bringing him to Bischio to run him in their race."

The silence that followed was . . . unexpected. The sight of Monticola suppressing laughter was more so. Antenami looked at his own commander. Folco, he saw, was biting his lip.

Monticola finally addressed the other mercenary. "Jad and all the Blessed Victims, d'Acorsi! You are guiding him there to do this? He thinks he is going to race his horse in Bischio?"

Folco said, tersely, "This is the first I have heard of it."

Well, really, Antenami thought, he didn't need to tell hired soldiers *all* his devisings, did he?

"I won't ride him myself, of course," he said. "Not proper at all. I've brought a rider."

"Have you?" said Teobaldo Monticola. He still seemed close to laughter. A slow dawning came upon Antenami Sardi that—again—he might have missed something others knew about.

He *could* have told his brother about this plan, he supposed.

He looked again at Folco d'Acorsi. Who drew a breath, managed a smile in his ruined face, then began to talk.

And so it was explained to Antenami, quite kindly on the whole, that the race in Bischio was unlike other races. That the horses were deliberately selected by city officials to *not* be exceptional. They were to be roughly equal in stamina and speed. The riders were picked by a drawing from a large group of candidates, randomly assigned to run on behalf of one of the ten districts of the city competing in a given year, and then—another drawing— paired with a horse.

You couldn't, in short, just *bring* a magnificent horse to race in Bischio.

It was, Antenami Sardi of Firenta thought, the strangest excuse for a horse race he'd ever heard of in all his life.

He said as much. He laughed, which appeared to free both of the mercenaries to also laugh. He was not, after all, unaccustomed to discovering that he'd misunderstood something. No great harm done. It was possible that he should have learned more about the race before impulsively making his plan, yes. There was that. There was often that.

He shrugged it off. He was good at doing so. You could be *far* too concerned about dignity, in his own view. It could get in the way of enjoying life. That was his brother's biggest problem, Antenami had always thought. And these two men? What was the point of living in such a way that your deepest desire appeared to be to carve someone else open and leave him bleeding to death on a road in the sun? He'd say that to his friends, later, or to one of the women he'd brought south with him. What was the *point* of such a life? he'd ask.

A shame, though, about the race. He had a thought. He'd ride Fillaro himself when they reached Bischio! Right through the city gates, a symbol (his father loved symbols) of Sardi wealth, and Firenta's power coming their way.

He could do that. Then enjoy their peculiar race.

CHAPTER VI

In the way of such things, the spring race around the city square of Bischio, especially given its eccentric rules, was subject to corruption and bribery—in all the obvious ways and a number of less-evident ones.

This was understood by the race administration, and so resistance to illicit influence on the result was fierce. It was a war of sorts, long before the horses and riders appeared.

From the moment riders' names were drawn and their districts randomly assigned, they were sequestered within those districts. These riders might come from anywhere in Batiara (and sometimes beyond). They had no link to the district whose banner and pride they carried, no loyalty to it, and only the winning rider won fame and glory (and a considerable amount of money). As a result, any offers of a decent sum from competing districts to ride slightly less well were going to be appealing. Hence the sequestering.

Of course, the stories repeated every year, pointedly, of riders killed after the race by an angry mob from "their" district, that mob having decided the rider had neglected to exert himself to the utmost on their behalf . . . well, these might be cautionary, yes. Or they might simply encourage more subtle approaches to deliberate losing. Still, it was understood by the riders that subtlety might be wasted on an outraged populace, some of whom would have lost money they didn't necessarily have wagering on their banner against ferociously hated neighbouring districts. They'd also usually be drunk by the end of the race.

It might be thought that this would dissuade would-be riders from even entering the draw to race. You could do your best and still be assaulted in fury. This would be to underestimate the extravagant levels of fame that came with winning the Bischio race. And, of course, if a rider won again, or many times, he would never have to buy himself a drink in Bischio, and if he wanted nighttime companions they would be varied, and extremely happy to be with him.

Until the next year's race, when dark suspicions might emerge again. After all, who better than a lissome night companion to suborn some foreign rider within the intimacy of a bedchamber, either with her own allure or with an offer she might bring? Or both. Desire and money.

There were many other ways to affect the race. Horses were guarded as soon as they, too, were assigned to a district in the draw, but guards and grooms could be approached, or threatened (through wives, children, parents), induced to look away when a horse was given some noxious substance.

Saddles were thin and simple for the Bischio race and there were no spurs or stirrups allowed, but the cinches that held those saddles could fray, slip. Riders fell all the time. Sometimes they were trampled, sometimes they died. Horseshoes were also in play, loosened a little. Not removed. That was too easily spotted.

The race captains of a district might identify a horse they judged better than the other nine and try to induce the drawer of the lottery balls to—purely fortuitously—assign it to them. There were ways that could happen.

The two starters who dropped the rope that held the horses back as the race began might drop it only after a rider signalled with a gesture or a nod that he was ready—facing forward, free, not hemmed in. In a race that involved significant levels of physical assault, rider on rider, breaking out first was a great advantage. Often a horse led from drop of rope to finish, three laps around the oval in the howling, thronged centre of the city.

It was a wildly unpredictable day in Bischio every year. The noisier trades would be moved out of the city centre a week before, along with the butchers and the lower sort of streetwalkers. Illustrious guests took houses near the square, paying exorbitant sums for the privilege. The entire population would be packed into that square on race day, amid people with freedom and money from across Batiara, all gathered to wager and drink and laugh in springtime—to celebrate the end of winter and the fact that they were still alive as another year began.

Some would be dead by day's end, but that was true of every day, anywhere you might be in the world.

ॐ

It was impossible to deny that Teobaldo Monticola was a magnificent-looking man, whereas Folco d'Acorsi was more alarming to look at than anything else. That had been my impression when I saw him that morning at our school, as well.

I found myself unable to take my eyes off him. When I went forward with Monticola to where we saw a small party waiting by a meeting of roads, it was Folco I looked at—stared at, in truth. I didn't think he'd notice. He seldom took his own gaze from Monticola.

This was the man who had sent Adria Ripoli into Mylasia. But it was more than my knowing this, that first day. There are men, I have since come to understand, who control and compel a room or an open space simply with their presence—and Folco was always one of those. So was Teobaldo Monticola, mind you.

The Sardi scion, Antenami, my age or a little older, seemed

inconsequential beside the two of them, though he represented, through his family, far more actual power in the world.

I was nothing at that crossroads. I just watched and listened. I did immediately long for Antenami Sardi's black horse. Not that it mattered. Some things are never to be ours: we love them, and dream.

There are moments I remember vividly from that hour. Monticola spoke first, amusement in his voice, "So, did she survive, your poisonous girl?"

It shocked me. I had no idea how he knew about her. I barely kept myself from gaping at him. Antenami Sardi, clearly confused, was looking quickly from one man to the other.

Then Folco d'Acorsi, answering with composure, "It is kind of you to ask. She is well, Remigio. And how are your various women? Which of them is with you? Shall we pay our respects and admire her . . . clothing?"

Teobaldo Monticola colouring, not making any reply.

But a little later, after the nature of the race in Bischio had been explained to the young Sardi, as they were turning back to rejoin their party, Monticola saying gravely, "Acorsi, you should know that if Bischio offers to hire me I will accept. You should . . . both of you should know that."

"What? What?" exclaimed Antenami Sardi. "What does that mean?"

I remember Folco looking at Monticola for a long time, then nodding.

"Of course you will accept," he said. "I told Piero Sardi this before we left to come here."

And I realized, *far* too belatedly, that we weren't simply riding to Bischio to watch a race. I was still young, as I know I've said. It excuses some things, not others.

EVEN THE CELEBRATED lord of Remigio had only been able to arrange accommodation in the city for himself and his mistress and ten of his men. The rest slept, among the followers of other illustrious figures, outside the walls. There were inns nearby, fully booked up; others paid to sleep in tents, farmhouses, even on straw in barns.

Bischio, in the week of its race, was famously disrupted. The city gates stayed open all night, there was no curfew, torches burned everywhere. Men and women of all kinds were in the streets: card players and dice throwers and jugglers and whores. Soldiers and acrobats. Loud sellers of potions to cause love or ease pain, or kill an enemy or an unwanted child in the womb. Clerics preaching and wine sold. Clerics drinking wine. Touts for the race offered betting odds in quickly assembled booths on almost every corner. Everyone laying wagers. The Tower district was favoured, because of its rider, apparently. The Fox district was also well supported.

Three bodies hung from a gibbet outside the northern gate. They bore inscribed wooden placards around their necks. Pickpockets. I doubted their deaths would forestall others from trying, there was too much to be gained in these crowds. I tucked the purse from my own race—the money I'd been given for Collucio's horse—inside my shirt on a leather thong. Not entirely safe, but nothing would be, and better than at my belt. I planned to sleep with it. I was to stay with Monticola in the house he'd booked inside the city. He appeared to have taken a liking to me.

Was it winning the race, or sorting out the problem of the cleric on the road? Or because I amused him in some way? He might have been evaluating me, I think, looking back. Gaetan was with us in the house. Collucio was sleeping outside the walls.

I still had no clear idea how I felt about being among the soldiers of the Wolf of Remigio. It wasn't a *decision* I'd made. It was a place fortune seemed to have assigned me for the moment, and I wasn't fighting it.

On the first night, I asked directions to a reputable house and bought time with a girl who seemed young and clean enough. I needed to be with a woman. I had been unsettled by the proximity of Ginevra della Valle. She was uncannily, and consciously, beautiful. She deployed her beauty.

I went there with three of the other men. There was a real danger of robbery or worse if you wandered the night streets alone, and I didn't wear livery—as the others did—that identified me as one of Monticola's mercenaries. Nor did I have a sword.

I had never been anywhere with so many abroad after nightfall. People didn't wander after dark in Batiara. Not in any normal time. It was exciting and unsettling, both.

The girl helped that night, as much as such encounters can. I was careful not to fall asleep beside her, joined the other three to walk back to the house. One of them told me, meaning well, I thought, that Collucio was still angry. It was suggested that he'd be delighted to have a reason to kill me.

I really didn't need to be told.

THE RACE WOULD be the third morning after our arrival.

Monticola went out to a meeting two days before. I didn't know where. I wasn't asked to go with him. I was someone he'd collected on the road, like a trinket or a toy. Collucio came into the city with ten others, and they accompanied him through the streets, along with Gaetan and five other men from the house. A large presence, not courtiers, fighting men.

Five stayed to guard Ginevra. She didn't really need *guarding*, but there was display to think of, and an escort for the expensively dressed mistress of Remigio's lord, should she elect to go walking among the shops and stalls of Bischio, which was larger than Remigio and had more to choose among for a woman seeking after fashion.

I went walking on my own. It felt safe in the daytime if I kept my wits about me.

The next morning, the day before the race, I went to a sanctuary for the early rites. I did try to do this when I could. The sanctuary

I found happened to be in the Falcon district. It was packed with people. I soon saw why. I did gape, I remember.

They had brought their horse to be blessed, *inside* the sanctuary.

The rider was mounted, wearing the Falcon colours. I had never seen such a thing, never heard of such a thing. It was—surely it was!—a sacrilege.

But there were four yellow-robed clerics by the sun disk and altar, and they had the usual cups of wine and water, and these were duly lifted as they offered incantations with pious intensity, and that huge gathering of Falcon district citizens chanted their responses. With a horse in their midst. "Let this animal receive thy blessing, most holy Jad . . ."

I was crushed into a corner by the main doors. I hadn't been able to get any farther in. I'd just wanted to join the morning prayers somewhere. The excitement was palpable, a force. I looked around the sanctuary, then more closely at the horse, the rider.

I knew the rider.

I WALKED OUT into sunlight, my mind in disarray like a jumbled room. I actually felt dizzy. The noise level was astonishing, even early in the morning. I needed to be calmer, I knew it. Needing and achieving are not the same. I sat down on the rim of a fountain in the crowded street.

I could ignore this, what I'd just seen. Watch the race tomorrow, take leave of Monticola, head north to Avegna and my teacher, then home to Seressa and a life there. A choice, a decision made.

Or I could make a different choice, amid the loud streets of Bischio, where many people seemed to be drunk already, the morning before their race. It occurred to me to pray for guidance, but I had just *been* in a sanctuary—where a horse was being blessed and celebrated. The same thing, I realized, must be happening in nine other districts.

It was not a time or place, I thought, for prayer and reflection.

But I still needed to choose a course of action. Right now. I stood up. Someone bumped me. My hand went to my chest to check the purse I carried. That would give its location away, of course, but what was a man to do?

What was a man to do?

My cousin Alviso would invite me to join him in the book trade, almost certainly. He was a clever, kind man. I even had money now (if it wasn't stolen before I got home) to invest in the shop. My father and mother would be extremely happy to see me home and starting a business, a trade. My mother would begin thinking of a wife for me. I would tell her I was too young.

Seressa was, by almost any measure, the most exciting city in Batiara—if not the world. Confident, expansive, wealthy. There was integrity, honour in selling books, binding them . . . reading them. Perhaps one day writing one?

I do not believe you are such a man. Not yet.

Teobaldo Monticola had said that, not knowing me at all. Having done no more than see me win a race up a hill and around a tree against a soldier with a knife.

"Not yet," I said.

I actually said it aloud. No one heard me in the tumult. It was punishingly loud in the streets of Bischio. I had never experienced anything like it, even at Carnival back home.

I made my way to the house where we were staying. I asked for the lord of Remigio. He had not yet left for his morning's meetings, wherever they might be, whomever they were with. He was with his lady, upstairs, in her chamber, I was told.

I went up. I knocked at her door.

"My lord," I said, from the hallway. "It is Guidanio. I have something you should know."

"Enter," I heard. Her voice, not his.

I opened the door and went in. A handsome room. A wealthy person's home had been assigned to Monticola—because, I now understood, Bischio might soon have need of him. And his army.

They were dressed; it was seemly, domestic, sedate. She sat by open doors beside a balcony above the thronged street. She couldn't be seen by anyone below, but was dressed to go out. He stood beside her chair, a hand on the back of it. They both turned to me. She smiling, he with a mild curiosity.

"Tell me, Danino," he said, using the boy's nickname he preferred. "What is it I need to know?"

I told him. That was a time I did make a choice in my life, and I knew it as I spoke.

"There is a woman riding tomorrow for the Falcon district. I just saw her on their horse, in a sanctuary. I recognized her. She will be doing this for Folco d'Acorsi, I don't know why."

I did not name her.

Part of the choice I made, or intended that way. I already thought she was unlike any woman I knew, perhaps any woman *anyone* knew. There was no point at all in thinking about her the way I wanted to think about her—but Adria was, looking back, a part of why I wasn't ready to become a bookseller.

Not yet.

"You have no doubt about this?" Monticola's expression was no longer mild or merely curious.

"None, lord."

"How? Why? How do you know her?"

Too much intensity that morning. Things happening fast. I hadn't considered he'd ask me this. I said a thing that was true, but not one that might be dangerous.

"She came to Avegna with Folco once. When he visited our teacher, his own teacher. I was there."

"And you remember her from then, seen now?" It was Ginevra.

"Yes, my lady. She is . . . distinctive in her appearance."

"Is she? How so?"

A complex question. I gave a simple answer. "Extremely tall for a woman. Red hair."

She thought about it. "She was not hidden or disguised? As a man, I mean?"

"No," I said. I hadn't even thought about that.

"Women have ridden here," Monticola said. "Once or twice. One died, or was injured, I forget. It is a violent race." He looked at me. "You don't know who she is?"

I lied. "No, my lord," I said.

"I do. This will be Adria Ripoli. Arimanno's youngest daughter. Folco's wife's niece."

"*What?*" I said. I dared not say more. I had been trying to be clever, while not thinking clearly at all. I cannot say why it was so important to me, but I had not wanted to betray who she was. I'd thought that much could be concealed. I'd forgotten that Monticola knew she'd been in Mylasia.

Your poisonous girl, he'd said to Folco, when we met at the crossroads.

"Teobaldo! That can't be. A Ripoli? Then she is . . ."

He turned to her, which was good, for me, just then, to not be scrutinized. "An aristocrat, yes," he said. "But not a woman afraid of violence. She killed Uberto of Mylasia for Folco."

"*What?*" said Ginevra della Valle, in her turn.

"Truth. He wanted to take it over. Claim a port city. I stopped it."

I'd had no idea. Of course I hadn't.

It wasn't hard for me to appear amazed. He didn't seem to expect anything from me, which was good. I was genuinely shaken. How had the story of that night—her identity, the link to Folco—reached Remigio?

So much, I thought, for my sheltering her identity like a hero.

"This is good," Monticola said, and again, "Very good, Danino."

He began pacing the room. Crossed it in four strides, turned back and did it again, and then again. Caged and coiled—and thinking.

"Acorsi never does anything without a plan . . . What does he want here? Racing. This race. What can he—?"

He stopped. Speaking and pacing, both.

I stole a glance at the woman in the chair by the balcony. She looked expectant.

Teobaldo Monticola smiled. He said, triumphantly, "He is going to wager on her! The Falcon district never wins this race, and now, with a woman riding? It will be treated as a jest, as though even they know they can't possibly win, they'll be amusing people by declaring it."

"But if they never win . . . ?" said Ginevra.

"She will be a very good horsewoman," he said. "This is a Ripoli, remember? And I suspect there will have been considerable sums expended by Folco, and wagered to win considerably more. Even to get her selected as one of the riders, he'll have had to bribe people."

"My lord, why does he need money?" I risked. "He's retained by Firenta. We learned it coming here. Isn't this a terribly elaborate—?"

"No war this year. Only next year, if Firenta does come this way. His fee will be small now, in a season without fighting, and he is building in Acorsi. Jad knows, the bastard is building and building."

"So are you, love," said the woman.

"Yes! Which is why I need funds too, in a season of no wars. And here we are! In Bischio. And there is nothing, *nothing* on Jad's earth under his blessed sun that will give me more pleasure than to make money tomorrow because of Folco d'Acorsi!"

He laughed aloud. Such a vivid, compelling man. I thought again of a bookshop at home, and I thought again, *Not yet.*

She smiled at him then, and I wondered if anyone would ever look at me that way at some point, at any point, in my own life.

He turned to me. "Danino, you have done me a good turn this morning."

"We don't know if she can actually win, or—"

"No. If he placed her here secretly, and bribed her way into the race, he will have bought her a good start, too. He didn't do this without thinking. Folco doesn't live that way. No, no. No. We have work to do now, all of us! Danino, I need you to go down and tell Gaetan to bring in ten of the men from outside the city and have everyone assemble here. And quickly."

"Yes, lord," I said. I turned to the door.

"Wait!" he said.

I turned back. His expression had changed.

"You didn't owe me this," he said quietly.

I met his gaze. I was ready for this question, at least.

"You have been generous, my lord. You have housed me with you. I am grateful."

"I had you stay with us because my lady likes you. She thinks you are pretty, though I confess I don't see it."

She was still smiling. At him.

I said, "I am honoured. I think she is the most beautiful woman I have ever seen."

A risk, perhaps, but I didn't believe so. She smiled even more deeply. He did the same, in pride. Not a man who worried, I had realized, about women, their affection. Especially not this one.

"What a sweet thing to say, Guidanio," said Ginevra della Valle.

"I don't think," said Monticola, "that this one is entirely sweet. I think there is more to him." He turned to me. "Do you wish to serve me, Danino Cerra?"

I swallowed. "I told you, lord, I am no soldier."

"I heard you say it. Any farm boy can be a soldier, get himself killed one way or another, be promoted if he doesn't die."

I remained silent, watchful. So, too, I saw, was the woman now. Something in how she knew him, his voice, change of mood.

"How long," he asked, "were you at Guarino's school?"

"Seven years," I said. I remember my heart had begun beating faster. "He kept me on. I taught some of the younger ones towards the end."

"Is that so? They taught you to ride, I know. Did they teach you anything else?"

"They did, my lord."

"Trakesian? Mathematics?"

"Both of those."

"Geography? Geography is important."

"Yes, lord."

A silence. I still remember the woman in that moment. Her posture had changed, as if she now was the one coiled, alert, attuned.

Teobaldo Monticola said, "You need not decide this morning. You can go home to sell books. But you can also come to Remigio with me. I have . . . I have two young sons who are of an age for a tutor. Would you like to do that?"

His older son, Trussio, his legitimate son, was in Sarantium, or on his way there. People knew it. The mother of the two younger boys was in the room with us.

"That is a serious task," I said. "There are surely—"

"There are tutors all over Batiara and beyond. I make decisions in my own way," he said impatiently. "There are many things a boy in a palace needs to learn, important as geography may be."

"You could send them to Avegna," I said.

"I am not sending them away from me," he said.

Ginevra's head was high, I saw. Her hands were clasped in her lap. I had the sense every syllable was registering.

I said, "My lord, I am . . . I am the son of a tailor."

"I know that. Does it matter to you? It doesn't to me. Not for this."

I lowered my head, looking at the carpeted floor. He had shaken me. My thoughts were scattered again, like morning feed for hens.

He said, "Leave it for the moment. We have much to do. Decide after the race. If Adria Ripoli falls off at the start, or comes in eighth or tenth, I'll likely kill you, anyhow." He didn't smile, saying that.

"That will spare me making a decision," I said. He laughed.

She didn't though, his mistress, the mother of those boys. She looked at me, at him, and her face was difficult to read.

I didn't even try. I left the room and closed the door on the two of them and went down the stairs to tell Gaetan what his lord wanted done.

HE SENT OUT fifteen of us, having first made his men change their clothing, no livery. We were to be unknown. He'd also—though I only realized why later—had Ginevra go out as well, to sell a necklace, a jade bracelet, and earrings at a Kindath jewellery shop. The Kindath tended to be fair, and there'd be less gossip. She couldn't very well disguise herself.

He needed money, immediately. Serales were best. Seressa's coinage dominated our world, but any larger city's was all right if you knew exchange rates, and a mercenary leader always knew those.

I learned a great deal that day about matters not addressed at school in Avegna, or in any Trakesian philosophy text or poem from Esperaña that I knew.

It was like a campaign. First, three men left, including Gaetan, whom Teobaldo trusted most, to determine two things: what the touts were offering as odds for different types of wager, and if any of them had accepted large bets on the Falcon district.

Then Ginevra went out, with her escort.

The rest of us remained in the house. The others changed their clothing. Tunics needed to be found. Not all of them fit especially well.

Teobaldo was in a main floor reception room, pacing. There was a kind of joy in him that day, I remember.

Ginevra returned. The three men returned.

He took their reports and her money. He wrote numbers down and considered them. He gave, crisply, commands.

It seemed there were, indeed, sums being wagered on the Falcon horse and rider. No single one was substantial, but bets were being placed with many different shops and booths. This was what he'd expected, I gathered, and what we were to do ourselves. Too large a wager would attract attention—especially a bet on a hapless district with a woman rider—and they'd change the odds.

The bets were to appear frivolous, Monticola instructed, drunken wagers for amusement. We were told to say that if the girl won, we'd give her a night of more pleasure than she'd ever known with a lover. Variations on such a thought.

I didn't do that.

There was more: the wagers that had been coming in—it was Folco's men doing this—were for the Falcon district's horse to finish in the first three, not to win.

It was called a triana wager. The odds offered on the Falcon horse winning the race were thirty-five to one, reflecting how slim their hopes were seen to be. For a triana they were only seven to the one. Strange things happened in this race, it seemed. Horses crashed into each other or into the wooden walls put up in the square. A district could find itself coming third if the rider simply managed to survive the chaos. No glory, no parade—but those with money wagered on a third-place result would be happy.

You could also bet, I learned, on which district's rider would fall first, or how many would, and even if anyone would die. People bet a coin on that last against the rider for the district they most hated. It was a tradition, apparently.

We went out just after midday, in sunshine and wind, going different directions in the city. I placed wagers and collected the slips of paper marking them all through the day. Small sums, one or two serales, five (not really such a small sum) once or twice at a larger stand or shop. We were to bet on a triana, but Teobaldo had decided that every fifth bet we each made should be for the Falcon district to win outright.

Folco wasn't doing that, and I wondered why. I'd asked Monticola before going out.

He'd looked up at me. He was standing at the table, studying sheets of paper with numbers all over them.

He said, "The daughter of Arimanno Ripoli of Macera will not ride to come third in a race. She rides for Folco but also for herself. It may be unnatural, but . . . there is something in her, or she'd never do this. We may not understand her, but I intend to make a fortune from Adria Ripoli. And at thirty-five to one, I might. And our careful friend Folco will not."

That last, I realized, walking the streets, was what was truly driving him. He would. Folco would not.

I wondered, not for the first time, what the history was here. Behind rumour. Many mercenaries, indeed *all* of them, might fight on opposite sides then find themselves working together on another campaign. It was the way of war in Batiara. But never these two. How did hatred for another man come to define so much of your life?

I thought about that and about Adria all day as I went through Bischio, with the sun in and out of clouds before it went down and lamps and lanterns began to appear, and torches in brackets on walls. And at some point, I realized that I knew—or thought I knew—something Teobaldo Monticola did not.

I was perhaps too confident, perhaps a little reckless, but at the last four large betting stands I wagered twenty serales of my own money, five at each, from the purse about my neck, on Adria Ripoli of Macera to finish in the first three of the Bischio race in the morning. A triana bet. Not to win.

"If it is ever known who I am, I cannot do any of these things any more."

She had said that to me. That was the thing I knew.

The four men seated behind their tables taking my own wagers each gave me a close, careful look. I was young, and five serales was a considerable sum to possess, let alone wager foolishly. Two of them said, in almost the same words, one grinning, one not, "She won't fuck you just because you bet on her. She'll never know your name."

It was true. She *didn't* know my name. That still bothered me. It was also a childish thing to be thinking about. There were greater issues facing me.

First among them, I was allying myself—now, today—with the Wolf of Remigio. Everything I was doing was designed to achieve a triumph for him over Folco—and Adria. I'd made that choice when I saw her in the sanctuary and took word back to Monticola. My own decision. Not life throwing something at me I could not avoid. Fortune's wheel might spin, but you acted—or did not—in response to where it went.

And because of my doing that, I now had an offer to go to Remigio, serve in the palace there. And a single day to decide. A day! Carrying the memory of a stairwell in Mylasia, her arm around my neck, a jest in darkness about a kiss without poison. And a different recollection, a second night there, killing a man in his bed, naming my friend as I did, so the one I knifed would know *why* he was dying. That had been outright murder. The choices we make. The person we become.

The crowds became even wilder in the streets as darkness came to Bischio on the night before its race. I bought chicken pieces on a skewer, ate them standing, allowed myself a cup of wine from a different seller in a covered arcade, and then another from a smaller stand I passed. I drank them both too fast.

My belief, of late, is that the young must be forgiven a great deal as they try to make their way into and through the world.

CHAPTER VII

There was another man who wagered significantly on the Falcon horse and rider the next day, during the mad morning's run-up to all of Bischio gathering in the centre of the city for the race.

His name was Carderio Sacchetti and he was a shoemaker, as his father had been. He was not very successful, and not from the Falcon district. Which is why he went a distance from his own Goose district to find a betting table for his wager—which happened to be all the money he could scrape together (by borrowing) in the world.

He didn't tell his wife he was doing this. He bet the Falcon to win, because he was in desperate financial difficulty, and a dreamer. But he did it principally because his aunt had told him to, and she was said to have become a witch since she lost the use of her left leg twenty-five years before and became dependent on the family's charity to live.

She'd been injured riding in the race. Crushed against the wall of the Fontena Curve, where so many accidents happened. Everyone knew the story of Mina Sacchetti.

She wasn't one of the *useful* witches or herbalists. No one paid her for healing or spells. That would have been good for the family, if a little risky. People just thought she was a crazed, bitter woman, not a seer or teller of fortunes.

Her nephew wasn't entirely sure about her himself. But two evenings before she had come to him in the small home seven of them shared and said, quietly, "The Falcon. The woman riding for them. I have dreamed it."

"What? Dreamed what?" Carderio said.

"Bet on them," she said.

"I have no money for wagers."

"Do it, fool." And she spat out the open doorway into the loud street.

Carderio Sacchetti had passed a sleepless night listening to the baby cry. He suspected it was going to die soon. Just before the sun rose he decided (perhaps because of lack of sleep) that he'd spend a day assembling all the money he could, then bet on the girl his aunt told him to.

Only after he'd made his wager, three serales and twenty doppani on the Falcon district to win, did he consider that Aunt Mina hadn't said the horse would *win*, only told him to bet on it.

It was even possible to bet that a rider would fall, just as his aunt had fallen twenty-five years ago. He could have done that. He might be, Carderio Sacchetti thought, the greatest fool Jad had ever placed on earth.

Two of the men he'd borrowed from might well kill him when he lost and couldn't repay, and there was no way he could repay them. His wife might kill him first when she discovered what he'd done. It would have been so much better, he thought, drinking on the morning of the race, early, if his accursed, crippled aunt had been given some sort of *healing* gift, so she could help the child— not tell Carderio to do something unspeakably foolish.

Yes, he could have refused. But they needed a doctor for the infant, and the two older children were bone-thin with hunger, and his wife was looking of late as if she hated Carderio more than she hated the demons who battled Jad at night, because of how poor they were.

He and his brother and his wife went to watch the race, in the section assigned the Goose district. Aunt Mina came with them, as always. The brothers carried her through the streets. People made way on this day for Mina Sacchetti, a woman whose name had been drawn to race years ago, and who had been sitting in fourth (third, some said) when she was ridden hard into a turn by the rider for the Bridge district, and her horse, going too fast, stumbled on the slope there, and her left leg was crushed against the wall, shattering her bones.

Men from the Goose district had found and beaten the Bridge rider that night, very nearly killing him, but it hadn't done Mina Sacchetti or her ruined leg and life any good.

Revenge, Carderio thought, was a proper thing, but it had limitations. It was surprising that Mina had lived. A tough constitution and the family's help and prayers. Always prayers.

They were given a place at the front among the well-off, right by the inner wall, and people, even from other districts, who normally cursed or ignored his aunt, came around to greet her, to ask her blessing on race day.

Carderio watched this happen as he watched it every year. There was a dishonesty to it, but it still gave him some pleasure to see, most years. A small, good thing for his aunt in a marred life.

Right now, he really wanted to ask her if she'd meant him to make a triana wager on the Falcon instead of a bet to win, or even something else, but he decided not to. The slip for the bet was in his tunic pocket. His life, he thought, was written there.

❦

Antenami Sardi mentioned, a couple of times, to the commune leaders he was seated with that none of the horses parading out now—to applause and cheering wilder than he had ever heard—would have kept stride for even a dozen paces with his own Fillaro.

They smiled absently, but kept their eyes on the racecourse constructed in their city centre, on the horses and riders now entering. To be honest, they appeared uninterested in hearing about Fillaro. He did now understand—he wasn't a fool—that the horses selected for this race were deliberately not exceptional.

That, he thought, was foolish.

A city that organized its great race in such a way would surely be an easy target for his father and brother, should they judge that it was time next year. He decided he'd say that to them when home.

Notwithstanding the indifference to his horse, Antenami couldn't complain about how he was being treated. Fear was the best explanation, of course. Everyone was afraid of Firenta and the Sardis now, and he was the family representative, accompanied by one of the most famed mercenary leaders.

Antenami wasn't used to being an object of apprehension. He wasn't sure he liked it, but it really wasn't in his hands, was it? He'd smiled often since arriving, and made conversation about horses and hunting and wine.

"That one!" shouted the commune member beside him (he'd forgotten the man's name, though his much younger wife, on the man's other side, was called Lina). The merchant was pointing. "See there? The grey? The rider is a woman!"

Antenami was startled. He looked more closely and realized that it was true. The rider was slim, undeniably female. Much too tall. The received wisdom on female beauty was that a woman's height should be eight times that of her head. This one would be easily more than that.

"Who is she?"

"Best I can gather, she's from Mylasia, daughter of a captain in Uberto's company."

Uberto of Mylasia had been called the Beast, and had done shocking things, by report. He'd been murdered in his palace last year. The world was a precarious place, even for those in power.

"Is that so," he said. He found it useful to say that when he had nothing better to offer.

"So they say. The man had no sons, taught her to ride as if she were a boy, that's the tale." They had to speak very loudly.

"She sits well," Antenami said. Horses and riders he was good at judging. "But why is she here?"

On the opposite side of the track, beyond the inner wall, the crowd was as densely packed as it was here, and as wild. It was really very noisy. He found it exciting.

"Came to compete for a place. Her father left Mylasia when the count . . . was called to Jad. Then he died, I think. It will have become difficult for Uberto's captains, I imagine. In all the circumstances."

"Is that so," said Antenami.

His host looked at him. The merchant's expression was difficult to read, but Antenami was used to that, reading people wasn't one of his own skills.

"Have you wagered, Signore Sardi?" the pretty wife asked prettily, from her husband's other side.

She was at least a quarter century younger than her heavy-jowled husband. She was probably restless and bored, Antenami Sardi thought. Had he had a few drinks, his mind might have . . .

He was lamentably sober, had been since arriving. His brother had made it clear (Versano was always clear) that at least one of those accompanying him would be reporting back on this subject. Antenami's allowance and future travels both turned on his staying sober enough to embarrass the family "as little as possible." That was how his brother put it.

He did think this woman was toothsome, though. Prostitutes knew more and demanded less, but there was something about riding a well-bred woman. And Antenami was young and strong. He could stroke himself into a girl a good dozen times before finishing, if he hadn't drunk too much.

"Not yet," he said, answering her question. "Tell me where I should wager!"

"Oh!" She smiled. "On us, of course! Bet on the Tower. We are the best. Bring us good fortune!"

Good fortune, he thought, was unlikely to be what his family brought to Bischio. It occurred to him: if his father and brother and their mercenaries did capture it next year, perhaps he could change the rules of this absurd race! Then everyone here could see how glorious Fillaro was!

A pleasing thought.

The merchant called over a stout, heavily perspiring man taking late wagers, and without paying any attention to the odds (betting odds were for those who needed to carefully judge their wagers), Antenami laid twenty serales on the Tower to win. It wouldn't do to make a *large* bet, it might make him appear too . . . malleable.

Malleable. A choice word, he thought. He believed he'd learned it from his brother. The woman smiled at him again, then turned her attention back to the track.

Down there, a rope was now being pulled taut by two men dressed in green and yellow. He and his hosts were—of course—situated splendidly on benches (most people stood) right at the start and finish line.

Antenami entertained a brief, arousing fantasy of Fillaro on the track, *springing* forth—to circle the course three times before any of these horses had even done it twice!

He looked around. Colours dazzled in the morning sunlight, banners were everywhere, for each of the districts. The noise was even more extreme. Shouts and roars, even screaming now. Two of the horses were disturbed by it, rearing and stamping. One rider was almost unseated before the start! There was nothing like this in Firenta, he thought. Well, give them their silly race, there was no denying it was exciting. He wished the pretty wife had chosen to sit between her husband and their guest. Shouldn't she have done so?

He noticed Folco d'Acorsi, not far away, standing, not sitting. The man had an intent expression as he regarded the track, but he almost always had that sort of look. Then, to his considerable surprise, Antenami Sardi saw their mercenary captain make the sign of the sun disk, as ten horses and riders came up to the starting rope.

☙❦☙

It might be a youthful thought, but this morning feels as if it may hold the most important moments of her life. More than killing a man? Adria chides herself; the comparison is irresponsible and she knows it.

But . . . she'd killed Uberto in secret, and here she's on a horse parading with nine other riders in front of the whole of Bischio, and men and women are screaming as if they want the world and the god and all the dead to hear them.

There are people from all over Batiara here, and she is being *seen* as a woman doing this, even if they don't know—must not know—who she is.

If her father or one of her brothers came down from Macera, which Folco had said was wildly unlikely, they might not even know her, though she's not disguised. It would never cross their thoughts that she'd be on a horse here! It is too wildly strange, the idea of a Ripoli daughter in this race. It would be inconceivable to them, make it impossible to *see* her. Folco had said that, as well. There were, he'd added, more substantial things for her to be concerned about. He had been uneasy, because this was not his idea.

She's been here since the end of winter. Her leg has healed. The healer was skillful and ultimately correct: a scar on her thigh, which hurts when pressed, but Adria doesn't limp, and there is no pain when she rides. She has been lucky, and knows it.

And *she* proposed to Folco, even before she'd fully healed, that she go to Bischio and race and—if he believed in her—he could wager on her horse and make money he badly needed. It was her plan. Hers.

She said she'd present herself as from Mylasia, a cavalry leader's only child—which would explain why she had been taught to ride. And be the reason she was in Bischio, to honour her father in the year he died.

When you proposed something to Folco you needed to have thought it through and be ready for questions. But there *had* been women who'd ridden in this race. She'd known that, so had he.

She said she would tell them in Bischio that she was headed to a retreat after, whatever happened. The rest of her life would belong to the god. This race would be the last dream she'd pursue in a tumultuous world before seeking peace among the Daughters of Jad—praying for the souls of her parents.

Her father had been an officer of the Beast of Mylasia. Uberto's officers had not been well treated in that part of the world since he died, not with the changes there.

Joining a retreat, abandoning the idea of a good marriage, that would appear an obvious—even a necessary—course of action to anyone she told about it. A good daughter, a pious, sweet, sad story. Many might even hope her name would be drawn to ride, she'd said, back in Acorsi.

Folco had agreed.

He is hard and precise and decisive with the world. With her—and with her aunt, whom he loves—he is easier, amused, attentive. If you considered *attentive* to include helping her live the way she does—as a weapon for him.

She has promised her aunt this will stop soon. She doesn't want to think about that. Promises are broken all the time, of course: you seek forgiveness from Jad and those you've lied to. But Caterina has written of that assurance to Adria's mother, who will have told her father. They don't know (of course they don't!) all she's done for Folco, but it might not be easy to avoid a return home to a life and expectations she does not want, or accept. There is, she has often thought, only so much forcing of the world a woman can do.

She'll deal with that when it comes.

She *knows* she's been given gifts by fortune and the god. Her lineage, and being the youngest. Had she been other than the youngest child there'd have been no possibility of being allowed to live in Acorsi for so long without going to a shrewdly chosen husband (as one sister had), or else taking a position in an important retreat.

To live as she is living now, Adria thinks, on the track in Bischio on a grey horse. To have found a way to be fully and intensely *alive* in a world that doesn't like that for a woman.

It will have taken a very substantial bribe to ensure her name was drawn as one of the twelve riders—ten to race, and two as alternates if something unfortunate should happen to one of those picked.

It is not infrequent that something does happen. The riders are guarded from the moment they are drawn and assigned a district, but your guards can be paid to injure you, or to permit an assault. For a rider in Bischio, refusing to be bought off can be as risky as taking a bribe.

She doesn't know how much Folco spent. Sixty-five people, including one other woman, had shown up on the first day of testing.

It had happened, though: her name was drawn from the drum two weeks ago. She was named to the Falcon district.

They never win this race, lacking the money and the stature to smooth the way for whoever rides their horse. This is *good* because her hopes, and Folco's, lie in the betting odds on her being long.

They treat their rider extremely well, however. They seem *grateful* that someone would ride for them, that they are even in the race. They'll parade and drink and scream happily, and they never win. Three or four districts take turns doing that, it seems.

She'd not had any communication from Folco until yesterday, when she was given a folded-over message by the woman attending her in the house where she had been sequestered. Adria's using the name Coppina here, for her own reasons, having to do with someone dead too young.

She knows Folco will be somewhere in this crowd now, and that his men will have been placing wagers on her for days. She also knows—from his note, which she burned—the rider she's to try to be beside at the start, and what signal he'll give the starters, to have them drop the rope only when he's ready.

The starters need money as much as anyone else, don't they?

Bischio's is a corrupt race, everyone knows it. Part of the unpredictability is seeing, as the horses start and run, which district has bribed best in a given year. But even with that . . . a favoured rider can misjudge the slope and grip of the track at a hard turn, or another might upset all plans and gallop his horse past all the money spent, with unexpected speed or by attacking the others with the club all the riders carry. It isn't for the horses, that weapon.

Some of the men on the track with her are very big, which might be harder on their mounts in a different sort of race. She doubts they'll be inclined to be kind to her if she isn't safely towards the back—where she and the Falcon belong. No, if she gets between any of them and winning this morning she'll be dealt with, or they'll try. You can do anything to another rider in this race; people have died. You'll be disqualified, though—and attacked by a mob, after—if you strike another's horse. There *are* rules.

She's a good rider. Very good, in fact. But she's a woman, and new here, without allies or friends on the track. Her horse is handling the noise well as they circle once around for everyone to see them, for the last bets to be made. She's been with the grey horse every day since they were paired, learning how to gentle it, how its footwork is on curves, what makes it startle, the way it responds to a shout or a slap on the neck.

They hunted and raced all the time at home. She has these skills. It is why she's here, why Folco has let her be here. If she falls badly, Adria thinks, or is hurt again in some other way, her aunt might kill the husband she loves.

Her heart is beating fast. Too fast. She needs to gentle herself as much as the horse. She's trying to block out the crowd, the *wall* of noise on both sides, and so she almost doesn't notice that someone is calling and waving to her as she passes a part of the inner stands.

She sees arms raised and moving urgently, and she does look over. It is an old woman, being held upright at the wooden wall by two men. The woman is gesturing for her to come nearer. This isn't even the Falcon section. It is . . . the Goose, she sees, from their banner.

Adria hesitates, then twitches a rein and moves that way. She stops at a distance. She can't be seen having a private exchange with people from a different district. Not right before the start! Riders have been torn apart by their district if it was felt they'd been suborned. If this woman has anything to say, she'll have to shout it.

She does. "I am Mina Sacchetti. I raced before you!"

Long before me, Adria thinks, looking at her, then decides the woman isn't so much ancient as worn down, withered by life. She can't even stand unsupported—and that makes a coin slot into her mind.

"You were hurt here? Riding?"

"Yes!" shouts the other woman. "Don't let them do it to you!"

Adria lifts a hand, salutes politely. No one, surely, will object to two woman riders speaking in public. "I'll do my best," she cries.

"*No!*" the other woman shouts, closer to a scream this time. "Don't *let* them, I said. Watch the Fontena Curve, and watch the Tower. He'll ride you into it! That's what they do! *They'll think you can't fight back!*"

The Fontena was the deadliest corner every year, the track sloping towards the wall, the turn hard. The Tower was a favoured district, always.

They always think we can't fight back, Adria Ripoli thinks.

She says nothing, however, just lifts a hand again in salute, then bows in her light saddle to a woman who has preceded her here, and had her life destroyed.

People are watching. They roar approval, sentimentally. A ruined old woman and a young one riding for a hapless district. You could surely hope she got safely around the track three times.

Then, having done that, let her go away and live a proper woman's life.

Trumpets sound, drums have been pounding steadily. The rope, Adria sees, has been drawn taut across the track ahead of them. She moves towards the start line with the others.

It is upon them. You can plan something far ahead, think it through, have dreams, premonitions. You could come to Bischio weeks in advance, set things in motion, wait on the results of a bribe. You *could* be selected, assigned a district, a horse, work with your horse (named, for some reason, Sauradia, for the wild lands across the water), and . . .

And with all of this, it can still come as a sharp, wild blow that it is happening, it is here, *now*. Wild blows are not to be permitted, not from within. She has a weapon in her hand for blows, they all do, but what she needs is clarity.

She rubs a hand along the neck of her horse, whispers to him. A good horse, none of them is supposed to be more than that, but she likes hers, his colour, his calm. He is calm even now. Sauradia is supposed to be a savage land, towards Sarantium. She has no idea how this grey got that name.

The calmness is partly her, but only a part. They are a team, horse and rider; they each bring to this track, to the chaos about to come, what they have—and they will see where it takes them, if it is enough.

She'd raced so many times at home, with her brothers and sisters, cousins. She was the youngest, awkwardly lanky for so long. There were years and years when she never won, was never even close, then there came an autumn when she began to do so. Her eldest brother said it was her horse one time, she remembers—that she had the best one, an indulgent gift from their father to his youngest. She'd shamed him, offering to switch and race again.

He'd had to accept; the way their family was when they were together and others were watching, the competitiveness, cold ambition. She beat him, riding his horse, with him on hers. He hadn't acknowledged her existence for half a year. It took a command from their father, who'd finally noticed, to change that.

That brother will be duke of Macera when their father dies, if events unfold as they are meant to. Plans, Adria thinks, sitting astride a horse in the centre of Bischio, don't always unfold. Men—or women—cannot control the world.

Folco tries, she thinks. She is trying now.

Her first goal, here at the start line, is to be beside the rider for Tower, who is favoured to win, with the Fox district also seen as strong this year. The Tower is the district nearest the square, the best houses in Bischio lie within it, most of the members of the governing commune live there. It is a matter of pride that it wins as often as it does—and money will always be spent in defence of pride.

He's not the biggest of the riders, the one for Tower, but he has a hard, seamed, southern face, and the look he gives her as she angles Sauradia closer is bleak, daunting. He looks *angry*. Adria knows he's been here for years, is usually drawn to ride—and has won many times. Given that, and the district, he will be heavily wagered upon. People will expect him to win.

His horse sidles to the right, and she uses that to slip neatly inside another horse on his left. She is beside him now. The crowd is—if this is possible—even louder. A dignitary is trying to speak. He has no hope of being heard. The horses jostle each other, crowded, some rearing as they approach the rope. The Tower rider glares at her. He wants more room, she knows, space on both sides, so that when the rope drops he can point his horse forward, whichever way it has turned.

When the rope drops. No. When he signals for the rope to drop.

She absorbs his look and smiles, her sweetest smile. "Don't like women next to you?" she says. "I'd not have guessed you that way. Not that it matters, of course."

His head snaps back. The Fox district rider, on her other side, laughs aloud.

"Watch your mouth! I'll fuck you with this stick," the Tower man rasps.

"Not my favourite," Adria says loudly. "If you must know. Is it yours? Is that it?"

More laughter. Not just the one rider this time. The Tower horseman swears. He turns away from her, starting to point his horse forward. He may be rushing it. She knows what he's about to do, she knows what *she's* doing. Men can be goaded so easily . . .

He has his horse almost aimed down the track, but she has her grey in position already. Still turning forward, he slaps his left thigh once—and the rope holders let go. The Tower rider gathers his reins, shouts at his horse, surges, positioned to go.

But Adria is ahead of him.

She is a Ripoli of Macera, is she not? She has spent her life riding. You *jump* in hunts—over walls, fences, streams, ditches, fallen trees. A different skill from racing along flat ground, or three times around a track. You learn how to get a horse up and over an obstacle.

Her grey has cleared the rope easily. It is only a rope, it is already dropping. A trivial jump.

And she is out on the course and ahead of them all. She slaps the grey's neck once, feels him respond. Sauradia, her joy for this morning. There is so *much* joy in her just then, a hard, bright rush of it. It is not a feeling she knows intimately, but it is there to be found, if life allows.

❦

I was astonished at how perfectly she timed it, taking the grey over the falling rope before it hit the ground. And there she was, in front of all the others, including the favoured Tower horse in the light and dark green colours.

"That clever bastard!" Monticola roared beside me. "He learned the signal!"

"*What?*" I cried.

He didn't look away from the track. He said, "Tower bribed the rope men! But Folco bought the signal he used to tell them when to drop it! Jad's blood and eyes, that woman can ride! Look at her!"

They were coming up to us now, on the first curve. I was remembering her arm around my neck on a dark stairway. She'd had a knife in her thigh six months ago, I thought, watching her urge her grey forward as Bischio went mad. It felt as if the air was shaking around me.

I stole a glance at Monticola. If she won, if Folco won, he'd win, too, probably even more—since he'd not have paid any bribes, and had every fifth wager on her to win not just come in the first three. He would undoubtedly let the other man know. With joy, I thought.

Tower was right behind Adria, two others close to him, the rest stringing out already. A bad start could ruin you in a race like this.

The leaders were at the trickiest curve for the first time, right where we were. It was brutally dangerous because the track sloped towards the wall even as you needed to curve away. Adria had her grey hugging the inside, the shorter path, away from that danger. Alone in front there was nothing to stop her, the track's slant to the outside wall would not be a problem—this time.

Behind her, the Tower rider was using his hand already, slapping his horse hard. He, too, was clear, no rival beside him. The two behind him were side by side. The one on the inside—the Fox district horse—was drifting deliberately out towards the wall in front of us. The other rider, for the Shell district, tried to beat him away with his stick. It was parried. But then he needed to stop, to concentrate on the track, the wall, where he was being pushed, and—

He collided, right in front of us. I could see his left leg hit. The crowd roared, but the rider stayed in his light saddle somehow and his horse came off the wall, still running. The Shell district people screamed rapturous approval. But he was in fourth place now, the Fox rider had angled off just before the wall and was chasing Tower alone as Tower went hard after Adria in Falcon's blue and white. Sky and clouds, I thought.

"He'll move on her next time around!" Teobaldo Monticola shouted, to none of us and all of us. "He's got the bigger horse. He'll try to take her down. She *can't* go down!"

So strange, I thought, the way things were that morning: both of them desperately hoping for a woman on a grey horse. Willing her to hold on.

Adria was taking the next curve, keeping low over her horse's neck. I saw her glance back to place the pursuit. Then they were on the far side of the course and hard to see from where we were. If she could stay cleanly in front she couldn't be hit, couldn't be ridden into the wall.

But I didn't think she could.

"Tower bought the best horse in the draw, too," Monticola said flatly. I only heard it because I was right beside him. "Fuck them," he said.

I wondered where Folco d'Acorsi was, if he was seeing the same thing. Saying the same thing.

⊙╬⊙

"*Look at that woman ride!*" Antenami Sardi screamed.

He was aroused, excited. He was abruptly aware that this could be seen, and he adjusted his clothing. He wished, again, that the woman not the man was next to him. She might have let her hand drift, as if by chance, with everyone distracted, and . . .

He wanted that girl on the track. She might be awkwardly tall but she was so *bold*. It was compelling! She was also in trouble now. Anyone who knew horses could see that the man behind her, in the green and darker green, had a bigger mount, and there were still two laps to go as they came around the turn to the right and past the start line for the first time. Also, she was just a woman, and they were carrying sticks as big as clubs out there. A thought occurred to him: with those sticks being wielded, it might be just as well Fillaro wasn't racing!

Watching, on his feet now, roaring with everyone else, he realized that the woman was about to encounter another problem—right in front of them. It was really very exciting.

"Giraffe is always with us!" said his host in his ear. He had to shout. "What?"

"The yellow! He is lagging deliberately, letting her catch him!"

"I see it! Why?"

"Slow her down or take her down. Watch!"

Well, of course he was going to watch! But for some reason he glanced over at Folco d'Acorsi again. The man was biting his lower lip. He was clearly *not* happy. Antenami had no idea why.

His brother, he thought, would probably have known. But damn him.

❧

Very well, Adria is thinking, *you know what you have to do here.*

Knowing and doing did not always marry, as her mother was fond of saying. Probably was still saying, at home, a long way north. She could be there now herself, enjoying the coming of spring to Macera, the woods and hills.

This is better. This is life. Whatever happens.

She is coming up fast on the Giraffe horse and rider, lapping him already. He has slowed, is waiting for her, helping the Tower. She'd been warned they'd work together. He is the biggest man in the field. The stick in his hand looks tiny, though they are all the same size, carefully measured. It is amusing, almost, how precisely the rules for this race are laid out—and how completely they are violated.

He isn't even pretending to race. Has turned in his saddle—to his left, she sees—and is watching her bear down on him with Tower behind her. He has his weapon in his right hand, reins in his left.

She comes flying towards him along the straightaway at the start and finish line. She's on his left because he's been keeping to the right, blocking the shorter, inside path. Now he starts moving wide, left, towards the wall. In fact, he pulls hard at his reins to do that because she has angled Sauradia closer to that outside wall to pass him and he needs to get *out* there or she'll go right by him. She's moving faster than he expected. He has his horse almost diagonal on the track now, hurrying to cut her off, force her to the wall. He moves to switch hands—reins and club. He wants to hit her. No malice. It's his task.

She's been waiting for that.

She'd grown up with brothers willing to do whatever it took to beat each other. She was mostly at the back of every race, for years. She'd watched.

The moment the man riding for Giraffe goes to change hands, when his control and attention are claimed for a heartbeat or two as he needs to glance down, take his eyes off her, Adria moves Sauradia *hard* back to the right—reins and knees and voice and leaning far over that way—and her grey does exactly what she's trained him to do, riding for two weeks here, twice a day, every day. He switches his lead—beautifully, for her—and *goes by the big man's horse on the inside.*

She hears a colossal roar as she passes, and because this is about joy and anger, both, because it might be the last time she is in the world like this, free to be what she wants to be, and because the Tower rider is still just behind, she swings her club hard, with her left hand, at the big man just as he is turning back towards her, too late, his own weapon in the wrong hand, and she cracks him on the near forearm, so that he cries out in pain (bones are broken, she knows it) and lets fall his reins and . . .

It almost works. His horse skitters awkwardly as she passes him. The oncoming Tower horse could easily have bumped it, or stumbled avoiding it. But the rider for Tower, that hard southerner who has won here many times, really is good, and he's been watching, has seen her cut back to the right, and so he is ready, he isn't too close, and he takes his horse wider left, and past, as well.

So, he is still there behind her, though he's lost ground, and she's smashed the rider she passed, his ally, taken him out of the game for the last laps . . . he won't be able to try this again with a broken arm.

Once more then, second time around the course. She stays safely away from the danger wall as they come to it. The Fontena Curve they call it, the one that other woman rider, the ruined one, had warned her about.

She knows about it, she is doing all she can. Knowing and doing do not always marry.

Her hat, worn so the brim would keep the sun from her eyes, flies off. Her hair had been pinned beneath it at the start, but not perfectly any more, and she feels it begin to stream out behind her as she rides.

Dear Jad, she prays, *let this not be the last true thing I do.*

⚭

He was preparing to take the woman down early in the last lap. He knew exactly what he'd do, and where. He'd done it before. There were advantages to having raced in Bischio for years on a course that never changed.

The useless fool for Giraffe had been tricked by her, and maimed (a clever move, he'd give her that), so he had to do it himself, and he would. He didn't like the way she'd spoken to him at the start, or gotten out ahead of him. Made him look bad.

It had nothing to do with disliking women. He'd do exactly this if it were a man on the Falcon horse. He'd loved his mother, he mourned his sister every day he lived. She'd been taken as a slave by Asharite corsairs.

The southern tip of Batiara, where he'd been born, was a different world. They had no idea up here.

Infidel raids—even far inland—were a continuous, terrifying fear. His sister had been thirteen years old. He'd been nine, and had been rushed away with his mother to hide when a raid came one spring. They'd killed his father in their farmyard. They'd found and taken his sister where she was hiding.

He still prayed for her every morning, every night.

By now, decades later, he didn't know if he was praying she was alive, or that she'd had a merciful death so that she might now be with the god in light.

He did know that he'd killed Asharites whenever he could when he was younger in the south. They were in the countryside where the so-tolerant duke insisted on employing them on farms and ranches, they were in the duke's palace guard, allowed shops and trades, even permitted their Jad-denying temples to worship the stars. The duke even had them fighting the corsairs of their own faith. The Asharites living among them did do that. Very well. So be it. He didn't care. Then, or now. It didn't change anything. There were limits to what honour would let you tolerate.

Their duke could do whatever he wanted, Carlo Serrana had decided, still very young. He would kill infidels in his sister's name. His father's, too, he supposed, but he'd never liked his father, truth be told.

He'd made himself one of the best horsemen in the south, learning on the ranchlands, even from Asharites, in fact. They were superb horsemen, some of them. A couple of those men—his teachers—he'd later killed. They'd trusted him, it hadn't been difficult. He was clever and careful, and young, no one ever knew it had been him.

When his mother died, Serrano headed north after laying her to rest. Eventually he'd found in Bischio a place to live and even flourish. He didn't have many friends, he wasn't a friend-making man, but by now every district prayed, come spring and the race, that his name would be drawn for their horse, and no one ever doubted his integrity. You couldn't bribe Carlo Serrana. It was known. And you didn't want to offend him, either.

You could fairly say he was a well-off man now, having won four times in nine years, using the money to buy land and build up a ranch south of the city, breeding horses for the well-to-do and for mercenary commanders, who always needed horses.

He had a wife, a son, a daughter who looked like his sister as he remembered her. His wife said his face was kind when he smiled.

He didn't understand why one would want to look kind. Perhaps to children. But on this track softness was a thing that would cause you to lose. If Tower had spent substantial money (he could guess how much by now) to have him drawn to ride for them, and the Tower district was where the powerful in Bischio lived, Carlo Serrana would win his fifth race for them this morning, and no woman riding for a useless district that never won would prevent it. You fought for everything you had in life.

That was just the way things were, especially if you'd grown up fearing raiders from the sea coming to take you as a slave, and a sister you'd loved, a sweetness in the world, *had* been taken.

He hoped she was dead, he prayed she was alive and well. He'd killed a great many men in her name. She'd never know. Jad knew. The woman ahead of him on the track—she'd never tasted, never would, a life built around fear and vengeance, whoever she was. The south was a different world.

They were on the far straightaway again, opposite the start line. His horse was running well. They were all meant to be more or less the same, but *more or less* did carry a range, and he was a breeder of horses, knew them, and the Tower had money to spend. He'd mentioned, casually, which one he'd want if—by fortune and the god's will—he should somehow happen to be drawn to ride for them this year.

Her grey was moving easily too, and she knew how to handle it. She was a rider. But she didn't know Bischio, this track, Carlo Serrana's life.

⚜

She's made a mistake. Adria realizes it from the sound of the crowd, which has changed to something darker, like an animal hunting. She is the hunted.

Coming out of the curve before the start and finish, one lap to go, she's done as she had before, as they are all doing . . . she's let Sauradia drift from the inside enough that she doesn't have to slow him or struggle to hold hard against the curving of the track. She'll go back tight to the inside when they straighten from the curve.

Except that the southerner riding for Tower chooses *that* point, improbably, to make his move to pass her.

He doesn't—he doesn't get past. It is very hard for horses on a track put together a few days ago, loose and uneven, to pass on the inside of a curve. It is why they are all letting their mounts drift a little.

This man has won many times here, however, and now she is learning why. The crowd warns her, the sound makes her glance back—to see him coming hard on the inside, straining to go faster *and* hold.

This race is about weapons, not just horses, and he is . . . he is suddenly too close!

She leans all the way left in the saddle, pulls Sauradia hard that way, with the track, so the heavy stick aimed at her whistles through space—as a crowd of people goes collectively mad.

He can't hit her horse. They banned you for doing that. Sometimes they killed you for it, she'd been told. But her evasion, his bold move with a big horse, has them almost level, and he is on the inside now, the shorter course. His horse will *have* to be exhausted, making that push, Adria thinks. Surely, surely it is!

Then she realizes that, indeed, it is, but the southern rider isn't going to try to outrace her the rest of the way. That is not his plan.

Watch the Fontena, and watch the Tower.

Yes. Well. Knowing and doing.

They are on the straight, hurtling past the start and finish line again, one lap to go, but the man on her right has no intention of letting her run that last lap. Why race with a hard-worked horse when you can take down the rider beside you right now? The rider on the wrong side of you. Because Adria is towards the outer wall now as the most dangerous turn approaches.

He isn't using his club, he can't, positioning needs to be too care-ful. He is controlling his horse as it creeps up, bit by bit, until it is *almost* beside hers. He's too close for her to come back away from the wall, to try to cut him off, he's too close for her to stop what is coming, what he wants to do.

She'd made a mistake on the previous turn, or he'd done something brilliant. It doesn't matter which, because she is about to pay the price.

❦

Serrana has no desire to kill or maim the woman, though either might happen when he takes her down. She's ridden well, bravely. What she did to the Giraffe rider (even if the man is a fool) was beautifully accomplished. He's a horseman, a trainer, has ridden all his life . . . he can admire technique and cleverness.

Doesn't matter, not when it comes to winning here. A wife and two children depend on him, and there is pride. He is the most feared rider in Bischio. He doesn't hate her for being alive and free, he just has to beat her on this track, and her being a woman can't get in the way of that. *She* can't get in his way.

How many times has he seen a horse hit the wall at the Fontena Curve? Everyone knows that turn. The first-time riders are warned about it, brought here ahead of the race by their district captains, shown how the slope of the track goes towards the wall there even as you will be struggling to keep your horse away from it, at speed—especially if you are running first and second and on the last lap and the horse is tiring.

He's second, just, right now, but he's too near for her to work back, or even try, and she needs both hands on her reins, can't give any attention to using her club against him as they near the turn or her horse *will* slide right into the wall and she'll be crushed against it by his. He can't surrender control to hit her, either, but it doesn't matter, he's on the inside. When she meets the wall, he'll pull off, can slow briefly for control, she'll be on the ground or her horse will be staggering, and the third- and fourth-place horses are well back of them.

He'll do the last lap alone, in glory.

He doesn't need her to fall or be hurt, although it is difficult for that not to happen at this speed. He just needs her helplessly behind him after that collision. Which is about to happen. Which is now. They are racing towards it. Still on the straightaway, the last of it, slope beginning, curve upon them. He allows himself a quick glance at her. He sees her look back at him, also quickly, in the same moment.

He doesn't see fear. He should be seeing that, he thinks.

◦✦◦

It was Ginevra's first time in Bischio. It was also the first time Teobaldo had brought her out into the world with him like this, displaying her beside him, dressed in her best, claiming eyes wherever she moved.

And there was more now: he'd spoken to Guidanio Cerra, with her in the room, about tutoring their sons—the way the children of a lord are taught. She'd had to work to keep her expression calm, try to seem just . . . interested. In truth, though, it felt as if it might be the most important time of her life, this journey west to watch some horses race.

But standing beside him (they had seats, as befit Remigio's lord, but *everyone* was on their feet), her thoughts just then were on the track—and with the woman riding there, on whom they had placed so much money, including some of her jewellery.

Ginevra della Valle had lain awake much of the night, after pleasing him (and herself) in love. She'd been afraid to fall asleep because she knew she'd dream of a future where they were wed, their sons acknowledged and legitimized, her older one named Teobaldo's heir and . . .

And that would mean his current heir, his eldest, would have died in the east, in Sarantium, and she mustn't *wish* for that, or dream of it, it would put her soul at risk.

Right now, this moment, she was not thinking about that, she was in a screaming crowd as she watched another woman and heard Teobaldo's loud admiration of her. She felt no envy, no apprehension. She did not doubt his affection, she only needed to be wed.

She, too, was caught up in the excitement, even though she didn't understand this race—the way the riders were allowed to club each other, or why Teobaldo and the young man they'd collected on the way here were *screaming* warnings to the girl as two horses, one of them hers, hurtled towards where they were standing, by the first curve past the start line. It had a name, this curve, it was apparently important, and dangerous.

"He has her! Jad rot his soul!" she heard the man she loved cry out.

Rage and pain in his voice. He rarely revealed so much. This was about more than a wager and money now, Ginevra thought, about more than spiting Folco d'Acorsi.

The crowd around her was a deafening thunder. The world shook with it. The woman's dark red hair was streaming out behind her. That was wrong, even disgraceful, but it looked beautiful, Ginevra thought.

"*Maybe not!*" she heard Guidanio Cerra cry.

Teobaldo called him Danino, a child's name. He did things like that to other men, asserting dominance. But she saw him look quickly at the younger man, who'd been allowed to stand with them because it was he—Guidanio, Danio, Danino—who had brought the information about a woman rider that might make them a great deal of money here.

Or not.

⚭

I do not, to this day, know what I thought could happen when I cried out as the two horses came to the curve. Why I denied what we were seeing: that she was trapped, approaching the deadliest part of the track.

Because Monticola was right, the Tower rider *did* have her.

But still I shouted what I did at the summit of my voice, raw with longing.

Perhaps I was *willing* it to be so. Perhaps I wanted Jad to hear me from behind the sun, as Adria raced towards us, and the wall.

⚭

"*Holy Jad of Light, what is she doing?*" Antenami Sardi screamed. He threw both hands in the air. He didn't know what else to do with them.

⚭

It was her father Arimanno, the duke, a man so prepared in life he made Folco look impulsive and careless, who had told her once— they'd been out riding, in fact, she'd been about fourteen years old—"Always try to have something in reserve, daughter. Wherever you are, whatever you are doing. There are always reversals."

This isn't a reversal so much as a catastrophe, but the idea is the same. She is about to be ridden into the Fontena Curve. Her left leg, her injured one, will hit first. Not that this is about an older wound. If they crash into the wall as hard as they are about to and Sauradia goes down, she can die here.

What she has isn't the soundest *something in reserve* one might devise, but it is all she can use right now. It occurs to her that life can be simpler when there are no responses but one, however frail it might be. And she *is* a good rider. Also—a complex thought—she is her father's daughter, after all, and it seems she always will be, however far away she goes, however hard she tries to be something other than a Ripoli of Macera.

Because she's practised this with the horse when no one else was on the track.

End of the straightaway. It has to be right now. This can't be done once they are into the curve. She prays. She does do that, what fool would not pray?

She throws away her club. She needs both hands.

She grips the pommel of her saddle with her left hand—she'd required a higher pommel than usual of the Falcon team leader. He hadn't asked why. She wouldn't have explained. She grabs with her right for the back of the thin saddle. Not much purchase there, but it has to be enough, it is what she has. She lets go of the pommel and swings her left leg (healed now) over the front of the saddle, over her horse's neck. Grabs for the pommel again. She is not holding the reins at all now, Sauradia is running free, but they've practised this and it has to be enough. Her head is towards the wall. She knows what that means, if they hit.

And then that screaming crowd in Bischio sees something never done before in their race. Something no one present in that morning sunlight will forget for the rest of their days, short or long, easeful or terrible, as fortune and the god decide.

She is strong. Long and lean, and strong. She holds herself in place with both hands as the two horses pound down the straightaway, near the wall, too near. Leaning back, she pulls both legs up to her chest, riding sideways—you can call it riding sidesaddle, the way courtly women sometimes do—but this is not that. This is not that.

And as the southern rider, four-time winner on this track, flings a startled glance her way, Adria *kicks*, uncoiling as fiercely as she can, gripping with both hands at her saddle, using her stomach muscles to hold and thrust, and she hits him *hard*, in the side, chest-high, with booted feet.

He doesn't just fall, he flies.

He actually flies off his horse. There is a moment when he is airborne, looking her way still, his dark eyes showing an incalculable astonishment. Then he falls to the track and *bounces*, and rolls, and lies there, as she swings herself back into the saddle, left leg over the horse's neck again, the other way, and reclaims the reins as the now-riderless Tower horse runs ahead of her, and in the space that creates she brings Sauradia off the rail, out of danger, slowing a little to negotiate the slope. And then she is free, still riding, safe, alone.

Alone in front of every rapturous, stunned, wildly transported person in the centre of Bischio. She is at the centre of all the god's created worlds for a moment, it feels like. It does.

They'll think you can't fight back, she remembers: the old woman, who had been crippled here, on that same wall.

And then Adria realizes something else, and what had already seemed perfection becomes even more.

⚭

Ginevra had spent her entire time here trying to convey detached elegance. She was adept at that—but that poise was gone now. She was shouting with everyone else. *How can you not?* she was thinking.

What the woman out there had just done was so . . . improbable!

"We will win!" she heard herself cry. "Teobaldo, she's winning!"

But then, to her astonishment, he shouted, "No! No! She is not! Come *on*, woman, ride! For me! Oh, Jad, *ride!*"

She looked at the man on her other side, the young one who might tutor her sons, who had told them about this woman riding for Folco d'Acorsi. He was not shouting, perhaps the only person who wasn't. She saw his face as he watched the woman on the grey horse gallop along the far side of the track towards the final turn to the finish line. There was wonder—but also something else in his eyes.

She felt, quite unexpectedly, some desire for a man who could close himself around a private awareness like that in the midst of a crazed tumult. She wanted to know what it was, that inner thing. Felt a wish to slip it out of him, prove she could be skilled enough, her allure mastering his will . . .

If he was coming to Remigio, she'd need him to love her, Ginevra della Valle thought—for her sons, their future, their fate. But watching him watch the woman with the red hair circle the track, she realized that wasn't likely to happen. He was elsewhere engaged. Lost.

It bothered her, a little.

And she still didn't understand what Teobaldo was screaming about.

∽∾

"Great glory to Jad in the sun!" cried Antenami Sardi. He became aware his hands were still high over his head. He brought them down. "*Did you see that?*" he shouted.

The man beside him, the dignitary from the Tower district, was also shouting, and smiling, and pumping a fist in joy. That was generous, Antenami thought: Tower had just lost the race, their rider lay on the track, but his companion was still caught up in the excitement of what they had seen the woman do.

"I'd take a lost bet to have seen that, too!" he shouted in the other man's ear.

"No!" the commune leader shouted back. "No, no, no! We are winning! We will win! *Look at our horse!* First to the finish, it doesn't *matter* if there's a rider!"

Antenami looked. It wasn't hard to see. The riderless Tower horse was still galloping, nearing the last curve before the half straight-away to the finish, and it was several horse lengths ahead of the woman.

Such a strange race, he thought again. Impossibly so! But what stories he'd have to tell!

He watched the woman slap at her horse's neck, working the reins, straining to make up ground. Antenami narrowed his eyes. He did know horses, and riding.

※

It is beyond anything she could have dreamed. No man will finish ahead of her. Folco will win his triana bets, she will be honoured and applauded, but *not* have to stay, be a part of parades for days after winning the Bischio race. Tower will win—and celebrate all day and night, all week. She'll slip away: remembered, but not thrust into the city's eye.

She lets herself appear to be working hard with Sauradia, urging him on, but her knees hold back and so he holds back. He'll look like an exhausted, gallant horse at the end of a gruelling race, chasing one that carries no rider, light, flying ahead of them.

She could catch up, she thinks.

She is entirely certain she doesn't want to, for *so* many glorious reasons.

※

I had known it yesterday, walking the streets, placing bets on the Falcon's woman rider, every fifth one a bet to win, at odds so great it would earn a fortune for Monticola. But my wagers with my own money had been the triana, to come in the first three, because I knew who she was.

And watching Adria Ripoli chase the Tower district's riderless horse—careful to be seen urging on her own—I knew I'd been right.

If it is ever known who I am, I cannot do any of these things any more.

She needed to stay hidden—which meant *not* winning this race. Too many people would see her if she did, so many questions would emerge. And this was the daughter of the duke of Macera, and she was doing this for Folco d'Acorsi.

But also for herself, I thought.

I wondered, suddenly, if Folco's cautious wagers had been based on this knowledge: that she was at risk if she came first. It might be so. I wondered if I'd ever be as subtle, as in command of stratagems, of the world, as that man—if he had anticipated this.

I watched her finish second to the wildly bolting Tower horse, ahead of all the other riders. She lifted a hand at the end, but only briefly. She hadn't *won.* But of course she had.

She didn't know my name.

◈

Carlo Serrana, four times champion in Bischio, riding for Tower that year, had fallen from horses a hundred times. He wasn't too badly hurt. Even walked off the track, moved awkwardly for a week or two, but he recovered.

Nonetheless, something happened to him that morning. He never rode the Bischio race again.

Nor did he ever explain why. He might not have been able to. He kept his breeding stable, didn't lose any of the mercenaries, aristocrats, wealthy merchants keen to buy horses. His horses were very good, he had a superb eye, everyone knew it.

He even passed the ranch on to his son because he trained him, too, and their business kept going. In his later years, he'd sit by a winter fire in a tavern in the city, or on his own loggia in good weather, and tell stories of his racing days, remind people that horses he'd ridden out onto the track in the square had won the Bischio race five times.

It was even true.

⚭

She lets Sauradia slow past the finish line. She comes up to the Fontena Curve again. They have removed the Tower rider from the track. Looking into the stands here, which are thundering still, visibly rocking as she approaches, she sees a big man under a wolf banner.

Perhaps she should resist, but in that moment she feels too exalted, too impossibly pleased with life, so she angles Sauradia towards the wall, to where he is standing in the first row, and she smiles at Teobaldo Monticola di Remigio, and holds up two fingers, for *second place*, and sees his head snap back. Then, to his credit, to his very great credit, he laughs.

Because the note she'd been sent by Folco the night before, by way of the woman attending her in the Falcon district, had not just told her what signal the Tower rider would use for the men holding the rope, it had also told her that Monticola had men wagering throughout the city on her, and that some were betting her to win. She'd been recognized by someone, in other words.

Now she smiles at the lord of Remigio, thinking of those lost bets. He'll still have done well, which is why he can laugh, but she decides that right now, out here on the track, she can let him know they'd *known*.

Beside him is a woman of extraordinary beauty. She is looking at Adria with a quizzical expression, but women have done that all her life, even her sisters, it is nothing new. What hits Adria harder is seeing the man with them. Because she knows him, and he'd saved her life in Mylasia.

And here he is, with Monticola di Remigio, looking at her with an expression she can't read, or perhaps doesn't want to. She's shaken, though. Of all things on this day . . .

She lets her eyes move on but not her thoughts. She sees the Falcon district leaders running across the track towards her and her horse, waving their arms, screaming and capering with joy, and it seems evident that a celebration is going to happen after all, because what has taken place this morning is unknown in the memory of anyone present, and Falcon coming second, with a *woman* riding for them, is . . . it is a miracle! Some of them are crying as they come up to her. A miracle!

⟡

One miracle did happen that morning.

Not an exercise in skill and courage and preparation. No, it was a true one, and understood as such in the mind and heart of the person who experienced it—who had thought his life was over.

Carderio Sacchetti the shoemaker, heart pounding madly, too hopeful and terrified to scream, had watched the woman chase the Tower horse—and fail to catch it—and he'd buried his face in his hands and wept.

His aunt was crying as well, though hers were tears of happiness. She turned to him and cried, "Our ticket! Your wager! Nephew, we have won!"

And Carderio thought that death could not come too soon for him. It was his time. He wondered what would happen to the children. The infant would die, that he knew. Perhaps his brother would find a way to care for Carderio's wife and the older two. His brother was a decent man. He'd be greatly burdened.

He reached into his tunic for his foolish, terrible wager. The blue ticket on Falcon to win. And what he saw, what he held in a suddenly shaking hand, was a green ticket.

A triana bet. Which he had not made. He knew he had not made it.

A sound escaped his throat. He had never made such a sound in his life. He turned the ticket over and over in his hand, which was now trembling so much he feared he would drop it.

It was green. It stayed green.

He had bet Falcon to win. Blue ticket. To win.

He looked at his aunt, who was said to be a kind of witch. But she wasn't, he knew she wasn't. She was a sad, maimed, angry woman who'd had her life destroyed here twenty-five years ago.

Then he thought, perhaps the betting stand man had made an error, had simply not believed anyone would be so foolish as to bet the Falcon woman to win, so had assumed it had to be a triana.

But no, he knew, he *knew* he'd been given, and pocketed, a blue ticket.

Which was now green. Which meant he had won, that they had more money than they'd ever had. He could hire a healer for the baby, buy food, and . . .

He began weeping again.

"Jad is good," he managed to say, to no one, to the blue sky. "Something beyond belief has happened. I must go to our sanctuary!"

"Yes!" his aunt shouted. "We will pray, all of us. Jad bless that girl!"

He and his brother helped her away, his wife making a path for them. He was still weeping. It took a long time to get free of the square, through the tumult. As they went, he saw the woman, the rider, on the track, carried on the shoulders of Falcon district men. They were laughing and singing as if they'd won.

Tower had their southern rider upright, he saw. They were helping him walk away through the crowd. They were celebrating too, but not hoisting him aloft. Not this year.

Carderio Sacchetti never took his hand out of the pocket where the ticket was. He was afraid to look at it again in this crowd. In their sanctuary, later, kneeling before the sun disk, he did.

It was still green.

The Sacchetti family never forgot that day. The day a woman the city knew as Coppina, from the countryside near Mylasia, a cavalry officer's daughter, did what she did on the Fontena Curve and came second in the race for Falcon.

They never saw her again, no one in Bischio did. She was, it was reported, gone that afternoon, unseen. She'd told people she was leaving to find a retreat, whatever happened. A virtuous woman. And *such* a rider! What she had done!

Kneeling in the Goose district sanctuary, Carderio Sacchetti promised his youngest child to the god if she survived. He promised it in a holy place, on that day.

She did live. Her mother's milk came in strongly as soon as she had proper food herself, and a healer they brought, and paid, gave them a balm to rub on the infant's body. She flourished. They all flourished, from that day. Carderio began selling shoes in a new style he invented—by accident (though he didn't tell people that).

That infant, Leora, entered a Daughters of Jad retreat when she was ten years old. She was soon recognized to be both brilliant and pious. She learned to read and write in several languages, to work with numbers, much more. After many years she became Eldest Daughter there, a shining, greatly honoured figure in her own retreat, and beyond. She corresponded with powerful figures among Jad's clerics throughout Batiara, and in many other lands.

It was said that by the time she died, at a great age and greatly loved, even the High Patriarch knew her name, and that prayers were spoken for her soul, with candles lit in Rhodias itself.

CHAPTER VIII

It was a tradition, openly discussed, that the man who won the Bischio race could spend that night, and many of the nights that followed, with pretty much any woman (more than one at a time, if he wished) in the district for which he'd won.

Some did decline this excitement, for a variety of reasons; one or two arranged nighttime encounters with men they liked. That was less talked about, but it happened. Victory came with rewards, not all of them financial, though there was that, too. The winning district would, after all, have a year of parades in Bischio led by their banner, lording it over the others.

Some years were more complex. If a riderless horse won the race—as had just happened—neither the district nor the rider would feel it entirely right to celebrate *him*. He was certainly paid—it would shame a district not to do that—but the nocturnal rewards were not as enthusiastically forthcoming.

In the present instance, the rider of the Tower horse, which had won today (riderless), was also in considerable discomfort.

Nothing broken other than ribs, which he'd dealt with before, but he really was in pain, and happier heading home to have his wife and a maidservant help him carefully into a bath—and out of it. No nighttime adventures ensued for some time, unless one deemed successfully turning over in bed an adventure.

Matters were equally complicated in the Falcon district.

They had not *won*, though their rider was the first person to the finish, and given that they had not had a result so splendid in half a century, they celebrated through the afternoon and night and for days after. Children were seen on window ledges and portico railings demonstrating, with varying degrees of success, the double-leg kick used to unhorse the Tower rider.

One man, trying to do the same, fell off an upper-level balcony and broke his collarbone late that night. Too much wine.

It was certainly the case that a great many men and a few of the women of the district would have been delighted to celebrate with their rider. To celebrate *her*, reward her with private company, should she have wished it.

Unfortunately, Coppina, their tall, red-haired wonder, was nowhere to be found after riding their horse in the procession back to the Falcon district sanctuary. She had smiled and waved to the cheering crowd, though she'd seemed obviously in some discomfort—and had used that as an excuse to withdraw, immediately after.

Of course they permitted that. It had been a hard, physical race.

But when, after darkfall, various persons attended at the house where she was quartered and knocked on the door of her rooms to invite her to dine with the district leaders, there was no answer.

In the morning, the owner of the house unlocked the door and they discovered that she was not within, and the bed had not been slept in.

This actually saved the Falcon district some money. They had assembled a sum as a reward for the woman even though she hadn't formally won. After discussion, half of it was given to the sanctuary and half assigned to next year's race funds.

Her disappearance (shutters opened, descending from the balcony) was understood as piety. Coppina had *told* them this race would be her last appearance in the world before she joined the Daughters of Jad somewhere.

She had evidently done just that. Perhaps sooner than expected, but . . .

She became, in Bischio, something of a legend. Girls—and not only in the Falcon district—were named for her, and a number of boys were named Coppo, the obvious equivalent.

She was never found, not by Bischio. There were rumours, later, about her perhaps not being who she'd claimed to be, including suggestions she'd even been of noble birth, but nothing was ever known for certain, and memorable moments accrue stories of all kinds. We are drawn to stories, we live for them.

❧

She wasn't in great pain, but she was exceptionally tired, and her mind was still racing with exhilaration. She wanted a hot bath, but that would have to wait. She did change out of her muddy clothes. She put on a fresh tunic and overtunic and then the riding trousers again; there were reasons. She pinned her hair back up. There was a plate of sliced meats and cheeses in the room and she paused to eat. She was, unsurprisingly, hungry. She drank only a little wine. She needed her wits about her.

Her rooms were at the back of the apothecary's house, over a laneway. She knew Folco would have determined where she was, and that he'd have someone waiting.

She didn't linger for nightfall. It would get busy down there after dark; laneways were for assignations. And she didn't want to have to stay mouse-quiet in this room when people came to her door. There had been offers and promises already. They were extremely happy in the Falcon district.

She opened the tall shutters. She stepped out on the balcony, as if giving herself some air in the afternoon light, in case someone was watching. She looked along the lane. Saw Folco's man almost immediately because he let her see him. He stepped forward from a doorway opposite. It was Gian. The only person there. Adria smiled at him. He didn't smile back; he wasn't a man who smiled much. Capable, though, possibly more so than anyone Folco had other than his cousin Aldo.

Gian held a cloak over one arm. He looked up and down the lane and nodded. She didn't wait. There was no reason to wait. She went over the railing and used crevices in the wood of the house to work her way down. Gian came forward and reached a hand to help her but she didn't need it. He gave her the hooded cloak and she put it on.

"He says it was well done," he said.

"What do you say?"

"The same." Which was pretty much what you could expect from Gian.

"Are you ready?" he asked.

"I'm here."

He gave her a sword and swordbelt to strap on, for the disguise. She was tall enough to pass for a man with her hair pinned and under a hood. There was mud on her cheeks and forehead, but the hood would hide it, and people weren't especially clean just now in the streets of Bischio.

It was crowded when they reached the square at the end of the laneway. She heard music. Gian led her out.

The city gates to the north were open. They made their way through in a crowd. She pretended to be talking to him. He didn't pretend back very well, but that was all right. Someone passed him a flask and he did the right thing and drank then handed it to her, and she took a pull from a bad wine—which was remarkably satisfying, just then.

There were horses waiting, held by another of Folco's men, about twenty minutes' walk beyond the walls. She really was tired, and her body was stiffening; it was even hard to mount the horse. She tried not to let Gian see that.

If he did, he didn't show it.

They rode through afternoon sunlight, passing thinning numbers along the road. Most people would stay in the city until late tonight. Adria wasn't paying much attention. They came to an inn and passed it, then they reached a second one and rode into a crowded courtyard and gave their horses to a servant there.

There was a room booked for her—in Gian's name. She asked the innkeeper if a bath could be brought up. She was told it was already in the room—he'd been given that instruction earlier, it appeared—and that hot water would be provided immediately.

She went up. The stairs were a slight problem by then. She was beginning to ache. Gian stayed in the common room.

She unlocked the door with the big key and sat on the large bed. She took off her man's cloak. There was a knock, almost immediately. She opened the door and sat down again on the bed and watched two girls bring water for the tub that had been set in the middle of the floor. They went back and forth several times.

There was a fire going. The two girls didn't show any surprise to discover she was a woman. It crossed her mind that people might meet here in secret for any number of reasons. She tried to pull her boots off, but needed one of the servants to come and help. She made a small joke about it, but the girl didn't laugh. She was very young.

When the bath was ready she undressed and slipped in. It was hot. Wonderfully so. She had one of the girls stay, to help wash her hair and back. She scrubbed her face and hands, watching the water darken. When she was clean, she had more hot water brought to warm the tub again, and she slipped down as far as she could, knees up, of necessity, and closed her eyes. She may have slept.

After a while—she wasn't sure how long but the water had cooled and the girl was gone—she heard another knock at the door.

"What is it?" she said. No point pretending not to be there.

"I might have been promised a kiss on a stairwell in Mylasia," someone said.

She'd assumed it was Gian knocking. It wasn't Gian.

⁂

I spent the first part of the afternoon, after we ate at the house Monticola had been given, joining the others in collecting our winnings.

It was evidently a good idea to do so quickly. Once, I was told, a tout had fled Bischio the night before the race, taking all the wagers made with him. He was unmarried, but his mother and father had been killed, also his sister and her husband and their infant child, and both houses had been seized by the city commune and sold, the profits going to make some redress for the theft.

The man was then hunted across Batiara. He was found in a room above a portside tavern in Seressa, awaiting passage across to Sauradia in two days. He was castrated and thrown into the lagoon. The money remaining, found in the room, was brought back.

Absconding with wagers had not been a significant concern since then, apparently.

But if bet shop proprietors might be disinclined to flee with their bets, they might still run out of ready money if they'd done badly . . . it was wiser to collect quickly, especially as Monticola didn't plan to linger.

Today his soldiers wore their livery with the wolf decal. I wasn't one of his mercenaries, but I did move through Bischio with four armed soldiers. We were collecting and carrying large sums of money on drunken, crowded streets. It was useful for people to know who we were.

We went back to the house regularly, dropped off our coins, went out again. It took some time. Along the way, I cashed my own bet slips where I'd made my wagers. None of the tout shop owners could be said to be particularly happy to see us. They'd have been even less so, I thought, if Adria had *won* the race and Monticola was cashing those bets at the outrageous odds given. He'd have ruined many of them, I thought.

I still believed she'd held back, while looking as if she was driving the horse as hard as she could. She didn't want to win, she wanted to be able to leave, slip back to Acorsi unknown, probably as soon as she could, and . . .

That gave me a thought.

I can't even claim to have been steered to folly by wine. We'd been moving too quickly to drink much. That was promised for the evening celebration. You can do impulsive, reckless things completely sober.

Or, well, I could, when I was young. I kept seeing her in my mind as we went through the city. Images, moments: on that grey horse today, going in to Uberto, on the hidden palace steps, walking away under stars outside Mylasia.

Once my tasks for Monticola were done, I went back into the city alone. It was easy to find where she'd been staying in the Falcon district. A number of men and women were singing outside a large house. She was in there, I was told. *Maybe*, I thought. I was offered a flask and took a long pull before handing it back.

I went around to the rear of the house, going some distance up the street before turning towards the laneway I expected. I stood in a doorway and waited. She might have left already, but I didn't think so. They'd taken her to the sanctuary with the horse first, someone had said.

After a while I realized I wasn't the only one there. I wasn't seen. The other man—same side of the lane, another doorway closer to the house where Adria was—was watching that house. If someone was here, I thought, she hadn't left.

So I was also watching when she came out on her balcony and then down to the street. He gave her a cloak and a sword to look like a man, and they walked up the lane and into the crowded square, for all the world like two more people celebrating. I had a moment to feel pleased with myself, and another to wonder what in the god's name I was doing.

I followed, keeping them in sight. Just another person celebrating. A woman kissed me, and then a man did, energetically. Adria and her escort went out through the city gate in the midst of that happy, noisy crowd, and I followed them along the road north, still among many people.

When they claimed horses I had to keep walking, but I had an idea what they were doing, what Folco would have arranged, and after about an hour, perhaps a little more, with the sun now setting on my left, I came to an inn beside the road. I looked into the stables, and saw the horses they'd ridden.

Clever of me to figure it out, I suppose, though I knew even then this wasn't the wisest thing I'd ever done. But neither had it been prudent to help her escape Mylasia, I thought.

Unsound reasoning, my beloved teacher would have said: an earlier folly does not make sense of a later one.

I think, looking back, I might want to argue that when we make a decision, a choice, folly or otherwise, there are paths that close off immediately. Others open up as possibilities—and some actions can even feel compelled, for one reason or another.

But there is no Guarino for me to discuss it with, not for years now. I live with certain memories. Surely we all do.

THE FRONT ROOM of the inn was packed with people loudly reliving the race. There were women, too, and not just serving girls or whores. Bischio's race upended many norms.

One man jumped up on the bar and demonstrated Adria's double-leg kick, for those who hadn't been there—or just because he wanted to. I saw the man Adria had ridden here with. He was sitting alone, with a view of the door. His demeanour was such that no one seemed inclined to share his table. *I need to be careful*, I thought. Mind you, had I been careful, I wouldn't be here, I also thought.

I waited for a group to cross between the entrance and Folco's guard on their way to the long wooden bar, and I went quickly up the stairs. These were also crowded; a prostitute smiled encouragement at me, and raised her eyebrows in inquiry.

I had no idea which was Adria's room, but fortune can spin her wheel for the foolish, not just the worthy or the brave. I saw a servant come out of a room, put down two pails, and close the door. She picked up the pails, flushed with exertion.

I took a chance. "Has she finished her bath yet?" I asked.

She looked startled. I added, "I am ordered not to disturb her until she has."

"Best wait, then," she said, and carried on down the hallway and the stairs. She might talk to someone below, but I didn't think so.

I did wait. I walked along the hallway, which was dark, no candles or lanterns lit yet towards day's end. Light was expensive. I went to the end, opened the shutters there, and stood as if looking out. I heard people come and go behind me; a door opened and closed, a lock clicked. No one came to ask what I was doing there. It was a busy, excited day, even at an inn a distance from the walls. Some people who'd come to Bischio for the race would be staying here, with rooms in the city impossible to come by or wildly expensive. This inn wouldn't be inexpensive either, I thought. Not this week.

The window faced west. I watched the sun going down. There was a crowd in the courtyard below. I looked at them in the waning light. Someone was lighting torches. After a while I realized I was lingering because I was afraid. That made me move. It often has, does so even today. I don't like letting fear guide me—though it can be a sound guide.

I turned. I waited for two men to walk along the corridor from a room and go down the stairs, laughing. Their laughter faded. I

went to the room the girl had walked out from with the pails.
I knocked.

"What is it?" I heard her say.

I drew a breath.

"I might have been promised a kiss on a stairwell in Mylasia," I
replied.

I hadn't known I was going to say that.

There was a long silence. Then I heard her moving about the
room. No reply, though. Time passed.

The door opened.

Her hair was wet, her tunic damp. I could see the bathtub in the
middle of the floor behind her.

She didn't smile. She said, "I don't recall it being a promise."

But she stepped back for me to enter. There was no one else in
the room. She closed the door. I stayed near it.

"How did you find me?" she asked.

I cleared my throat. "I went to the Falcon district, there was a
crowd in front of one house. They were singing, some of them."

"I heard that."

"It wasn't very good."

"No."

"But they were happy."

"Yes. You found the house and . . . ?"

"I went to the laneway behind and waited."

"You knew I would be leaving?"

"I thought so, yes. If you hadn't already gone. It . . . it fit what I
know of you."

"What you know of me," she repeated. "And Gian never saw
you."

"I saw him first."

She was really very tall, even barefoot, as now. Wet footprints on
the wooden floor. The wet tunic showed her body too well for my
concentration.

"Well, Guidanio Cerra, I admit this is unexpected."

That was unexpected.

"I . . . you know my name, my lady?"

She flushed. I knew my own colour was high.

She said, "I asked, after Mylasia."

"You . . . how?"

"I sent a letter in the winter to Avegna. To the school. Where you said you saw me."

"You asked Guarino who I was? He answered you?"

She smiled, a little wryly. "He wasn't going to refuse a Ripoli."

Which was true. And served to calm me. The reminder of who she was.

"You told him we met in Mylasia? That I'd said I was at the school? He didn't ask why you had been there or why you wanted to know?"

"He wouldn't ask me questions."

I nodded. I said, quietly, "I can recommend my father in Seressa for any clothing you need expertly tailored, my lady."

She didn't reply. In one sense, I wasn't sure why I'd said that, either; in another way, of course I knew. Her eyes were grey or green, it was hard to tell in the muted light. There were two lamps lit, one by the wall, one near the bed. She had opened her shutters. We could hear sounds from below. My coming here, following her, seemed absurd.

She said, "I asked him who you were because it seemed proper that I know who saved my life, at risk of his own."

"Of course," I said. "As you can see, I've survived that risk, to this point."

"Yes," she said. "I'm pleased, of course."

I said, "I'm also wealthier than I've ever been, because of you, so you've . . . repaid any debt you might think you owe me."

I could see her putting it together. She had an *alert* face, I thought. I was seeing her clearly, up close, in some light, for the first time.

"You wagered on me?"

"I did. The triana."

"Not to win? No faith, Signore Cerra?"

"Not that. Faith you didn't want to win."

"Oh," she said. "I see."

What I know of you, I had said.

She was standing two or three paces away. The day had darkened further just in the time since I'd left the other window in the corridor. Twilight now.

"I was wagering for Teobaldo Monticola, as well," I said. I felt I needed to say that. It was embedded in this, it seemed to me.

"You work for him?"

"I met him on the road. I won a horse race of my own, against one of his captains. Won the horse, which Monticola bought back, so I had money. He invited me to join him in Bischio to watch the race."

She looked even more alert. "And should I guess you are the reason he knew who I was?"

"I saw you in the sanctuary when they blessed the horse. I told him if you were riding it would be for Folco, I didn't tell him who you were."

"But he already knew." It was a statement; she wasn't asking.

"Yes," I said. "I don't know how."

"Of course you don't." A sharpness.

She didn't explain. Why would she? The mood had changed. I had known it would when I named Monticola. She was Folco's niece, worked for him. I had just helped the man he most hated in the world, who most hated him.

I said, "He wagered trianas but also laid bets on you to win."

A slow smile. "I know he did. So that he'd defeat Folco that way. And then tell him, of course. You didn't share with him your thought? That I wouldn't want to win?"

"No," I said. "I . . . am not his man yet."

"Yet?"

"He has offered me a post . . . as tutor in Remigio."

"Monticola's son is older than we are."

"And in Sarantium. No, this would be the young ones, the sons of Ginevra della Valle."

"Ah," she said. "That means something. So, you will go to Remigio?"

"I haven't decided. He's allowed me time to think about it. Until tonight, in fact."

"What is there to decide? It is a great honour for someone so young. What . . . what else would you want to do, instead?"

Her voice had changed.

"I don't know." I realized mine had, as well. "I had thought of going home to Seressa. My cousin . . . has a bookshop. I have money now. Because of you. I can buy an interest, not just work for him."

"A bookshop," she said, but not with anything dismissive that I could hear.

"I'm not a soldier," I said.

"But you ride well enough to win a race with a mercenary captain?"

She'd registered that. She also smiled, a little wryly again.

"I know horses," I said.

"From the school?"

"Yes." I hesitated. "But I'm not a courtier. I have . . . no status at all. My lady."

She shook her head a little. She said, "They brought me wine. Will you take a cup?"

I said (I don't know where it came from), "I am light-headed already, my lady, in your presence."

She opened her mouth, closed it. "That is polished flattery," she said.

"For a tailor's son, you mean?" I said it too quickly.

She looked at me a long time before replying. She said, "We are what we are and the world is what it is."

"I'm sorry," I said. "I know that. Both things."

She said—I will remember it all my days—"Did I really promise? In Mylasia?"

I cleared my throat again. I *was* light-headed. I said, "Honestly? No. You—"

"I said I regretted having to defer it," she said. "I remember."

"Yes. Because of the poison."

A beat, as of musicians waiting. "Somewhat because of that, yes."

Somewhat. My heartbeat was absurdly fast. The lamplight in the room was erratic. It was difficult to tell, but it seemed to me her colour was still high.

"You did save my life," she said.

"You feel gratitude?"

"That must be it." She drew a breath, then said, "I have a thing to say, and a question to ask, Guidanio Cerra."

"Yes, my lady."

"You can't call me that. Not just now."

I nodded.

She said, "I have no poison on my lips, though I am dangerous in a different way . . . you will know it . . . in who I am. My family."

I nodded again. Speech had left me.

"I also . . ." She seemed awkward now. She cleared her throat. She said, or tried to say, "I should tell you that I am . . . that I have never . . . we cannot do . . ."

"We cannot make love," I said, "because you never have and must not be gotten with child."

"Yes," she said. It was barely audible. "Those things. Yes. Thank you."

"And the question?" I asked.

She lowered her head, lifted it again. "There are still . . . that is, there are . . ." She swore suddenly, like a soldier, said, "Do you know how to please a woman?"

And, as I remember it now, looking back, it seemed, just then, as if so much light had come into the room. I looked at her. I said, carefully, "I have some thoughts. And I am willing to learn."

IT IS ALMOST DISTURBING, how aroused she feels hearing him say those words. She doesn't feel fatigued any more.

She says, keeping her voice steady, although it takes an effort, "In that case, I believe you should kiss me."

She thinks he is trembling. She knows she is. He takes a step towards her and stops. She has no idea why he stops. She doesn't want him to have stopped. But he is smiling now, a good smile. He is a little taller than she is. They are alone in a room with a bed, on the day she's raced to glory in Bischio. He saved her life half a year ago.

He says, "A question of my own, if I may?" He pauses. "Do you know how to please a man?"

This is the dance. One she knows from home, from the world of courts. She has resisted it as a way of living, leaving home for Acorsi and a different existence, but she knows it well, and it is not always displeasing, she decides.

She says, gravely, "I have some thoughts. And I am willing to learn."

And she is the one who steps forward and puts her arms around his neck and her mouth to his, safely, not safely.

PHILOSOPHERS HAD WRITTEN about time, how it didn't have to be seen as steadily *flowing*, might be said to speed up or slow down, even rest suspended. I was entirely certain, entwined with Adria Ripoli on a bed in an inn near Bischio, that these ideas were all very wise, worthy of reflection, of being carefully weighed against each other.

That wasn't going to happen just then.

I was aware that the world existed outside that room and I would have to re-enter it, be *thrown* back into it, carry on with my life, decisions to be made in a violent world. And that such a life, mine, would not—*could* not—include this woman and what I felt about her, what I'd felt—however improbably—since Mylasia half a year ago.

"You must have been a very good student at Avegna," she said. We had been quiet, just breathing, for a time. One of her hands lay on my thigh.

"And you say this because . . . ?"

"Because you are a quick learner, Signore Cerra."

"Two of those here," I said. "If I may be permitted to say."

She laughed. "You are permitted."

"I suppose someone might be killed for simply touching you."

"Then someone would have to want very much to touch me."

"Yes," I said.

The sound of her laughter kindled desire again in me. Not that kindling was greatly required. I lifted her hand to my mouth, kissed her palm, her fingers. Then I shifted downward along the bed, which was quite large, it could have held four sleepers, many nights it probably did, at a country inn.

I kissed her breasts, moved down along her belly and kissed her there. I brushed my lips along the scar on her thigh. I let my fingers drift and circle in the space between her legs, as she had just taught me to do. She made a wonderful sound, somewhere between a sigh and a plea. I slid farther down and let my mouth go there.

"Danio, you don't have to do that again," she whispered.

I lifted my head. She was looking at me, along the length of her body. Her nipples were hard, as they had been before.

"You don't want me to?" I asked.

"YOU DON'T WANT me to?" he asks, and she can hear he is teasing, and it is . . . it is . . .

"I didn't say that," she hears herself whisper. "Dear Jad, I did not."

His laughter is soft, warm, then he finds other things to do and it is her own breathing she hears, then her own voice as she says things that seem to urgently require saying, however inarticulate they might be.

After, when she feels mostly able to deal with breathing and her body again, he is up beside her once more and she lets her hand touch him, as if idly, and feels how pleasingly excited he is again. She explores him with one finger only; down, and back up, and very slowly down again.

He says, a little desperately, "You don't . . . you don't have to . . ."

She doesn't even dignify that falseness with a reply.

She, in turn, shifts down the bed and his body.

"You will destroy me," she hears him say, and she is inexpressibly pleased with the world just then, even given the awareness of what is hovering—always—beyond them, like a shape, a shadowing where the light does not reach.

We are what we are and the world is what it is, she had said, in that time when they had been standing, not yet touching, not in this bed.

She wants him inside her. She knows she cannot do that. This will end, just as her time with Folco at Acorsi will end. She says, after his shuddering release has come and subsided, "Do not ever forget this. I promise I will not ever forget this."

She sees him shaking his head, he seems to be searching for the capacity to speak.

Finally, he says, "I cannot. I am . . . branded with you, Adria."

First time he's said her name. And such a thought. Such a lovely, such a sad thought. Why is there always sadness, she thinks, entangled with joy? Why is that how life must be?

She moves back up and kisses him again. Eventually, though not quickly, they rise and Guidanio dresses himself (she does not), and he walks to the door, and she goes there with him, in a long, pleased, luxurious nakedness, and they kiss again there, slowly, sweetly, and then he goes back out into a world that is not this room and is—always—what it is.

As if to prove that this is so, almost mockingly, only a little later she hears loud voices in the corridor and then there is a knocking again at her door, and a voice she does not know. And soon after that, a voice she does.

❦

The proprietor of The Cannon's Bell inn (the name had a long history, mostly lost) was a gaunt, long-faced fellow, belying any expectation of a portly, cheerful innkeeper in the countryside. He was used to people telling him to look happier. He didn't see much reason for doing that.

He undermined another assumption by being honest, serving decent, unwatered ale and local wines that were better than the run of such things. Also, if he was bribed to keep quiet by patrons, he kept quiet.

He expected to find his god in light when he died. He lived in hope of that and carried a well-worn sun disk always, even at night. His wife said he touched it in bed more than he touched her, but that was a private matter.

On the other hand, as to not betraying those who had bribed him, he had never been tested by a sum quite so substantial as this just now—offered by the well-dressed, insistent person before him.

Someone of considerable wealth, the kind that made judging quantities of money seem an irrelevance, wanted to know who had come into the inn and taken a room any time from mid-afternoon on. He suggested they had probably ordered a bath.

There was only one such person. A man who'd kept his hood up when he entered, and had gone straight upstairs. People had various reasons for wanting privacy, it was hardly unusual. The man's companion was still in the room, to the innkeeper's left. This caused the proprietor to urge the new person to keep his voice down.

He did accept the money offered.

You would have to be a blue moon's mad fool to refuse so much, and this man didn't look dangerous. He was a little drunk, slurring his words, but most people were today, and he kept saying, "I mean no harm. I mean no harm at all, as Jad sees my heart."

That was pious enough. The innkeeper told him the room, asked him to delay a bit, have a drink, not make it obvious what he was doing. There was someone watching by the far wall, he said.

"Aha!" said the well-dressed one, too loudly again. "A guard! I have found her!"

Her? thought the innkeeper.

Slipping the heavy purse into his tunic, he did resolve to go to his own quarters, where he had a sun disk on the wall, to pray for forgiveness. And, of course, for the god's safe journey under the world, where he defended mankind every night from demons.

Those evening prayers didn't happen, in the event.

Other men strode loudly into his inn shortly after the first man went upstairs. Half a dozen of them, five with swords and horsemen's bows. They were led by someone lean and imperious, older, balding, with a neatly trimmed grey beard, also well dressed, if dusty from travel. He made the same demand of the innkeeper—without offering money.

Instead, this one said, coldly, "I am looking for someone. You will be hanged from a tree in the courtyard and your inn burned to the ground unless you tell me who came here this afternoon and took a room that had been arranged for them. If there is no one of interest we are gone, but I urge you not to test me."

The innkeeper looked quickly over at the guard sitting by the eastern wall. He saw that this man was sitting up straight now. He saw that the fellow had gone rigid, as if fighting a sudden pain. He felt the same way.

He didn't test this tall, cold man, clearly accustomed to being obeyed. He said what room had been taken, again. These men, unlike the earlier one, did look dangerous. They went up the stairs immediately, three soldiers, the grey-bearded man, two soldiers.

It was only after they disappeared, followed by angry voices upstairs, that the innkeeper realized he knew the livery they wore.

He swore. It was extremely rare for him to do that. But this man *could* burn the inn down if he decided to, with no risk or consequence.

"Who the fuck is in that room?" was what he said, softly. Only his wife, coming back behind the counter, heard him.

She laughed. "What do you know about that word?" she said.

He didn't *think* anyone heard her say that.

❦

Antenami was very pleased with himself, hopeful that *two* desires could be assuaged now that he had found her.

He had little interest in the family business. The ledgers and bookkeeping rules his brother had tried to teach him seemed desperately tedious. He understood them (in fact), but he didn't *care*.

At the same time, he was entirely happy to deploy the wealth generated by their banking empire. They were beginning to rival Seressa, it was said—which could be dangerous, but that would be for his father and brother to address. Antenami had elected to be undisturbed if he was left to the side regarding such decisions, as long as he had money to spend. His older brother defined him as incapable. That was all right.

He'd spent family money this afternoon in the Falcon district. Three men had been paid sums. The third reported seeing their rider come down from a balcony in back of a house while singers were serenading her in front.

No, he had no idea where she'd gone, but she'd walked off in a cloak beside another man—and a third person had followed them, he said. North, he said. At a guess, to spend the night outside the walls. An assignation? He smiled a tavern smile. He hadn't said anything to anyone because it amused him to see all those Falcon fools in front, more arriving all the time, hoping she'd come out to them. He was from the Goose district, adjacent. Let the Falcon people sing to her—pointlessly.

Antenami truly hoped there was no assignation. He didn't think there was. Not a romantic one, at any rate. He believed himself to have instincts about women and horses. Better with horses.

He rode out with two of his men, north along the main road. Nothing useful at the first inn they checked. At the second one he found her.

⚜

I ought to have left, yes, but I'd gone back to the window at the end of the corridor. No one had closed the shutters I had opened before. There were lamps in the corridor now. The one nearest the window flickered in the breeze but didn't go out. I leaned out into the wind. More torches in the courtyard, and many more people.

I wasn't sure why I was lingering. Perhaps a wish, a longing, that she would open the door, step out looking for me. That she'd call me back to say . . .

To say what? This was dangerous folly—for her almost as much as for me. I didn't want that. But I wasn't ready to face the world again, walk down those stairs into the inn's front room and hear men shouting excitedly about the brilliant ride of the Falcon's woman in the Bischio square that day. And how they'd love to ride *her*, given half a chance!

From the wide bed, as I was dressing, she'd said, "Are you going to go with Monticola?"

"I haven't decided. I need to decide."

"You should do it," she said. "It puts you in a palace in an honourable position. There are opportunities there."

"I was in a palace in Mylasia."

"Different. You know it. Folco hates Monticola, there is a history, but the man isn't Uberto."

"I know that. Do you . . . do you know why they . . . ?"

"Want to kill each other? Not entirely. There was a battlefield some time ago, but there have been many battles. There are other stories."

"His eye?"

"Monticola didn't do that."

"So you don't know . . ."

"They are mercenaries, rivals, they made their fortunes that way, they still do. There may be something about his sister, Folco's. He has never told me. Neither has my aunt."

My aunt. Adria was what she was.

I'd finished dressing by then. I said, "I should go. It will be bad for you if . . ."

"If a man is found here? Maybe. Only if they know who I am."

I was looking at her. I was trying to memorize her. Against never seeing her again.

As if hearing me, she said, "I will want to know where you are, Danio. Will you try to let me know?"

It was generous. Courteous. I didn't want to feel sorrow. I nodded.

She added, "I'll tell you a thing about today. Folco knew Monticola was wagering on me to win. He sent me a note, with the start rope signal."

I adjusted my belt and the knife there. I looked at her. I could have stayed all night, and beyond, with this woman. I said, "That's why you didn't want to win?"

"No. You were right about that. I'd never have been able to get away if I'd won the race. People would have worked hard to figure out who I am. But . . ."

"But it was an added pleasure, knowing Monticola's bets would be lost?"

"For Folco it will have been."

"And you like to please him?"

She didn't smile. "I owe him for this life, the chance he gave me."

She said *gave me*. I ended up thinking about that at the corridor's end, by the window, in the wind. Not *is giving me*.

It wouldn't have been an accidental word. A race, a triumph, and done, finished—on her own terms. Was that it? Today marking the end of a part of her life. And: *I will want to know where you are.*

People spoke words like that, I thought, to be kind, at parting.

I had a choice to make. Where would I be? This could mark an end and a beginning in my life, too.

I turned from the window to go back downstairs. It was time. I was thinking these things, distracted by the memory of her, sight and taste, scent and feel, when I saw Antenami Sardi come up the stairs and go to Adria's door.

There was a lamp in the wall just beyond. I knew him from our meeting at the crossroads. Folco had been escorting him to Bischio.

He took a breath, put a hand on the wall to steady himself. He wasn't sober. I didn't know how he'd found her, but—

"Open for your greatest admirer!" he called abruptly, loudly. "I am Antenami Sardi and I have a proposal for you! *Two* proposals! One is . . . one's about a horse . . ."

Easy to guess what the other was. But he might mean it about the horse. He'd been so proud of his own, coming this way in ignorance, to race it in Bischio. He could want her as a rider . . .

I stayed where I was. I considered climbing out through the window. I hadn't checked for handholds that would get me down the wall, though, and you could break a leg jumping from here.

I could walk past him, I thought. I could go by quickly, as if leaving my own room, and . . .

I stayed. I didn't think he was a *dangerous* man, I was certain Adria could deal with him, but I had just left her bed and . . . I stayed.

What we do in a given moment, what we don't do, different paths in life.

There was no reply from the room, or none that I heard where I stood. Sardi knocked, five raps, five more. He said, "I mean only to honour you! To show my admiration. To *reward* you!"

Money, I thought. This man would be about money, and assume it would speak for him. He'd usually be right. And what he knew, what Bischio knew, was that the woman who had ridden for the Falcon district this morning was the orphaned daughter of a mercenary from Mylasia.

She'd said she was going to a retreat. But men like this one could propose alternatives. Still nothing from within, if his manner was a clue.

He drew himself up. He said, "You *must* let me in. There is so much we have to talk about!" He hesitated. "I know you did not try to catch the other horse. I know all about horses!"

And that, I thought, was dangerous. He'd be a rash, foolish man, with wealth and a sense of invulnerability, and he could do careless harm.

Except that he wasn't invulnerable, even wrapped in money and power. Not to everyone. Not to mischance.

A clatter from the stairs. Men bursting into the corridor at the far end. Three, then one, a tall man. Two more. And they were armed. I stayed where I was. Too late to disappear now. I could only hope no one would look this way.

"Step back from that door!" the tall man said in a high, authoritative voice. I didn't know him, but I knew that tone.

Antenami Sardi turned to him. He was not, I guessed, accustomed to being given orders. He said, "Go about your business. Do you have any idea who I am? Go piss in an alley somewhere and leave me alone!"

"Shoot him," said the other man.

All it took. Two words. Two arrows.

Sardi fell, with a thump not a clatter, to the hallway floor. I saw his head hit hard. He made no other sound. My jaw dropped. I closed it. I was aware that my life was in extreme danger now. Why would they hesitate to kill an observer?

They almost certainly had no idea of his identity, but a very important man had just taken two arrows and might be dead. Probably was—with implications for all of Batiara.

The tall man moved forward, stepping fastidiously over the body on the floor. He knocked at the same door, Adria's.

He said, clarifying many things, "Daughter, open now. You are coming home with me."

Holy Jad, I thought. And then, *This is impossibly bad.*

The duke of Macera had just had a Sardi shot, possibly killed. Also: Adria, and the end of a life she'd lived.

She'd guessed it was ending, I thought. She'd probably been planning it herself. I didn't think she'd imagined it would happen this way—and not by her own choice.

The door opened. She stepped out. She looked down at Sardi, then at the man in front of her.

She'd clothed herself, in what she'd worn coming here.

"This is unexpected. How pleasant to see you, father," she said, with an unsettling calm. "I do regret you've seen fit to expose who I am, and to have your men—in livery I see, easily identified—shoot someone you really should not have shot."

He seemed taken aback. "A drunken man trying to bed you? Of course I will have him—"

"That is Antenami Sardi you've just killed, dear father. Piero's younger son. Tell me, how much money do you owe the Sardi bank?"

I was holding my breath.

"Oh, Jad," said Duke Arimanno of Macera. "Oh, holy Jad! How could I . . . why didn't you . . . ?"

"Why didn't I what? *Tell you?* What are you doing here, father? What could possibly have made you leave home? *Why are you here?*"

The duke looked at the fallen man again. He stepped back a little. He gestured, almost helplessly. "Your . . . your mother . . ."

"Ah! *Mother* demanded you come fetch me home?" Adria laughed. Very different laughter from when we'd been together in that room. She pointed at the man on the floor. "This is a disaster. For everyone!"

"It may be," came a different voice, from behind the Ripoli guards. "It probably is."

The guards turned quickly, one drew his sword.

I saw Folco d'Acorsi at the top of the stairs, another man behind him. The one who'd brought Adria here.

Folco said, calmly, "Has anyone troubled themselves to confirm he is dead?"

"How lovely!" said Adria. "Let's *everyone* come to the inn where I was to spend a night unknown!"

"Folco!" cried the duke. "It's you! Jad be praised!"

"Arimanno," d'Acorsi replied, nodding his head. "You are far from home. And have placed me in a difficult position."

"*I* have placed *you*?" The duke's manner changed, his voice went higher. "Given what you had her doing here? Folco, it'll be worse for you when I—"

"Arimanno, stop. Listen to me. I am retained by the Sardis this year. This man is under my protection. You just put arrows in him."

"Oh," said the duke of Macera, after a moment.

Oh, I thought.

I'd actually forgotten that Folco was both Ripoli's brother-in-law *and* the Sardis' mercenary captain, paid by them to prevent anything remotely like this.

"Who," said Folco d'Acorsi, "is by the window? Show yourself or be killed."

He didn't miss much, even with one eye. And if he didn't kill me, the duke of Macera would. I was a witness.

I walked forward towards all of them. I was thinking as fast as I ever had in my life.

SHE IS THINKING as fast as she ever has in her life.

She believes Guidanio will die here. Her father's men are tense and uncertain and so is her father and that can lead to violence. Folco seems calm, but he always does, and she knows this is bad for him.

She still can't believe her father is here. Folco had assured her that no one in her family would come to Bischio. It is not the sort of thing the Ripoli do, especially not her father, who *never* likes leaving Macera, or even his palace, except to hunt. He is a man who has his food tasted and his bedroom searched by guards before he goes to sleep at night.

Her mother is different. Her mother terrifies her father (not Adria, not for a long time). But . . . how had she learned Adria was here? Who could have . . . ?

There may have been, she thinks, more than one spy in Folco's palace in Acorsi.

It makes sense, that her parents will have assigned someone to keep a distant, careful eye on their daughter. Folco has probably figured this out by now, she decides.

But he hadn't, before, or had known and wrongly judged what her family might do. A mistake. *I make mistakes*, he'd told her, more than once. *Never assume I don't.*

She says, "No one is to harm this man."

"Why?" says her father.

"Why?" says Folco.

She has an answer, but not one she wants to say, about his saving her in Mylasia. It opens up so many other problems. But Guidanio speaks first.

"Because I am the tutor of Teobaldo Monticola's young sons, here innocently, and I must assume neither of you wants a war with him, especially if he is in the right. You will not remember me my lord Folco but we met at two roads coming here. Signore Sardi spoke of wishing to race his horse?"

"I remember that. Not you. Why," says Folco, "are you here, so innocently?"

Danio has come forward into the light. He says, "To express the lord of Remigio's gratitude to the young woman who rode for the Falcon district. He won a considerable sum wagering on her. He sent me with a purse. Even though she said she intends to seek out the Daughters of Jad, money can be of assistance in retreats. I was instructed to say that."

"Then why were you at the end of the corridor?" Folco's voice is hard. She can see he is dubious, though he knows about the wagering.

"My lord, I heard someone on the stairs and I withdrew, to be discreet until he left."

"How did you find her?" Folco's arms are crossed in front of his chest.

"It was not difficult, my lord," Danio says. That is reckless, with Gian right here, Adria thinks. "We were looking for her in the Falcon district and saw her leave with your man."

We is clever. Suggests Monticola's men had been with him, able to observe all around the house she'd been in.

"And you, dearest father? How did *you* find me?" She needs to take some of this attention from Danio.

"Money," he says. "If that is really a Sardi he'll have done the same."

"It is really a Sardi," Folco says.

"This is," Adria says, genuinely angry, "desperately foolish, what you have all done. Do you *want* to drive me to a retreat?"

"I see no better place on Jad's earth for you," her father says grimly. "We can leave you at one on the way home."

"Very well. And from there I can tell the world I rode in the race in Bischio, and other things I have done. Think more carefully, father. Of course, you could kill me, instead."

"Jad's blood and his chariot wheels!" her father snaps. She'd known he'd say that. She knows him very well. She loves him, as it happens. She knows he loves her. He is very unhappy right now.

She sees Danio kneel by the fallen man. First to do so, though
Folco had asked. He puts fingers to Sardi's throat.

"He's not dead," he says.

Folco nods. "Good. We have a chance."

"Are you," her father says quietly, "so certain it is good? Perhaps, if
he dies . . . no one will know who . . . it might have been this tutor!"

The duke of Macera, her father, is subtle, clever, cold, and can
make mistakes when unsettled. Everyone can, she thinks.

"Your men are wearing your livery, father. They walked in with
swords—and bows. Bows, father? Arrow wounds? *Everyone* will
know who did this," she says.

"Jad's blood," he says again. He looks at Folco, married to his
sister and employed this year by the family of the man lying on the
floor. He wants help. She knows that look.

She understands her father. He can be vicious, but never to his
children. A dangerous man, however, because he is always afraid.

She sees Folco working through possibilities. She knows the
expression on his face, too. There are no good choices that she can
see, but she waits, they all wait. People do that for Folco.

Eventually he says, "Very well. My best thought. Arimanno, leave
now with your men. The road north as far as you can tonight, then
straight home. A hood to cover your face when you go downstairs."

"I don't have a hood," her father says.

"I do," Adria says. She goes into the room and returns with the
cloak she'd worn coming here. She hands it to her father.

"It won't fit very well," he says.

"My apologies," she replies. And sees the faintest glimmer, like a
ghost at the edge of where moonlight falls, of amusement in his face.
He is clever, he just hates being abroad, and has made a bad mistake.

She also remembers—never really forgets—that he gave her permission to do what she's doing with Folco. Perhaps not as to the
details but he'd let her go to Acorsi and her aunt, and Folco. It
would never have happened without that.

She steps forward and adjusts the cloak and hood for him. She kisses his cheek. "I will see you at home."

"You are coming home?" he says.

"Perhaps. For a time. At the least."

At the least. She doesn't know, just now, what she needs to do, wants to do.

He nods. "That will be good. Did you really win their race?"

He loves horses, riding, hunting.

"I was the first rider across the line," she says. She'll explain later.

Her father looks at Guidanio, still kneeling by the fallen man. He has shifted Sardi onto one side, so neither arrow presses against the floor. "And Monticola wagered on you? Why would he do that?"

Too shrewd a question. He must not be underestimated.

Nor should Guidanio Cerra, she is learning. He stands up. "He knew she was with the lord of Acorsi. My lord of Remigio decided Acorsi must know something concerning the race. My lords, please, while you talk, a man—"

"May be dying. Indeed," says Folco. "Arimanno, north, quickly. Gian, bring me the innkeeper."

Gian goes quickly down the stairs.

Adria's father looks at her again. "I cannot approve of this," he says, "but well done if you won this race. Don't take a purse from Monticola. We don't do that."

"I am just a girl from Mylasia."

"No," he says, "you aren't." He kisses her on the cheek and turns to go.

He stops beside Folco. "I think it is enough, for her, don't you?"

"It might be. We need to deal with this first."

"Then deal with it," her father says, as if commanding, as if this isn't a chaos of his making.

Folco looks as if he might say something about that to his wife's brother, but only nods. "Have your soldiers hide their bows until you are horsed and away."

Her father nods. He and his men go down.

She feels a strangeness within. It has been a long time since she's seen her father. This has been such an eventful day. And is not yet done.

Folco is looking at her. He says, "It *was* well done this morning."

She has a sense he wants to smile, but there is a man here with arrows in him.

"I was happy," she says.

She knows he will understand that. He says, "You are all right? You'll be able to ride if we need to leave quickly?"

She makes a face. "I rode three times around the Bischio square, that's all."

"That's all," he repeats, still not quite smiling, but it is in his voice. He turns to Guidanio. "You have a purse for her?"

She'd known he'd ask. Testing the story.

"I do, my lord." Guidanio reaches inside his tunic. She realizes what's there. His own money, from his own wagers. He's very clever, she thinks. She likes clever men. He says, "Though if this is a Ripoli, I have to say . . ."

Also shrewd. Since he'd heard what had been said by her father, and could be expected to react.

Steps on the stair. The innkeeper, with Gian. Gian, she thinks, will be extremely unhappy. He was followed here. *It was not hard,* Danio had said. That will have stung.

The innkeeper is perspiring, though it is a cool night. "My lord," he says, wiping at his forehead. "My lord, what may I—?"

He stops, a hand to his mouth. He has seen the man on the ground.

"Oh, Jad!" he exclaims. "What has happened?"

"An unfortunate mistake," Folco says calmly. "You must help us remedy it. The nearest capable doctor? Where?"

"Tonight, my lord? Tonight? It is . . . it was the race today! All the physicians in Bischio are—"

"Tonight. Now. A name. Gian will bring him. Quickly, or someone important may die in your inn and there will be an investigation."

Investigations, Adria thinks, are never good for an inn.

"Important, my lord?"

"I said that."

"The physicians in Bischio will all be drinking and abroad, my lord. The city tonight will be—"

"Outside Bischio, then. A name, man!"

Another voice answers him. A woman's, from the top of the stairs. They all turn, again.

"I know of someone." It is a small, capable-looking person, hair tied back, hands at her sides.

"You are . . . ?" Folco asks.

"My wife," the innkeeper says.

"To my sorrow," she says.

Folco does not smile. "Tell me," he says. "This physician?"

"There's a healer, just arrived in Dondi, north of here."

"How far?"

"A few hours on a good horse. At night."

"His name?"

"Hers. Her name is Jelena. She came at winter's end. Has delivered babies there, done other things. We've had word of her."

Adria's heart thumps hard.

She is looking at Folco. This time he does allow himself to smile.

"Of course that is her name," he says. "The god amuses himself with our lives."

The innkeeper makes a quick sign of the sun disk, hearing impiety.

Folco shakes his head. "Gian, two horses, pray she can ride. Get directions, find her, tell her it is arrows. As quickly as you can in the dark. We *really* don't want this man to die."

Gian and the two from the inn go back down. Adria finds herself alone with Folco and Guidanio Cerra and the arrow-pierced body of Antenami Sardi—who they really don't want to die.

Folco looks down at him. "Very well. Let's get him off the floor and onto a bed." He turns to Danio. "Can two of us lift him?"

"Three of us," she says.

They do that. He does not die when they move him. He does not awaken, either.

"The injury to his head may be as bad as the arrows," Folco says inside the room, looking more closely at Sardi. He calls for hot water and clean linens. Also food for the three of them. Adria is grateful she'd straightened the bed linens before opening the door to her father. Sometimes, she thinks, she can be prudent. Not often enough, perhaps.

She is looking at Antenami Sardi lying on her bed. *The god amuses himself with our lives*, Folco had said, in the corridor.

CHAPTER IX

Folco says to Danio, "Signore, your name?"

"Guidanio Cerra, my lord. Of Seressa."

"You didn't come here to give her a purse from Monticola, did you, Guidanio Cerra?"

Danio doesn't answer immediately. He doesn't betray anything, either.

Adria knows she needs to speak. "No," she says, "he didn't. Folco, this is the man who saved my life in Mylasia."

He stares at her, the one eye. "Jad's blood," he says, as her father often does. He turns to Danio, his voice cold. "You followed her to Bischio?"

"I had no idea she was here," Danio says. "I had to leave Mylasia, I am on my way home to Seressa, I thought I would see the race first."

"Why did you have to leave Mylasia?" Folco is a good listener.

Danio says, "I was brought to Mylasia to serve one of the men who was killed when the count died. A friend of Guarino's in Avegna. It became dangerous for me."

"You are important enough to kill?"

"I am beyond unimportant, my lord." She hears a note there, but it was clever of him to mention Guarino, whom Folco loves. Danio adds, "Unimportant men were dying, my lord."

Folco is taking his measure, she sees, or trying to. "And Monticola? Why with him now?"

It is as if he is hunting, Adria thinks—whenever that man becomes part of a conversation.

"We met on the road not long before we encountered you, my lord."

"So, what you said about tutoring is a lie?"

"It is not, lord. He has offered the post. I have not decided yet."

"Offered it why?"

"I cannot speak for him, my lord."

Folco's expression eases, a little. He likes cleverness too. "Your best guess?"

"Because I studied at Avegna."

"Ah." She sees a piece slip into place for him. "You said that. I did, as well."

"I know this, my lord. We saw you—and the Lady Adria—in our courtyard. You came visiting our teacher."

"You remembered her from then?"

"She is . . . Yes, my lord, I did." Danio is carefully not looking at her.

Neither is Folco now. And Adria realizes something, and is afraid, because she knows Folco d'Acorsi and how his mind works.

"And the lord of Remigio offered you a post for that reason? Because you studied at Avegna?"

"I told you, I cannot say. Perhaps also because I won a horse race against one of his captains. And because . . . he may have only just decided to do something about his younger sons?"

There is a silence. Folco turns to her, finally. He hesitates for the first time.

"You have not been foolish?"

She lifts her head. "It would be foolish for you not to withdraw that question."

He looks away. That rarely happens.

"I'll take it, then, that you haven't been."

"Take it any way you choose," she says coldly.

He looks back at her. "Adria, you understand your aunt is the only person I fear."

She thinks that there are two people he fears, one he loves and one he hates, but she'd never say that.

She says, "You lay claim to all the folly I have, uncle."

He shakes his head. "I am so fortunate!" He turns to Guidanio. "Do I need to kill you?" he asks.

Which is what she has feared.

"Because you believe I will tell the lord of Remigio what happened here? Why would I do that?"

"Why would you not?" says Folco. "If you are at his court and seeking favour? If he learns the duke of Ripoli did this to a Sardi—perhaps killing him—he has the power of that knowledge."

"That *would* be a power," says Danio. "He will not learn it from me."

"Because?"

She holds her breath.

"Because it might do harm to the duke's daughter, here with us, and I will never do that."

Said simply, and Adria feels—again—how richness and sorrow can be entangled in the world.

Folco is thinking hard. He doesn't like untied ends, things he can't control. Danio is now one of those. She should speak, she thinks, but doesn't know what to say.

"Work for me, then," Folco says.

She hadn't expected that.

He adds, "I can use a man in Remigio."

She looks at the man she has lain with in this room, the man who'd saved her life in the autumn, and she sees he is struggling with this. She wonders if he's aware he can die here with the wrong answer. Folco is calm, but he can kill a man calmly, and this is Monticola they are talking about.

"Will you," Guidanio Cerra asks, "kill me if I do not agree to spy for you?"

And Folco laughs. She had not expected that either. He says, "I might have you killed on the road. There's a body here already. But when did the young people become clever? Isn't that supposed to take time?"

Guidanio doesn't smile. "Wisdom does," he says. "People can be clever at any age. My lord, if I go to Remigio it will be as a teacher, not a spy. But I will never speak of this evening. If word emerges of what happened here it will not have come from me. Do you want an oath?"

"Men lie under oath."

Adria looks from one to the other. She realizes what she wants to say. She says it. "Folco, it is simpler than that. If you harm him, I will reveal that I murdered Uberto for you."

"*What?* Why would you do that?" It is Danio who exclaims, not Folco.

Folco is just looking at her. He says, softly, "That would do harm to your own life."

"I think not. It would explain my guilt, and repentance, why I became a Daughter of Jad, to pray for my own soul and those of others for the rest of my days."

"Adria," he says. She knows that tone.

"Uncle," she says.

"That," says Guidanio, "would be such a foolish thing to do!"

"Be quiet," Folco says, not looking away from her. His forehead is furrowed. "I am not going to ask again if you have been foolish here."

"Good," she says coldly. "Very wise."

There is a knock at the door. Folco nods and Danio goes to open it.

The innkeeper and his wife. They don't want others here. They appear to be trying to avoid looking at the man on the bed, and the blood. They have food, the linens Folco wanted. Hot water is coming.

"I should go," Guidanio says after the husband and wife have left. "I have a walk in the dark ahead of me."

"Where?" she asks.

"Where?" Folco asks.

Danio looks at her, not him. He is tall, dark-haired and dark-eyed, amusing and alert. He may even be wise, or on the way to that. His father is a tailor in Seressa.

"I don't know," he says. And leaves, leaves her again, after bowing properly to both of them.

The door closes. After a moment, she looks at Folco, who is looking at her.

"You are right," she says, with a heavy sigh. "Alas the day, I lost my maidenhead here. I think I am with child already. My body feels as if—"

He swears. Quite vulgarly. She's pleased.

"Folco, I told you, I've not been foolish," she says, and it is almost true.

"I believe it." He smiles a little. "Or else he'd have agreed to spy for me, lost in love."

She swears at him this time, which seems appropriate.

They eat the food that has been brought. Antenami Sardi does not awaken, but neither does he stop breathing. There is blood, but not such a great deal from two arrows, much less than there had been with Uberto, when she'd stabbed him where she had.

After, she rests on the servant-bed at the foot of the large one, genuinely exhausted. She thinks about the day, about many different aspects of the day. She sleeps.

Some time later—she's awake again—there is another knock. Folco opens the door this time. It is most of the way to morning, and Jelena, the healer, is here, with Gian in the corridor behind her. The blue moon has long since risen, is setting by then. Adria can see it through the window where they've left one shutter ajar.

❦

Jelena saw Folco d'Acorsi first. He was as she remembered. Not a man you forgot.

"Be welcome," he said, "and thank you."

He did not smile. Neither did Jelena. She was not fearful, but she was disturbed, shaken by what was happening, and a cold night ride. This was too unexpected. Yes, you could be summoned at any hour as a healer, but this was . . . different.

He added, "I am pleased to see you. And grateful. I had thought you might decide to leave Mylasia. Was it because of us? That night?"

"Not really," Jelena said with a shrug. "I don't seem to have left you, in any case."

"I hate when capable people leave me," he said. A brief smile. But he was showing strain, Jelena thought. She looked towards the ceiling for the presence of death in this room, or a ghost. She didn't see either—yet.

She was cold from the ride. She saw a man on the bed. There appeared to be, as she'd been advised, two arrows. He was lying on one side, which was good. But a mercenary leader would know to do that. It wasn't a difficult idea, ensure the arrows weren't pressing on anything. There was blood, of course.

The man who'd come for her, offering a good-sized purse and a promise of more (a wealthy man injured; archers, he'd said), had not offered any further details. Certainly not that Folco d'Acorsi would be waiting. He'd been under great stress when he found her. Agitation and fear, vivid even in the dark.

He'd brought a horse for her. Jelena could ride but not well, and it was night. She wouldn't go as fast as he wanted to. She'd had to pack her kit. There were implements she needed, given what he'd said. He carried them for her on his horse, then up the stairs when they reached the inn that was their destination. It was not yet morning, there was still a handful of people in the downstairs front room, the fires were lit.

At the doorway to the bedchamber Folco stepped back. She walked in—and saw Adria Ripoli.

Jelena drew a breath. The capricious wheel, she thought, was spinning tonight.

She said, calmly, "My lady. Your leg is recovered?"

"It is. I remain deeply appreciative," said the other woman. She'd been sitting on a cot, now she stood. Jelena had almost forgotten how tall she was. "As you see, we need you again. And again at night."

"I am not a surgeon," Jelena said.

"I imagine you are more skilled than most of those." It was Folco. "Also, he hit his head on the floor when he fell. There's a wound there, too."

She nodded. Walked towards the bed. These two, the memories of last autumn, could be addressed later—if she chose. Right now, she had a task, and she could very much use whatever payment they ended up offering. It would be generous. She knew that much. The man on the bed was extremely well dressed. Damask silk for his doublet, red, and not from blood. The fabric and the colour spoke of money.

She was in a new place this spring, looking to settle in a city, not a hamlet in the countryside. Testing that life. A large fee to start would help. You needed to think of such things if you were a woman alone, relying on yourself.

She said to Folco d'Acorsi, "I don't intend this to become a habit, but I will do what I can. Arrange for more light, please, very hot water, and as much clean linen as you can."

"We have the linens," Folco said. He nodded towards a neat pile on a chest under the window.

Adria Ripoli went out. They heard her call downstairs for the water and lamps. She came back in. Behind her, quite quickly, came a man and a woman, each carrying two lamps. They left these and went out, as if they wished to pretend never to have been there. Folco placed the lamps near the bed.

"Close the shutter and come hold him down for me," Jelena said. She removed her cloak and set it aside. "The arrows have to come out." She pushed her hair back and gestured for Folco's man, still by the door, to bring her bag with the implements.

"Wait," she said. "Should I know who he is?"

"Perhaps better if you don't," Folco said.

"I'll become fearful and unsteady?"

He looked at her. Smiled again, that wry smile. He was an ugly man, but there was so much *life* in that face, Jelena thought—for a man whose life was so much about killing.

"This is Antenami Sardi," he said. "Piero's younger son. You might understand why we are anxious to have him live."

And with that, Jelena suddenly did feel unsteady.

She tried to cover it. "So many important people I seem to be meeting. Where," she asked, "is Teobaldo Monticola tonight?"

His smile again. "So many clever young people I seem to be meeting. He is in Bischio, as it happens. I hope he doesn't join us."

"I can imagine," Jelena said. She wondered who had loosed these arrows. If Folco was here, and so concerned . . .

She took a large pair of tailor's scissors from her bag and began cutting away the clothing of the man on the bed. When his doublet was free from both arrows (one in the shoulder, right through, one in the ribs on the other side), she took out an instrument she'd had made, following instructions in a very old book she'd found in a library in Varena, and set about dealing with the second arrow, which would be more difficult, because it had not gone right through. She used a knife to expand the entrance wound, which would—always— be painful. She wasn't a surgeon, but she'd done this before.

Antenami Sardi stirred, and cried out, a low-pitched moan. The two men held him down. They'd have done this before, too. Soldiers.

"Most thoughtful thing I've ever heard this one say," muttered Folco d'Acorsi.

Jelena was startled, almost laughed. Not good, given what she was in the midst of doing, sliding a metal probe into an arrow wound.

"You aren't helping," she said.

"Forgive me," he said, but he didn't sound contrite. She didn't look to see if he was smiling again. *He* would not suffer if the man on the bed died. Or . . . perhaps he would. Perhaps that was why they were here?

"I may not forgive you," she said. She felt what she was probing for in the wound. Drawing a steadying breath, she pulled the arrow out in one smooth motion, the gouging flanges of the arrowhead sheathed in the cup of the long, thin device she'd had made after reading about it and seeing a drawing. It had been a book based on an even older text by a physician in Esperaña centuries ago.

There were things you could learn from the past. Mistakes to avoid, paths to pursue. That applied to your own life, too, she thought. She wondered if she'd have come here, summoned in the night, if she'd known these two were waiting.

Then she admitted something to herself: of course she would have. Fortune's wheel might spin, but you could also *choose* to spin it, see how it turned, where it took you, and she was still young, and this was the life she wanted.

❧

The world was blurred. It wobbled, and there was a great deal of pain. He had no idea where he was. When he opened his eyes, he couldn't see. He was aware of light, which was causing some of the pain. There was a scent in the room, something herbal? He seemed to be lying down. His left arm hurt terribly, and his side. He couldn't understand why this was so. He couldn't make his eyes work properly.

He was unhappy. He moaned.

A voice, a truly gentle voice was beside him right away. The voice said, "You are in an inn near Bischio, signore. You were wounded by arrows. The wounds have been treated. Can you hear me?"

He wanted to *keep* hearing her. It was a woman's voice, and so soothing, so kind.

"Have I died?" he managed. He didn't think so, but . . .

"Not yet," she said. He heard amusement, but that also seemed gentle, he thought, not a hard thing at his expense.

He was still trying to make his eyes work so he could see her. Then he realized there was a thin wet cloth over them.

"Eyes," he said.

"I'll close the shutters first," she said softly. "You will be sensitive to light." She was being so *good* to him, Antenami Sardi thought. He suddenly felt like crying. He heard the wooden floor, then shutters creaking. His hearing seemed to be all right. He heard her footsteps coming back. She took the cloth from his forehead and eyes.

He could see. It was not bright in the room, but he looked up and saw a woman of surpassing grace and beauty standing above him, smiling.

"Welcome back, Signore Sardi," she said.

"Will you marry me?" Antenami replied.

She laughed, but gently, so gently.

HE STAYED THERE three weeks to recover. She stayed with him. The woman rider was gone, and so was Folco d'Acorsi. It appeared that Folco had come here after Antenami was attacked, and had arranged for this healer to be brought to him.

Folco had provided her with a considerable sum to remain, and left three men to escort Antenami home when he was ready to ride. Fillaro was being tended to in the stable of the inn. Money was always a factor in such things.

He had only the vaguest memory of what had happened. He'd been outside the door of the woman rider. He remembered a tall, unpleasant man. He was the one who'd had Antenami wounded by arrows, if such a thing could even be imagined! He could have died! He had no idea who the man had been—the archers had worn livery, but he didn't remember it clearly. He recalled a high, imperious voice.

His brother Versano sent a man to ask about this. The identity mattered. The man also asked the innkeeper, but it seemed the would-be assassins had been cloaked downstairs, no one knew who they were. They'd come in and gone out quickly, then away on horseback. North, was the thought, but no one appeared certain.

Folco had reported arriving too late to see them. He had sent for a healer (wonderful healer!) and she had saved Antenami's life.

It was possible—it might even be useful—that the assassins had been from Bischio, a bold (foolish) thrust at Firenta in the person of a member of its most powerful family, Antenami was told. They might declare it to be the case, regardless of truth. He wasn't sure what to think of such matters normally, and especially now. His head hurt in the first days, but that eased.

No one knew who the woman rider had been, either. His brother's man spoke of trying to find her in Daughters of Jad retreats between Bischio and Firenta. Antenami was alert enough by then to say there was no point, she'd had nothing to do with what had happened. It was, in his view, likely that a rival for her company had taken exception to Antenami being at the door first. That sort of thing happened.

He knew what his brother would say about his behaviour, but he *had* brought two guards with him to this inn. He hadn't been reckless. They had since been dismissed, he was told. They were fortunate not to have been executed for remaining downstairs, uselessly, then going back (uselessly) to the larger party. He didn't like his brother dismissing his own men, but he supposed it was proper. He had almost died!

His brother's man left. The healer stayed.

He was in love with the healer. He told her so, frequently. She told him it happened all the time, men or women feeling affection for their physician or healer, that he needed to put his mind to getting well.

He told her he *was* getting well, and he didn't care if it happened all the time, it had never happened to *him*. He asked her, every day, if she would marry him. He made sure she knew who he was, his family.

She knew, she refused. Partly because of who he was, she said. It could not happen, would never be accepted. He knew it, she said, surely he knew it. She was so gentle.

He knew that she was right, but he didn't *want* to know it.

One night, towards the end of his time there, when he had clearly recovered, she came into his bed from the small cot where she slept, and made love to him, riding above him, gently (then a little less so). Afterwards, she began teaching him some things he'd never known about the act of love with a woman one had not paid for. He liked learning these things. He liked when she began to reveal that she, too, was deriving pleasure from what they did.

He wanted to do this every day, many times. She'd smile and tell him his healing needed to take precedence. He told her she was healing him this way.

One morning he woke and she was gone. She left a note. She told him that his shoulder might ache for a time, possibly even always, but he was unlikely to be impeded in the things he liked to do, such as riding or hunting. She asked him, as an act of courtesy and grace, to leave her to her life and the memory of their time together. She called it an interlude, and wished him good fortune.

Antenami Sardi, in the greatest exercise of self-restraint in his life to that point, accepted this. He did not pursue her to her city nearby, though he knew where it was. He went home as spring was turning towards summer, riding Fillaro north between hills and vineyards, among bright-green leaves, flowers, birdsong, seeing fortresses and towns perched above the road. One of the small cities along the way was hers. He kept riding. She had asked him to.

It would not be excessive to say he was a changed man from that time. Even his brother acknowledged it, eventually. His father did so even sooner. So, too, did some of the women who had been his preferred bed-companions at home. He enjoyed these things being said. His shoulder did hurt at times, more as time went by, especially when the winter rains arrived each year, but few men were permitted lives free of pain or loss.

When spring came the next year, his father intended to have Firenta go to war against Bischio, their forces led by Folco Cino d'Acorsi. Pain and loss were likely to attend.

ᐒ

It was reckless to walk back alone in the moonlight with no sword and a substantial purse hanging about my neck. My winnings were hidden inside my tunic, but if anyone did decide to rob me they'd give wild thanks to the god for what they found.

I could have booked a horse at the inn but it didn't occur to me until I was some distance south already. I needed time to think, in any case. Looking back, that night road feels like another interval, my life lying before it, and after.

I was not in anything resembling a tranquil state of mind, but I had a decision to make. I think that when we're young we often have the sense that what we do when faced with a choice will define our lives forever. This can be untrue, sometimes amusingly so, but not always.

Events since then have proven my feeling that night to be true, I think, even if we concede that no man can know what would have happened had he turned north or east instead of south at some place where roads divide.

TWO OF MONTICOLA's soldiers were guarding the door when I returned to the house. I knew there'd be others around the back. It was as much a show of force as any actual concern about threats. People feared this man, and he was here to possibly take a contract *with* Bischio. He might be their champion next year, if Firenta came with an army. That army would be Folco's, of course.

It occurred to me, distracted and tired as I was, to wonder if that was *why* Monticola might take this on. Their long feud playing out on a stage offered by wealthier cities, paid for by them? Batiara is still like that. Matters of high policy and power, but with personal hatreds (or loves) added to or opposing them. And who knew which one took the lead in that dark dance?

I didn't. I still don't. The guards nodded at me, one made a crude joke and gesture. It was obvious where they thought I'd been; most of their fellows were at brothels that night, spending money before heading home to Remigio. Those on guard had drawn the short lots or rolled bad dice to be posted here, sober, on a wild night.

I was feeling fear as I walked in. I thought about my parents, Seressa, the life I thought I'd been born to. And here I was, entangled with Monticola and Acorsi. Folco had asked me to spy for him. Adria had been looking at both of us when he did. I was a tailor's son, having been given the lucky gift of an education. But what did that mean? What could it be caused to mean?

Not the hour to weigh all that. I really was tired, it had been a day of days, and I'd walked a considerable distance, as well. Had the race been only this morning? I thought I would go up to bed and deal with my life when I woke.

What we think we'll do is often not what we end up doing. It isn't always in our own control, our life.

Monticola di Remigio was in the front sitting room to the left of the stairs. The door was open. He was in a high-backed, cushioned chair of the newer sort and he was looking at me, a cup of wine at his elbow, booted feet outstretched, crossed at the ankles. It was as if he'd been waiting for me, though I knew that couldn't be so. Ginevra della Valle was standing near him in a deep blue robe with pale green sleeves. No jewellery at home at night.

"*Danino!* Here you are at last!" he cried enthusiastically, using the boy-name. It was immediately obvious he was not sober. I thought I saw a warning in Ginevra's eyes. I had no idea what to do with that.

"My lord," I said, stopping in the doorway, bowing to both of them.

"Where were you?" he asked. It could have been a mild, inconsequential question.

I managed a smile. "Abroad in the city. I am reluctant to say more with the lady—"

"She's no innocent," he said. "Was it a pleasing whore?"

"Teobaldo," she said. "I may not be innocent, but I have my preferences as to that sort of talk."

"Indeed?" he said with a short laugh. "Share them with our friend?"

"No," she said. "I think not. I believe I will retire. You should, as well. Come with me?"

"Not yet," said Monticola. He was looking at me, not her. "We leave in the morning, I have finished my business here. Our young Danino has yet to tell me whether he will accept my offer of a post. So, our young Danino, will you? Will you tutor my sons? This lady's sons? I believe it may even be her preference."

She didn't move. She was standing still, hands by her sides. She, too, was looking at me now.

I had never seen him like this. I felt an extreme sense of danger. How not?

I refused him. I had not known I would. I had walked back under two moons not knowing.

I said, "My lord, I am still a student learning Jad's world, not a teacher of it. I am neither proper nor worthy as tutor to the sons of a nobleman. I am . . . I am sailing to Sarantium, lord."

I hadn't known I was going to say that, either.

He smiled. It was not a soothing smile. "And how do you mean that, student of Jad's world? Are you going to fight Asharites on the walls there like my son, or are you just using an old saying?"

I'd underestimated him. It *was* just the old saying I'd meant. Guarino had taught us the phrase. It meant a feeling that one's life was about to alter greatly, that a change was coming. I hadn't thought he'd know it. I suppose I'd hoped that because of his son he might just think me heroic and leave it at that.

I was entirely sober. A good thing.

I said, "I do not know my future, lord. I am not a soldier and—"

"You continue to say that," he said.

"It . . . continues to be true, my lord. I intend to visit with my teacher, then go home to see my parents, and make a choice there of what I'll do."

"You'll pray for guidance, of course?" He was mocking me.

"I will, my lord."

"And what sort of guidance would have you turn down a position in the palace of the lord of Remigio? What are you not telling me?"

Both of them in one wild night. Acorsi and Remigio. I look back and I wonder how I lived. Well, in a sense I know how. Two women saved me. Adria at the inn, and now . . .

"Teo, we cannot force a man to serve us," she said. "He is allowed to be unsure of what he wants to do or be. Remember when you were young?"

"I knew with certainty what I wanted to do and be," he said. But his voice was quieter.

"Because your father was lord of Remigio," she said, "and raised you to command men. As I hope you will raise our sons."

He turned to look at her. I drew a careful breath.

There was silence for what seemed a long time, then he stood up, the chair creaking, and the floor. He said, "If need be, love, I will. Some of it can begin when we are home."

If need be.

If my other son dies in the east.

Almost indifferently, he said to me, "Go to bed. I am grateful for what you did, as to the race. It was a service and I will remember it. If you have need of me, ask. I have never been called ungenerous."

"My lord," I said. And turned to go.

"Wait."

It was the woman. She took two steps towards me. She said, "If you decide, after going home and taking counsel, that you do wish to be a teacher of the young, let us know. We may find a suitable tutor before that, we may not." She smiled. "I will be happy to see you in Remigio, in any case, Guidanio Cerra, and to pour you a cup of wine myself."

She could stop your heart, that one.

"My lady," I said. And fled, although moving slowly for the sake of appearances to the stairs. I went up, entered my chamber, closed the door behind me. I leaned back against the door.

I was shaking. I remember looking at the trembling of my hands.

And I had just decided, standing before Monticola in that hallway, not to go to him. Because all of these events were suddenly overwhelming? Because he frightened me? The sense that a wrong word spoken . . .

He terrified just about everyone. So did Folco. They were the same in that. I think, looking back, that they frightened each other, though both might have killed a man who said so.

I had been in a dangerous palace in Uberto's palace in Mylasia, men had died there, two of them by my hand. Perhaps I didn't feel ready for another one? Perhaps my brief taste of the wider world felt like enough that night? Home might be better, quieter. My parents, my cousin, a shop, books to read, the canals and bridges I remembered.

I don't know. I don't know.

We like to believe, or pretend, we know what we are doing in our lives. It can be a lie. Winds blow, waves carry us, rain drenches a man caught in the open at night, lightning shatters the sky and sometimes his heart, thunder crashes into him bringing the awareness he will die.

We stand up, as best we can under that. We move forward as best we can, hoping for light, kindness, mercy, for ourselves and those we love.

Sometimes these things come, sometimes they do not.

I LEFT IN the morning without seeing them again. I found Gil in the stable by the walls with the other Remigio horses and I saddled him and rode out. The sun was rising on my right as I left Bischio on a mild spring day. Going north, I passed the inn where Adria Ripoli might still be sleeping, or lying awake, or gone in the night.

I should not have ridden alone, not with the amount of money I was carrying. By the measure of any brigands I might meet, I was rich. I could easily have been robbed on that ride, with a valuable horse under me and no companions or guards, no weapon.

I wasn't robbed, all the way north. Sometimes the wheel spins you good fortune for a time, even when you're foolish. I decided, as the sun climbed on that first windy day's riding, as I left them all behind me, that I might be feeling happy. I had escaped, I thought. I'd been caught up with Remigio and Acorsi and what lay between them, and I was free of it. I might have started singing as I rode. I don't remember, but it is a thing I did when I was younger.

❧

A young man appears to be telling his story. Others are having their stories told.

There is a maker, a shaper, behind all of them. It is the same with art on a dome, or a portrait done on a wooden surface, with gesso and not oil, for a reason. It is the same with a sculpture of hands. Someone made this, made choices doing so.

A song remembers a home, another conjures fear that home will fall to those who would destroy it. A poet places wine glasses on a fountain's rim under stars. An artist sets his lost wife on a dome . . . amid stars. A dancer lets the music be what she is, until it stops. Someone made the music, someone plays it while she dances.

And there is also this, as to stories told . . .

There were once two young men, both exceptional, promising, more than that. They had already led men in battle. One was tall, well made, good with horses and weapons and tactics. Hot-tempered, but learning to harness that, use it. His father took a city-state and passed it on to him so he was already a lord, that father having given him the added gift of living long enough for the boy to become a man—and so survive, and hold his city, which was Remigio.

The other, from Acorsi, was shorter, broad-chested even when young, slope-shouldered, never handsome, with both eyes then, and a subtle, quick, incisive, trained cleverness. He was also very strong, celebrated for it. No one wrestled him for sport; he'd killed a man (mischance) in a bout at the court in Macera. He wielded a heavy, punishing sword. His grandfather, also a mercenary, had married the daughter of the lord of Acorsi and inherited there, so this one had two generations of lineage to assert a claim to nobility, one more than the other.

Such things have mattered in the world.

He did not lose his eye to the taller man. Their long war is not about that, though it is long and it is a war, and some do think it must be because of the eye. It is not.

There is a bitter tale to tell of how this feud began. It goes back before the two of them. They inherited it, with all else that they inherited. That mercenary grandfather in Acorsi had seduced the aunt of the other, and boasted of it after—leading to her death at her husband's hand in Remigio.

It is often the telling that begins such things. Stories matter.

The tall one, the handsome one, not yet Remigio's lord, still very young, went to a certain holy retreat not long after, to find the other one's sister there among the Daughters of Jad, and he . . .

Ah. You see how this begins another tale? How one gives rise to another, and then others? Because he did not assault her that night, though the story told to the world was that he did—and it never stopped being told, because it suited some people to tell it.

But when the girl, Folco Cino's sister Vanetta, first spoke to her father and brother she said Teobaldo Monticola had entered her chamber at night, having scaled the wall, and had terrified her at first, but that he had—she swore it before Jad by her hope of mercy and light when she died—never laid a hand on her.

They had talked, she said, for a long time. She did not say what about. Then he had bowed and expressed regret for frightening her when he left.

And her father, the lord of Acorsi, had told her, forcefully (a forceful man, that one), that she would say this to no one, ever, this denial of an assault.

She was ordered to keep silent to the end of her days about what had really happened, to let the world construe her silence as piety or shame, whichever they chose. But she would never speak of it, did she understand?

And so the girl became another weapon in a war. Then she died, very young, in a plague year, although after a life more interesting than one might imagine in a Daughters of Jad retreat, because she didn't simply stay there placidly.

Her brother, along with their cousin Aldo, used to help her leave at times (yes, over the same stone wall at night) and bring her back, once or twice after several nights away (money changed hands on those occasions). Vanetta tasted the world that way, knew a different sort of laughter. Returned to her prayers.

But she did keep silent as to that night in her chamber. Perhaps she should not have obeyed her father in this. Much might have unfolded differently had she told the truth. (It was the truth.)

Or not. It might not have mattered. There was also a certain battlefield, when both men were still young . . .

So many stories that can be told, in and around and braided through the one we are being given. Don't we all know that stories can be sparks leaping from the bonfire of an offered tale to become their own fire, if they land on the right ground, if kindling is there and a light breeze but not a hard wind?

Someone is deciding what to tell us. What to add, what not to share at all, or when (and how) to reveal a thing. We know this, even as we picture in our minds another young man, a tailor's son from Seressa, remembering a spring ride, how he used to like to sing . . .

We want to sink into the tale, leave our own lives behind, find lives to encounter, even to enter for a time. We can resist being reminded of the artificer, the craft. We want to be immersed, lost, not remember what it is we are doing, having done to us, as we turn pages, look at a painting, hear a song, watch a dance.

Still, that is what is being done to us. It is.

Even so . . . we do turn the page, and can be lost again. And in that deep engagement we may find ourselves, or be changed, because the stories we are told become so much of what we are, how we understand our own days.

So, here it is again: a man on a horse in springtime, riding alone, and he is young and a breeze is blowing.

We turn the page. We learn that a year has passed. Flowers have died and returned. Green leaves again on the trees, another spring's sunlight. A falcon soars, dives to kill.

It continues . . .

PART THREE

CHAPTER X

Seressa on its lagoon was often damp and rainy in spring, with fog in the mornings or a wind off the sea driving hard along the canals that ran that way. It was not a *healthy* place, thought the acting duke of Seressa, looking out from a window in the palace. Doctors did well there, without necessarily being useful.

It remained, however, the pre-eminent mercantile city in the Jaddite world. The wealthiest, shrewdest, most opulent in its display. No one wanted to offend Seressa—or be targeted as a threat. And when fog or mist burned off under the sun rising beyond the lagoon, he believed his city was terribly beautiful.

He loved it. He knew it well. Dangers and glories, gold and stolen art, wharf rats and miasma, Carnival, canal-side murders in the night.

He might have taken a different path, had he not felt so much pride and love. The dukes elected to lead the Council of Twelve carried a heavy burden, sometimes had to do harsh things that placed their souls at risk. And the office certainly limited time and energy for commerce, where success had made them eligible for political power in the first place.

His father was dead, murdered in a political struggle years ago. He had an uncle, two brothers, nephews, a son almost of age to play his part in expanding and defending the family fortune. They could deal with it, he had decided. And, of course, his taking the position of greatest power in the city was not . . . well, it was hardly a negative thing for the family.

Some might aspire to a position on the council *for* the pursuit of greater wealth. He hadn't. Duke Ricci (he was growing accustomed to the title) was where he was because he saw threats to his city everywhere (there *were* threats everywhere!), and a corresponding need to be vigilant and acute in fending them off.

He was a vigilant, acute man. He also wasn't actually the duke yet. His was a more informal position carrying a formal title. The duke of Seressa, Lucino Conti—respected, honoured, venerable— had had what doctors were calling a stroke these days. It had left him paralyzed on one side and unable to speak. A lesser man would have simply been deposed—or smothered. The Council of Twelve, not ready to do either, or to hold the vote as to his replace- ment, had named Ricci to act in his stead. The fiction was that Conti was advising him. It was expected that the aged duke would soon go to the god, and there would be the usual voting manoeuvres then.

Ricci had no idea how long he'd hold this position but he was boldly certain he was the best person for it. Considerable sums had been spent to place him here, even temporarily, buying votes. It was now a matter of proving himself worthy of eventually ascending to the full rank and title.

He was in a study he had set up inside the palace, a smaller, more sequestered room than the one normally used by the dukes, cer- tainly nothing like the great chamber where the council sat to debate and govern, or to receive emissaries, or those they'd summoned.

People didn't much like being summoned by the Council of Twelve.

When he had someone brought to this comfortable room overlooking the lagoon they were less likely to be frightened, though some of them would have been if they'd known his thoughts.

Ricci had studied the philosophers and history. He admired and paid for art and architecture (some of what he'd bought was pure display, but not all of it). He had read poetry and even written verses to women and the god (when younger, much younger). But among the lessons he had learned in his years of life under Jad's blessed sun was that attacking before you were attacked was generally a good thing. His father might not have died if he'd done that.

Another lesson, connected to that: you needed information to act wisely. You could never have too much information. Seressa was notoriously good at spying. He intended to make it even better, granted enough time.

This morning he was reviewing reports, a stack of them from within the city and beyond. These came three times weekly. Briefings on the arrival of ships, what cargo they carried. On merchants, or anyone else of possible note entering overland. Sudden departures.

There were also reports on events considered untoward among the citizens: erotic, financial, otherwise. Smuggling was common, punishment extreme. He was preoccupied, already, by pirates across the narrow sea in their small, walled, inaccessible city of Senjan. They were a nuisance, a growing one.

He was also trying to get a better sense as to the health of the Holy Jaddite Emperor in Obravic, and whatever they could discover about his eldest son, and heir, Rodolfo. An eccentric man, it was said. He wanted to know more. Such things could matter.

Plots and schemes and diplomacy of one sort or another were a large part of what Seressa was. Challenges and threats existed, shrouding the world's truths. They needed to be burned away by knowledge, as the rising sun of Jad burned away the mist along the canals.

Right now, at his desk, he found himself staring at what was noted to be a third report on a citizen who had returned home last summer with enough money, unexplained as to origin, to buy into a business and then—this past week—pay for repairs and an addition to his father's shop and home. They knew the son had paid, they knew his bank.

The father was a tailor, one Cerra. The son, Guidanio by name, was evidently a bookseller.

Evidently was a word he used with intent—in his mind, in speech. Some resources had been used by way of inquiry with the father, while he fitted one of Ricci's brothers for a new dress robe. It was established that the son had attended the celebrated school at Avegna and had gone from there to Mylasia at what turned out to be a *very* dramatic time in that city's recent history.

He had left Mylasia at some point after the count was murdered—with no indication in the notes of where he'd gone, what he had done. And now he was home, with considerable funds for a young man without any obvious means of having acquired those.

The matter was ambiguous but was likely nothing. Young Cerra might have gambled well, stolen cleverly (if it wasn't in Seressa they didn't care much). Or . . . he might be in the pay of someone, which *would* matter.

It was also possible he was the sort of person who could be useful to his city. His education was significant, certainly.

Ricci was a man who prided himself on reading people well. He decided he ought to have a conversation with this young bookseller. At the very least, someone who'd attended the school in Avegna ought to be diverting. He found himself to be lacking in certain kinds of *intelligent* conversation. It wasn't important, but of course it was.

❧

My cousin, now my business partner, was a kind man. You could call him sweet, he was willing to be teased about it. At the same time, Alviso was no fool. He mentioned to me, shortly after I joined as an owner of the bookshop, that a man examining unbound coastal maps in our stock, on a morning when I'd been out riding Gil, hadn't looked like a mariner, and had asked a not-entirely-casual question or two about me.

He'd bought a map of Sauradia and left.

I'd expected this. Seressa prided itself on being a free republic, but it watched its citizens carefully. You didn't only monitor threats from abroad if you were the Council of Twelve.

I was no threat to anyone, but they'd want to decide that for themselves. Guarino had told me, when I stopped in Avegna on the way home, that there might be an election coming within the council for a new duke, that I should pay attention to it.

"I'm planning to be an owner of a bookshop, Teacher. Why would I pay attention to such things?"

"Because you live there, and because you spent many years here. They will know you, Guidanio, or want to. Best if you learn what you can about them."

We had already spoken of Mylasia and Morani di Rosso. That happened on my first night back at the school. I told my teacher about killing a man in a palace on the night the count died. I didn't tell him what I did six months after, killing another, in revenge for Morani.

Guarino was honest and virtuous. I didn't want to burden him with that second murder. We choose what to tell when we tell a story.

He wept when he heard about Morani and his family. We went to the sanctuary and prayed for them. It didn't ease me very much, to be truthful.

I didn't tell him about seeing Adria Ripoli, either, in Mylasia or in Bischio, or what she'd done in either place. Not my secrets to share. If Folco wanted to visit his old teacher and tell him that story for some reason—he could.

It felt odd, being cautious with Guarino, the man I trusted most in the world. It felt like yet another moment of transition, an entry into responsibility—because I was doing it to protect him, and others, not myself. And it came as I decided to turn my back on the wider world, to sell books on medicine, poetry, texts of holy Jad.

The world can come to you, however, even if you ride away from it. I've learned that.

I rode away from Guarino after kissing him goodbye and promising to return. I did not tell him how fear had been a part of what made me turn for home. There, I was protecting myself, my pride. I don't know what he would have said. He had been the one who wanted me to go to Mylasia. He felt his pupils had a duty to serve the world and the god, that everyone had such a duty.

I went home.

I gave my cousin Alviso what he asked for a half share of the business. It was a very fair sum. We then made an offer for the shop next door, which sold an odd collection of goods—writing implements, soap, spectacles. We broke down the wall between the two shops, cleaned up the dust and damage, and expanded our stock. Alviso and his family lived upstairs.

At my suggestion we continued to sell the pens and spectacles. They seemed to belong with books. We discontinued the soap but I took a box of it to my mother. We found a supplier of good candles and added those. We used the larger space to better display the loose sheets of books we sold and the leather bindings we could put them in. We had a number of books already bound, for those in a hurry (visitors to Seressa often were), or less concerned about the colour of the leather than they were about the words inside.

At the port, over by the armoury, I had a boy hand out information about our shop to merchants with ships headed across to ambitious Dubrava, or down the coast. There were markets for books beyond our lagoon, and nowhere in the world was better placed to service them than Seressa, where all the ships of the world seemed to come.

I placed Gil with two brothers who stabled horses outside the city, inland. I walked out that way and rode him three or four times a week, even in winter.

I stayed with my mother and father and sister for a short time, then found a place on the top floor of a three-storey building not far from the shop. It was the first time I'd ever lived alone.

I was well-off after Bischio, and I had funds left after buying my share of the business. We were making money, as well. You might not grow wealthy in Seressa with a bookshop, but if you were good at what you did (including binding the books) you would not starve, unless everyone starved. I began to think about one day investing in shares of a merchant voyage. I was Seressini, after all.

I bought a small painting by Viero Villani, of Jad as Warrior, pictured in the sky above Rhodias. I hung it on the wall beside the chair in my apartment where I read in the evenings by the light of one of the candles we sold. It made me feel I was arriving somewhere in the world, to own a work of art. I ate, most often, at one of two establishments on my street. One specialized in pork, the other in dishes from the east. You could find many things in Seressa, including varieties of food. I set about locating friends from childhood. Some, it turned out, I still liked. Some still liked me. We talked politics and trade; everyone talked about those things in Seressa.

I was happy enough. There were taverns towards the artists' quarter (rougher, more interesting) where they served decently priced wine or ale, unwatered once they knew you as a regular, and one or two of the girls were agreeable to me.

Once a week I ate at home. My mother's cook was the same one we'd had when I was growing up, before I went to Avegna. It seemed a long time ago.

On one of those evenings, as spring returned that first year, my father told me, proudly, that he'd received a commission to fit and cut a robe for the brother of the temporarily appointed duke. It was possible, he said, that if this was a success, he might even be asked to tailor something for Ricci himself.

Tailors went to their clients; the best known were welcomed in the finest palazzos in Seressa. It was a relationship, a reason my father's was a trade of some respectability.

"What did you talk about?" I asked.

My father smiled, stroked his beard. "You, some of the time," he said.

I was not, because of this, entirely surprised when I received a request to attend upon Duke Ricci a few days later. I knew the ways of my city, even then.

The surprise came the night before I was to go to the palace, when I very nearly walked in on someone looking for me, and carrying a sword.

I HAD HEADED towards the artists' quarter at the end of the day, after closing the shop. I seldom went all the way to that district. Few did, if they didn't have to. That part of Seressa was also the tanners' quarter and the smells were noxious. A reason artists lived there, of course, inexpensive rooms in an expensive city.

But halfway between our shop and that district lay a sequence of taverns and brothels I liked, a little back from the Great Canal. I crossed the arched bridge just before them, walking past the barrel used by the young, blind one-time mariner who begged there every day. He had gone to wherever his dinner and bed were by then, but he did a decent begging trade, sitting on his barrel. He told good stories, was a splendid gossip, knew people by their voice and even their tread. His name was Pepolo. I spoke with him often, gave him coins when I did.

The story he never told was why he'd been blinded. It was almost certainly for a crime at sea; blinding was a punishment for something grave. I wasn't inclined to ask, or judge. I'd killed men myself.

I saw three new friends and another from boyhood in one of the taverns, and went in to join them. I joked with the women as we drank, but decided not to go upstairs that night, so I left earlier than I otherwise would have.

Who can know which idle decisions we make will play a role in our lives? That feeling of randomness is surely a reason we pray, or carry objects meant to bring protection or good fortune, why we live in terror of demons.

I was going to the palace in the morning. I suppose my vague thought might have been to stay sober, get a night's sleep.

I accompanied a friend as far as his own building, not far from mine. It was always wise to go with someone at night in Seressa. I walked faster when alone. I entered my building and started up the stairs. There was a lantern lit on each landing, it was a better sort of building. A windy night now, moving clouds hiding stars. I rubbed my hands to warm them as I went up. There was a smell of cooking on the first floor. We weren't supposed to cook, the horror of fire in a city, but people did—and were reported for it if someone didn't like them.

I heard voices above, on my floor. Loud enough that I slowed to listen. Then I saw that Maurizio, on the second floor, had his door open. He held a finger to his lips. I raised an eyebrow. He gestured—the drawing of a sword.

I shouldn't have, but I went halfway up, careful where the stairs would creak, to hear better.

"I told you, Signore Cerra is not here! You are intruding and will be reported for it. That's probably happening right now, someone down below. This is a respectable building!" That was Petronella, who lived next to me with her husband and small child.

I looked back down. Maurizio had come as far as the stairway. I pointed outside, made a gesture of handcuffs. He nodded and started down—to find the night watch.

"I have done no harm and intend none," said a voice I didn't know.

"You are a stranger in a building after dark, with a sword, demanding to know about a resident. People don't *do* that at night if no harm is meant. If you were Seressini you'd know it. You aren't, are you?"

Petronella was a spirited woman. Perhaps too much so just now, facing an armed man at night. I wondered where Ilario was, her husband.

I couldn't see them from where I stood. It occurred to me that if this man did turn to leave and come down, he'd find me on the stairs. I had no idea why anyone would be looking for me at night.

He said, "I will leave, signora. I mean you no evil. Just tell me, has a letter been given to you, to hold for Signore Cerra?"

"You asked that, I answered! No, and I'd not have opened my door for anyone wanting to leave one! I mean it, go! People will have heard us, the watch will be on its way."

"In that case, I must also be on my way. Here's a doppani for your trouble." I heard the clink of a coin hitting the floor.

"Fuck you!" said my neighbour Petronella.

"A kind offer, but you aren't my sort," the man above replied. "I like more flesh, myself."

I heard the floor creak. I spun and went down quickly, then along the second-floor corridor. I flattened myself against the wall halfway along, in the darkness there. I saw him walk past, continuing down.

He walked straight into Maurizio—and the watch.

I heard it happen. So did Petronella. I saw her go past, down to the entrance. Her voice was loud, angry. He ought not to have tossed that coin, I thought.

I went to join them in the small square outside our door. Perhaps not the wisest thing—he was looking for me, after all, whoever he was—but his crudeness had also angered me. I had no idea what letter he was talking about. I had received none besides the duke's summons two days before, by way of a palace courier to the bookshop.

There were three of the night watch in the courtyard before our entranceway. One held a torch and Maurizio had another. The wind was blocked a little here, they flickered but held.

"Good," I said, stepping outside. "You have him. This man was threatening a woman, refused to leave, demanded after me, insulted her honour. You may want to question him."

The man was not tall, but he was well built. He was clean-shaven under a hat pulled low to hide his face. I walked closer and looked at him. And I knew who this was.

I opened my mouth to say that, but did not. Instead, I said, "I am meeting with Duke Ricci in the morning, gentlemen, it is possible this person had reasons to prevent that. It should be looked into."

The guards gaped. With the duke named, a minor incident had suddenly become much more.

"*What?*" said the intruder. "I know nothing about—"

"Best you come quietly now, you," said the biggest guard. "And we'll be taking your sword and that dagger."

"You will not!" the man exclaimed.

"Wrong about that," said the same guard, and without warning he threw a punch at the other man's midriff, then another, also heavy, to his jaw as the stranger doubled over.

Seressa had well-trained civic guards.

"Will you be wanting an escort to the duke in the morning?" the big one asked, rubbing his knuckles. The other two set about taking the stranger's sword and dagger from him as he lay on the ground. The first guard's expression suggested he might be testing the truth of my words.

"I will now, thank you," I said. "This has been unsettling."

"What is the nature of your business at the palace?" he asked.

I stared coldly at him. "You exceed your rank, I think. Not wise. Hold this one until I speak to the duke about him. No questioning until then. Have men here to meet me an hour after sunrise."

I was, to be honest, imitating Teobaldo Monticola's manner of giving orders. How would I have had any experience of doing so?

The guard stared back, but without conviction now. "Yes, signore," he said, looking away. I believe he was close to saying "my lord."

It was good enough.

They dragged the intruder to his feet, shackled his wrists, and began walking him towards the canal and the bridge and their station nearby. Or they might take him straight to the palace cells, I thought. Those were not pleasant places, by widespread report.

I stood with Maurizio and Petronella. He held his torch, looked at me by its light.

"Going to the palace?" he said skeptically. I was a bookseller, after all.

"I am," I admitted.

"Why?" asked Petronella, same question the guard had asked.

I smiled at her. "I'll tell you when I know," I said.

She smiled back. She had a good smile. A forceful woman. More evidence of that tonight.

We went in, it was cold outside. We said goodnight to Maurizio at his door and went on up the stairs. Outside my door Petronella said, "Danio, wait."

She went into her flat and came back out.

"Someone did bring a letter," she said. And handed it to me. She winked. "You'll break hearts before you're done, Guidanio Cerra. Just remember I told a lie for you."

"Why did you?" I asked.

She didn't smile this time. "I didn't like him. I like you." She paused. "So does Ilario. Come visit us one evening when the babe's asleep, we might find ways to please you."

She turned and went into their room and closed the door.

I stood alone in the dark corridor, dumbfounded, fighting a nervous laughter. But I was also holding a sealed envelope with my name written on it in a firm hand.

I knew who had written it. Not hard to work out, once I'd recognized the man who'd come looking for me.

He was one of the two who'd put an arrow in Antenami Sardi last spring.

Which meant he served Duke Arimanno of Macera. Adria's father. The letter would be from her, and someone didn't want me seeing it. My heart began beating fast. A year had passed, but some things aren't changed by a year.

I wondered if the guards would listen to my instruction not to hurt him. It might be a bad idea to interrogate that one, given the duke he served, and noting that he hadn't actually harmed anyone.

In bed later, it crossed my mind to wonder, belatedly, why I'd assumed he was alone. I didn't sleep well, but nothing happened before morning other than my keeping a candle burning and reading a letter many times.

☙❧

They were well into the rains of winter before she'd realized her father was intercepting her letters.

She was confident that Guidanio Cerra would not be ignoring her. She didn't know where he lived, but had found out where his parents did. A tailor named Cerra, not difficult. That address ought to have been sufficient to reach him. Her letters to Folco and her aunt in Acorsi had gotten through; she'd had replies from both.

Three letters to Danio had gone unanswered.

At home in Macera, and with time to think, Adria realized it would be a mistake to confront her father's courier to Seressa. If she did that, he'd lie to her and they'd know she was aware of what was happening. One of the things she'd learned from Folco: when you discovered something, it could be useful if others didn't realize you knew.

In one way, it wasn't an *important* matter, these letters. She was writing to keep contact, let him know that she hadn't forgotten him, wherever their divergent paths might lead. Danio Cerra was a memory of a life she'd lived for a time. One that was likely over. A vivid memory, yes, but she wasn't that person any more, or . . . she wasn't supposed to be.

But she had been away and independent for too long to simply *accept* the seizing (and reading?) of letters she wrote. Perhaps it was important, after all. Her father needed to know that she might be home again but was still what she was, what she'd become.

She could tell him, or she could use what she'd learned in a different way.

Of course, once she did choose a Daughters of Jad retreat and withdrew behind its walls, acceptance would become her life. But she knew enough about the retreats to believe she could—entering with a position of rank—navigate those requirements, one way or another.

She had decided she didn't want to marry, would not accept *that* submission. Eldest Daughters at retreats had considerable power. There was a freedom that came with power, along with responsibilities. It was a dance, she thought.

It was reasonable to expect that the daughter of the duke of Macera would assume a dominant role somewhere, sooner or later. Money would play a part. It would become a matter of choosing which retreat—to achieve the *sooner*. Negotiations could be as delicate as a marriage contract. She would be binding herself to the god, after all. That was the teaching, wasn't it?

Taking lovers in a retreat was a transgression, of course, but those were not always avoided. The world was what it was.

On the whole, she was ready to accept all of this. It had not been possible to continue the life she'd had in Acorsi. She'd always known it would end. The race in Bischio had felt like a farewell even at the time.

Also, Monticola di Remigio knew about her, what she'd done in Mylasia and in Bischio. His hatred of Folco could easily lead him to risk making an enemy of Adria's father, by revealing what she'd done, which included murder. It was—there was no way to deny it—extremely bad that he knew. He hadn't said anything, but he *held* it over her, and Folco. Knowledge was power, the recurring lesson.

Her parents didn't know about Mylasia. Folco and his cousin Aldo and some of his men knew. Monticola did. A healer who lived near Bischio now. And a young man from Seressa.

A thought occurred to her at some point as the seasons turned: if her father did learn of Mylasia, and that a tradesman's son in Seressa was somehow aware of it, he'd have him killed. There was no doubt about this.

Folco would not harm Danio: she'd made that as certain as she could at the inn. If he did anything to Guidanio Cerra *she* would reveal the story, she'd said—and take refuge in guilt and contrition with Jad, leaving him to deal with the aftermath.

But she'd known, riding out of that inn yard in the morning, that it was time to go home. A door had opened, and had now closed behind her. Her own decision, at least. Or she could tell herself it was. She needed to see what other doors could now be found, and be made to let her through.

And as to that, she did *not* have to accept that her correspondence was being intercepted by her father. She'd been careful in what she wrote, no need to put Danio at risk. Although if she truly felt that way she'd not be writing him at all.

There were, Adria had decided, limits to her acquiescence. Someone who wished to know her better would have to live with an awareness of that, she told herself.

It was possible that Danio Cerra, who had studied in Avegna, might find a weakness in that argument, but she didn't care. A shrug was as good a reply as any other sometimes.

She sent a fourth letter to Seressa in the spring. Not by her father's courier.

The duke of Macera was, however, a shrewd, suspicious man, and he knew his daughter to be clever and willful. The man she sent did manage to leave Macera with a day's head start, but the palace guards learned he'd gone (he was the longtime groom for Adria's horses), and her man was followed.

They knew where he was going, and by now they knew (even if she didn't) where the man she was writing to lived. They almost caught up to the groom before he reached Seressa, but she'd told him to ride fast, and he did. They didn't bother looking for her messenger among Seressa's canals and bridges. He wasn't why they'd been sent, and he'd end up back home in any case.

Based on Adria's letters, the bookseller didn't seem important—just someone encountered with Folco—but sending him four letters meant *something*. Duke Arimanno ordered him killed, just to be safe. He had long since acknowledged that absolute safety was impossible, even with thick walls, troops well paid, a taster for his food, guards in his sleeping chamber, and cannon aimed both outside the city and towards the citizens he ruled. Nothing was absolute in the lives they lived, but a man could certainly be prudent.

To Guidanio Cerra:

I send greetings. I have begun corresponding with people now that I am home from a long stay with my aunt and uncle in Acorsi, during which time, of course, we met and had an engaging conversation in Avegna, one that I recall gave me pleasure.

I have written you earlier, but now believe those letters went astray in autumn or winter, or perhaps you did not continue with your plans to return to Seressa? I send this with a different courier.

If you are indeed home yourself, and a bookseller as you intended, I would be pleased if you would provide me a copy, bound in crimson leather, of The Book of the Sons of Jad, *printed on good-quality paper. My own future will likely be in a holy retreat and it is expedient for me to begin acquiring a deeper knowledge of many things, including the liturgy of our*

*god, from whom all blessings and pleasures—from sunlight to
springtime to the power and speed of horses—come.*

*I believe myself willing and able to learn how to find
pleasure and instruction in many ways—and will hope my
new life affords me opportunities to do so.*

*The man who bears this is named Jacopo. He will attend
upon you, to see if you have an inclination to accede to my
wishes and needs in this matter. He will bring any letter, and
the book, back to me and has funds to pay you. I, of course,
will happily render whatever recompense you deem proper for
your services.*

With my salutations, and a hope that Jad defends you,

Adria Ripoli,
Macera

❧

There were three guards from the palace waiting by the door of the
building when I came down in my best clothes. My father had tailored them; I was better dressed than someone of my status might
otherwise have been. I stopped, eyeing the guards. They saluted me
formally. Not a thing I was accustomed to. It was a bright morning,
the mist had gone already.

I had never had an escort anywhere in my life, but I was relieved
they had come. That late-night thought about another man from
Macera wouldn't leave me. If Duke Arimanno didn't want his
daughter writing a tailor's son from Seressa, there was an obvious
way to stop it.

He'd been prepared to order a man killed at an inn last spring
without even knowing who he was. He knew who I was from her
letters. His man—or men—knew where I lived.

Holding great power can cause people, men and women both, to behave in ways most of us would never consider. I thought that then; I haven't changed my views.

I looked at the tallest of the guards. "You still have the man taken last night?"

He stared blankly at me. "I imagine you'll be told what you need to be told."

I could have accepted that. I almost did. A daunting morning lay ahead of me. But Adria Ripoli had written me a letter—had written several, it appeared—and there'd been a message coded in last night's. That reference to our encounter in the inn was one of the things that had kept me awake.

I didn't feel inclined to be dismissed just then.

"No, I think you'll tell me now, if you know anything. Also, has a second man been found? There were likely to be at least two."

He stared at me again. He had, clearly, his own disinclinations. He said, "I repeat. I imagine you'll be told—"

I lifted a hand to silence him. There was no point being angry. These men would have their orders and routines. They were just here to escort some commoner to the palace after an incident in the night.

He wasn't happy with my stopping him like that. I didn't care.

I was in the doorway of my building. There were trees planted in boxes of earth on either side of the door, for shade when summer came. And for green, which was rare in Seressa.

I stepped forward. I looked up.

It was luck, mostly. And alertness. Fear, you could also say. I saw movement and the glint of sun on metal on the roof of the building to my left. I saw it because I was looking for it.

I threw myself towards the nearest tree, bumping one of the guards.

A crossbow bolt lodged in the door frame behind where I'd been.

"*Up there!*" I cried, pointing. "You useless turds! Rooftop!"

Someone *had* just tried to kill me. I offer that in my defence for harsh language in the moment.

They reacted swiftly, I give them that. Two turned to block access to me from the square, drawing swords. The third raised his voice in a shout all Seressinis knew. "Palace guards! City guards! *Call for them!*"

All citizens were to respond to that cry. It was a crime not to do so. We heard immediate shouts for help from towards the bridge and the canal, then from ahead of us, and to the left. The cries would spread fast.

I peered carefully around the tree.

And another bolt flew past, only just missing me, even from a distance and on a rooftop. I had a memory of arrows hitting Antenami Sardi. I realized abruptly that they had likely not aimed to kill him that day. From so close, they could have, easily. I didn't believe that same restraint was in play now.

But it took time to rewind a crossbow. I looked out again.

"Stay sheltered, signore!" the tall guard said. "I see him! We know the roofs he can reach from there. He's not going to get away."

His tone had changed. He was a badly shaken man. If I had died, it would have been on him, and our city-state was not a for-giving place.

I believed him, about the man not escaping. Already we could hear running footsteps. More guards, some palace, some civic. It didn't matter (though they hated each other).

They made me stay there. They really wanted me back inside, but I remained by the tree in the morning air. Not that the air of Seressa was wonderful, but I wanted to be outdoors, not hiding in a hallway. I *was* hiding, but it wasn't the same. Or so I felt. Probably foolish, yes.

We stayed there, five guards now, and me. The sun rose, a breeze rose. From the bridge and the Great Canal I could hear a rising hum and rattle, a great city coming to morning life. People began to fill our square, moving through it quickly when they saw the guards.

Then another guard came, walking briskly. He saluted and spoke to the leader, the tall one. He told him the man with the crossbow had been taken.

We left for the palace. I was late, of course.

"BOTH MEN ARE being interrogated, and those reporting to me do not believe there was a third," said the currently acting duke of Seressa.

We were in an unexpectedly small office, one floor up in the ducal palace. I had never been in the palace. There was a window overlooking one of the smaller canals. Duke Ricci sat behind a large desk. It was covered with papers. I was seated in a hard chair in front of him.

He looked younger than I'd expected. I knew he had only recently been named to office during the infirmity of the old duke, but he'd have been on the council for years. He'd have to have been, to be sitting here, with this title now.

He had blue eyes, a neatly trimmed beard, a high forehead, dark hair, long fingers. His voice was measured. He had a notebook open, he'd been writing in it when I was ushered in.

"They told you this, my lord?" I was nervous for many reasons and trying not to show it, for as many reasons.

"Yes. I said this."

"What will be done with them?"

He stared at me. "A good question. What do you think should be done, Signore Cerra?"

And with that question, and the watchful expression on his face as he asked it, I realized that this encounter was not what I'd thought it would be.

It didn't make me less anxious, at all.

GUIDANIO CERRA, THOUGHT the acting duke of Seressa, was indeed young, and looked it. He was a well-built young man, brown hair, short beard, a prominent nose. Evidently observant (he'd looked around the room as he entered, registering details).

He ought not to be asking questions, and probably knew it, and was still doing so. Twice, right from the start. The duke was not distressed. It made the man more interesting.

Abruptly, after Cerra's second query—*What will be done with them?*—Ricci changed the planned course of the interview, or added something to it, like a tributary to a river. A good leader, he'd always thought, needed to be able to respond to new information, even if it was just an instinct that arose.

But he knew, from the notes before him, that this young man had been well educated. One of the council had recommended him to Avegna's school, where they accepted some children of tradesmen, and Cerra had stayed longer than most. It was worth finding out what that meant.

The young man said, carefully (the duke could see him being careful), "It is not my place, my lord, to—"

Ricci interrupted briskly, to see how he'd handle that.

"It is your place when I ask you, Signore Cerra."

Cerra drew a breath, but kept his gaze level. He was, the duke realized, trying to read *him*. Also interesting, also did not disturb. Ricci waited. Waiting was as useful a tactic as there was.

His visitor appeared to come to a decision, which suggested he had considered doing something different. He said, "They are Duke Arimanno's men, from Macera. His own guard, I believe."

Ricci kept his face expressionless, but this was genuinely startling. They had not yet established it in interrogating the first man, and the second had just been taken.

"You know this how?" he asked, making a note.

This time there was no hesitation, as if the young man had chosen a course and would see it through. A good quality, though there was something of interest, still, in that he had thought about going a different way.

I REALIZED I HAD already made a choice. It felt like a kind of release. Indeed, from the moment the duke of Seressa asked my view on what to do now, I'd felt something shift within me, unlocking.

I was Seressini, I thought. This was my city, my *home*. If loyalty was to exist in me . . .

I said, "I saw them with him near Bischio, my lord. Or one of them, the one taken last night."

"Duke Arimanno went to Bischio? He left Macera and went there?" I could hear surprise in his voice.

"Yes, lord," I said. "Last spring. He arrived the day of their race, though too late to see it."

"That is not like him at all," said my own duke. He made another note. He looked down to write, then back up at me.

If I was doing this, I thought, I needed to do it fully. This was not a man I could safely dissemble with. I had decided this immediately, although, in the event, I did dissemble a little, or try, in that first encounter. I suspect, looking back, that he knew it and allowed it, for his own reasons. In my view, which has never changed, he is one of the great men of our age.

I said, "He had come south to bring his daughter home."

Duke Ricci stared at me. "Go on," he said eventually. But then added, "The lady Adria?"

"Yes, my lord," I said.

"Who has been with her aunt and uncle in Acorsi?"

"Yes, my lord."

He knew a great deal, I thought, and then I thought: of course he does.

"And *she* was in Bischio?"

I had made my decision.

"She rode in the race, lord, she did it for Folco d'Acorsi. He wagered on her to finish in the first three. She came in second, he won a great deal of money."

He began writing again. I could see, leaning forward a little, my name at the top of a page. He said, not looking up, "Can you read upside down?"

I sat back, flushing. "Not well, my lord."

He did look up then, smiled a little. "It would be a useful skill to develop."

I believe I knew something from that moment. A hint, at any rate. He said, "So Folco placed Adria Ripoli in Bischio's race. People did not know it was her?"

"No, lord."

"But you did?" Very blue eyes on me.

"I did, lord. I had seen her in Avegna with Folco."

"And remembered her?"

"She is not easily forgotten."

He smiled again. "Especially for a young man?"

I shook my head. "My lord, I doubt you would forget a Ripoli, either."

He glared at me. "You presume to say I am not young?"

I froze, then saw he was suppressing a smile.

"In truth, lord, you look younger than I had expected."

He grinned now. "That might earn you a purse." He paused. "What did you do, knowing it was her? And why were you in Bischio, and wherever it was her father came—with his men, as you say?"

I had made my decision.

"I was with Teobaldo Monticola, lord. I told him she was with Folco, that I had seen her before with him. He then wagered on her as well. For the money, and to spite d'Acorsi, I believe."

"You believe?" He was writing again.

"He said as much, my lord."

"And why did he say anything to you at all? And why were you with him, Signore Cerra? You seem to have placed yourself among interesting men."

"Not ever planned, my lord."

"Really?" he asked. "Just good fortune?"

"Or bad, lord."

And so I told him how I'd met Monticola and his mistress on the way to Bischio, and about the race I'd won myself, and wagering in my own name, which was how I'd made enough money to buy a share in a business and help my father expand his workshop.

Because I had expected to be asked about *those* things when I was summoned to the palace. These were answers I had prepared. I was young to have such funds at my disposal, and Seressa was a place that tracked someone's money.

He listened, he made notes. When I stopped, he looked at me in silence. I tried to sit still, not to show anxiety. He said, "So your money is honestly come by? You have not robbed anyone? Or been paid to spy on us?"

I cleared my throat, which had gone suddenly dry. "Lord, in the chaos of Mylasia after the count was slain, I was one of those who added to my store of funds. It is how I bought the horse I raced against Monticola's man. For winning that race I was paid a sum equivalent to the other man's horse, which was our wager."

He wrote it down. He wrote everything down. He said, quietly, "That is half an answer."

"My lord," I said, "I would never spy on Seressa, and no one has ever asked me to. Both Acorsi and Remigio asked me, when we met, to join them. Remigio to tutor his young sons. Acorsi to accept that position in Remigio and report to him from there."

"That might have become delicate."

"Yes, lord," I said.

"And you decided . . . ?"

"To come home and be a bookseller, lord."

"Because?"

I had been trying to answer that myself for a year.

I said, "I did not believe . . . My lord, they are dangerous men, consumed by each other more than anything else, it felt like. I did not want to be consumed by them."

He nodded. Didn't write this down, kept looking at me.

"Are you afraid of life?" he asked. His voice was quiet. "Of opening a door your hand is on?"

That actually angered me, even given where I was, who he was. "Is that not a part of what it means to be a tailor's son, my lord? Not a wealthy merchant or an aristocrat?"

He considered it. "You blame your father?"

"I do not. I am grateful to him every day I live. I simply did not want to be a piece in the game those two are playing."

"Simply?" he asked.

He is a remarkable man. He always listened carefully, then, now.

"Perhaps the wrong word, lord. There is another thing."

He waited.

"My lord, I am Seressini. I am not of Acorsi or Remigio—or anywhere else. This is my home." It felt true as I said it. It felt as if it had always been true, and had only needed knowing.

He smiled a little. He touched his beard. He said, abruptly, "Tell me, Guidanio Cerra, have you any thoughts on young Rodolfo in Obravic? The emperor's heir?"

I blinked. I stared at him. I cleared my throat again. "None, my lord, of any worth at all. I should need letters and memoranda before I had anything to say that merited hearing."

He looked down at his papers. "A good answer," he said. "Have you heard anyone's thoughts?"

"Only that Guarino, our teacher, believed he would be underestimated when he came to the throne, and should not be."

"He said that?"

"He did, lord."

He made a note. "You correspond with Guarino?"

"I do. He is good enough to write in reply."

Another note.

He set his pen aside and leaned back in his chair for the first time. He looked out the window at the dome of our own great sanctuary and the waters of the lagoon beyond. He said, "I believe you, Guidanio Cerra, about feeling Seressini in your heart. I have thoughts, and some further questions."

He asked these and I answered them. I appeared to satisfy him, doing so.

And that is how I became, while still extremely young, an official of the Council of Twelve, sent by sea, with guards and a secretary, to Teobaldo Monticola in Remigio.

My task was to collect Remigio's annual payment for the right to have merchant ships dock in their harbour on a sea that Seressini galleys protected from coastal pirates and Asharite raiders.

Also, I was to spy.

JACOPO, ADRIA'S MAN, attended upon me at the bookshop two mornings after this. He appeared neat, unobtrusive, a bit awkward among so many books, perhaps. I was certain he knew about the men who'd followed him, and that they were in custody. He was unlikely to know what had been decided concerning them. I did know.

I had already written my reply to her. I gave it to this man, along with the liturgical book she had requested. He paid me for it, counting out the coins. I had spent the previous afternoon binding it for her, in red leather, as requested.

He nodded politely and left.

I also left, three days later, by ship for Remigio.

◈

Lady Adria,

Our respectful greetings to you. Thank you for the order placed with our bookshop. We are honoured to serve. Enclosed with the book is our itemization of the cost.

I hope the binding satisfies. It is our desire to always satisfy. Payment for any future orders may be made at your convenience, of course. We are eager to be a supplier of anything you might require, whether seeking instruction or pleasure. I take the liberty of including a document that indicates a number of titles we have for immediate delivery. Needless to say, we would endeavour to gratify any other wishes you have, even if they should take time to fulfill. What we do not yet know as to your needs in these matters we are very willing to learn.

I note your expressed intention to seek a religious life. If it is not too great a presumption, I would like to say that any retreat that receives you will bestow honour upon itself.

With appreciation,

Guidanio Cerra, Bookseller,
Seressa

CHAPTER XI

Scarsone Sardi, High Patriarch of Jad in Rhodias, pre-eminent cleric in the world the god had made, lifted his hands over his head, brought his fingers together, and made the sign of the sun disk, ending the morning rites.

The usual rustling followed in the elegantly painted chapel of the Patriarchal Palace. People rose from their knees and stretched.

He was the only person who was supposed to raise his hands in this way, signing the disk at the end of prayers, but apparently the Eastern Patriarch in Sarantium also executed the gesture with hands above his head. Sarantium was under Asharite siege, but was apparently weathering it behind its triple walls of fabled thickness.

Others in the Jaddite world, including dukes and kings, made the sign of the disk before their hearts. The High Patriarch, heir to a thousand-year tradition, was to offer Jad's symbol aloft—on behalf of all the god's children.

A number of people had evidently been killed in the working out of this distinction, but that had been a long time ago, as Scarsone understood it. *May Jad in his wisdom and benevolence defend those who worship him properly*, thought the Patriarch virtuously. It seemed the right thing to think.

He was hungry and annoyed, however, and he didn't linger over pieties. There had been a report, early that morning, about Bischio. An unpleasant one, about a grim forthcoming siege by his uncle's hired army, headed now towards the subjugation of that city.

Weren't sieges always grim? Were there any pleasant sieges? He had no idea what people wanted him to do about this. His Uncle Piero terrified him, for one thing. For another, everyone had *known* this was coming.

In the event, his cleverest secretary devised a phrasing for a letter. It expressed the urgent hope that all participants in any conflict that emerged to trouble the peace of Batiara ("*What* peace of Batiara?" Scarsone had said, eliciting the laughter he liked) would do their best to avoid unnecessary suffering among the innocent.

Scarsone signed three copies, one each for Firenta and Bischio, and one for the archives here. He had never seen the archives. He understood they were very old. He pictured dust and faded, crumbling paper, rats.

He went to dine. He did think, briefly, about what *necessary* suffering might look like, among the innocent.

⚭

Jelena had never been in a place where war had come.

You had to call that fortune, since war was just about everywhere. It was a condition of their time. Spring meant armies, everyone knew it. She'd heard stories all her life, but this was not just a story, it was a threat to her walled small city of Dondi, as spring came that year.

For one thing, the ruling council had begun ordering the beggars and the homeless out of the city. Also, the Kindath were being forced to leave. There weren't many of those, and they weren't poor or homeless, but they were expelled as well.

It was explained to her—by one of the Kindath, in fact—that when starvation came in a siege, and it *would* come, it was policy supported by faith that feeding an unbeliever was wasteful, close to heresy.

This man, whose name was Cardeño, and who traced his lineage to Esperaña before the Kindath had been expelled there, had been one of the first to leave Dondi. He hadn't waited to be forced out. He'd gathered his goods as winter drew to an end and departed, with his family, four carts, and six guards. He'd sold his house and mercantile rooms. He would not have been paid much, Jelena imagined, under these circumstances.

They had become friendly when she'd delivered his third son. He was going to Firenta, he told her. There was an irony in this, and he let Jelena hear it in his voice. Firenta was the city whose army might be besieging them here, on the way to Bischio. But brazen, growing Firenta liked the Kindath, it appeared—for the moment, at least.

Financiers were needed by smaller tradesmen and merchants, too, and the Kindath filled a money-lending niche below that of the banks. Firenta was expanding under the Sardi family. It was making war, in fact, to do so. Trade, mostly in textiles, was what underlay all of this. Dondi lay between. It paid taxes to Bischio. That was not, it seemed, acceptable any more.

Mercenary soldiers were paid, in part, by being allowed to sack a city after a siege. Looting was obviously valuable, but Jelena wanted to ask some soldier how rape and murder counted as *payment*.

A town could surrender, of course, but then their goods would simply be taken—including any food they'd stored. Food was critical. Armies could starve, too. Supplying them could be a nightmare.

It was always a difficult judgment for the people of a town. Could a small city like Dondi, even with a garrison and walls, withstand a siege? Would there even be one? Might they not be too inconsequential for that? Be seen as a delay in setting up outside Bischio itself?

She'd asked her Kindath friend. He'd advised her to leave. Offered to take her with his family and guards to Firenta.

It was tempting. For one thing, Jelena knew she had a friend (more than that, if she wanted) in the Sardi family itself. Antenami might not have any power within his family, but he was Piero's son and she'd saved his life. He could protect her.

She also liked him, somewhat unexpectedly. She thought about going. She had complex dreams as winter ended: of ghosts, fires on hills, two full moons arcing swiftly across the sky, unnaturally. She saw unknown stars between them.

She stayed. If this small city, where she'd been accepted, was about to face a siege, healers would matter. They had two doctors here, and her, and one of the doctors was desperately incompetent.

"Understand that when people are starving, ugly things happen," her Kindath friend had told her.

"I'm sure they do," she'd said.

"No. You do not understand if you have not lived through it. Do not say you are *sure* of anything, Jelena."

She recalled nodding her head.

"They will," Cardeño had added, "name you a witch and blame you for their suffering."

"A witch," she remembered saying.

And he'd been the one who nodded then.

She was frightened, but she stayed. She did send two letters with him. One to Firenta, one to be entrusted to a messenger going farther north.

She'd woken early and left her house to watch Cardeño and his family leave one cold morning, frost still on the grass outside the walls, a weak sun rising. It had seemed to her there was something hovering, not over the Kindath family, but above the gates of Dondi as they passed through.

No one else seemed to see anything, but Jelena was used to that.

✥

Ariberti Boriforte was a modestly competent military leader. (He thought he was more than that, but he was wrong.) He had been hired by Firenta to serve under Folco d'Acorsi in the campaign to subjugate Bischio. He would be in charge of bringing up the artillery. Boriforte didn't like being second to anyone, but it was difficult to object to this with respect to Folco.

He and his men were being paid adequately, but it was a small sum compared to what rumour reported their commander had extracted from the Sardis to command this long-anticipated assault.

It rankled a little—what proud man would not feel a sense of being slighted?—but he kept telling himself, and various women in various brothels through the winter, that his time would undoubtedly come. He was still young. Folco wasn't any more, and neither was Teobaldo Monticola, who would command the force that defended Bischio. No one was certain how Bischio was able to afford the fee Monticola was certain to be charging them.

If he was honest with himself—and he sometimes was, usually in the mornings in a sanctuary—Ariberti Boriforte was happy to have Folco d'Acorsi lead this campaign if it was to be against Monticola. They would one day die, or weaken in the field and withdraw to their own cities, but neither of these things had happened yet.

Folco remained at home in Acorsi through the winter. Letters went between him and Piero Sardi, Boriforte knew. He himself was in Firenta, waiting, his six hundred men in barracks outside the walls, forbidden to enter the city in groups of more than ten (this was customary). He was not privy to what the letters shared or debated. He would be given his orders when the time came and that was that.

He did receive those orders, when the weather turned properly towards spring. He had nearly a thousand mercenaries by then. A good number. Fighting men gravitated towards the anticipation of pay and plunder. More men added to his own lustre, but you did need to pay them—or find a way to let them pay themselves. A successful leader kept his soldiers alive (mostly) and fed and clothed and shod, and offered the promise of either money or looted goods. That was how people could be drawn to your banner, the way they had been for Folco Cino or Teobaldo Monticola over the years.

Boriforte's was a modestly known banner, so far. He did intend to change that. Jad knew, there were wars to choose from in Batiara, year over year. And enough small cities to offer protection to in exchange for a contract and a city house, perhaps eventually a well-born wife.

He had his examples, didn't he?

The instructions he received were to proceed towards Bischio with the artillery and siege engines, destroying some fields once they'd left Firenta's territory, but not to linger doing so. Farmers and villagers were to be driven into Bischio where possible. The more mouths in the city, the sooner hunger would bite.

They were not going to be able to break through those walls, not with Monticola defending them. This *would* be a siege, which meant cutting off supplies, and adding to those who would go hungry in Bischio.

Nothing new in any of this. It was what he'd expected.

He consulted a map again before he set out. Doing so gave him a new thought, or the beginnings of one. There seemed to be a city, walled but quite small, it would have only a modest garrison. It lay just west of the main road. It paid tribute to Bischio—which meant that this city, Dondi by name, could be considered a proper target for him. He'd argue that point with anyone, though he didn't mention it to anyone.

Folco was going to set out from Acorsi with the main body of their force. He'd planned for one delay, apparently. He didn't explain that, or Boriforte didn't learn it, if he did.

Monticola was also going to be coming west from Remigio.

They might meet. There might be a battle over that way.

If so, thought Ariberti Boriforte, it had been a long time coming for the two of them. And there could be opportunities for younger mercenaries, bold ones, if events fell out in certain ways.

◈◈◈

Antenami Sardi received a letter from Dondi, sent in the care of a Kindath moneylender, of all people. He read it carefully.

He also accepted a second letter from the same man, entrusted to him in order that it might make its way to Macera safely. He did not read this one, though he was puzzled, since it was addressed to Lady Adria Ripoli, and wondered what possible connection Jelena could have with Duke Arimanno's youngest daughter. Still, curiosity had never been a dominant trait for him. He sent two of his household guards north with the letter.

His guards were also to inquire in Macera about imported Ferrieres saddles and harnesses. There were, apparently, new styles in the north. They'd reach Macera first, and these *did* intrigue him.

Had he known who the woman riding for the Falcon district had been in Bischio's race he might have been more interested in that second letter.

He'd gone to a roadside inn hoping to entice a splendid horse-woman as a rider, and perhaps to his bed, and he had been wounded (by unknown assailants!) then healed by a different woman, and bedded by her. His feelings about all of this . . . ? Well, Jad worked in ways not to be understood by his mortal children, wasn't that what one said about such things? He had changed, there was no real way to deny it.

In the year since coming home he had attempted, with unexpected success, to take a more engaged approach to the finance and politics that consumed his father and brother.

He knew their armies were headed for Bischio this spring. He had known *that* since last year, when Folco d'Acorsi had escorted him south to the race.

Now he had a letter from the healer who had saved his life, had changed it—made him a better man, you might even say. And she was expressing fear of their army, his family's army, from within the city of Dondi where she lived.

He could send men to bring her to him here, but in her letter she said that was not what she wanted for her life (she had said the same thing a year before). She wrote to ask him to intercede to protect the innocent souls of a small, imperilled city.

It was his family and city that endangered them, after all, she wrote in her letter. That was true, Antenami decided. There was no way around agreeing.

He bestirred himself, arriving in his father's workroom quite early. His father appeared to have been there for some time, as always. His father never slept, or so it seemed. His brother wasn't in the room yet. Antenami wasn't certain which of them frightened him more. Their father, probably, but Versano had *such* a command of scorn . . .

He greeted his father, who was at his desk reviewing documents. Piero Sardi looked up at him. Surprise could be seen in a normally impassive face.

"Antenami. You are very early. Why?" he asked.

"To learn more about what we are planning this spring," Antenami said, as he'd rehearsed on the way from his chambers. "I should not remain ignorant of such weighty matters."

"You've been content to be so before," his father said, but he did not look displeased.

"I know. But we have not waged a war of this sort."

"We have warred before."

"Barignan. I know, father. This seems . . . weightier." He was repeating a word, which his brother would have mocked.

His father removed the spectacles he wore to read. He looked at his disappointing younger son for a time, and then his mouth moved and it was very nearly possible to say that he smiled. He pointed to another desk. "There are copies of the orders for our troops. Read them, then share your thoughts. This . . . this pleases me, son."

He hadn't said *that* in . . . well, possibly forever, Antenami thought.

He had feared the documents would be lengthy and confusing but they weren't, and he was looking for a specific name, in any case.

Folco was heading from Acorsi along the major roads towards Bischio. He would not come to Firenta, his route would be south of them. It might or might not intersect that of Teobaldo Monticola, which was interesting.

Folco wrote that he would not seek out a fight, but if it happened he was of the view that with ground properly chosen he could prevail in an open engagement—and strip Bischio of its relieving force before it got there.

Of course, a major battle between *those* two men would be more than simply a tactical encounter. Even Antenami knew that much. He tried to picture it.

Absent such a meeting, Folco wrote, he proposed to join forces with Boriforte, who had been retained to lead their smaller army based in Firenta. They would either engage Monticola outside Bischio if the other commander came out, or commence a siege if he did not. Monticola's army would be too large for an assault on the city. But its presence would also mean a very large number of additional mouths to feed, and they might well be forced out in summer by hunger. There *would* be a battle if that happened. The issue was what ground near Bischio would see it, and Folco intended to choose that.

He sought his esteemed patrons' views, he wrote, but his own was that this was the manner in which they ought to proceed.

Antenami Sardi wished to be at such a battle, and also to be a considerable distance away from it.

He consulted an attached set of documents. These were Folco's detailed orders for Ariberti Boriforte, who would be bringing up their cannons. Antenami had seen the man many times over the winter; he frequented the better class of brothels. They were obviously paying him enough to do that.

Boriforte's orders, he saw, had already been countersigned—and thus approved—by Piero Sardi. The man was to proceed south, quite soon in fact, harrying people into Bischio before the siege. The expectation appeared to be that Folco would besiege Bischio through spring and summer—by which time the city would be starving, or Monticola would have come out to fight.

It was hoped that surrender would come before that. Monticola *could* surrender, or just negotiate a departure for his army, leaving Bischio to its destiny. Mercenaries did that sort of thing all the time.

But in this second set of instructions Antenami found what he was looking for. No towns or cities between the two warring cities were to be attacked or looted, Folco had written. Those paying taxes to Bischio would be required to do the same to Firenta after they triumphed. That was a large part of what this was all about. And the memory of an ugly period after the siege of Barignan was still with them. It hadn't been so long ago.

This meant, as far as Antenami could grasp, that the small city of Dondi ought to be safe. His father wanted townspeople to survive, flourish, carry on with their markets and trades—and pay taxes here, perhaps as soon as autumn if the campaign went well.

He was a little surprised to discover that it all made sense to him. He ventured to say as much to his father. He added that it did indeed seem proper to be careful with the towns between, since they needed them amicable, or at least not hostile, if allegiance and taxes were to be transferred.

His father removed his spectacles again. He nodded briskly. "Exactly so. We handled things badly at Barignan. It cost a great deal of money to address that." He didn't speak of the deaths caused in the sack of that city, but he wouldn't do that.

Antenami said, "Was that Folco's fault?"

His father shrugged. "He commanded, so, yes. Or you could say it was mine."

"Hardly, father!" said Antenami.

"No. No. I paid and retained him, so . . . But the error, once we were inside the walls, was the lesser commander's. Massato. Folco entrusted him to keep order when the soldiers went in. He failed, or he chose to fail, to keep his men happy."

"What happened to him? Where is he?"

"Buried," said Piero Sardi. He smiled. "He kept the wrong people happy."

He had a particular smile that wasn't pleasant at all. The one he'd just used. In a world full of clever men, Antenami's father was seen by many as the shrewdest. He added, "Folco d'Acorsi dislikes living with the blame for that violence, even today."

"Is that a weakness in him?" Antenami surprised himself with the question.

Surprised his father, too. Piero looked at his younger son. "Do you know," he said, "it might be." He put his eyeglasses back on and wrote something down.

They heard a sound. Antenami turned. His brother came in. Versano nodded at their father, ignored Antenami.

Piero Sardi was still looking at his younger son, however, the spectacles removed again. He said, "Would you like to accompany Boriforte? We require an official to report back, and deal with supply requests. You might take on that role."

"My *brother*?" Versano said quickly. He was, clearly, astonished.

"I would be honoured to be trusted," Antenami said, looking only at his father. Thinking back, after, he realized he'd said it because of Versano's interjection as much as for any other reason.

He had no real idea what the city official with a mercenary force was tasked with doing, but it turned out not to be so difficult, either. He wasn't sure why he'd thought all these matters would be *hard*.

He took Fillaro as his principal horse—you needed three—and a dozen of his own guards and attendants.

They set out a week later along the same road he'd taken a year before towards Bischio, winding through the green and birdsong. Summer's heat would dry the grass and flowers later, but right now they were beautiful. He saw men and women working in fields by the road. He thought about how springtime meant war and death for many, not a returning of life. That, too, was a new thought for him.

On the first night, he had Boriforte dine with him. He made a jest about the man having the same name—in the male form—as a Blessed Victim. He didn't think the mercenary was amused. Had probably heard it too often. No matter. Antenami did bring out the orders to review them. He stressed that they were to drive farmers ahead of them as soon as they crossed out of Firenta's hinterland and reached Bischio's, but were to leave all cities and towns along the route untouched, for reasons set forth.

Ariberti Boriforte's expression darkened at this, Antenami noticed. He wondered if he was becoming more of a *noticing* sort of man.

"We have to make all such decisions based on what we encounter," the commander said. He drank from his wine. "It is what soldiers are trained to do."

Antenami nodded his head, said nothing. But he decided that it might be a good thing, after all, that he was here.

After dinner, as Boriforte was leaving, Antenami asked, as if idly, whether the other man knew where that mercenary they'd once employed, Ciotto Massato, was buried, and had his family been looked after?

Boriforte said that he didn't know. His expression (Antenami noticed) became thoughtful, even after a quantity of wine.

Before going to bed he dictated a letter to the man he'd brought for this purpose—the one with the best handwriting and spelling.

He sent this with a rider to his brother, a second copy to their father, overnight, putting it on Versano to confirm with Folco d'Acorsi, and send Antenami that confirmation, that the towns along the route were to be left untroubled.

He had never, as best he could recall, instructed Versano to do anything before. The copy to their father meant that Versano likely *would* do it. It felt as if he was learning new things every day.

He went to bed. He slept surprisingly well, given he was in a tent and on a hard cot. He woke with the sunrise birdsong, ready for more of whatever this was.

⚭

One of the things Eldest Daughters did at important retreats was correspond widely, sometimes with important figures. It was a reason a retreat could be a pathway for an ambitious woman. One who sought not only to control her own life, but possibly influence the world beyond whichever walls she found herself behind—or chose, if she was the daughter of the duke of Macera, and had that privilege.

Adria didn't know if she'd arrive at a Daughters retreat and be named Eldest immediately (though being young was not necessarily a problem in that regard, there were precedents). She wasn't even certain she wanted to be. There would be a great deal she'd need to know about power first, just as she'd learned from Folco and her aunt (and her parents, in truth, though she was angry with them).

A strong, clever woman—an aged one, perhaps—leading at a retreat, a woman she could observe, that was her own ideal. The donation her father was about to make (he was saving himself her dowry, after all) could ensure she arrived as the tacitly anointed successor to such a woman.

There was a great deal of politics involved in this.

Careful investigations were done when a daughter of an important family chose the serene life of serving Jad. One could be amused, knowing that actual piety was often just an option, or take the process seriously. Adria went back and forth between the two attitudes.

What didn't change was her conviction that this was the path for her. Once she'd left Bischio behind she'd had an increasing certainty of that. An interval in her life had ended on that racetrack. She knew it, Folco knew it. Her Aunt Caterina had known it even earlier, Adria suspected. Women like her aunt and her mother *could* find power and influence in the right marriage, but that was often out of their control, so much good or bad fortune went into it.

If you married a fool? Or another Uberto of Mylasia?

No, this course was better. It was even possible, she thought, that she might find piety within herself. Unlikely, given her family and her nature, but . . . life could change you, couldn't it? She had no idea what being old would feel like.

In the meantime, she had been writing letters, a kind of preparation. She didn't dictate them, she wanted her own hand to be clear, strong. Separate letters went to Folco and her aunt. A long one to the mother of Coppo Peralta, who had died outside a healer's house in the dark, killed by Teobaldo Monticola.

She didn't know if Coppo's mother could read; she probably couldn't, but she was at a retreat, working for the Daughters there, someone would read it to her. Adria sent money, as well. She knew Folco had done the same.

She'd also written a bookseller in Seressa, three times, and had those letters seized by her father (or her mother, which was possible).

She'd used her own man for a fourth letter as spring came. This one reached him. She knew this, because Danio replied, cleverly, carefully. Distractingly, also, as to knowing and learning things. He sent a book, bound, as she'd requested, in red leather.

Not long after, she heard that two of her father's guards had returned from Seressa (secrets were hard to keep in a palace). Each of them had had his right hand cut off.

This was, given that they served the duke of Macera, extremely serious.

It appeared they had been found guilty by the Council of Twelve of attacking a citizen of the republic, *in* Seressa. A bookseller, apparently. They carried back a letter for her father from the acting duke of Seressa. This violent punishment was, it appeared, a Seressini provocation. Or it might be something else. If guards from Macera *had* assaulted a citizen inside Seressa, and the two men had talked about it under questioning, the provocation would have been theirs . . .

Earlier that same day, another letter had arrived for Adria, unexpectedly. This one from Firenta, which was *not* a city allied with them. It was from Jelena, the woman who had healed her and then had done the same for Antenami Sardi—whose man carried the letter.

Adria read it, then did so again. She spent the morning thinking about many things, but mostly of assassins sent after a tailor's son who sold books now.

She went to her father. He would be in an anxious, angry mood because of his two men. But so was she, and she did *not* fear him, even if others did.

ARIMANNO, THE FIRST duke of Macera (*first* because he had paid a truly mad sum for the title—to vest in him and his heirs forever), saw his youngest daughter approaching through his garden on a spring morning.

He loved his gardens. Gardens were an island of order imposed upon the chaos of the world. He spent time here whenever he could, consulting with and instructing those he employed to devise and maintain them. He enjoyed these conversations greatly.

Duke Arimanno loved many things. Hunting, of course. Horses. Dogs. Cooked pheasant and good wine. Truffles in autumn. Large, generous women (his wife was neither). He was a reader: out of doors, or by lamp and fire at night. Music eased his anxieties, if well performed. False notes distressed him, elicited anger. He was quick to anger, often out of fear.

He feared many things. More than he loved, in truth. He was terrified of large rabbits (one had been rabid, had menaced him when he was young, he had a memory of shouts, screams). He disliked travel, inns, the castles or palaces of others. Not sleeping in his own bed. He was afraid of erect penises not his own. He was frightened by eclipses of the god's sun. Everyone feared those, but the Ripoli family tale was that his grandfather had died during one, so there was *reason* to fear. Such things had meaning! He feared being poisoned, used a taster for his food. Also, portents and the possibility of ghosts frightened him. He lived in terror of his soul's fate when he died and came to be judged by the god. His sister Caterina, married to Folco d'Acorsi, frightened him. So did his wife.

He had not expected to be afraid of his youngest daughter's fire and force as she grew up. He told himself he wasn't uneasy now, seeing her approach, long-legged, head high. Adria was very tall, it always came as a surprise when he hadn't seen her for a time. Not as tall as he was, though, and she *was* his child, and much too headstrong, needed curbing like a horse.

He turned from his flower beds, waved two gardeners farther away, and crossed his arms to receive her in the sunshine, preparing a necessary rebuke.

"By the blood of the god and all the Blessed Victims, father, how *dare* you?"

She stopped directly in front of him, too close for his ease of mind. The duke fought an impulse to take a step backwards. It would look wrong—also a flower bed was behind him. She had spoken loudly; the gardeners might well have heard.

"Mind your tongue, child," he said. "Remember who you are."

"I am the daughter of a fool," Adria snapped, not quietly. "Even if my mother is surely not one."

He was caught between his own anger and the distressing awareness (from this morning) that he might have made a large mistake, and that this was what she was addressing.

"Mind your—" he began again.

"I will not!" Adria said. Her colour was high. She had a face more expressive of energy and vigour than grace, but there was no denying the . . . well, the vigour. She was glaring as if she meant him harm!

She said, "You sent men to kill a bookseller? A *bookseller*? Men who could be questioned and discovered to be yours?"

There it was. He attempted to wither her with a glance.

"I am very angry about what Seressa did to our poor men," he said coldly.

His daughter laughed. "If I learned anything from Folco, I'll wager the letter you just received says that they could have been sentenced—properly!—to death, and that was commuted to maiming only out of respect for you!"

This was, unfortunately, correct. The duke cleared his throat. "Even so. To assault men of my personal guard and—"

"Men who tried to kill a Seressini in *their* city, father! And Seressa has a leader new to his position who must not be seen to be weak! *We* appear weak because of this! Dear Jad, a *bookseller*?"

"I am allowed my own decisions as to who has done me harm!" He meant the book person.

He saw that she understood this. Her hands were clenched at her sides. She had ridden in the Bischio race last year, had come first of all riders. He had felt great pride.

Adria took a breath. She said, driving the words at him like a wind in winter, "That man saved my life, father. Folco knows it. I was sending business his way, out of gratitude. Tell me, how has a tailor's son done the duke of Macera harm?"

He hadn't known about that first thing she'd just said. He felt unhappily at a loss to answer her question. He didn't like the feeling.

He said, "My daughter's virtue and honour matter to the entire Ripoli family."

"And your daughter knows it, and is about to choose a Daughters of Jad retreat with her mother and aunt. But you, father, *you* have caused Seressa to wonder . . . how could such an insignificant man possibly be a concern for Macera? What might make the duke want him *dead*, risking his own men and relations with Seressa? And then some in Seressa, which is a name in the world for shrewdness, may ponder and think . . . think that perhaps the daughter who ordered a book from this man had offered him more than coins?"

He looked at her. He swallowed. "Did you?"

"*No!*" she shouted.

One of the gardeners quickly moved farther away, towards the cypresses, then right in among them out of sight, the duke noticed. He experienced a wish to be there, too.

Adria said, "Father, this is the second time you have exposed me in a year! Do you understand how *hard* Folco worked to hide that it was you who almost had Antenami Sardi killed?"

He had nursed a vague hope she wouldn't mention that.

She pushed on, forcefully. She was always forceful, he thought.

"And using the same men, father? Men known to be your guards? Do you want Seressa set against you as much as the Sardis would be if last year's incident were to become known? You'd risk that much for this folly?"

"The Sardis don't know," he said, aware it was lame and knowing what she could say.

She did say it.

"The Sardis don't know because *other people protected you*! Including me, right now!"

"What does that mean?" he demanded. "Why you?"

Another mistake. He made those. Didn't everyone?

She said, her voice cold as a loveless life, "Because, father, if any-thing happens to that bookseller I will tell the world who put two arrows in Piero Sardi's son last spring."

He felt himself growing pale with outrage. "That would be a betrayal of your family! Of Macera!"

"Yes," she said. "It would. So, don't make me do it. I told you, he saved my life. I am not going to forget it." She closed her eyes and opened them. Her voice changed, grew gentler, at last. "Father, he really did. I would not lie to you. Folco knows, because it involved something I was doing for him. Trust me. Stop this. Draft a clever letter to Seressa's duke, send them money and gifts. Buy books from the bookseller."

She seemed to have composed herself. Arimanno took a breath. She was impressive, his daughter. She was going to be a daughter of the god. That might help him as age and death drew near. Every man needed help, or his soul did. Candles and prayers, intercession invoked in a holy place. Jad knew, his errors were many.

He said, seeing her soften, "Will you sit with me?" He gestured to a stone bench by the bright flowers.

She smiled. She had a rewarding smile, he thought. She said, sweetly, "Of course, father."

SHE LET HIM see her smile when he asked her to sit. Men could be handled that way, even her father. Perhaps especially her father. And she still had something she needed from him.

They sat beside each other. She said, "Of course I would never reveal secrets to our enemies. You know that."

He nodded. "It would surprise me, although you become impul-sive when angry. You always have."

Which was true. It was important to remember he was a fearful man but a very clever one.

"Perhaps the Daughters of Jad will calm me." She smiled saying it.

He shook his head ruefully. "Unlikely. But growing older might. And having responsibilities, which you have never had."

Also true.

Then he said, "I would like to live long enough to see what you are like when you are older." That gave her pause. He went on, "How did he save your life, this Cerra?"

He was like this, her father, filing things in his mind to bring back. She'd hoped that question wouldn't be asked.

She said, "I was doing something for Folco, as I said."

"And met a bookseller?"

"He wasn't a bookseller then. Father, it is better if—"

"It would betray Folco if you told me?" An eyebrow raised, and a fair point.

She answered with truth. "It would betray me."

He was silent, looking around his garden, coming into spring. Eventually, he said, quietly, "The world will lose something when you go to a retreat, Adria."

She hadn't expected that. She felt herself flush. She said, "Thank you. I hope I will . . . that I can achieve things there. Isn't that why we . . . ?"

"Why we are doing this? Yes. But even so."

It was as good a moment as she was going to get.

She said, "The woman who saved Antenami Sardi's life at that inn is the same woman who healed me."

He looked at her. "After you did what you cannot tell me?"

"Yes, father. She has helped us twice now."

"Should we send her money?"

"Folco paid her, both times."

He made a wry face. "Of course he did. And . . ." She could see him thinking. "And he is commanding his army for the Sardis now."

Being fearful, she thought, could make a man perceptive, alert, if the fears did not rule him. She said, "She has written me, it came this morning. She's in a small city near Bischio. She fears it will be attacked. I intend to write Folco about this, but I need one of your couriers."

"You sent your own courier to Seressa."

She made herself smile, to ease the sting. "Do you want to discuss *why* I was forced to use my own?"

He turned away again. "Not really."

"Good. Then we won't." She heard a sound, looked up. "Mother is here."

He glanced the same way. "Jad help me," he said. "Both of you at once?"

Adria laughed.

But the tidings her mother came bearing were for her, about her.

They'd found what Corinna Ripoli, duchess of Macera, believed to be the best retreat for her daughter. A large, well-known one near Rhodias. They would take her this summer, and the understanding was she'd follow the current Eldest Daughter in that role. The proposed cost, the duchess added, turning to her husband, was high.

"Of course it is," Adria's father said.

"We will negotiate," her mother said.

"Of course we will," said her father.

This summer, Adria was thinking. It was upon her, then. She could almost picture the garden around them in its summer hues, and she'd be gone. A life could change—your life—so quickly.

She realized her father was looking at her. She turned back to him. She thought she saw tenderness in his eyes. *He loves me*, she thought.

"It seems we all have letters to send in various directions," Duke Arimanno said to his youngest child. "I'll have them carried wherever they need to go."

Adria wondered if she was about to cry. She excused herself before that could happen. She went riding later. Midday was not the best time, but it wasn't hot yet. It wasn't summer. Not yet.

After, she wrote two letters—one to Folco, one to Seressa. She ordered another religious text in the second one. She named the retreat near Rhodias where she would be going.

It was odd, writing down the name, saying it aloud to herself. She would be expected to live and die there.

She joined her parents and brothers for sundown prayers in the palace sanctuary. She prayed for forgiveness, she always did, for the killing of Uberto of Mylasia. She sought within herself, she always did, for any contrition, failed to find it.

I am, Adria Ripoli thought, *not ideally suited to become an Eldest Daughter of Jad*. For some reason the thought made her feel better.

There was music after the evening meal. She danced with her father. He loved music. He was a good dancer, better than her.

"I propose," he said as they moved apart on the floor, then came back together, "to write the duke of Seressa that I feared my headstrong daughter was forming an attachment to a tradesman, and sought—foolishly—to forestall it."

"You have a headstrong daughter?" she asked.

He smiled. "I can write a different letter."

She shook her head. "It is all right. You will give the bookseller an undeserved reputation, but men like having those."

"Sometimes, some men."

Her turn to smile, but it took an effort. She was still feeling . . . difficult things. "You may have to send me to a Daughters of Jad retreat. To curb my excesses."

She saw, to her surprise (a day of surprises, this), that he was also dealing with emotion as they danced.

"Rhodias," he said, "is very far, Adria."

He hated travel. She hadn't thought about that.

She said, firmly, "If you do not visit me I will not pray for you."

He squeezed her hand after she spun through a turn and came back. "Then I will have to visit, because if you don't pray for my soul there's no point to any of this, is there?"

He was, Adria realized, close to tears. So was she again, but only because of him, she told herself.

SHE WENT UP the small, winding staircase that led from her rooms to the palace roof, something she liked to do: mornings, sunset, sometimes in the dark, as now.

They'd dined and danced late. It was night when she came out onto the flat roof, the waxing blue moon risen among the stars. It was windy but she had a cloak.

She'd always liked the night, its stars and moons. Jaddites prayed for the return of the sun, for the god's safe journey, but Adria had sometimes thought how you could also need the nighttime, the intimacy of it, the privacy. Lovers did, surely. *Needful as night* was the phrase that came to her.

She could remember a cleric teaching her, a child in this palace, how Jad's pre-eminence was shown by the way the rising sun chased away the stars and the two moons (or dimmed those two to pale, weak things in the daytime sky). She'd asked—at eight or nine years of age—why it couldn't then be said that Jad was chased down in the west by them, and they ruled the night as his sun ruled the day.

The cleric, indignant, had instructed her father to have her beaten for that impiety. He'd not dared to touch her himself, of course. Her father had heard the story, suppressed a smile (she'd already learned to recognize when he was doing that), dismissed the cleric, appointed another.

Her mother had called Adria into her chambers (she still remembers how wonderfully scented she'd found those rooms, always) and told her, also smiling a little, that her thoughts were clever but that girls—and women—needed to be cautious as to cleverness. Not to deny it, but to use it shrewdly to affect the world, tilt it subtly. If one was known to be confrontational, obstinate, challenging, it made it hard to do that tilting, Corinna Ripoli told her daughter.

She hadn't done particularly well as to *cautious*, Adria thought on the palace roof. But she was no longer a child, and there were different lessons to learn now. Her mother and aunt still had things to teach her, just as Folco and her father did. Her father—a sudden thought—truly *loved* her. It wasn't just about usefulness, or the possible lack of it. She considered this, looking out. He would have a long way to travel to see her near Rhodias. He'd promised he would.

She was on the city side of the roof, above the palace wall, though all the towers rose higher. From here she could see Macera in the dark. Some lights still flickered in the city but not many at this hour. To her right she could have seen far out into the countryside if it had been day: fields, forests, as far as the river. If she crossed to the other side of the roof, she'd be above the walls and towers that defended against foes from without. A palace was a fortress in their time.

She didn't feel tired. It had been an eventful day. She now knew where she was going, for one thing. A new life far away from here, an *entirely* new life. It would not do, she thought wryly, to propose in a Daughters of Jad retreat that the sun god might be balanced equally by Kindath moons or Asharite stars. She looked out and down, smiling a little.

And so Adria became the one to sound the alarm that night, and save the palace and her family, and thereby change the course of history in Macera, Batiara, possibly the wider world—for who can know how far the ripples of events can run?

She saw torches in the city, moving towards the palace. This was unusual at night. There *were* lights in any city after dark, but these were all coming this way, converging, and could only have been seen from up here, or by guards on the city-side wall or towers.

Then she saw the main palace gates below swing open. Something that should not have happened, *ever*, at night.

Six of the nine night guards there, it was later learned, had been suborned, and the three who had not been were the first to be killed.

She knew what this was, what it had to be.

"*Guards!*" she screamed. "*The city gate! We are under attack!*"

She kept shouting it, down to the forecourt. As soon as she saw men moving in response, she wheeled and ran as fast as she could across an uneven roof to the far side, and screamed from there at the guards on the wall that faced the countryside. There were barracks outside the city where her father's best troops were quartered. She shouted to the wall and towers, to anyone below, her heart pounding.

She heard responses, saw men moving. Arimanno of Macera had good soldiers, he paid them well and on time, always, and they were effectively led. This was a substantial part of where the taxes on his city and hinterland went. Macera paid, some had said in secret gatherings all winter, for its own subjugation.

Almost all of the soldiers turned out to be loyal, which, with Adria's warning, turned out to be enough, in a hard, close, savage fight.

Her father had always feared his city as much as any threat from outside. One is not foolishly anxious or afraid if there really are those who want one deposed and dead, who see themselves ruling. The Abbato and Conditti families of Macera were loftier in lineage than the Ripoli. They could—they did—regard Arimanno as a clever upstart, taxing them to pay for his own wildly expensive elevation to a dukedom.

They could take a cue—it later emerged that they had—from events in Mylasia following the assassination of Count Uberto. True, Mylasia had no ruling lord now—it was a commune led by merchants—but the lessons you extracted from history were yours to choose, weren't they?

The rising of those two rebellious families—and those who cast their lot with them—was defeated, in the event.

It was, however, a near thing. The rebels did get into the forecourt through the opened gates on the city side. They rushed through it with purpose. Some did make it into the palace and started up the main stairs towards the family's living quarters. If the duke and his three living sons could be slain, the soldiers—it was believed—could be told as much and would change allegiance towards those who could pay them, since the Ripoli would have no one left.

A soldier's loyalty is more fickle than a girl's was the saying.

Sayings are not always true—as to soldiers, or girls—and the rebels never did get up the main stairway to the duke's chambers. Some went up a second, smaller staircase; they all knew the Macera palace well.

There, also, they encountered guards, if a smaller number. And there they also found the duke's youngest daughter, holding a sword on the stairway.

Adria had been stabbed in Mylasia, a knife in the thigh. A good healer and the god's mercy could get you past something like that. She was feeling strong and angry (and fearful for her family) as she came down to join the two guards defending the back stairwell. Two guards and the duke's daughter, for the moment, against half a dozen coming up towards the family quarters.

There were other guards arriving behind her, she heard them shouting and clattering through the living quarters, headed for this stairwell and the main one. *Behind her* was the thing that mattered. You couldn't help from too far behind, and their loyal men below would have to fight up here through the courtyard. They'd need time.

One of the men in front of her engaged an attacker to his left. Killed him, in fact. But that engagement left room for another rebel to shoulder past against the wall of the stairwell. Adria thrust with her sword. She felt it drive into flesh. But the man—she never saw him clearly—thrust back with his own blade.

There was a shocking degree of pain. She fell backwards and to one side as reinforcements came running down to join the fight. One of these saw her and swore savagely. He dropped his sword to pick her up. He carried her, still cursing, up past the others, back the way he'd come, towards the family quarters. She cried out as he stumbled on the top stair. There was pain with every movement, she felt blood pouring from her. Again. But this wound was in the stomach, below her ribs. It was bad, she knew it was. She thought of Jad. You were supposed to think of the god, weren't you? He was under the world now, far away.

Men and women die every hour of every day, but Adria Ripoli's was a brilliant, restless, still-growing soul, and there were differences she might have made in the world from a retreat near Rhodias, or anywhere else.

It is possible to contend that the sweep of time will do what it does regardless of who is there to observe it or try to shape it. But it is also possible to believe that people make a difference. They can offer others safety and calm, shelter in a wild wind—or be the ones bringing death on that wind, because making a difference is not always benign.

It can be, however.

She'd raced down from the roof to her room to claim the sword she'd insisted on keeping there, and trying to learn to use, from late in childhood. She was never skilled with a blade. Not every gift is ours, even with desire.

She ought to have stayed in her rooms, guarded, or crossed that upper floor to join her parents where they were. Or remained on the roof. She did not do any of those things. Her nature, her pride. We are what we are in the world, when it allows.

Their soldiers were fighting the rebels in the courtyard, having run through the ground level of the palace from the barracks outside. Some of them did break through to both stairwells, up behind the attackers there—and they did stop them, meeting the duke's guards above, slaughtering men.

But not before one of those rebels, an Abbato it was later learned, put his sword into the youngest daughter of the Ripoli, whose name was Adria, and who had shone brighter, by a great deal, than was normally permitted one so young, and a woman.

She was set down in the largest sitting room. Her parents were there, guards around them and at the doors, with weapons drawn. Her brothers were fighting below. She was breathing with difficulty and cried out again when the man bearing her put her gently down on a cloak someone spread on the marble floor.

Arimanno, weeping, knelt by his daughter and took her hand between his own. He had held it, dancing, earlier that night. Her mother—Adria heard her voice as if from a distance—was calling urgently for their doctors. She thought of the healer who had helped her two years ago, outside Mylasia. She knew where Jelena was now, too, she'd written a letter on her behalf earlier today, to Folco. In that time before the sun had set and the blue moon had risen through stars, and . . .

There were lamps, but the room seemed oddly dark. She closed her eyes then opened them again, but there was no greater light. She heard her father saying, also from far away now though he was right beside her, "Child, hold strong! The physicians are coming!"

But she knew by then. She knew that being strong or brave was sometimes not enough. She looked at him, at love and terror in that known face. She reached for breath and said, as clearly as she could, "I am sorry I wasn't what you both wanted me to be." Her mother was here, too, somewhere in these shadows.

"Not true!" she heard Corinna Ripoli say. "Never think it, Adria!"

But her father, nearer, mouth to her ear, said, "You are so much more. But do not speak. Marshall strength. See, they are here now! The doctors are both here!"

Strength, again. But it was too late for that. It had been, she thought, too late when the sword went into her.

She offered no more words before she died. There are not always wise or meaningful words spoken at the end of a life. Nor does courage always find a reward, except in the memory of others, perhaps, and that is a tenuous thing.

SHE WONDERS WHO ELSE is here, wherever she is. She seems to be suspended in a space above her body. She can see her parents weeping, and others. This is no time to be weeping, she wants to say to them, there is an attack *taking place!*

She ought to be afraid, she thinks. She is dead, she knows it. But fearful is no way to prepare to meet your god, is it? And she has not lived that way, it's not what she has been, and she won't take this next step that way, either. If she can help it. Perhaps there is, being honest, some fear, just now.

But there seems to have been so little time. Time, she thinks, was the thing, wasn't it? She'd needed more. Probably most people wished for that. There was always more to learn, and be. Places, people. Love to find among men and women. Knowledge, laughter, horses to ride.

Not about to happen, it seems. Not for her. Even now (not enough time, even here!) the people below, around her dead body, appear to be fading, or blurring, they are disappearing. From her. Whatever is coming is beginning as something ends. Life. Life ends. Hers. Such a great shame, she thinks.

Now she appears to be outside that room entirely, to have passed through the ceiling, amazingly! She is hovering above the palace, the city. They look very beautiful, she thinks. She is above the whole world, looking down . . . a long way now, at the roof where she'd been standing when . . .

Horses, she thinks. She'd so much loved their courage, power, grace.

Light, she thinks. The god who offers it. To some.

There is no more pain, at least. She can hold to courage, to her own nature, the memory of it, and look to see what will come next.

Then it does come to her, for her, and she is air, moonlight, lost, gone.

ARIMANNO RIPOLI'S TWO older sons also died that night. They, too, had seized weapons and hurtled down the main staircase into the courtyard to meet the first wave of rebels there. The third son, the youngest, was wounded in the arm, but was pulled back to safety inside and upstairs, and he survived.

There is an aspect to this, too, showing again how seldom men and women can confidently shape or even anticipate the future.

That third brother, just a year older than Adria, was much the most capable of the Ripoli sons. He would almost certainly never have come to power, but with his brothers dead he was named Arimanno's heir, and became duke of Macera when his father went to the god.

And it was because of this, because of him, that the Ripoli dynasty survived, grew stronger, lasted as long as it did—which had a great effect on Batiara and the world, in so many ways.

It is harder to measure what his sister's life and death meant.

It was said at Adria Ripoli's memorial service, some time after that rebellion had been savagely crushed, with two hundred and forty-six mutilated bodies rotting in the city square and severed heads spiked on the city walls, that she had died as she'd have wanted to, defending her family and home, braver than any woman known (speeches in honour of the dead are always thus).

There was both truth and an old, sad lie in this, since she'd not have wanted to die so young at all. She had a life to look forward to and live, savour, the way one tastes fresh fruit in mid-summer or new wine in autumn, or observes the two moons after love as they shine through a window, riding through clouds in the night.

She lies in the Ripoli Chapel in the great sanctuary of Macera. On the slab of marble set into the wall there are only her name and the year she'd been born and the year she died. Someone looking at this after enough time had passed wouldn't know anything about her at all. Only that she'd lived and—by the dates shown—died young. And because she'd been a woman they'd be likely to think illness, or childbirth.

Unless they looked at the fresco above—and connected it to her. Because on one wall of the family chapel her father had had the celebrated Matteo Mercati paint a woman, tall, with dark red hair (it faded to brown in the fresco after many years passed). She was shown riding a splendid horse, which was highly unusual.

She looked fierce and proud, and even carried a sword in one hand, because her father had wanted her painted that way.

THE HARSHNESS OF Duke Arimanno's response to that night was in good part due to his daughter's death. This was generally understood.

It was because of Adria that the women of the Abbato and Conditti families were killed in the square with their fathers and brothers and sons, dragged from their homes and hacked apart. They were not sexually assaulted—which was also because of Adria, since he'd never have wanted her so treated. They were simply killed, as she had been. He mourned his youngest daughter the rest of his days, felt her absence, lived her loss.

So did others. Folco d'Acorsi and his wife Caterina among them, her aunt and uncle. And also, a Seressini tailor's son who had known her only briefly, and only on two occasions, but had been aware from their first meeting on a stairway in a different palace that this woman had claimed him, his heart, a part of whatever life he would live. This is a recognition that sometimes, if rarely, does come to some of us . . .

◉◈◉

The sailors say the rain misses the cloud even as it falls through light or dark into the sea. I miss her like that as I fall through my life, through time, the chaos of our time. I dream she is alive even now, but there is nothing to give weight or value to that, it is only me, and what I want to be true. It is only longing.

We can want things so much sometimes. It is the way we are.

CHAPTER XII

It was true that the twin brothers who ruled Avegna had generously supported the celebrated school there, educating their children along with the sons and sometimes the daughters of other aristocrats, and a number of others, as well. The brothers honoured Guarino Peselli, who had founded and still led their school.

Notwithstanding this, it would have been a dangerous error to think them soft or particularly kind-hearted. Especially where the security of their city-state was concerned. Or the revenues that were a good part of that security—and of their own comforts.

Because of this, when the city of Rosso, southeast of Avegna, was late for a third season in paying taxes properly due (by agreement!) for their protection, it became necessary, the Ricciardiano brothers agreed, to make a strong statement. Such statements, in Batiara in that time, generally meant destruction and people dying.

Rosso was a fair-sized city, however, and it had maintained and repaired its walls—very likely with some of the monies due!

In short, it was not a trivial military exercise to either compel it to submit or to break through the walls. For various reasons, mainly to do with other commitments of their preferred mercenary leader, a siege was not going to be possible that spring and summer, though destruction could certainly be visited upon the farmland and water mills and logging nearby.

Their preferred mercenary leader was Folco Cino d'Acorsi. He'd attended the school, of course, and maintained cordial relations with Avegna's lords afterwards. There had even been a time when a marriage between him and their sister had been discussed, but d'Acorsi had done better (they'd had to concede it), marrying into the Ripoli of Macera. The Ricciardiani were well-respected, style-setters in a time when style mattered, but Macera was significantly larger and wealthier.

Still, Folco fought for them when he was in a position to do so, and often just the threat of his name and army had been sufficient to quell unpleasant signs of dissent in cities from which they claimed taxes.

With Rosso, unfortunately, that had not been the case. It was another of those self-governing communes that seemed to be proliferating in Batiara. It evidently chafed at the level of taxation Avegna required (always requested politely, and with style!). The citizens of Rosso appeared to think they deserved to be free of Avegna, and that they could be.

Not a useful idea, the twins agreed, and this would be so even if other towns and cities owing them taxes were not watching with interest.

Folco had been engaged by Firenta and the Sardi family this year for the subjugation of Bischio. (There were divergent views as to just how bad this would be for political balance in Batiara, but it was fair to say no one *liked* it.)

Nonetheless, d'Acorsi agreed to assemble a small force and make an effort before the walls of Rosso for his old friends. His fee (very fairly) was for a set period of time he could commit, with a signifi-cant additional sum if he broke through, or induced surrender and the payment of the sums owed. He undertook to return with a larger army the next spring if he did not succeed, for a fee to be negotiated.

The lord of Acorsi was, as always, a pleasure to deal with, in person or by correspondence, although you really wouldn't want to be late, or underweight, in paying him.

HE HAD TWELVE hundred men, four hundred of them mounted, outside Rosso.

It was early in the spring. He needed to start west for Bischio soon with an army of twelve thousand. He had only a little time here, accordingly, but he had promised to try, and was being paid.

He did not yet know—no one did—what had happened in Macera. The uprising. Word had reached Acorsi in two days and messengers had been sent by his wife to find him immediately. It was news Folco needed to learn, for many reasons.

He would weep, though not where anyone could see him doing so.

Right now, he was staring at the well-maintained walls of Rosso. He could take it, of course he could, but not in the time he had, or with these numbers and without artillery.

He had been executing campaigns like this, with variations, for a quarter of a century, since he'd crossed out of childhood.

It was a way of life, of sustaining their family, protecting Acorsi, allowing things he wanted: wealth, a measure of power, renown, the things that brought renown. Also pride, being aware that he was extremely good at war, and that the world was aware of it.

He was known to be pious, and a patron of artists, architects, poets, alchemists, philosophers, bringing them to Acorsi. He had also killed, over the years, a great number of men and women, had burned cities, let his men run wild after a conquest.

There was, in Batiara, no contradiction seen between this love of art and thought, and a violent life, and Folco Cino d'Acorsi might have been offered as an example of this truth.

Also, if he was honest with himself—and that became more important as you grew older, and nearer to your death and the god—he still loved it. War. Even now, after so many seasons in the field. Spring came, and his heart quickened, and not just for the return of flowers and leaves and light.

His wife, whom he also loved, said he preferred being on campaign to being in her bed, or with her in a garden or by a window at sunset. He denied it. He felt his denial as truth. He looked her in the eye when he said it, but it was . . . it was not entirely simple.

There was a fire, a ferocious brightness to existence when you were at war, carrying a sword, riding a good horse, knowing your life might end that day or the next. The *keenness* of how the world appeared to a man at such times.

Of course, this was also a little dishonest, since the leaders of a mercenary company, especially one as feared as his, rarely faced any extreme danger of dying in a battle.

They were at greater risk of stomach flux, or crippling back pain from a bad night on a cot following a long day in the saddle. Battles were rare. The art of war in their time was to achieve one's military goals without fighting at all. That was how you kept your army mostly alive, and your horses (horses mattered a great deal), and brought money home.

The great captains all knew each other, were all engaged in the same war-for-profit dance. There was seldom need to have anything so unruly and unpredictable as a battle in open country. Your employer one year might want one; that didn't mean you did.

There were formal rules for sieges. A city might agree to surrender by a certain date, for a certain fee paid you, if a relieving army did not arrive for them. If such a force did come, you went away. If it didn't, you let the city open its gates and surrender. Their defending garrison marched and rode out past you—and you did no great harm inside.

There were many ways to avoid fighting. For the right sum, you could switch sides and join your current foe. A city won a war, often, just by having more money than the other side. It wasn't as if the city-states or the High Patriarch (perhaps the best employer of all) were going to refuse to hire a strong captain the next year. Their options were limited. There were many leaders but few good ones. It was a dance.

The dying, when matters came to that, tended to be done by others. Farmers whose fields were ruined, harvested crops seized, and who starved, accordingly. Or men and women in a city like Rosso, now, which was refusing—obstinately, recklessly—to yield to him and simply deliver the taxes they owed Avegna. If they forced him to come back next year and breach their walls there'd be a terrible price paid here. There would have to be. You couldn't allow these refusals.

He'd sent his cousin Aldo, his longtime deputy commander, to the gates to deliver that warning just now. Aldo was a daunting man with a hard voice. He was good at this (at many things), and utterly loyal to their family. He had no extreme ambitions beyond what he was doing, and hated their enemies perhaps even more than Folco did.

He was accompanied to the walls, for the experience of it, by the younger son of one of the prominent families in Acorsi. Having sons of noble families in the field with him was a status boost for a com-mander, but for those who ruled cities it was also useful with respect to forestalling trouble at home: sons with the army were hostages against their family's good conduct while the lord was away at war. Cities were restive places, needed to be monitored.

The threat Aldo carried was simple. If Rosso did not yield and pay their arrears, d'Acorsi would be back next year with a vastly larger army. They would bring artillery and engineers. They would destroy the countryside around Rosso, not just a few symbolic farms as they'd done coming here now. They would live off the land during a siege. People would die in great numbers.

And they would not accept a surrender then because the honourable brothers ruling Avegna would have to pay a *very* large sum to Folco for such a force, and there would be legitimate anger concerning that. And then the soldiers of that army would demand their customary privileges, the most important of which was three days' looting in a taken city. Rosso would be a taken city.

Had any of the citizens of Rosso lived through a sack? Aldo would suggest that he didn't recommend the experience—for them, for their wives, daughters, young sons.

Paying fairly assessed taxes was much the wiser option. Unless they had reasons to prefer crossing to the god in suffering. The Blessed Victims had done that, of course, but the victims of a city's sack were not blessed. They were fools who died badly.

Aldo had said this many times outside many city gates.

It did not work that morning. His cousin came back and reported as much, sourly. The commune leaders had called down, courteously but firmly, that Avegna had doubled their taxes the year before. They had paid the original amounts on time, but could not sustain the increase. This resistance, as they described it, was not a rebellion of any kind, only a plea for fairness. There had been some desperation in the voice of the man who had spoken to him from above the gate, Aldo reported.

It was not Folco's place to assess any of this. Had he been here on his own behalf, for Acorsi, he would have done so. The demanded increase might well be unfair, unmanageable. Doubling taxes tended to be.

But he was a hired soldier here, enforcing a demand by a stronger state on a weaker one. It *was* true that one of the Ricciardiano daughters was being married (quite well) into a powerful family in Rhodias, and her dowry would undoubtedly be costing them a great deal. Raising taxes on subject peoples tended to occur at such times. Still, not his concern.

Aldo looked angry. He wasn't used to failure, it rankled. A good thing in a senior officer. He was also hot-tempered, not always as good. Folco shrugged, touched him on the shoulder, invited him to eat. They did, in sunshine and a brisk north wind.

"What now?" his cousin asked.

"I'll take Gian and try something." He had a slight headache, and the socket of his missing eye ached, which it sometimes did. On the windiest days he wore an eyepatch, but he didn't like doing that.

"Be careful, then. I saw at least one arquebus, and crossbows on the walls."

As expected. Those were part of his thinking, in fact.

"Of course," was all he said. "How many men defending?"

"Real soldiers? I'd guess a hundred."

One hundred good men could defend a walled city unless artillery was brought up and the besiegers had time. They had neither here.

He finished eating, wiped his face, went and pissed behind his tent. He came back and put on his breastplate, no helmet, no sword. He started walking towards the city, waving Gian to come. Bringing Aldo again would look weak, since his cousin had already failed. He had done this so often over the years, he thought.

There were two pikes struck into the earth some distance from the gates. His own innovation from early in his career. You had a man good at such things mark where a bowshot and an arquebus could reach. It made things safer for anyone sent to parley, even under a flag of truce.

He told Gian to stay by the farther pike and walked ahead himself.

"My lord!" Gian called. "They do have—"

He said, without looking back, "I know. I see them. They won't hit me."

"My lord, there will be trained—"

"Look at the banners," he said.

It was sometimes wearying to be the only one to notice things. On the other hand, it was also why he was as successful, and as feared, as he had been for so long. It was inconsistent to lament it.

The banners above the gate, two of them, the boar crest of Rosso, were flapping briskly in a wind from the south. Down here was that breeze from the north.

He said to Gian, still not looking back, "It happens sometimes here, crossing winds, high and low, usually in autumn."

"They might know it too, my lord."

"No. They aren't down here. And it is springtime. I'll be all right."

He walked past the two pikes, up the hill, a hand in the air to signal a desire to talk. He didn't go right to the gates—that might mean a bullet or crossbow arrow wouldn't need to try to account for the (false) wind. You didn't want to make it too easy.

Just have it *appear* that way, if someone was foolish.

He called out, "I am Folco Cino d'Acorsi. Who speaks for Rosso?" They would be aware of who he was if they could see his eye, but he was still some distance off. It was important they know it was him.

A voice came from the walk above the gates. "I do, lord. I am Goro Calmetta, merchant of Rosso, leader of our commune. I believe you will have been told by your captain why we are doing this, and that we've paid Avegna the taxes assessed at the fair rate. We beseech you, in Jad's holy name, and in simple decency, to withdraw from our city."

An intelligent man, to affirm what they'd told Aldo, without repeating it in detail. Probably a good businessman.

"He did report this to me. You understand it is not my task to judge Avegna's taxation of its subject cities."

"Before Jad it is," said Goro Calmetta. "But we will leave that. I have another thought." He appeared to be an older man, but his voice was clear.

"I am listening," said Folco. "But what my captain told you is truth: if you do not yield now and pay the taxes assessed, if Avegna needs to hire me to bring an investing army next year, there *will* be terror in Rosso. You will be destroyed."

"But if Rosso offers itself to Acorsi, Lord Folco? What if we do that? Your reputation as an honest lord who defends his cities is known through Batiara."

This, he had to admit, was unexpected. Perhaps it shouldn't have been.

He heard Gian behind him make a sound. He didn't look back. Much of this was about one's manner, it was a performance.

It was also, appealing as the offer might be, impossible. He protected Acorsi and the towns subject to it with his mercenaries, and he could pay those men because of commissions such as this one (and, rather more, the current one from Firenta). A mercenary would be forgiven for changing sides a few times—they had all done that—but not for robbing the city-state that had hired him. If he claimed Rosso he'd be stealing it from Avegna.

Besides which, the Ricciardiano brothers were his friends, since they were young together. Not the *best* of friends, but there had never been any ill will, even when he'd declined to marry their sister in favour of Macera and Caterina.

Tempting, however. Almost absurdly tempting. Rosso was not on the sea (he still needed a port) but it had a straight road to the coast and a village harbour they used for smaller craft.

No, he thought. Cannot be done. Not unless a great deal changes.

And in that moment, on that thought, someone was foolish.

A bolt from a crossbow hit the earth three paces to his right—because someone *did* try to adjust for the wind from up on the wall. The wind that wasn't blowing down here.

With some regret—because the image of controlling Rosso from Acorsi, the revenue, some access to the sea, the enhanced stature, lingered—Folco lifted a hand and pointed at the gate and let his voice carry menace now, which was a thing he could do.

"*How dare you!* You have sealed your fate with that treachery! What man does such a thing?"

"It was not ordered, lord! It was not!" Goro Calmetta's tone was vivid with fear.

"And I should believe this? You are Jad-cursed violators of a truce!"

"We are not! It was one foolish person!"

Foolish was what he'd been hoping for. There did tend to be one or two such men in moments like this.

"Then give him to me."

A silence. Then, "He is the son of one of our commune leaders. He is . . . he's just a boy, lord!"

Desperation now. As if Calmetta knew what was coming.

And it *was* coming. Folco had done this, too, before. With variations, but pointing towards the same end.

"Boys can kill men, Signore Calmetta. You know it. They can also destroy their cities."

"It was not ordered!"

"Ah. Not ordered. And if I had died, it would have eased my city and family to know that?"

"My lord, truly, I can truly . . ." Calmetta's voice trailed off.

There was a stillness in the world in the morning light. He saw bees among the flowers.

He walked forward a few more paces. They needed to see him do that. He was coming for them.

"Here is what will now happen. The man who loosed that arrow will be thrown from the wall. Immediately. The gates will be opened and you will collect and send out, before the sun sets and we all withdraw to our prayers, the taxes owing to Avegna. *All* the taxes, Signore Calmetta. It will be counted, by us and by them, I assure you. Then I will go away from here and you will not be harmed. I undertake it, on my oath. Failing this, the commune of Rosso will be attacked next spring by an army far larger than this one, with weapons of assault, and we will not accept a surrender. We will destroy you, signore. With cannons or by siege. You *will* have heard of the pillaging that follows, perhaps some of you have survived a siege somewhere, somehow. The famine. You will end up eating parchment and books, you will boil the heads of drums to eat, after all the rats have been devoured. You will eat each other before the end. Do not invite it upon your city and your children."

He'd always had a good, strong voice, and he knew how to use it, make it implacable, convincing.

As it happened, what he was saying was also true. If he did have to come back, it *would* be to sack this city, and three days of looting was the rule in their time. Not one he loved, but you lived with the codes of war as well as those of peace, and an army needed to be kept loyal.

He heard other voices above the gate. Urgency, anger, fear, which was as it ought to be.

"My lord Folco," Calmetta called down, "one moment, I beg. If you please!"

"A moment is all," he shouted back. "Then I turn and leave here, and you know I will return."

He waited.

"Lord," Gian said quietly behind him, "you should step farther back and—"

"No," he said, still not turning. "Not now. Cross your arms, legs wide. Look angry."

"I am angry, my lord," Gian said.

Wind in the banners, the scent of wildflowers, white clouds moving, the rising sun. A sweet time of year in so many ways. Then Calmetta's voice again: "My lord, we have decided it is . . . proper to pay the assessed taxes. We will send emissaries to Avegna to discuss the amount going forward."

"Good," he said. "Now the man who loosed an arrow. Throw him down. Do it. Your city depends on it."

"My lord, can you not see a way to—"

"No," he said. "I cannot."

It mattered. He might wish it otherwise, but he lived in a dangerous world and had not survived so long without taking measures such as this. It was necessary to send a message about what happened if Folco d'Acorsi was attacked—or even resisted. A message not just for Rosso. It was for the world, their part of it. What happened here this morning would be known everywhere, soon enough.

"He is a boy, lord! Truly. And he—"

"Do you *want* me back? I gave you two conditions. One for Avegna, one for myself. Meet them both, Signore Calmetta, and call yourselves fortunate when you pray tonight."

Raised voices again, fierce dispute. He could imagine. Nonetheless . . .

Nonetheless.

He took a brief, professional satisfaction but no pleasure when he saw a man thrown over the wall to plummet, screaming and spinning, into the ditch below. He might be alive, Folco thought.

"Gian?" he said. "Deal with him?" And added, "They will not harm you."

"I know, lord," said Gian.

He walked past Folco towards the city. He went down out of sight into the ditch. He came up a moment later. He cleaned then sheathed his sword, not hurrying. He walked back.

"How young?" Folco asked.

"Old enough," Gian said.

THEY STARTED TOWARDS the tents and the camp. Folco was thinking of how they'd deal with the tax wagons when they came out. They would be coming now, of course they would. They'd killed one of their children already.

He didn't really need to count the money, but he'd said they would. He'd report a sum to the Ricciardiano brothers, to ensure that what arrived was what set out, but he wouldn't escort it. Rosso could get its wagons to Avegna without him, they had enough soldiers to guard them. He'd send a pair of messengers ahead to report success. This had gone more smoothly, he thought, than one might have expected. You could be grateful for fools sometimes.

Then, walking back to camp, he saw that two men had arrived and were waiting for him. You could see how tired they were. Their horses, behind them, were exhausted, heads low. They'd have ridden through the night, then. A bad sign. They came from home, he knew both men, they were part of Caterina's guard.

And it was in this way, when he reached them, that Folco learned what had happened in Macera, the uprising and who had died there. One person, especially. And within his head—or it might have been his heart—her name began tolling, very much like a bell.

CHAPTER XIII

The supporting army of Firenta, led by Ariberti Boriforte and accompanied by the city's administrative supervisor, who happened to be (unexpectedly, for everyone, including himself) Piero Sardi's younger son, moved slowly south. Bischio was only a few days' ride if one had good horses, but they were going to take longer.

This had everything to do with the ordnance this smaller force was bringing. The heaviest cannons required sixteen to twenty-four oxen each to pull, even on dry roads, and spring roads were seldom dry. Oxen pulling cannon were never to be associated with speed.

The cannons were, however, very much a part of taking cities. You could conduct a long siege, with its problems of feeding and supplying your army while starving the enemy inside the walls, or you could try to smash through those walls with your artillery and the colossal stone balls they were also bringing. These, too, needed wagons, oxen, men to supervise.

There was nothing compelling about this part of warfare. One lumbered along, the cavalry bored and impatient, the engineers and gunners worried and short-tempered. Even in a mild spring the mood of such a force was seldom cheerful—much less so if they knew, as this one did, that facing them at Bischio would be a defending army led by Teobaldo Monticola.

It remained unclear how Bischio had managed to pay the sum Monticola would surely be levying for his services. There were rumours, but there always were.

On a brisk, windy day that force led by Boriforte, twelve hundred strong, reached a place on the road south where a smaller road forked west a short distance towards the city of Dondi.

It was late in the afternoon of what had been a difficult day. The difficulty having to do, as usual, with the gun carts and the animals, on a road that was no better than most of the roads in Batiara.

A commander needed to be able to deal with this, and Boriforte congratulated himself that he was as capable as anyone . . . but he hated this work.

He wanted to be raiding with his best horse and his cavalry. Cutting down enemies, setting fire to farmhouses and barns, seizing goods and food—and women. The things you became a soldier to do! Always remembering that commanders had first pick of everything, which was only as it should be.

They hadn't raided and burned *anything* yet. They'd been in lands offering allegiance to Firenta. Only now, near Dondi, had they reached countryside Bischio claimed. Most of the territory owing taxes to Bischio lay south and west of it, not this way, towards Firenta.

In other words, there had been no pleasures or rewards at all thus far, and when they met Folco and the main part of the army, Boriforte's ability to make decisions, claim things for himself, would—well, it would be gone, vanished. It wouldn't exist.

It could make a man of spirit angry and looking for trouble towards evening on a spring day.

☙❧

That same afternoon, inside Dondi (which had guards on the wall-walk now, at all hours), Jelena finished a day's work in her treatment room. She put on a cloak and went for a walk in the sunshine and breeze. She was one of those who felt reduced, constrained if she had not been outdoors at some point in a day, and springtime made her restless.

Dondi wasn't large. Inside the walls you couldn't wander far, and with the threat of war you weren't supposed to leave the city at all. People did go out, of course. Jelena was one of those. No Firentine force had yet been reported.

On the western side of the city was their smaller gate; farmers from that side came in with market goods in the mornings. The city's secondary market was on that side. Dondi opened that gate briefly, closed it until the market closed, then let the vendors go back out. Men on the wall kept watch. The hope was that the Firentines would just pass them by. There was no extreme confidence that this would happen.

Jelena joined the last of the farmers with their carts and went out with them, walking towards the setting sun. She knew a way to get back in after the gate was closed. One of her patients (a man with a rash she'd eased) had told her about it. There were almost always ways in and out of towns and cities.

It was liberating, it was wonderful, to get outside, even amid fears. She'd never lived in a walled place before. It mattered to her to be able to leave and come back by her own choice. The fear was real, however.

She had no idea if the letters she'd sent with her Kindath friend had reached their destinations. Bischio had sent a messenger with encouraging words—but no soldiers. If Dondi was attacked it would fall. It was that simple, and very likely that deadly—if they didn't surrender. They would *have* to surrender, and hope.

She ought to have gone with the Kindath family and their carts. She hadn't been here long enough to feel intense loyalty to Dondi. She wasn't certain why she'd stayed.

She didn't like running away, she'd decided. She liked moving on by choice. *Choice*, again, that word in her life, but she knew the distinction could be hazy. People drew sharp lines in the world, Jelena thought, even when there was no justification for them.

There was an abandoned sanctuary a little to the south of the farmers' track. It dated back to when Dondi had been just a village, two hundred years, at least. The last clerics living beside it had moved to the city—or gone away. It was a ruin now, empty and quiet. Jelena liked being there. There were animals sometimes, a threat of wolves, but not this time of year, and not until twilight in any case. She'd seen a very large boar once, from a distance. She knew enough to stay away from them.

There was a cemetery behind the sanctuary, with a crumbling, low stone wall around the graves and headstones, some still upright, some fallen. Jelena walked that way. It was a mild day, though with a wind, and there were wildflowers by now. The pale blue flowers of flax plants were all around her, brightening the world. She carried a basket, looked for herbs as she left the path and cut through a field. A healer knew what to look for. It was a large part of what she did.

She didn't see anything useful today, but she picked anemones for her house. A favourite, that flower, associations going a long way back. It was linked with boars, in fact, and a goddess and her lover dying. There had been Jaddites once who'd linked the flower to Heladikos—the son of Jad who'd fallen in his father's sun-chariot to his death. The red of some anemones was his blood.

Heladikos was a heresy now. She was a heretic herself, if it came to that. At risk. Who was ever not at risk?

There were said to be sanctuaries in the east, across the water, towards Sarantium, that had images of the god's son on their domes or walls. She wondered if she'd ever see one of those. It was a large world and most of it she would never know. That was the way it was in a life. You could only experience so much.

She saw a falcon hunting with the sun behind it. She watched it for a while, then walked around the broken walls of the sanctuary.

The roof was long since gone; it lay open to the sky. The stone altar still stood, exposed to the sun.

She went into the graveyard through an opening where a gate would once have been. It was cooler now, late in the day, though not twilight yet—she'd need to be back in Dondi before dark. The wind had died down a little. There was a stone bench she liked to sit on, look out over hills and fields, west and south. She went that way and she saw, with real surprise, another woman there already. She'd never encountered anyone here before.

This woman had long brown hair which she wore loose, as Jelena did. She was tall, older than Jelena but not old. She wore a hooded robe of the same colour, more or less, as her hair. Sandals, a silver necklace, large silver earrings. It was foolish to wear jewellery outside the city, Jelena thought, but it was reckless even to be out here, so . . .

She said, "Greetings. I see you like the same bench I do."

The woman turned her head and smiled briefly. She had a long face, pale-coloured eyes, long fingers, too. Three rings. More jewellery to tempt an outlaw.

"I do," the other woman said. "Especially this time of day, this season."

"I haven't seen you before. I've been coming often."

"I've seen you. Left you to your thoughts."

"I don't mind a conversation."

"I think I do. Always have. Why I like it here."

Jelena kept her eyebrows level. That sounded like a dismissal. "I should leave you, then. Enjoy the quiet."

The other woman looked at her again, more closely. "There is," she said, "someone who has died. I see her ghost above you."

Jelena froze. After a moment she said, "You can see such things?"

The woman nodded. "Can't you? As a healer?"

Jelena cleared her throat. She felt afraid suddenly. This was a long-kept secret, casually voiced by a stranger.

She nodded. "Sometimes." Then, "Can you tell me what she looks like?"

She was thinking of her mother and sisters and her heart was beating fast. She never, for a moment, did not believe what the woman had just said. How could she? She *did* see spirits herself. Sometimes.

The other woman looked above Jelena and a little to one side. "Young, tall. Too young to be dead, but it happens. She doesn't look like you."

Jelena bit her lip. She was trying to think who might have been in her life who could—

"Her name was Adria," said the woman on the stone bench. "I suppose it still is. We don't lose our name, only our life."

Jelena sat down abruptly. There was room on the bench. The other woman wore a scent, violets and something else, fainter.

"Adria Ripoli," she said. "Oh, my."

And still she never doubted. Adria was dead and this woman had seen her ghost. The world was not to be understood in simple ways, however much one might wish to make that so. Someone encountered outside the walls of a small city—in a graveyard, even—could know a death, see a spirit, name it.

The other woman shrugged, indifferent. "Was she kin? A lover?"

Jelena shook her head. "Someone I healed."

A first hint of surprise. "That is all? Why would she be here? With you?"

"I don't know."

Which was true. Although she dreamed of Adria often. She dreamed of many people, however, on nights when she'd have preferred not to be alone.

The other woman turned so she could look directly at Jelena. Her long fingers were laced in her lap. One of her rings had a dark red stone.

"I was a healer, too," she said.

"Here?"

"Yes."

"And . . . ?"

The other shook her head. She was looking overhead now. Into the blue sky where white clouds were moving quickly and the falcon was still hunting. She said, "You will be leaving soon. A longer journey than most ever take. You are meant to conceive a child with a man you meet at journey's end."

"*What?*"

Another shrug, as if the woman was bored. "Surely you can see these things, too?"

"No," said Jelena, shaken. "No, I can't."

"That will come. You're young."

"Where . . . where am I to go?"

"East. Somewhere. Carry the child to term. She will comfort you later."

A girl. She was to have a girl. Somewhere.

"What did you mean *meant to*? How is it . . . ?"

A smile this time. "I'm sorry. I speak that way. Habit. You *will* conceive one. You could choose not to birth her. I am telling you that you should."

"And that I am . . . meant to be there?"

"You *will* be there."

Finality. A future seen and known, at least a part of it.

"And . . . and the man?"

"I see nothing of him. He will have a name."

"Everyone has—"

"A name that matters. He will not stay. That is why you should have the child, to not be alone. Also, there is an old god nearby. Be careful."

Jelena stood up. Her hands, she saw, were shaking. "If everyone has a name, will you tell me yours?"

"Of course. I'm Niora. Baschi is my family name." She looked at Jelena. The sun was behind her. "I did not ask for my gifts, as you never asked for yours, I am certain. We are children before our power, however little we have." She looked back over her shoulder. "You should leave, before the sun gets too low. I saw three wolves yesterday."

"Walk back with me?"

"I left Dondi some time ago. I'll be all right. I don't have far to go. Your journey is longer. Be careful, be blessed." She made a gesture, not that of the sun disk, using the hand with the red ring.

"Will I . . . may I see you again? I have much I think I could learn from—"

"No," said Niora Baschi. But she smiled again. "I told you, I don't like conversations. I'm sorry about the one who died."

Jelena stared at her. She opened her mouth to ask another question, but the other woman had turned her head and was looking west again, towards a wood in the late-day light.

Jelena left. Walked back through the open space where a gate had been, past the roofless ruin of the sanctuary, across a field. She was in time to come back into Dondi through the still-open gate. The guards there smiled at her. She was a healer, a city needed those, questions were not asked about faith and beliefs as long as you helped people, and Jelena did.

She managed to smile at them as she went past. Then she stopped and turned.

"Do either of you know a woman named Niora? Niora Baschi?"

"Of course," said the taller of the two. "She was a healer here before you came."

"And she left? Moved outside the walls?"

"Is that how you say it?"

"What do you mean?"

"That she *left*?"

"How would you say it?"

A chill now, and it wasn't the breeze.

"She died ten years ago, at least," the tall guard said. "She's buried by the ruined sanctuary, people still use the cemetery there."

Jelena stared at him for so long his expression became worried. "Thank you," she said, eventually. Then she turned again and walked through the streets to her home and entered her house and closed the door.

SHE SLEPT BADLY that night. It was hard to come to terms with the death of Adria Ripoli *and* with the idea that a woman, an aristocrat seen only twice, and only briefly the second time, would be one of her own ghosts hovering, to be observed by someone who knew how to see the spirit world.

She didn't know why Adria's ghost had been with her. She wrestled for understanding through the dark hours. But why *should* she know the way these things worked? And then there was the other thing the dead woman had said among the headstones and the flowers, about Jelena's journey to come, and a child born far away.

A girl, she'd said. Perhaps the two things together were about being a woman and making dangerous choices. Your decisions in life could kill you, however brave you were? A woman couldn't *force* the world to fit her needs and strengths?

Could try, though. You could try.

She lay in bed remembering Adria Ripoli with more clarity and sorrow than she'd have expected. Courage there, to have done what she'd done in Mylasia. And the Bischio race. Almost no one knew that had been her, Jelena thought. Things done in the world, affecting the world, but kept close, secret, private.

She'd had arrogance, too, that one, born to power, but the fierce, reckless nature had been her own. How did people, men or women, become that way? How, Jelena thought, had she become what she was, herself?

She wondered how Adria had died.

In the morning, when she saw the light through the shutters that meant sunrise, she got out of bed and prepared herself to address the needs of the day.

It never occurred to her, then or after, to doubt what she'd been told by Niora Baschi. She had seen ghosts herself. Why would there never be one above her—or speaking to her on a stone bench wearing silver earrings and a red stone in a ring?

It was, Jelena thought, another kind of arrogance to believe you could understand the way the world was made. It could not be done, there was too much. You needed to be open to it, though, to what your life gave you and demanded. She'd had thoughts about travelling east for years! What the other woman had said to her was a confirmation, not a revelation. Jelena told herself that as she dressed and ate.

She unbolted and opened her front door and stepped out to see what the morning had brought.

Firentine soldiers, it turned out.

They were at the eastern gate. But it was not just that. Jelena saw a guard approaching quickly, purposefully, pushing through people in the street, as she stepped out into the fear and chaos there.

"My lady," he said, coming to a halt, breathing hard. "Someone has asked after you. You must come to the gate! It is very important."

The demands of the world. And so Jelena learned, following that man through the streets, that it was Antenami Sardi who was here.

No one else from their army, it seemed. Just him and a small escort. Which was why the gate was open, a little, for her to walk through. Two of their own men, armed, stood by the wall outside but Jelena went forward alone. She felt as if she was still just waking up. *Antenami?* It was so improbable. He was wearing a soldier's breastplate, she saw, no helmet. One man stood behind him holding the reins of a superb horse.

Antenami Sardi, whom she had healed of wounds at an inn south of here a year ago, and had made love to many times when he was recovered (enough), smiled at her. He seemed a different man. In a year? But that calm smile, the soldier's armour, the way he was standing. His being here at all!

In a sense, she thought, looking back afterwards, this meeting by the walls surprised her more than speaking with a dead woman in a graveyard the day before. Which could be amusing, of course, considered a certain way.

The sun rising behind him, he said, "There you are. Good. I wanted to be sure you were still here and all right, before moving on to the next thing. *Are* you all right?"

She managed to nod. She cleared her throat. "You look different," she said.

His brow knit. "Is that good?"

A hint of remembered hesitance. He'd been confident about horses, his knowledge of them, about his family's status and wealth. Food and wine. Not a great deal more.

She nodded again. "Yes. It is . . . you look very well."

He said, "You started it. I wanted to be better. After. Even my father noticed. Or I wouldn't be here."

"Why are you here?"

"He named me supervisor of this part of our army. And the . . . our commander isn't someone I trusted to leave you alone here. So I came myself first. He'll probably be here soon, when he discovers I've gone."

He smiled, she saw. He didn't seem uneasy, saying these things.

This was, Jelena thought, Piero Sardi's son, after all. Maybe he had realized that, grown into it.

He added, "I did send your other letter north, to Macera."

She looked at him. "Do you know . . . has anything happened there?" She felt tentative, hesitation in her, too.

"In Macera? Not that I've heard. What do you know?"

It was easiest to shake her head and say, "Nothing. What are . . . Antenami, what *are* you here to do?"

"I need an agreement from the city leaders, the commune, to give us a great deal of food, and ten thousand gold serales."

"*What?*" she exclaimed. Ten thousand was a fortune for a small city.

He didn't look dismayed. He even shrugged. "I am going to propose that if we capture Bischio and the tax money comes to us going forward, to Firenta, you will be given credit for this sum. I'll sign for that. If we fail at Bischio, it will be a sum you've paid an army to leave you alone. I think I can make our commander do that, but the food and money have to come first. Armies," he said earnestly, "need to be kept happy."

"You know this now?"

He blushed a little. "I think I do. I also think Ariberti Boriforte would like nothing more than to sack Dondi. Jelena, I can order him not to, and he's *likely* to listen, because of who I am. But I need the food and the gold. You have to give them. To survive."

"Are you negotiating with me?"

He smiled again. This smile was new to her. "No. I wanted to see you. And to ask if you wish to leave. I can give you an escort anywhere you like. You said . . . you said last year this was a new place for you. Do you feel it is home now?"

"Not truly. But neither will I leave if danger comes."

"But that is when people *should* leave," he said.

Which was, she thought, sensible.

She said, "I'm not certain I know this man you've become."

He looked shy. "I'm not, either. I think I like him."

She smiled this time. "I do, too."

The sun was above the trees along the east-west road behind him now. It occurred to her, and it was strange how sudden the thought was, that this would be a foolish, unnecessary place to die.

She'd leave it for later to think about what places might be wise or necessary ones for dying.

She said, disliking the words a little, but saying them, "If you fail to get them to agree to what you require, let me know. I'll leave with your escort. You're right, 'Nami. I can be too stubborn."

"You've had to be," he said. Which was a little bit astonishing as well. "Go back in and have someone with authority come out to me. I'd like this decided before Boriforte shows up with however many men he brings."

"You've *really* changed," she said again.

She wasn't used to repeating herself so much.

He nodded. "Will you consider staying with me? If you think I have?"

She shook her head. "You're a Sardi. I'm not a mistress. And I'm going east, across the water."

"What? Now?"

She hadn't expected to say it. To make it a thing in the world so quickly.

"Soon, I think."

"To Sauradia?"

She nodded.

"Sarantium?"

"Maybe later. If it is safe."

"Why?"

Really. Why? Because a ghost had said . . . ?

"I have things to learn there," Jelena said. And favoured him with her best smile.

She turned back and told the guards at the gate to have the commune leaders come out to talk to the administrator of the Firentine army immediately, before soldiers came and the morning altered in a bad way.

In the end, they invited Antenami inside. He entered willingly. No harm would ever come to him from them. His family would level their walls, burn the city to ash, salt the ground, hack each one of them into pieces for dogs and corpse birds if anything happened to him. They knew that.

THE COMMANDER OF the artillery-escorting portion of the Firentine army did consider—if briefly—killing the civic administrator attached to his force. He entertained this thought when he saw

Antenami Sardi walk out alone from Dondi as he himself galloped up, at speed, raising dust on the road at the head of twenty riders.

Sardi's servant, leading the magnificent horse Boriforte lusted to own, followed him out. It was stunning—the city actually opened its gates! Notwithstanding the presence of Boriforte and his men. It was almost an insult! They feared him so little? Sardi had— clearly!—gone inside alone and undefended.

What were the world and warfare coming to?

Piero Sardi's younger son strolled, as if out for a pleasant morning in the countryside, towards where Boriforte halted his men, carefully out of arquebus and crossbow range. You learned those distances early. It was fundamental knowledge. Sardi was smiling. He lifted a hand in cheerful greeting.

"Captain!" he called. "I am pleased to see you. I can share good tidings the sooner."

What Boriforte wished to say was, *Fuck you, you rich, interfering fuck!*

What he said was, "Good tidings are always welcome. But you must never again ride out like this, my lord. I am responsible for your safety."

Sardi came up to him. His smile did not waver. "Sometimes we take risks," he said, waving an aristocrat's careless hand. He stopped smiling. "In addition, I was informed last night of your intention to approach these walls with hostile and deceptive intent, despite my instructions, which are also my father's. We will discuss this in my tent at camp, and your explanation will be attached to the letters I send home and to Folco d'Acorsi. Dismount, please. I will get a discomfort in my neck looking up at you."

Anger could disappear quickly when extreme apprehension replaced it, Ariberti Boriforte thought. He also thought, *Oh, dear Jad.*

It had seemed such a good idea the day before, to approach the city then allege, galloping back to camp, that a casual reconnaissance, a signalling of their presence, had been met by arquebus fire and crossbow bolts—and that this disrespect to Firenta could not be permitted. Not at the outset of a campaign!

Then they'd take and occupy this city and do what soldiers did and reap what soldiers reaped, before Folco arrived at Bischio to take over the army and most of the profits to be found.

It became important to discover who had talked to Sardi.

It might have been an error to have so many men privy to his plans. Spies were legion in an army, especially spies for the city officials accompanying them, interfering with what soldiers needed (or desired) to do.

"Dismount," said Sardi, again. "My neck . . ."

He did not say *please* this time.

This man was not, Boriforte thought, the person he'd seen singing late at night, a cup of wine in his hand, in several of the better brothels in Firenta during the winter just past.

He dismounted.

He really did want to kill the other man, but there were twenty cavalry here and Dondi's guards could see them from above the open gates, and . . . well, he didn't particularly want to be castrated and beheaded and have his head spiked on the wall of Firenta.

"We were coming to do a sighting of the ground here, in case we needed to know the terrain," he said.

"Were you?" said Sardi. "Let's discuss it, shall we? And you can put that in a note to go with my letters. Do it all properly, right?"

"Properly. Yes," Boriforte managed to say. His horse shifted and stamped beside him. He gestured with his free hand, and a rider came up to take the reins.

"Check the left rear hoof, I think," said Antenami Sardi. "Shoe might be a concern."

This man was, Boriforte thought, going to drive him mad.

He said, "You mentioned good tidings."

"I did!" The young Sardi smiled. "Dondi has agreed to give us— today—eight thousand gold serales and then twenty wagonloads of grain in sacks—their own wagons and horses to pull them, too. It was all *very* easy. They have no desire to offend us. Or," he added, quietly, "to have us do violence in a city that should soon belong to Firenta and pay taxes there."

"Eight thousand?" Boriforte repeated.

It was an enormous sum for a small city to assemble immediately. He was doing numbers in his head.

"I believe," Sardi said, smiling again, "our soldiers will be pleased when we tell them. No siege, no fighting, no delay, no wasting cannonballs we'll need at Bischio. And a sum for each of them. And for the captains, of course, however you normally divide it."

"Eight thousand serales. Today?"

"I said that. The grain to follow. We will leave men to wait for their wagons and escort them after us. I do have questions about how Folco intends to prevent Teobaldo Monticola from being ahead of him to Bischio. If we encounter his force before our main army arrives, are our cannons not lost? Aren't we lost?"

"I wouldn't worry about Folco," said Boriforte, clinging to some pride as a military man, speaking of his superior.

"Good," said Sardi. "If you say not to, I won't. Shall we ride back to camp? I find I'm hungry. I was going to eat in Dondi, they invited me, but then someone saw you coming."

Eight thousand. Twenty wagons, Boriforte thought. The idiot had done amazingly well.

He still wanted to kill him. And he really needed that letter, as described, to not be sent to the father, or to Folco. The world, Boriforte thought, could be challenging. A man might be hemmed in on all sides sometimes.

They rode back. At the camp, Sardi, unexpectedly, let him be the one to share the news. The army cheered loudly and for a long time. But it would be known quickly, if it wasn't already, who had negotiated this—that it hadn't been their commander.

Hemmed in. All sides. You might as well go be a cleric in a Sons of Jad retreat, wear a scratchy yellow robe and a disk around your neck, light candles at all hours, wake in winter nights to kneel and pray . . . bound by so many pious *rules*. No horses, weapons, fires, blood. No life.

CHAPTER XIV

I left Seressa for Remigio by ship before word arrived of what had happened in Macera. So I hadn't heard about Adria before I met Teobaldo Monticola again.

I don't think I'd have done anything differently, but it is impossible to know. We cannot go backwards in our lives then unspool them in another way, to compare. There is no life where I did not go with her down a stairway in Mylasia, or find her at an inn near Bischio, where she didn't ride in a springtime race long ago, or die on another stairway at home.

I was truly unimportant, in any case, whatever I might have felt. A minor representative of Seressa sent to address certain money matters with the lord of Remigio. Sent because Duke Ricci had decided, for his own reasons, that I seemed promising, and because I'd told him I'd met Monticola and he'd shown me favour.

Seressa has always been good at finding even the smallest advantages. I began to learn that then. I know it extremely well by now.

Brunetto Duso was with me on that journey, for the first time. He was the leader of those guards who had been in the square to escort me to the duke. The ones who had missed the presence of an assassin on a roof.

"Do you want the guard leader executed?" Ricci had asked me at the end of our meeting, after he'd offered me a post, and my first journey by sea.

"What?" I exclaimed, genuinely dismayed.

"He failed. He was assigned to bring you to me safely."

"He did bring me safely here, my lord," I said.

"Only because you saw the man on the roof. Neither he nor his men did."

I stared at him. He was new to his great office then but it didn't seem that way. He sat calmly at his desk, holding the spectacles he used. I said, "Would you really kill him if I said I wanted you to?"

"Of course. Or I'd not have asked."

"Not even to test me?"

He smiled. "I could note your reply and have him killed, regardless of what you say, Guidanio Cerra."

"Don't," I said. "Or don't for any desire of mine. They did catch the man quickly."

"They did. Very well. Would you like him assigned to you? I will have him advised that he owes you his life."

I blinked. "I am to have a guard?"

"And an escort. As befits a representative of the council."

I swallowed. This was happening quickly. "That would please me, if he . . . if he wishes to be . . ."

"His wishes," said the acting duke of Seressa, "do not matter at all."

They've come to matter to me. Brunetto is a presence in my life, a constant, a friend. He's still with me all these years later, neither of us young any more.

Adria is an absence. No one living knows what that means, how often I remember her, even now. It is foolish, I concede it. Sometimes we are foolish. But isn't it also true sometimes that the only way a person survives after they die is in the memories of others?

IT TURNED OUT I was comfortable at sea, which has been helpful in the years between then and now. Brunetto was continuously unwell, still is if a sea is rough.

We poured oil over the railing to bless the journey, then hugged the coastline south, pulling into harbours at day's end. There were raiders from Senjan in these waters, they even crossed to this coast, we were told, and we did have commercial goods on board. (Why waste a voyage by not carrying goods to sell?)

I liked watching the dolphins that flanked and followed the ship, and I liked the taste and bite of salt in the wind. I was still working to deal with what had happened to me. I had been a bookseller, and now . . .

One evening, the white moon rising over the water, we moored in the harbour of Mylasia, paying the port fee to do that.

I had complex memories that night, seeing those walls and the lights of the palace in the dark. I'd killed two men there, had a friend slaughtered in the square by a mob.

We were a Council of Twelve ship, we didn't take on passengers, and no one entrusted mail to the Seressinis, they knew it would be opened. On the other hand, we were the ones who guarded this sea for all merchants and ports, our war galleys defending against Asharite raiders and—as best we could—against the Senjani pirates. Mylasia and Remigio, all the cities down the coast, were permitted to have trading ships pull into their harbours only on payment of an annual fee to us.

That was—in part—why I was on my way to Remigio. Mylasia's taxes would be collected by someone else, later in the season, by contract. Which was just as well for me. There could be people who knew me there, and I really didn't want to be known.

A few days later, a wind whipping our sails from the east, we saw Remigio on a rise of land above the water, the dome of a new-built sanctuary gleaming in the late-day sun. We swept into the deep, sheltered harbour of Teobaldo Monticola's city, flying the flag of Seressa, Queen of the Sea, and bearing an official envoy—me.

"OH, TEO, SEE who has come to us! It is my darling Danio!"

She recognized me the moment I entered, from the far end of their reception room. I hadn't been announced yet. It was, I will admit it, deeply flattering. But Ginevra della Valle was that sort of woman. My sense is she'd had to be observant from the start, to emerge where she now was . . . sitting beside the lord of Remigio, married to him as of the winter.

That had happened, yes. Word had crossed Batiara swiftly, because such things mattered. The Wolf of Remigio was married again, claimed and tamed by a longtime mistress of celebrated beauty. Tamed in this regard, at least.

She was a remarkable person. Dangerously attractive and dangerously clever. Being called *my darling* here could be good or bad for me. I wasn't in a position to know. I did see men turning to look at me, closely.

Monticola, in hunting clothes on his throne, was smiling, unruffled, although I was certain he'd needed her voiced alert to recognize me in formal clothing and a new office. He'd only known me as a hanger-on to his men, one who'd amused him on the road then done him a service—winning him a great deal of money.

"Danino it is," he said. "You have risen far in a year. Come forward."

I had only a basic idea of protocol, though one of those on the ship, a man named Queratesi, had been advising me in a perfunctory way. I had the sense that it was his considered view that he, not I, ought to have been appointed the council's representative on this trip, not merely one of those accompanying me. Still, he was too experienced to visibly sulk, and he'd told me a few things.

I walked to the edge of the carpet below their cushioned chairs and bowed, removing my hat. "My lord," I said, "I have risen only

enough to be permitted the pleasure of seeing you both again."
That sounded about right.

Ginevra della Valle, in green and gold beside her lord, smiled
prettily. "*Such* a sweet man!" she said.

She stood up, as if impetuously, came down the three steps, and
kissed me on the cheek, rising on tiptoe. She wore golden earrings
and a scent that offered a hint of the east. There was a murmur in
the room.

"Do you want me to kill him in a rage?" Monticola asked. He
was grinning.

"I would poison your wine if you did!" she exclaimed, laughing.
She gathered her skirts and went back up to her seat beside him.

I took a chance on a jest. "Doing that would hardly help me, if
I was already dead."

Monticola laughed, but briefly. "As I recall," he said, "you were
going home to be a bookseller when you declined service with me.
And now . . . ?"

Dangers, always. How swiftly they could come. He could see me
as having rejected him—and his children. And he was not one to
be easy with that.

"I *was* a bookseller, my lord. Until very recently. Someone tried to
assault me in Seressa, and Duke Ricci summoned me to speak about
it. He then decided I was worthy to be tested with a mission."

"To our court, because we knew you and might share more than
we would with a stranger." It was the woman, not the man who said
this, and it was a statement, not a question.

Both of them, I reminded myself: the need to be cautious.

I wondered if I would ever be like these people, in this quick,
probing way. Or in any way that mattered. Would I become a figure
drifting on the edges of their world? Or be binding and selling
books again by summertime?

I said, "My lord, my lady, Seressa lives by gathering information. So do you. But I have no task in that regard. I am too

inexperienced. I am here only to address a matter of . . . monies owed this spring."

I had been told by the duke how to put that last phrase, even to the pause. He'd rehearsed me in it. There were reasons. He'd explained them and what I was to watch for. Seressa was what it was, my city.

THERE WERE ABOUT forty people in the audience chamber. Monticola didn't order it cleared. We withdrew, instead, into a smaller room through a door behind their chairs. Himself, me, Brunetto as my man, two officials of the court. One, very well dressed, had a twisted hand; that would be Gherardo Monticola. I'd been told about him: his brother trusted him more than anyone alive. He had a benign look. I had been advised it was misleading.

I said, after the door closed behind us, "Have you found a tutor, my lord? For the children?" It seemed an important thing to ask.

Monticola looked at me. His expression was not welcoming. With his size and reputation and that narrowed gaze, he was genuinely intimidating. He said, "Why would that matter to a representative of the Council of Twelve? Or a bookseller?"

I cleared my throat. "We can have interests beyond our roles, lord. I was honoured to have been asked. I am sorry if the question is an intrusion."

He stared, but I could see something change. He was a changeable man. Towards violence sometimes, sometimes the other way.

"We have a tutor, yes. From Varena. For half a year, now. I am modestly pleased, not more than that."

I thought of a jest, an apt quote, and didn't say it. I waited.

He said, "To business. I owe Seressa eight thousand. You are bringing me . . . ?"

This was why we were in a private room.

"Fifteen thousand serales, lord, to supplement what Bischio is paying you. Macera has proposed the same."

"And you are carrying the sum from Macera, as well?"

"I am."

"So, we will receive bank drafts for twenty-two thousand serales from you today? Fifteen from Macera, seven from Seressa—fifteen less the eight we owe?"

I turned. It was the brother who had spoken, a deep, strong voice. Gherardo, who administered the affairs of Remigio while Teobaldo was away—and in good part, also, while he was at home, I'd been told.

"Yes, lord," I said to him. "My man has them here."

"Not, I trust, drawn upon the Sardi Bank of Firenta."

That was Teobaldo. He did smile, saying it. He was being paid by Bischio—and us—to fight the Sardis' army.

I didn't smile. This was an important exchange, the heart of my mission here. I was, to be honest, more than a little afraid. I was just carrying the money, but I was carrying it to *him*. For a war. Because Macera and Seressa had decided, alone and then together, that neither viewed Firenta capturing Bischio and the areas it controlled and taxed as a good thing.

Helping the smaller city retain a major commander—pretty much *the* major commander, with the possible exception of the one he was to face—was judged to be in their shared interest, and worth money spent. Within reason, of course. Fifteen thousand each felt like reason, I had been told by the duke. It did need to be done with discretion, given that the High Patriarch was a Sardi now.

"Not drawn on the Sardi Bank, no," I said. "Brunetto?"

He came forward, head lowered, as was proper, and withdrew the papers from his satchel. He gave them to me. I gave them to Gherardo, who had come forward. He put on eyeglasses and read them beside a lamp. It was morning, but this room had curtains drawn. He looked at his brother and nodded.

Monticola smiled. "There are reasons why I have been looking forward to this war, and now you have given me another. Good. I do," he added, "have a condition, however."

I had been told there might be conditions. I had been told I was not to accept anything to do with money. On other matters I was told to use my discretion.

I had no idea what *my discretion* could even mean. Did I have any worth the name? I suspected if I did badly here I was a bookseller again. It didn't seem like such a bad thing, just then. Ambition, I had decided a year ago, was complicated.

"Conditions, my lord?"

"Yes." He continued to smile. I didn't trust it, that smile. Handsome, assured, he said, "You will come with me part of the way west. Not to Bischio. I intend to find d'Acorsi on the way. I want you there when it happens."

"Why, lord?" I asked, controlling my voice. But I knew.

"Because Seressa's role will be known eventually. Bischio could never have paid me enough on its own. But I want it known at the right time for me—or for Bischio, if you prefer."

Bischio was hardly beloved, it was much more that Firenta was feared. I was thinking hard, trying to do so usefully. "Macera's role, too, lord?"

"You have no link to Macera, but he'll figure it out. Say what you like about Folco, but he figures things out. And so does that clever bastard Piero Sardi."

"I was tasked to do this transaction and return, lord."

"And will have doubtless been instructed to react and respond to events. I know Seressa, remember? I have worked for you before. My condition is now an *event*. React and respond. Send the ship back with a letter, Danino of Seressa. I want you with me. We'll be leaving soon, now that I've been paid."

React to events. To conditions. Binding books was easier.

"Yes, lord," was what I said. "I will do so."

"I had no doubt you would. Now, sit down. I have a thing to tell you."

"My lord?"

He seated himself first, by a large table with two lamps on it. He gestured to another chair. I had no idea what this was about. Looking back, I understand he was offering a courtesy, a kindness, because he didn't know *that* much . . .

I sat down.

He said, "There was an uprising in Macera. We learned last night. A rebellion. The Abbato family, with the Conditti. It was always possible."

I felt a chill. Like a wind in the room.

He said, "Arimanno defeated it, but two of his sons were killed. Also," he said, "his daughter Adria. It is said she died wielding a sword. Remarkable, if so. A remarkable woman. I believe she was someone you encountered, and might have cared for in some fashion. If this is true, I am sorry to report it, but thought you'd want to know."

And that is how I learned.

The rain misses the cloud as it falls through the world.

SOMETIMES HAVING TASKS and duties is useful. I have found that many times. When my first wife died bearing our second child, who also died, I needed very badly to be busy. I found ways to be. We hurl ourselves like stones from a cannon into work, until we crash into some wall of the self, and then we grieve . . . if I may risk overstating my imagery.

I went back to the ship and wrote my letter to the duke and council. I was as precise as I could be in recounting the morning in the reception room and in the smaller room behind—except for the detail about Adria Ripoli and my sorrow. Some things, even in office, are allowed to be your own.

I still believe that, though it is also true that you can think something is private and it is not.

I told Queratesi he was in charge of the ship returning home. I would be accompanying Teobaldo Monticola west. He asked me why. It was a fair question, there was no denying it. I did deny him an answer, however. It was in my letter to the duke, I said.

He would not appreciate my giving him orders, but he'd like being in command. And he would never open a letter under seal to Duke Ricci. You died badly if that came out, and your family was dispossessed of all they had. There'd be spies on the ship. Seressa spied on its own people, too, not just those beyond our canals and lagoon.

Monticola was right, I'd realized. Our involvement in the defence of Bischio *would* be known soon. It was probably surmised already, ever since the Wolf of Remigio had ridden to that city the year before to watch a race—and have discussions with the commune leaders. He was expensive. They were not poor, but . . . he was expensive. And it was hardly a secret that other powers would not be enthused about Firenta expanding in this way.

I wouldn't be *revealing* anything by being seen with him. I might be making something explicit, and that could even—I thought, wishing I had someone wise to talk to—prevent a war or siege. The Sardis were bold, might test the will of other city-states, but Piero was a banker first, which meant boldness tempered by prudence. Or so I finally decided, without guidance or support, and thinking about Adria, helplessly.

We left three days later. But something else happened on that first afternoon, down by the harbour.

I was writing my letter to the duke and council. The first of a great many since that day. I was trying to imagine how my teacher would have phrased things, as I wrote.

Brunetto appeared in the low doorway of the small chamber and said someone wished to speak with me on the dock. Then he told me who it was. I went up on deck and down the ramp.

It was late in the day by then, the sun lighting Remigio's towers and domes and the ships around us in the harbour. There was a handsome carriage at the bottom of our ramp. Beside it, standing exposed, waiting for me, was Ginevra della Valle.

I went up to her and bowed again. I couldn't have said what I expected. I was too far out of my depth.

We were alone there, afternoon light, gulls overhead, a breeze from the sea, sounds of a busy small harbour. She said, quietly, crisply, what she'd come to say, then turned to leave me there.

I swallowed, and called after her. She did turn back, slowly. Her glance was calm, attentive.

I asked her a question, awkwardly.

She raised her eyebrows. "Because you are Seressa now, Signore Cerra, and your city is a nest of snakes. And I want you to know that I know it, and will not forget."

I, not *we*, or *Teobaldo*.

I just nodded. What was I to say to that, which all Batiara believed to be true—with cause? I bowed again. She turned and entered her carriage and it rolled away, wheels, horses' hooves.

I went back on board my ship, our ship, Seressa's. I had thought, childishly, that she liked me, that perhaps I even appealed to her in some fashion. I might have, but that was so far down any measure of what mattered to her that it hardly registered at all. I understand that better now.

IT WAS A LARGE, well-equipped army Monticola di Remigio was taking to the support of Bischio. Cavalry with armoured horses, pikemen and shield-bearers among the infantry, his celebrated mounted archers. No artillery. Bischio would have cannons and bringing them made you slow.

The army had been waiting outside Remigio, encamped in tents. Waiting for me, it seemed—and the payments. Large armies were expensive and commanders did not move without money. After which, a good leader went quickly, especially if he had an intent to surprise an enemy and needed to be somewhere first. That much I managed to figure out as we headed west.

I was riding a good horse. I believe Monticola gave instructions as to that himself. I remember him as a man who could surprise you, in many ways.

They both were, he and Folco. Matched and ferociously opposed, dramatically different and much the same in skills, in what they wanted, in what they'd achieved.

We did get to where Monticola wished to be though not before Folco arrived. I didn't understand about the place at the time. I do now. I'd been there before, too.

And there, where they met, much changed, because we are not in control of all or even most of the elements of our world: earth and air, water and fire, light and dark. Fortune and the turning of her wheel.

❧

Folco d'Acorsi still has nightmares at times. He never talks about his dreams, but others do about theirs, and some have written them down, going back to the Ancients, so he has always known that this is a normal thing. He's not unusual. People's nights *are* troubled, variously.

He would prefer to not be ordinary in this way, but he is only mortal, and must accept that truth with humility—and pray for Jad's light when he dies. There is no soldier he has ever known who does not think about dying.

His nights can also be troubled by fears for his wife and the children who have survived. He sometimes dreams of Acorsi besieged by a great, fog-shrouded army sent from one or more of the larger city-states—because his city is *not* a major power. He is a military leader whose father and grandfather were also that, and their family claimed a small city and made it theirs. He exists as the lord of Acorsi at the sufferance of Macera, Seressa, Rhodias—even Firenta now, given how wealthy the Sardis are. He serves these powers in the field, plays a role that keeps them in balance with each other—and away from his own walls.

Yes, if he takes Bischio for the Sardis now it alters that balance, but sometimes you need to cast your lot with a power you see rising. And sometimes you may want it to *seem* that way to them. Because Folco d'Acorsi owes as much to cleverness as he does to skill at war.

He doesn't believe he'll capture Bischio this spring.

He's just about certain Seressa and Macera will together fund a force too large for him to defeat. He will take Piero Sardi's money, go to war for him, then negotiate a truce before Bischio's walls— before the heat of midsummer arrives, bringing illness and hunger for the troops of a siege. Money to induce him to go away will change hands.

That is his expectation. That is what *should* happen if he has anticipated properly. The sty in his eye, the thing that makes it hard to see unfolding events clearly enough, to plan *properly*, is that it is Teobaldo Monticola opposing him, and . . . too much lies behind and between the two of them.

The past can destroy the certainties of the present.

One of his dreams, hardly a nightmare, is of killing the other man. Different weapons, different ways. He has no doubt Monticola dreams of killing him.

The other man has his own city to protect, and will also have no desire to be an enemy of larger powers, but he is so dangerous. Brave, tactically brilliant. Prone to impulse and therefore unpredictable. And Folco *had* made a sally in his direction when he had the Beast of Mylasia assassinated, in the hope of taking Uberto's city in the chaos that might follow his death.

It was a bad thing, that Monticola had learned of this by way of a spy (very much dead now) in Acorsi. That woman in Folco's own palace, in Caterina's chambers. You could have bad dreams about that, too. He can't imagine life if his wife dies. Not a good truth, but a truth.

The worst nightmare, the one that keeps coming back, is not about this, however. The dream that too often returns isn't about a bereft future, it is a reliving of the past . . .

HE'D BEEN VERY YOUNG.

When he wakes in terror, he always tries to remind himself of that: as forgiveness, explanation, understanding. He'll have sweat on his face and body wherever he has been sleeping, as now, in a tent, leading an army towards Bischio, all these years after.

Twenty years old that summer. Not new to war, for his father had been bringing him on campaigns for years, had taught him (brusquely), then entrusted him with small commands: collecting tribute, dealing with brigands, serving under a senior commander with men they'd agreed to send to a war. Jad knew, there were enough wars.

He had learned quickly. He paid attention, remembered things, had never lacked courage. He was good on a horse and with a sword. He was very strong, even when young. The lost eye, from a joust during a midwinter feast at Macera, he had adjusted for. You turned your head more often, and swiftly, you learned other cues for depth in a swordfight, you made yourself better with a bow than before. Fortune's randomness gave things to a man, took things away. What point lamenting? You offered thanks for gifts, prayed for light at the end, carried on.

He'd had his largest army yet in the heat of that summer long ago. It was late in the season but they'd been paid to join a significant force fighting on behalf of the Patriarch. Rhodias wanted two cities subdued. They'd expressed unacceptable desire for independence, which meant not paying taxes to the Patriarchal reserves. There were religious sanctions in place—denial of access to clerical blessings at deaths and births—but those seldom caused men to pay what they owed in a sadly impious world.

Soldiers were needed for that. The threat of death opened coffers.

His father had agreed to send a force to supplement one already out under another leader. He let Folco command Acorsi's company. His father had gout by then, in summer's heat a painful affliction. Folco didn't think it would kill him, but he turned out to be wrong about that. He was lord of Acorsi himself by the next summer.

Carrying a memory that still entered and defined too many nights.

Teobaldo Monticola had also been young, though by three years the older man. In later times, when they were the acknowledged great commanders, people would assume Folco was the older of the two. An easy mistake to make. As the years passed, Monticola di Remigio remained strikingly handsome, had his hair, good teeth, no missing eye, no vivid scar. Three years was nothing later, but when you were both young those added years at war could matter.

The army of Remigio had been hired by the two cities the Patriarch sought to discipline. Since being *disciplined* in those days, in that part of the world, tended to be violent, they had pooled resources and retained an emerging, allegedly brilliant young commander to protect them.

Teobaldo Monticola *was* brilliant in the field. Later years enshrined it as deeply as any truth whispered to the god before an altar, but even then it was something those who knew war could see in him.

Folco's army had considerable cavalry, three horses for each rider, two men on foot to assist each horseman, one of those carrying a pike in the newer fashion. Including infantry and archers, he led almost five thousand men. He needed to be aware also of the usual followers of any army—present to make sure his soldiers were kept happy—but they couldn't be allowed to slow him down. He had a woman with him himself. It was pretty much expected. A commander needed to appear a man among men in all ways, especially if he was very young. Later that year negotiations would begin for his marriage to Caterina Ripoli. It became a coup for Acorsi, eventually, their young lord marrying into the family that controlled Macera.

The fact that it became a love match was irrelevant in the dance of city-states, however life-defining it might be for the man and woman.

He'd had scouts ranging in front of his army. Two of these alerted him, racing back one afternoon in a white midday heat, that Monticola's army was encamped ahead of them in a wide, flat field.

There was a wood to the north, the river was south. That army, they judged, was a little larger or a little smaller than their own.

It was not usual to encounter an enemy this way. It was also frightening, though he couldn't show that. A force defending cities (two cities) ought to be inside already, strengthening defences, arranging for food to be brought in. It was extremely rare for armies to fight in open country. Mercenaries didn't like dying any more than anyone else did. You wanted your payment. If a city surrendered, it was on terms that tended to be honoured. Sometimes walls were breached in an assault and then you sacked the city. It didn't happen often. Soldiers died in assaults. It was wasteful.

If the young lord of Remigio (Monticola's father had died when he was seventeen) was here in the open, blocking their path, it was a direct challenge, a mocking of the even younger son of the lord of Acorsi. Teobaldo Monticola would be assuming he could put Folco's army to embarrassing flight, or smash enough of them to badly disrupt the joint forces attacking the cities he was defending.

So, Folco had been twenty years old and was being challenged, before his own army—and the world—by a man already reported to be dangerous in battle.

It would be possible, he had judged, to go around the woods, let Monticola chase him, then choose his own ground if he turned to fight. His sense was that this was what the other man would expect him to do, and that he wouldn't follow. Monticola had a contract to be south and west of there, behind two city walls with a force he'd have to divide.

That forced division could have been a part of his thinking, Folco later decided. Monticola trying to defeat a less experienced commander with his full army before splitting his force. Also, burnish his reputation—which would be worth money in campaigns to come.

They had never met before that day.

Already there were stories, a tale that it was Teobaldo who had taken out his eye in a duel. And, of course, Teobaldo Monticola's nighttime assault on Folco's sister Vanetta at a holy retreat was known. Their father had made certain of that. It was useful.

By the time they met on that field in summer their families, and the two young men, already hated each other like death.

Folco hadn't withdrawn. Hadn't gone around the other side of the wood to avoid a foolish fight or choose better ground if pursued. You could offer many reasons.

But the ground Monticola had chosen, according to Folco's scouts, was level, even, as if the other man was *daring* him to fight. The armies were equal. And if he beat Teobaldo Monticola there, or even damaged him enough, this campaign could be over.

Also, he was twenty years old. A withdrawal would be noted, known, remembered. Monticola would cause that to be so. Young Folco d'Acorsi was prudent and calculating by nature, but prudence needed to factor in how you were seen at the outset of your career.

Also, he was not a man to decline a challenge.

He ordered his army forward.

They camped at sundown on low, flat ground within sight of the Remigio force. There had been sown fields here, but not this year, the ground had been trampled. Nothing grew on brown-baked midsummer earth. He had men slip forward before dark to bring him a more precise count, and they reported it was true: this would be an even match of forces.

He *could* win this war in the morning. That decided him. He was doing the right thing, he told himself. He went to sleep after telling his officers how they would deploy at daybreak. He was crisp and precise. He knew what he wanted.

He actually slept, though sunrise would bring his first major battle as a commander. But in the dark of night he woke, heart pounding with a terror he could not attribute to anything at all. Was it fear of war? Of dying? That was not him! He'd fought before!

He lay on his cot in the commander's tent and listened to what seemed like thunder in his blood. His mouth was dry. He called hoarsely for a drink and a man brought that for him in the darkness. He rose and walked from the tent to stand under the blue moon, looking out over what would be a battlefield.

And something—an instinct he could never explain or understand (and this, *this* was a cause of his nightmares after, that he'd had no control over the thought at all, it had just . . . come to him under that moon)—caused him to call for his cousin, his second-in-command. He instructed Aldo to quietly, immediately, take eight hundred infantry and archers back behind their line then into the woods north of them, and stand ready there, at the edge of the trees, hidden, for whatever might come.

No, he said, he didn't know what might come, but he had . . . he had a feeling. He could not put it better than that. Aldo, who was loyal to death, and who hated Teobaldo Monticola as much or more than Folco did, would later say it was his cousin's military genius showing at the very start.

Folco knew better. It had been fear, and an impulse to do *something* to allay it. He'd lifted the flap and gone back inside the tent. He'd even slept again, fitfully.

The sun rose, and with it came the waters. He woke to a flooded tent. His boots were floating past his cot.

He scrambled desperately into clothing. His heart was pounding. An aide helped him put on breastplate and helmet. There was shouting outside. He pulled on the soggy boots and rushed, squishing, from the tent into a sunrise nightmare.

There was a shallow lake out there, in the midst of which his forces were encamped. Some tents had been dislodged from their poles. He watched one of them float by. He saw more boots drifting past.

Then arrows rose and descended from the west—where Teobaldo Monticola had pulled his force back in the night, to be elevated enough so they were not similarly swamped by the rising water.

Folco's aide sloshed to his side, shield up to protect his commander.

Later, they would understand.

Monticola had opened the sluice gates along the river that the farmers here used to irrigate their soil before planting season—in years when the land was planted. The other commander had noted these and figured out how to use them if faced with a young opponent who might be induced to camp in *exactly* the right place.

Face burning with anger and humiliation, Folco began giving orders as quickly—and as calmly—as he could. His own archers could return fire from here. Monticola's men could not advance into the swamp without suffering the same problem with movement. He sent the infantry pikemen forward a little, behind shields, to block any such attempt by cavalry.

It made sense to retreat to higher ground. The Remigio forces couldn't follow; *they'd* be vulnerable if they moved after him. This would be, he decided, an embarrassment but not a rout. Not deadly. Monticola would have decided last night that an open battle didn't serve his needs. Setting up a rival for mockery did, splendidly. It amused, diverted. It could also last, Folco thought, for a lifetime, both their lifetimes, when the story spread. As it would.

But then the story changed, as stories do. It changed because Jad—it seemed—did not want young Folco Cino d'Acorsi ruined in this way.

His archers from the wood—the ones he'd sent there in the night with Aldo—began loosing arrows at the Remigio force. They arced and fell in rapid waves. Then Aldo sent his infantry out of the trees to hit the Remigio cavalry on the flank. Hit them hard, before they could react, adjust, and suddenly, wonderfully, mockery was gone. The other army was shouting and flailing in its own disruption, and some of them were dying.

Monticola's cavalry couldn't get their horses turned and clear swiftly enough, and pikemen were deadly against cavalry in a situation like this. Losing too many horses was its own disaster for an army.

Folco had the horns blown, he ordered his forces to pull back.

With a counterattack on the flank launched and effective, it became strategic, not weak. He gave a flurry of orders. He had men collect all the gear they could, including the tents. Tents could dry in summer heat. Everything could, just about.

Ahead of him, he saw Monticola reorganizing to face Aldo. But his cousin knew what he was doing: he pulled his pikemen back into the trees. Then he started back through the woods to rejoin the main body of the army, the same way they'd gone out in the night.

Remigio's army *could* have tried to go after them, but fighting in woods was difficult, and Folco's main force would have no trouble launching arrows at their flank if they moved that way. Folco gave another order, to have his archers ready to do that.

But no, the other man knew it, too. And suddenly both sides were pulling back. Both sides. Thanks be to merciful Jad, *both sides*.

It became a story told, sluice gates opened in the night to flood the army of Acorsi, that dangerous situation forestalled, anticipated, by a young commander having placed a large group in the woods under cover of night, those men doing damage with unexpected arrows and an infantry assault.

Two clever commanders, then, with a clear edge in casualties inflicted going to the younger one, d'Acorsi, even if amusing tales were told of his soldiers (and their leader) floundering about in water as they woke of a summer morning.

In the event, no grievous harm had been done to his men or his reputation—but only, *only* because he'd woken in the night with a fear he could never understand.

He had been desperately close to a terrible defeat, even capture, at best an embarrassment he might never have lived down—on his first major campaign.

Life can hinge on such moments. It is sometimes that close, in our lives, in the lives of others. Sometimes the arrow or the sword misses us, or wounds instead of killing, the earthquake smashes the world flat a little distance away from where we are, and there is a life for us . . .

He mounted his horse, looking over towards the way they'd come to reach this field. They'd passed a Brothers of Jad retreat. Its sanctuary dome gleamed now in the sunrise light.

He turned then, the sun behind him, towards the figure of Teobaldo Monticola, also mounted. The other man had a hand raised, a salute. Folco thought he heard him laughing. It was unlikely, it would have been too difficult to hear laughter over shouting men and at that distance, but he has heard it in his dreams since that day.

He cannot now remember if he'd returned the salute. He thinks he must have done so. It would have been the right thing to do, sent the right signal back.

CHAPTER XV

With no oxen pulling cannons we went quickly west from
Remigio. Speed is dictated by infantry and by those who supply an
army (you don't want to separate too much), and we had wag-
oneers, cooks with portable ovens, bakers, smiths, grooms and doctors for the horses. But, unusually, we had no women or merchants
following. Monticola was going into Bischio to repel an assault or
deal with a siege, and there was no place for the usual followers.
Useless mouths was the term.

I'd heard stories of commanders throwing the women following
an army off a bridge into rushing water when they refused to turn
back on orders. I'd wondered if it was true, and if the soldiers had
then rebelled, or deserted. Could you follow a man who sent a
woman you cared for to her death, just so his forces could move
faster?

There was nothing pretty about war.

But it was exciting. I'd be lying if I denied that. There was something about rising (the weather stayed fair as we went), eating quickly,
mounting up, knowing an enemy lay ahead somewhere, and a test of
courage, fame, and wealth to be gained. Or death.

Not for me. I was an observer, and a symbol. Monticola wanted me with him so that if he met Folco d'Acorsi on the way west (and it seemed he intended to), the other man would see me and know me—and understand that Seressa was opposed to him. Or to Firenta and the Sardis, whom Folco was serving. He would probably realize that Macera was a part of that, too. I had time, as we went, to work this out.

Thinking about Macera took me back to Adria, however, and pleasure in the quickening spring would leave me then. It was foolish and I knew it. I'd met her twice. Her life had had so little to do with mine.

But our meetings had not been ordinary, either one, and her last letter had invited me to keep writing her—with a hint of wanting me to visit one day. I knew I hadn't imagined that.

I was young, and she had laid claim to some deep part of me, and taken me to her bed. And at the heart of all of this was the feeling I might never know a woman like her again.

Which, as the years have passed—quietly at times, and at other times less so—has proven to be true. She did not live her life to be a memory for me, or anyone, but she is. Some people mark you as they go by.

I also thought, as we went west, about Ginevra della Valle and a moment in Remigio. What she'd said to me on the dock, sun setting, wind rising. A very different woman, a different kind of memory.

"*You need to know: if he dies on this campaign I will have you killed.*"

I had not been composed in my response.

"Me?" My voice had swirled upwards, embarrassingly high. "Why would . . . what can I . . . ?"

And she'd given me her answer. That I was Seressa among them that spring. A nest of snakes, she'd called us.

❦

Folco knew exactly where he wanted to go as they headed west from that quick, successful, small campaign at Rosso. His cousin Aldo, with him most of their lives, took the view that Folco always knew what he wanted to do in war.

There was a story, going back to their childhood, that Aldo was actually his commander's half-brother, another son of Folco's father (who had left a number of children scattered through Batiara). There had never been anything conclusive, and by now it hardly mattered. Aldo would die for the other man, whether cousin or brother.

Aldo Cino was one of those rare men whose sense of his strengths and limitations was an accurate one. He was aware that his position at Folco's side had been, for all these years, the perfect place for him. He felt as if Jad had looked kindly upon him when he was born. He was, accordingly, exceptionally devout, in an age where passion for the god often arrived for powerful men only late in life, as they turned their minds towards death, and what might come after.

Aldo ensured that his cousin offered the dawn and sunset invocations whenever possible. In Acorsi, the palace cleric took charge of this. Out here, riding and marching, or before a battle, it was Aldo's accepted responsibility. At such times he always offered a prayer for the soul of Vanetta Cino, whom he had loved, and he made sure her brother heard him and did the same.

They had prayed this morning before moving their very substantial army into a position just past where the road southwest met one coming up from Remigio.

There was a large religious retreat near this meeting of two main roads; Aldo could see its walls as they went past, the sanctuary dome, smoke rising from chimneys on a cool day with a breeze.

This was, of course, a place he and his cousin knew extremely well, from long ago. Aldo looked at the river to the south, and the woods north, and his memories were vivid. He remembered slipping into those woods in the night with eight hundred men. He had his own anger and fears associated with this place. They had lasted a long time.

Folco's would be deeper. It was why they were here.

Aldo set about deploying their force. He knew what his cousin wanted done. He detached three thousand cavalry under Gian's command (Gian was very good) with precise instructions. They rode south, fording the river, crossing the other road, riding across newly sown fields to be out of sight. They would ruin those fields, but armies did that. The farmers and their labourers were nowhere to be seen. Prudent of them, Aldo thought.

He watched Gian's horsemen until they disappeared behind a ridge. A ridge Folco had remembered, and specified. Aldo returned to his cousin's side. Folco had been watching the riders too.

"And now?" Aldo asked.

"Won't be long," the other man replied. "Today is likely, tomorrow if not, I think. He'll be here."

Folco was, Aldo understood, in a mood to kill people. He was, uncharacteristically, hungry for a fight. It was because of his niece, the news that had come to them at Rosso.

Aldo wanted to say Adria's death had no connection at all to Folco, to his allowing her to be one of them for a time (by her wish and desire). It had been treachery in Macera, only that, her father's lack of attention, if anything, and likely her own brave recklessness (he didn't say that).

Nothing to do with anything Folco had done, or had her do for him.

It didn't matter. Gone was gone, and Folco was grieving and they were where they were and Teobaldo Monticola was coming.

Aldo hated Monticola di Remigio. Possibly even more than his cousin did.

❦

It did seem strange to me, how hard Monticola was pushing west. It was still early in spring, surely there was time to get inside Bischio before any investing force arrived. Perhaps, I'd thought, he wanted to try to cut off the smaller part of the Firentine army bringing the artillery? But then he'd have sent cavalry ahead, not limited their speed with the infantry and wagons.

I reconciled myself to not understanding, just being present. Why should I understand war? I thought. Did I even want to?

In a way, though, I did. Warfare was, then and now (all these years later), a theatre for men to perform, test themselves, a way to advance in and through the world. Over the bodies of others, of course—but none of us had been born into a time that offered peace and seemliness.

My teacher, Guarino, had tried to instill in some of us the idea that there were other ways to excel and rise, even end up governing the affairs and relations of cities and states. Almost all of his pupils had been the children of powerful families, however, and he hadn't made much headway with those teachings. He had been tacking, I might put it now, against headwinds towards a narrow harbour.

Late one morning I realized, because it had been only a year ago, and because it had marked one of the important places of my own life, where we had come.

Ahead of us lay remembered fields on the left side of the road; a river was flowing on the right, with more low-lying level fields beyond it, then the land rose towards a forest. It was here that I had caught up with a small party from Remigio, all of us headed to see the Bischio race.

We passed the hill and the lone tree I had raced towards to keep a horse I still loved. Not far from here would be the retreat from which a young cleric had come out to stand in the roadway before Teobaldo Monticola and a company of men (and his elegant mistress).

I wondered what had become of that cleric. Most likely nothing, I thought. He would be proceeding, behind those walls we would see soon, through the endless routines of prayer. So little time had passed. He'd be pursuing piety and calm to the rhythm of bells and seasons.

A horseman was galloping back, dust on the road. He reined up hard before Monticola. He said, loudly enough for anyone nearby to hear, "He's here already! Just ahead, my lord! Other side of the river, in a field past the holy retreat. D'Acorsi! His army!"

Monticola di Remigio smiled, and then he laughed. "Of course he is," he cried. "Let us go and see dear Folco. My life has been lacking that pleasure for too long!"

I went too, which is why I can tell this story.

TEOBALDO MOVED FORWARD along this bank of the stream. We saw the holy retreat, on the far side, as we went by. A little farther west we began to cross the narrow, swift river. The artillery remained on this side. I'd actually wondered if we might be attacked while crossing but that wasn't what would happen here, not with the two of them. Messengers on horseback were also sent across, to meet those sent by Folco.

I saw our soldiers begin forming ranks in the field. Folco's army was already arrayed on the western side, we took the east. Or, Teobaldo Monticola's mercenary army took the east. I thought that way for a moment, that this had nothing to do with me, and then turned the thought around: I was Seressa here, and Seressa was with Bischio against Firenta, which meant I *was* aligned with Monticola. I'd be seen that way.

How I felt about the two of them didn't matter. I was an office-holder, my role defined me. It was a new feeling.

I was also trying to deal with the size of the two armies assembling between water and wood. Surely, I thought, *surely* these two forces were not going to battle here. The slaughter would be immense, and mercenaries deplored losing men, everyone knew that. The retreat, with its domed sanctuary, was easily visible from where we were. So they'd have seen us all from there. I wondered what they were thinking behind their walls.

Monticola stopped by the riverbank on our side, watching the meeting of messengers on the other bank.

"He's never forgotten it," he said. "That's why we're here. A quarter century gone and it still burns."

I had no idea what he meant. He wasn't speaking to me—or to anyone else. The wind had dropped. Our wolf banners lay against the poles on which they were carried. Folco's was a falcon, and those, too, were draped and curled. It was past midday. Not hot, a lovely afternoon, I remember. Sweetness in the air. Sunlight, high white clouds.

Our messengers came splashing across the stream.

"He says he will be delighted to meet with you," the older of them said.

"That was his phrase?"

"It isn't mine, lord," the man said. "Two companions each, he suggests."

Monticola smiled. He named two men. Gaetan of Ferrieres, his second-in-command, was one of them.

I was the other. I was the other.

I told myself it had nothing to do with who I was. He wanted d'Acorsi to see someone from Seressa and know what that meant. Mostly, I still think that was accurate.

We rode across the river, three of us. The rest of Monticola's cavalry had also crossed, farther back east, to not interfere with the meeting, or be seen to be doing so. The water was swift and cold, the banks quite steep. I saw sluice gates, and channels leading north from them. They could be opened to irrigate the fields on that side.

I saw Folco riding towards us, two men with him as well. Monticola stopped, not far from the river. We waited, on our horses. My mouth was dry. I wanted to be there, and I wanted to be anywhere else in the world. Birds were singing. It was spring, why would they not be?

MONTICOLA SPOKE FIRST. He was always the more impulsive. "Greetings! Shall we open the sluices to make this interesting?" he asked.

"I thought you'd say that," Folco replied calmly. "Let's not. I neglected to bring watercraft."

The other man laughed, genuine amusement. "So did I." His expression changed. "I heard about Macera. It seems to have been dealt with by the duke, but I am sorry about the girl, d'Acorsi."

I hadn't expected that right at the start. I swallowed, hoped no one noticed. It was unlikely they would.

"Good of you to say so," said Folco, still calmly. Then he was looking at me, the one observant eye. "You've brought someone who will also be sorry to know of it."

Was he exposing me? Trying to? Monticola *knew* I knew who Adria was, I had told him about her in Bischio before the race. I'd only lied about how I knew her. Was there more to this . . . ? I was, again, out of my depth.

I said, "I am, my lord. She had even begun buying books from me in Seressa."

"You are far afield for a bookseller, Guidanio Cerra." I hadn't thought he'd remember my name.

"I am no longer a—"

"He is the representative of the Council of Twelve, sent to collect my port fees." Monticola's voice was crisp.

"Ah. And to pay you for this army?"

Folco had been looking at Monticola, but he turned back to me. He shook his head. "Would you imagine it is unexpected, that Seressa—and Macera—would prefer Bischio not be taken?" He looked at Monticola again. "Did I need a *message*? Does Piero Sardi?"

The other man shrugged, but I had a sense he was displeased. There had been too little impact to his bringing me here. None at all, really. I said nothing. I remember feeling afraid. Those two could do that to people.

"Ah, well. I suppose he can go home, then," Monticola said.

"Why would I care what he does?" said Folco d'Acorsi.

He looked at me again, and what I remember seeing—or thinking I saw—was disappointment. I didn't understand it. I still don't, remembering. Why were they even talking about me? To me? Or was I just a way in to something else, as you might ask a man about the state of his vineyards or horses, before killing him?

"You'd like to kill me here, wouldn't you?"

It was Monticola who said it aloud. It might as easily have been the other man, I thought.

Folco smiled, at ease in the saddle of his own splendid horse. "And you are free of such desires?"

Teobaldo did not return the smile. "I am not. It is always with me, d'Acorsi. All I need do is think of the lie about your sister. Using her that way."

"Do not," said Folco, "speak of her."

"Why? Out of fear? I am to *fear* you? Or is it because whenever I do I expose your father—and you—as liars before the world?"

"No. Out of simple decency towards the dead, Remigio. Have you any?"

"I do. I always have. Did your father? Do you, even now?"

I saw the man beside Folco pull at the reins of his horse, as if fighting anger. Monticola saw it, too. "Aldo Cino!" he said brightly. "Helped any Daughters of Jad over any walls after dark lately?"

I had no idea what that meant, either. The named man, who would be Folco's cousin and second-in-command, said nothing. He was white-faced, however.

Folco's expression as he looked at Monticola was not one I'd ever have wanted directed at me. He said, "Let us leave the dead, recent or long ago, at peace. Pray they are with Jad. Can we do that?"

Monticola's expression became odd. Defiant, angry, aggrieved? He said, "The dead have been your tools, d'Acorsi. Both recent and long ago. It lies ill in your mouth to speak piously."

Folco swore crudely. "What is it you want, man?"

Teobaldo laughed again, not with amusement this time. "What I want? To defend Bischio against Firenta. I'm paid to do that. If I kill enough of your men here I'll be done."

"You would like a battle?"

A gesture with one hand, almost of outrage. "Folco, in Jad's name, *you* assembled here! I am headed for Bischio. What do *you* want? Redress for shame twenty-five years ago? I can't *give* you that."

I still didn't understand, but I saw something in Folco, a tightening of his face. His cousin was looking at him.

Folco shook his head. "No. It amused me to be here. To let you see what we are bringing to Bischio. But if you want a fight . . ."

Monticola snorted. "I knew what was coming to Bischio. I know your numbers. And the artillery? Led by that vain fool, Boriforte? *He* was the best Piero Sardi could do for you? And you knew what I'd be bringing, once you realized I had money for a larger force." He gestured at me, saying that. "So . . . now you don't want to fight?"

Another headshake. "I thought I did, but it would be wasteful. Although I'd beat you."

A short laugh. "You have never defeated me in the field in your life."

"And you've defeated me? Will you say that? Before Jad? We'd slaughter a great many men here, Remigio."

"We would. We *could* fight alone, of course. Then let your cousin bury you here, or carry your body home. The clerics over that way could chant the rites for you." He nodded towards the retreat. "D'Acorsi, I still believe you deserve to die badly for what you did to Vanetta's name and memory."

Another motion from the cousin, but also from Folco this time, a chopping gesture with one hand. "I told you not to speak of her! Do not put my sister's name in your mouth."

Monticola reddened. "You hold to the lie? I suppose you have to, after all this time. Very well. Fight me, then. But know this: I will be the one fighting for the honour of Vanetta Cino, not her brother."

"Do not! Do *not* speak her name!"

"But I will! I am weary of this, it has gone on too long. I *will* speak of her, and declare her memory tarnished by her father and brother—for their own purposes. Fight me for saying it! With an army, or with a sword. Your choice. Nothing happened in that retreat!"

"You went there! For revenge!"

"*And nothing happened.* And you knew it then—from her! Fight me!"

"You are a vicious son of a vicious family. You destroyed her by *going* there! It was over for her the moment you climbed a wall and went to her room. What value denials after that was known?"

"What value? Her word, my sworn word. The First Daughter would have also spoken before an altar for her—and for me—if asked. But your Jad-cursed father decided otherwise. *He* destroyed his child to damage me and Remigio, and *you* have sustained it for all these years! Honouring him by sullying her? Well done, my lord!"

Folco was trembling now. So, in fact, was Monticola, I saw. *The past*, a hard, sudden thought, *can kill men today.*

"Just the two of us, then," said Folco, forcing the words out. "It is past time."

"It is," said Monticola.

"I should have killed you years ago."

"You should have died trying. Do you want to pray first, my lord of Acorsi? Are you at peace with Jad?"

"As much as I will ever be."

"Folco . . ." began his cousin.

That chopping hand gesture again, and the cousin was silent.

I realized I was shaking too. I heard the birds, the sound of the river behind us.

And then I heard, we all heard, another sound, and we came to understand that everything had changed. For all of us living through our days in that time, that place, in the world as it had been given to us—or the world our choices had made.

It was a calm day, the most tender thread of a breeze. The sky was high, distant. And in that calm, down where we were on the god's earth, beside a river, we heard bells begin to toll, the sound coming clearly to us from the walled retreat and sanctuary, over the fields between.

We still didn't know. Not in that moment. But we turned that way and we saw that three yellow-robed clerics had come out through the gates of the retreat and were making their way towards us.

Two of them were carrying bells, heavy ones held in both hands, and they were ringing them steadily as they came. The third was a tall, lean man, quite old I saw as they drew nearer, and I also saw that he was weeping, tears streaming down his face, and so, too, were the two clerics with him, they were also weeping as they swung their ponderous bells. And they came across the springtime earth towards us under the sun and those high clouds, and they stopped near to where we sat astride our horses, and the tall one, the Eldest Son of Jad in that retreat, spoke to us.

And so I learned, we learned, that word had just come to them of the fall of Sarantium and the changing of the world.

MEMORY IS A TROUBLING THING, I have found. Some moments, even long ago, are vividly recalled (or we think they are); others, as important, perhaps even more so in our lives, are difficult to recollect with clarity.

The day when I was with the lords of Acorsi and Remigio and learned that the City of Cities had fallen to the Asharites was a bright spring day, I know it was. But trying to reclaim the moments after the cleric told us what they had just learned . . . it feels as if there is a mist, like fog off our lagoon or the greyness of a day of winter rain, shrouding everything when I try to see back through the years.

I was shaken. I was shattered, it might be better to say. We all were. How not? Truly, how not? We were as glass, dropped from a height to break on a stone floor.

My first clear memory is of having dismounted from my horse (but I don't remember doing that), standing in that field and seeing Folco Cino and Teobaldo Monticola kneeling. So I did the same. The old cleric was weeping still, and the younger ones were still swinging their heavy bells, and the great bells from the sanctuary were still tolling. Or so my memory says. I may not be reliable in all of this.

I think it was Folco who spoke first. I remember him as saying, "Forgive us all, most holy god. This is our great sin before you, and it will weigh upon us forever."

Then, as if he'd been struck by a thought, he turned his head quickly and looked at Monticola beside him, who had not spoken, whose face was covered by his hands.

"*Teobaldo!*" he said—I had never heard him use the name— "Hold to faith and the god! He may live! They will not all have remained, and not all who did, surely, not all of them will have—"

"Yes!" cried Gaetan, Monticola's longtime companion, kneeling beside me. "Yes, lord. Trussio might have survived! We must not—"

In my memory Teobaldo Monticola lifts his handsome head and looks at Folco beside him, and he says, "No. My son will have stayed, and died on the walls. I know him. I . . . knew him. I can only . . . I can . . . will you pray with me, Acorsi, for his soul? Will you do that?"

"For him, for all of them," Folco said. "And for forgiveness, which we do not deserve."

And then I remember us inside the walled retreat, though I don't recall how we came to be there. We are within the sanctuary and offering prayers before the altar with the clerics: for Sarantium and all those who will have died there while we went about our lives, pursuing our wars and ambitions and grievances, as if they were the things most worthy of our attention and desire.

City of Cities. I knew from my teacher something of what it must have been like once. He had shown us chronicles, descriptions. We had read from them. *We cannot forget that beauty*, one ambassador from Moskav had written home, after seeing Sarantium. Guarino had taken some of us to Varena, shown us mosaics there, of two emperors and their courts.

Even in our own time, long since fallen from its glory . . . even a thousand years after those glittering courts, Sarantium had remained the greatest city on earth. A triple-walled stronghold of Jad in the east—even if the god was understood differently there. And now . . . it was gone. Fallen. I saw fires in my mind. The unbreachable walls had been breached. And it was not hard to imagine what the conquerors, bearing the star-strewn banners of their own faith, would have done there, triumphant after so long and bitter a time.

MY MEMORY, TO NOW, to this night in Seressa, still holds the sound of the two of them singing as they knelt beside each other. Teobaldo's voice unexpectedly light, tuneful; Folco's deeper, carrying faith in it, I thought, like a heavy branch.

> *Let light be our mercy,*
> *Let it be thy grace,*
> *Unworthy as we are.*
> *Let your presence be the destiny*
> *Of all who love you.*
> *Let our weaknesses and errors be forgiven*

As a part of what we are—
Because you have made us so.
Be merciful, most holy Jad,
Because without your mercy we are lost
In the world you have given us.

I was feeling undone, destroyed; that's why my memory is sporadic, blurred, uncertain. I knew my own feelings were nothing, they didn't matter, except to me. I thought of the clerics all around us, and what this calamity would mean to them in their deep faith. And that was before I discovered, standing afterwards at the doors of the sanctuary, preparing to go back out into a different world, how they had come to learn of the fall.

One of their own had gone east a year ago to Sarantium. Last spring, when I was in Bischio with both these men and with Adria Ripoli, watching her race, following her to an inn, being consumed, altered by her—again. *For life,* I'd thought. I'd thought it even then.

At some point that same season, we were told, a young cleric had left this retreat and gone east to defend Jad against assault—as none of the rest of us had. Well, almost none of us. Monticola's son had been there. Remigio's face as we stood by the doorway looked as if it had been pulled taut against his bones.

That young cleric had evidently been writing home to the retreat all the year, letters slow in winter but coming through. And the latest one had been sent on what he'd said would be the last ship, the night before the final assault—which could not be, he'd written, which would not be stopped.

The wall was breached, he said. There were not enough of them left. Sarantium was open. Morning would see it taken and they would die. So he'd written to them here.

There were brave men beside him, he'd said, some from Batiara. The empress mother had been sent away—against her will—to safety by her son. (She would live a long time, that one. She is still alive now, in Dubrava, as I find myself remembering that day, telling a part of this story.)

But the emperor and the Eastern Patriarch were still with them, their cleric wrote, leading all those left alive to fight for Jad and the City, and when death came for him in the morning, he would greet it with his soul at peace, knowing he was serving his god among brave, strong men. He asked for prayers in their sanctuary for all those who fell in the City of Cities, not just for himself, but he asked to be remembered, not forgotten. So the old man told us. I heard this, and my soul felt small, trivial.

They'd have died weeks ago. That was part of the horror.

These tidings were about a moment in the past, however new and raw they were for us. Time was strange when distance became a part of it. You learned of something, it destroyed you on a day when spring was ripening in the world—and it had happened long since.

Folco Cino d'Acorsi walked through the open doorway of the sanctuary and stood looking out at the grey stone walls of the retreat and the trees in the sunlit courtyard. Monticola followed him, went past, also looking out, before he turned.

Folco said to him, "I will not make war anywhere this spring or summer. Not for the Sardis or anyone else. I will return what they have paid me, or ask to apply it to next year. None of us should be fighting now."

"We will next year, though?" the other man asked.

Monticola smiled with his mouth but not his eyes; his voice was flat, thinned out. The rest of us had followed them outside. I was last, reluctant to leave the sanctuary, that place of peace and prayer, with the sun disk and the altar offering something other than . . . what the world did.

"We are as we are," Folco said in front of me as I came forward. I was looking at Monticola. "I am not a man to pray in a retreat for the rest of my days."

"You could assemble a force to recapture the City!" the elderly cleric said suddenly, his voice strong. "The two of you could lead it!"

The commanders looked at each other.

"It will not happen," Monticola said wearily. "There will be talk among those more powerful than we are, but it will not happen. Just as it never did when we might have sailed to lift the siege."

Folco nodded. His cousin was beside him, I saw him in profile; Aldo Cino's face, too, was harrowed.

Folco said to Monticola, "Will I cost you your own fees if I withdraw?"

The other man shrugged. "Probably not. I don't know. I can do the same thing you do, face you at Bischio in a year."

There was silence, then, "I deeply regret your loss," Folco said quietly. "It is good you have other sons."

"It is," said Monticola.

"You need to live, to let them grow up."

"You are advising me now, d'Acorsi?" A hint of anger. Or pain.

"I am sorry. I did not mean—"

"I can still kill you. In this courtyard, outside these walls. We were about to do that, remember?"

Folco looked at him. "We were. Is it what you want?"

Monticola's mouth was a thin line. He said, "What I want? I want your admission, before this holy man on this terrible day, that you and your accursed father lied all these years about your sister. Failing that, I *am* of a mind and mood to kill someone, yes. You will do, better than anyone else I know."

"And your sons? Your city? If you fall?"

"That won't happen. Admit the lie, the Cino family lie, and we both ride home. Do not, and we fight—and you *will* die. Never doubt me. You will end your days here."

What happened next is easily told. The words are simple, they are only words.

I heard a strangled sound to my right, beyond Folco, and I turned that way. I remember that. Then I actually moved, some instinct. I did. The elderly cleric lifted a hand. That I remember too.

And Folco's cousin Aldo cried out, in raw, racked pain, "*It was no lie, bastard! You ruined her!*" And as he did so he drew his dagger from his belt and threw it.

I recall my hand moving, *reaching*, towards his arm, his shoulder, for some way to make this not happen—but I was on the wrong side. I had come out the door and stood on Folco's other side. The accidents behind or beneath who lives and dies, what happens in the world.

I think I also cried out, but I can *see* Folco turning at his cousin's words, towards the movement on his right, knowing already—moving swiftly but too slow (forever too slow)—his own hand flung out, desperately.

And I remember, I will always remember, Aldo Cino's knife, thrown by a man celebrated for his skill, burying itself in Teobaldo Monticola's eye. I will never not see that, for as long as I remember anything at all, I believe.

Probably some poets have since written about an eye taken then and an eye lost long ago . . . I haven't heard such verses, but it is such an obvious association with those two men, and truth dies before good images, or stories.

FOLCO KILLED HIS cousin (whom he had loved since their childhood) with a dagger to the throat. Aldo was wearing armour that day, he couldn't be stabbed in the chest. There was a great deal of blood, I remember some of it landed on me because I had moved that way, uselessly. It was on my cheek, like a stain, a mark.

I saw two clerics rush to Monticola, but he was already dead. We all knew it. He'd been dead before he fell. The elderly cleric was on his knees again, wailing in pain, both hands covering his eyes, as if to unsee horror in a holy place.

I wanted to do that.

I looked down at my hands and saw that, without realizing it, I must have drawn my knife. Folco had been faster—of course he had—and had killed his cousin for killing his lifelong enemy.

I looked at him, then I had to look away.

DO YOU RISK *or lose your hope of light, he thinks, if you curse when you are dead? When you seem to be looking down on your own body and are swearing about the stupidity of dying here? Now? A blade in the eye— from Folco Cino's cousin! Bitter fruit of a hard—lost—world.*

But his pain, his anger—his grief, to use a truer word—is somehow still about Trussio. He is hovering above his own dead body—and thinking of his son, who will have died in Sarantium.

Weeks ago. Weeks ago. If he'd been a truly caring father, shouldn't he have woken in some night at the beginning of this spring and felt— known!—his son was dead?

But no, he was, or had been (he is dead), a caring, a proud, a loving father. He had hated to see his son go over the water to Sarantium. He had been unable to deny him the right to do so.

And a moment ago Folco Cino, born arrogant and subtle, both, had reminded him he needed to live to protect the younger children. That they would be terribly vulnerable if he was gone before they came of age and showed their own prowess. If they did do that.

And now he is gone. No use to them at all, no shelter. He is looking down in some in-between strangeness, and his small sons will be naked before the world, and he knows the world. Had known the world.

There is no chance for them, he thinks, and it makes him want to weep (do the dead weep?). No way they will survive his dying. Ginevra might live—as someone's trophy. His brother, whom he has also loved, will probably be killed with the boys. Remigio will be too brilliant a prize. The cities of Batiara will fight like slavering hounds to claim it.

He has done all that he's done to no purpose in the end. He is leaving no legacy, because of stupid, bitter, murderous Aldo Cino—who is lying on the ground by the sanctuary door, dead at Folco's hand.

If he could see Aldo in this space, if the other man were somehow also hovering here (wherever here is), he'd risk his hope of Jad and light by telling him exactly what he thinks. You can't kill a dead man, he supposes, but perhaps you can tell him what you'd have wanted to do to him, and let the god also know.

He ought to have been watching for something like a thrown blade when he mentioned Folco's sister again. Everyone knew Aldo had loved her.

The truth of that thought burns, even here, unseen above the living.

It was because of Trussio. He had not been paying attention. He hadn't even really known what he was saying. He had spoken violently to Folco about wanting to kill him, but the truth—his heart's truth—is that he'd been thinking about being released from sorrow into . . . this.

Unworthy thought, since so many had depended on him—his children, Ginevra's—and Folco had said as much.

And now there is nothing he can do except wait to see if Jad will forgive his sins because he'd loved some people truly, and had not committed nearly half the crimes alleged through the years.

A thought comes to him. A drifting tendril of an idea. And because he'd always been impulsive, had always believed that he could do things others could not, he bends what remains here of himself—of Teobaldo Monticola di Remigio, the finest commander of men in Batiara if not the world—and he aims his will at Folco, and at the young man, the Seressini he'd liked, standing beside d'Acorsi. He tries to make his thought, his desire, into a kind of dagger from beyond.

He hurls his need towards them for as long as he can, as hard as he can, with longing and despair, but even as he does he feels the shadowy space begin to change. This is not, it seems, a place where you can stay.

He sees those around his body, where it lies, becoming smaller, more distant. He can do nothing more to them, or with them. He can only drift—and wait for what will come now, and forever. It occurs to him that he had loved the world Jad had made, and his place in it.

He shapes a true prayer then, asking Jad's blessing upon Ginevra and the children, and upon his brother who had been dear to him all his days on earth. And he wishes that he might be remembered as honestly as might be in a dishonest time. Probably too many things to want, he thinks, as thought comes to an end.

He looked towards what seemed to be a light, and did not know if it would be his, if mercy existed for such as he had been. He yearned, as we all yearn, but he did not know, since none of us can know.

෯

The Asharites had overwintered outside Sarantium's great walls, continuing the siege through the cold months, cutting off supplies to the city.

In spring, with new soldiers and additional artillery, they resumed their assault. The resources required to have wintered here, Trussio d'Acorsi had explained to Nardo the cleric, were colossal, wasteful. They made no sense, given the loss of men and animals that winter's cold and disease imposed, and the cost of providing (inadequate) food and shelter and heat to allow at least some of the invading force to survive.

It could only be justified by a ferocious passion, Trussio said. But they knew by then, inside the city, that Gurçu the khalif had passion to spare. He wanted the city, he wanted them dead. He did not care how many among his own army died in winter or in battle— so long as he took Sarantium.

And he was going to do that. This morning. A morning several weeks before an encounter outside a sanctuary and retreat far to the west, where Trussio's father would die, thinking of his son. The same retreat Nardo Sarzerola had left to come to the City of Cities. How could any man claim to understand the ways of Jad's world?

Nardo was not a soldier, but prayers and piety would surely help save the city, he had thought, journeying here a year ago. He didn't think that any more, though his faith was still with him. He would die with it, he knew.

They had spent the night, the last night, in each other's arms, he and Trussio, too weary, too terribly hungry, to make love, but still alive in darkness, still needing the shelter another soul could offer, especially when there was love. He had known the son of Teobaldo Monticola was here, the father had told him as much in that road-way a year before. He had sought out the other man to salute him when he arrived, tell his story, why he had come. What had happened between them was a world removed from anything he'd thought would happen. It was a blessing. Had been.

Now, at sunrise, assembled before the gaping wound in the walls that the enemy cannon had torn, they stood with those who remained, and he knew it was the end. Last sunrise, last birdsong heard, dawn wind felt. The great walls and the sea had defended the city for a thousand years. They would not do so today.

The noise from the enemy beyond was another kind of wall, rising where the stones in front of them lay broken and exposed. Nardo felt Trussio squeeze his arm as the Eastern Patriarch finished the dawn invocation with the words and melody they used here. Nardo would have called it heresy, worth a pyre, once. Not any more, though a burning was coming.

They stood up. Everyone was so weak and frail with hunger. Gaunt men helping each other rise. Nardo looked at the tall man he loved, the one so unexpectedly found as his heart's companion here at the end, and he saw in Trussio's eyes that he, Nardo Sarzerola, was also loved, astonishingly.

A sound behind them. The emperor, coming from beside the Patriarch, approaching them. He saluted Trussio Monticola, heir to Remigio, among the highest ranking of those who had come to Sarantium—and had stayed. He offered him a kiss on each cheek, and then on the mouth, and then he did the same for Nardo, unworthy as the young cleric knew himself to be. He was *here* though, standing with these two.

The emperor said, in his light, mild voice, "We will see our god today, and can tell him we kept faith."

No one else in the Jaddite world had done so, Nardo thought. He didn't say it. Not now.

The emperor moved on, to salute and speak to others.

Nardo, holding a spear awkwardly, feeling heavy in the armour they'd made him wear, looked at Trussio.

"Goodbye," said the other man. "You were an undeserved gift of tenderness. I am here and I love you. Try not to be afraid."

Nardo shook his head. "I am past fear. You and I will be with the god in light today."

Trussio offered his half-smile. He shook his handsome head. "I have too many sins to my name. I will not, I think."

Nardo, with an effort, managed a smile in return. "But I do not have many sins, and you belong to me. I will bring you to Jad in light. Wait and see. Wait and see, love."

Drums beyond the gap in the wall. Shouted commands heard, then the sound—a roaring—of many men coming for them. Coming now.

The emperor was calling them to form ranks. The banners of Jad and Sarantium were beside him, held by boys. They must be so afraid, Nardo thought. Trussio turned and went towards the very front, to take the initial charge when it came, and because he did that, so did Nardo, armour over his yellow cleric's robe, and they died together that morning beside the last emperor of Sarantium, as the city fell.

CHAPTER XVI

I will swear until the last breath leaves my body that a wind rose in the courtyard just after Teobaldo Monticola died.

I have no idea what I could have done to change what happened there. But I dream, even now, in restless nights, of jarring Aldo's arm or body with mine, or being next to Monticola, seeing the dagger drawn, pushing him, shouting the warning that let him live.

And what would our world have been, if so?

Perhaps as often as we dream of things we wish might come to be, we dream of what we wish had been otherwise. We are carried forward through time, but our minds take us back.

I will not say—it would be a lie—that I cared for Teobaldo Monticola. I respected and feared him. But he had been good to me from the time we met on the road so near to where his life ended. He was such a *compelling* man. He should never have died in such a way.

Neither should Aldo Cino d'Acorsi, if it comes to that. A bad end to that life, too, slain by the cousin he'd loved, his body later given to Monticola's army to do whatever they chose with it—and everyone knew that certain things done to a body imperilled the soul. They did mutilate him. It was widely reported.

And what if Monticola had not said what he'd said in that moment—about Folco and his father? I think about that, too, and not just when I'm awake at night. Would Aldo have held his peace? Would the two men have fought in that courtyard? I don't think either of them wanted to. Not then.

Words spoken should not be a death sentence, but they can be, they have been.

Both things—killing his cousin, surrendering the body—would have wounded Folco grievously. Giving Aldo to the men of Remigio was proper, it was necessary—but even that, and killing him, might not have been enough to stop Batiara from hurtling into an ugly war. One that could have started that day, west of the walls of the retreat, where two great armies had gathered.

But no. The bells were tolling above us. Sarantium had fallen, and the towering awareness of that cast a shadow over everything, even the murder of the lord of Remigio.

That wind did rise, however, I swear to it.

And it wasn't a *normal* wind. I cannot tell you how I know this but I do. Perhaps because with that swirl and gust—a cold wind on a mild day—a thought came to me. Was given to me, imposed upon me. I have never had the right words. But I knew in that moment what I was going to do. What I seemed to have no choice but to do.

Folco d'Acorsi turned from looking down at two bodies and his gaze met mine, the one eye. *He feels it*, I thought. And I believe he saw it in me.

That same day he dictated a letter to the clerics and they began making copies. Folco would sign all of these and have the Eldest witness them. He gave me two, with instructions. He was calm, precise. But after, he went back into the sanctuary and prayed all night. I did the same, beside him.

Sarantium had fallen. Had been allowed to fall. At one point, towards dawn, he looked at me and we walked out, stiffly. We had a quiet conversation under the last stars, in the chill, standing by the doorway where two men had died.

He spoke, I listened, mostly. He already knew where I was going. It was why he'd given me two copies of his letter. I nodded when he was done talking. I was ready to leave. I had already decided to do so. That wind.

I begged two horses of him before he went back in. He called to someone I hadn't seen in the darkness. Gian came forward and took instructions. I went with him to their camp and was given horses. Brunetto found me there; I'd known he would. He would have been watching for me. We left in the last of the dark, riding towards the sunrise.

Ginevra della Valle would be in Remigio—a city exposed to the world now. She had two small children, fatherless.

If he dies on this campaign I will have you killed, she had said.

I rode there.

☙❧

"It has nothing to do with me!" the High Patriarch of Jad shouted from his throne in a crowded, anxious room of his most senior advisers. "I wasn't even here for almost all of what happened in the east!"

Not entirely true. He had been Patriarch in Rhodias for more than two years now. But what could he have *done*?

They had received word of the fall of Sarantium.

Horror was starkly visible on faces in the extravagantly decorated room. It was not, for once, a display. The Patriarch saw men weeping. It made him even more anxious, and angry. Were they really going to blame *him* for this? Some would try; he knew it!

He abruptly announced that he was cutting the meeting short. They were going to pray again, he declared. It would be seen as a pious response—and would give him time to think!

Not that the added time, as he led them all through the routines of the rarely used afternoon invocation in the sanctuary of the palace, offered anything in the way of ideas.

He demanded solitude after. He did the evening rites with three clerics only, in his chamber before the small altar there. He ate by himself and went to bed early, without a companion. In the darkness, alone except for the guard and a servant, he was astonished to discover, at a certain point, that he too seemed to be weeping.

Becoming Patriarch had been a young man's delicious pleasure amid trappings of luxury and useful power. There had been little he could desire or request that was not offered to him by someone keen to please.

In darkness, on the night of the day they learned of Sarantium's fall, Scarsone Sardi realized (one could say belatedly) that power might have implications. Also, that some events could not be undone, and could change the world.

He gave up on sleep. He called for light and his favourite Candarian wine (some things were not going to be altered, there was no reason, surely?). He had his principal secretary summoned. Yes, it was the middle of the night. The City of Cities had been taken, amid death and fire. A secretary could be roused to his work!

The first letter was to his uncle in Firenta.

He ordered Piero Sardi (he had never given him an order before) to abandon the siege of Bischio. It was *not* to take place this year. The Jaddite world would be instructed to dress in mourning until autumn, and any military action, any conflicts pursued, would lead to a Patriarchal ban from all rites and services, including those for weddings, births, funerals, and the memorials for the souls of the dead.

Every leader in every city-state and every country that worshipped the god would receive the same notice, he had his secretary write his uncle. The west would mourn Sarantium—and atone for its collective failure.

Next year would be next year. But the world, Scarsone declared, could pause, even if it could not stop.

He liked that phrasing. He did not go back to sleep. He had servants summon the palace clerics for an extremely early start to the morning rites, startling them, and himself a little bit.

It had occurred to him that although his thought had been true—that he hadn't been in Rhodias during all the years leading up to the Asharite conquest in the east—he *would* be remembered, perhaps forever, as the man who was High Patriarch when Sarantium fell, having received no support from the west despite its repeated pleas. He didn't like that.

They observed the rites with particular intensity all week, even adding that midday service of the Ascendant Sun. Scarsone was busier than he'd ever been with correspondence. He intended to enforce that year-long truce in Batiara and beyond, and was telling everyone who mattered.

Then, a few days later, came word of a different sort of death.

It would be dishonest to say that many people would mourn the sudden passing of the violent, uncontrollable Teobaldo Monticola. But there *were* issues associated with his death.

Two of the Patriarch's advisers were quick to point out the obvious: there was no clear leader to follow him in Remigio, because Monticola's son and heir would have also died this spring. *In the east*, was how they put it.

Scarsone Sardi wasn't impressed by this evasion, though he knew why they did it. Trussio Monticola had fallen as a hero of Jad in Sarantium. His father's other sons were very young, only just legitimized following a marriage to their mother. So Remigio was exposed to many possible futures, and yes, being governed from Rhodias was certainly one of them.

The High Patriarch could generously take on the task of protecting the boys and their poor mother in the god's holy name—and obtain control of a good port and harbour in the process.

This was, however, before another letter arrived from an unexpected source, changing all such calculations.

It was a turbulent time. Looking back, Scarsone Sardi would remember that spring as a blur of prayer and activity, during which—it could be said—he himself changed greatly.

It unsettled people, that changing, which was not always wise (or safe) in a place housing the sorts of ferocious ambition Rhodias did, but the young High Patriarch came to feel that this was not a concern.

The fall of the City of Cities was. He remained acutely aware that how he was judged by the god, and generations to come, might turn on his response.

He never did rally the west to the rescue of Sarantium. There were too many conflicting goals and desires at various courts, too many hatreds embedded, too much fear of the Asharites, also. Any war in the east would be ferociously dangerous. They needed to have defended the city properly before, not try to reconquer it.

No mighty, unified, avenging force of Jad ever went east.

Scarsone Sardi did what he could. He cajoled and commanded and scorned. He wrote letters, thundered denunciations and bans. He summoned kings and princes to Rhodias. Sometimes they came. They spoke proper words, committed to nothing at all. He never in his life used the word *Asharias*—the infidels' new name for the city that had been Sarantium. He refused to let it cross his lips or have anyone speak it in his presence.

He invited the empress mother of Sarantium to come live in a palace in Rhodias, once it was confirmed she'd escaped the sack and burning. She declined, choosing a Daughters of Jad retreat in Dubrava across the water. Nearer home, perhaps. Nearer what had once been home. She was an arrogant, bitter woman, Scarsone was told. It was likely for the best that she wasn't in Rhodias.

Scarsone Sardi would go to his god able to declare with truth that he had tried. That he'd changed from a dissolute man placed on the throne in Rhodias *because* he was seen as easy to control, indifferent to the complexities of the world so long as he had a ripe companion for his bed and comforts and entertainments to hand.

He didn't ever reject the pleasure of a woman or a boy at night, he took the view that Jad would want him to have *some* easing of his great burdens, but his working days in the palace were long and became disciplined. Rhodias and the Jaddite world found itself with a spiritual and political leader of determination and all the signs of piety.

This disappointed his Uncle Piero and his Sardi cousins, of course. There were (as there always are) rumours of various sorts when the High Patriarch died suddenly, twelve years later, in the middle of a winter feast.

His monument in its chapel in the sanctuary was magnificent. One of the best things the great Matteo Mercati ever did, was the general opinion.

❧

Folco's letter to their smaller force that was to join him at Bischio was addressed to the civic administrator, who was Antenami Sardi, of course. When Boriforte brought it to him, he saw that it had been opened, which angered him, but then he saw the other man's face. He said nothing, read the letter.

He made himself draw several breaths before trying to speak. He failed, he had no words. He read the letter again. His hand holding it was shaking. Boriforte was silent. What Folco d'Acorsi had just told them altered the world, far away and here at home. Sarantium had fallen, and Teobaldo Monticola was dead.

Folco was taking his army home; he would not make war this year. He wrote that he could not tell the Sardi family and Firenta what to do, but he advised them to go home also and mourn for the fallen city. He said he had written Antenami's father directly, and they would make arrangements regarding his fee.

Antenami looked up. He still wasn't ready to speak, to frame thoughts. Sarantium had been under threat for so long it had come to seem an element of the world. It would always be threatened, always be requesting aid, it would not—it could not—fall.

"I should not have opened the letter," Boriforte said. "I'm sorry. I saw it was from Folco and . . ." He trailed off.

"It doesn't matter," Antenami said. It did and it didn't. But mostly, right now, it didn't. "Monticola is dead," he said. Another colossal thing, something that was only smaller next to the news from the east.

"He . . . doesn't say how," Boriforte said.

"He doesn't. I'm certain . . . well, we'll all know soon enough, I'm sure."

Boriforte nodded his head. He was visibly shaken. Antenami imagined he seemed much the same.

"Do we turn back?" the other man asked him.

"How do we not?" he replied.

It was late in the morning, a beautiful day. They were not far south of Dondi, close to Bischio. Dangerously close, Antenami had thought, but Boriforte appeared to know what he was doing in this regard. He had taken a strong position on a rise of land, in the event the city recklessly tried a sally against them. He had the smaller cannons aligned and ready to fire. Antenami had asked what would happen if Teobaldo Monticola sent a part of his force ahead to attack them, take the artillery. *Folco won't let that happen*, he'd been told.

Monticola was dead. Bischio would have no feared commander defending it.

Didn't matter. They wouldn't have one attacking it, either.

"Ensure the courier gets food and drink," he said.

"Of course," said his commander. Boriforte looked curiously childlike, as if he might be about to weep. That, thought Antenami, would be embarrassing. He kept telling himself to breathe deeply.

He said, "Why don't you and I ride back to Dondi? They should be told. Perhaps we can pray with them in their sanctuary."

"I'd like that," said Ariberto Boriforte. "Should we also send word to Bischio?"

Antenami considered it. "It is a good thought. They will have a messenger coming there, I am sure of it, but I think it would be right to let them know we are not going to be attacking now. It . . . yes, we should do that."

The other man nodded.

"Will you choose a messenger, write a note?" Antenami asked. Boriforte nodded again.

He didn't like Ariberti Boriforte. The man was a fool, and not especially trustworthy, but he was still someone living out his allotted days under the god's sun as best he knew how. *As are we all*, thought Antenami.

That felt sanctimonious, even as a thought, but how were you supposed to *be* after tidings such as this? His father might have an answer. In the meantime, there was nothing wrong with prayer, and much that felt right. The two of them, with a small escort, headed north to Dondi a little later.

But just as they set forth Boriforte held up a hand and they stopped. There was a breeze, young leaves on the trees.

"Listen," Boriforte said.

A moment later Antenami Sardi heard it too, coming from the south. All the bells of Bischio were ringing, distant, unseen, sending sorrow out over the countryside. They knew.

❧

Jelena did not go into the sanctuary with everyone else when the news came to Dondi. Antenami had brought it to them, in fact. He was in there, praying with the others.

It wasn't that she never went into a sanctuary, it didn't *threaten* her to be inside a Jaddite holy place, it just wasn't somewhere for her to find comfort or guidance. All around her now were people who did need, in a time of fear and sorrow, that domed space and altar and sun disk and the rituals enacted there. It made her feel detached, unconnected, and she felt too much so most of the time.

She shared the sorrow, of course. She had a frighteningly vivid image in her mind of what it might have been like when those fabled walls were breached and attackers, repelled for so long, broke through like a river might when a dam broke.

But images of floodwaters, however destructive, didn't carry the full horror. Even if she stood, or tried to stand, apart from the wars of Jad and Ashar in the world, she lived in Batiara, in this city, among these shaken children of Jad, and some allegiance, some affinity had to slip into a person.

Into her, at any rate. She didn't know any Asharites, and only a few Kindath. Her world was the Jaddite world and for the most part it tolerated her, allowed her the life she seemed to be in the midst of making for herself.

She could grieve with them. Surely anyone could, for the loss of life and what would have been terrible destruction. Changes would come from this. There was no way that she—a young healer in a small city in Batiara—could know what those would be, but the fall of Sarantium would surely shake the world.

She had intended to go east some day, perhaps, if circumstances allowed, as far as the great city: see the mighty sanctuary Valerius had built a thousand years ago, the even older walls, the place where chariots had raced before fifty thousand people (*fifty thousand!*), the palaces and gardens, the sea where dolphins had been said to carry souls when men and women died.

That last was a belief that pagans held, it was a heresy now. She didn't believe it herself, not truly, but it was closer to her sense of the world, how everything could be numinous, holy, engaged in the unfolding story.

Her own changes, Jelena thought, plans needing to be altered, were a small thing. She might see that city one day—or not. She did decide, listening to bells ringing through Dondi and the chanting from within the sanctuary as she sat in a courtyard nearby, that she was still going to go east.

And yes, a conversation with a ghost outside the walls was part of this. Who ignored words from the half-world?

She waited for the services to end. She was standing outside the sanctuary, waiting for Antenami, when they did. He saw her immediately. He was, she thought, a decent man, possibly growing into an important one.

He walked over to her. *I can give you an escort anywhere you like*, he'd said when they'd last talked, when he was here to save them from attack. She had told him she would not be a mistress, that she was going to Sauradia. Perhaps even to Sarantium, if events allowed one day. She remembered saying that.

Not a hard thing to remember. It wasn't long ago, in that time before the world changed.

IT WAS POSSIBLE, he thought, walking towards Jelena through a square crowded with grieving people, that he was in love with this willful, solitary woman who had saved—and altered—his life.

It was also possible this was just passion shaped by how they'd met, when he'd nearly died, and the lovemaking that had followed when he was healed. Lovemaking as a part of healing?

On the other hand, that wasn't, Antenami Sardi thought, such a terrible reason to fall in love with someone.

"This is very bad," he said to her, after they greeted each other.

"Of course it is," she replied.

People were all around them. The square was crowded. It was an oddly private moment, despite that. You could be alone in a crowd, he thought. They stood close, to hear each other over the voices and the bells.

He said, "Forgive me, but this is not a time for you to go to Sauradia."

She nodded. He'd been afraid she'd resist. He had no way of stopping her, of course.

"I know," she said. A faint smile. "I'm stubborn but—"

"We have no idea what will happen, over that way."

"I know," she said again. "I think, if you are still willing, I'd like an escort after all. To Firenta, if you are really heading back, and then home to Varena from there. Is that all right?"

He hadn't expected this. "You know it is. I may try to persuade you to stay with me."

"I might for a little, then."

"As . . . a thank you?"

JELENA HEARD THE note in his voice. She said, and found it was true, "No, I'll stay because I like being with you."

He flushed. A scion of the Sardi family, wealthiest bankers of their day, ruling Firenta, one of them as High Patriarch . . .

He said, "I'm going to leave Boriforte to bring the army and the cannons. I'm riding home with half a dozen men. You'll come with us. Can you be ready by morning?"

She nodded. "But if you are going fast, I have to warn you, I don't ride well."

"I can teach you. I know horses."

"I believe you."

He smiled. But when he spoke it was gravely. "*Will* you not stay with me, Jelena? At least consider it? This is not an impulse."

She stood looking up at him. Someone jostled her and apologized, moving on.

"I think it is," she said, "but an impulse you really mean. And I also mean it when I say I like being with you. But that is not my destiny, or yours. It is also true that I will miss you when I go."

HE TRIED AGAIN, in Firenta, to induce her to stay. They spent nights together in the house where he placed her, but he knew it was only for a limited number of days—and nights. She gave him pleasure, and comfort, and he thought he might be offering the same to her. He had a sense, through that spring, that his life would be so much better for her presence.

He wasn't wrong, but it was equally a truth that the purpose and direction of *her* life was not to make his better, and in time he even came to understand that.

One morning, while Jelena was still in Firenta, he was meeting with his father and brother in the palace. His father looked up from ledgers—they all had numbers in front of them. "Tell me who she is," he asked, without warning.

Antenami didn't bother pretending he was unaware of what this meant. He was doing better with his father than he ever had in his life, there seemed to be some sort of understanding, as if shutters had been thrown open, letting in light.

"Do not worry. She is a healer, a pagan, but she will be leaving soon, home to Varena."

His brother looked up, smiling thinly. "A pagan?" Versano said. "That's useful. We can give her to the clerics. It is a good time to let people vent some rage against infidels."

Antenami kept his temper. He was discovering, among other things, that he didn't fear his own anger as much as once he had, but it did need controlling. He said, quietly, "I'd kill you first."

It was the calm tone, he thought, that caused their father to keep silent, watching and listening.

"What? For a pagan woman?"

"She saved my life," he said.

"Oh," said their father. "This is the one?"

"Yes."

"Then we all owe her a debt."

Versano grinned again. "Well, if Antenami is gritting his teeth and fucking her out of gratitude, he's paid any family debt, I'd say."

It was easier than one might have expected to put a remark like that into a . . . context of understanding. He did think he understood his brother better now.

He said, his tone measured, "You know, this may all be my fault. Father had to depend on you only. I was of no help in anything. I was distracted by the trivial, paid too little attention. But at some point, brother, it seems you became a mean little man. It ill becomes a Sardi. I've been remiss, but not any more. I'm going to keep an eye on that from now on."

He thought he saw, from the corner of one eye, that their father's mouth quirked briefly, before he lowered his head—as if to hide it—to his ledger.

"Fuck yourself," Versano said.

Antenami let his brother see his smile, then returned to his own work.

SHE KNEW SHE couldn't stay, interesting as Firenta was. It turned out she wasn't afraid of a bigger city after all. They even needed healers here, though there would be real rivalry with the physicians in a city so wealthy. She sensed she might be in some danger, in the season of Sarantium's fall.

War was suspended in Batiara, possibly elsewhere. Folco d'Acorsi had taken his company home, and the army of Remigio had also gone back, with the body of their lord. There could still be violence, many different kinds, Jelena thought.

With unpaid mercenary bands moving about, it would be genuinely reckless to be a woman on the roads alone. She told Antenami, after two months in the house he provided her, that she was ready to go home. Varena was just a stop, but one that mattered. He arranged for twenty men to escort her through the summer heat. She thought it was extravagant, far too many, but she didn't deny him the gesture. On the morning she left, he wept in the bedchamber they'd shared.

To her surprise, Jelena was close to tears as well. She kissed him with all the tenderness she had in her.

His men took her home. She had written her family; they were surprised to see her but not astonished. That was all right.

She stayed two years, living in the house where she'd grown up. It was a violent, uncertain time across the water. Asharite forces were enforcing submission all through Sauradia. Submission meant paying taxes, mostly, including a head tax unless a family converted to their faith. It could also mean you were killed if you were rebellious. The taxes mattered to the Asharites. Empires were expensive.

She claimed a room in their house as a treatment chamber: the one with the old artifacts and the mosaic floor with birds. They were well outside Varena's walls, but people began coming to her: from the city, from the countryside, from farther away after a while. She was skilled at what she did, had instincts and experience now.

One morning, in summer rain, she woke knowing it was time. She'd had a dream, but couldn't remember it. A few days later she kissed her mother and sisters goodbye and hugged her father hard, and she left her family and home and went to the coast. She took ship across the narrow sea for Sauradia. Things were better there, by report. Some merchants were even going to Sarantium again, although there was supposed to be an embargo. The city was called Asharias now. A change in the world, that. There were always changes, Jelena thought.

Her mother had asked her why she was doing this. She ought to have had a good answer by then, but she didn't. She repeated what she'd said to Antenami Sardi: *I have things to learn.*

It was true, at least; maybe a deep truth. She wasn't sure.

She had three guards with her. She'd made money in two years, saved some even after insisting on paying her parents for her lodging and treatment room. She could have contacted Antenami, even after two years, asked for another escort, but that felt wrong by then, an incurring of obligation with nothing offered in return, and she didn't do it. She had—everyone who knew her said it—a foolish measure of pride. *That* wasn't about to change, she had long ago realized.

She had no idea where she was going in Sauradia. She knew little about it, which became a bit frightening as she went east from the town where the ship docked, into remote, wild countryside. The trees were different, and many of the autumn wildflowers (it was autumn by then).

She could have stayed on the coast, gone south to Dubrava, by all accounts a splendid city, and one that wanted healers. She wasn't certain why she didn't do that, what she was looking for—or being summoned to.

One day, on a wide east-west road, the party of merchants she had joined with her guards came to a place where the forest was being cut back by loggers, up a slope to the north, and there, right there, Jelena felt a presence. Something huge, a power in the wood. She didn't understand. With that came a fear different from any she'd ever known. She thought she heard a roaring in the forest. It took her breath away. She was trembling.

She had to stop in the road to regain control of herself. Her guards stopped, too, looking at her. But a moment later she realized that what she really needed was to keep moving, to get *away* from this place. She had no idea what was in the forest, and no one else appeared to hear anything. It was only her. That had happened before, but not like this.

Her terror receded a little, and then a little more as they moved on. Jelena took a cloth and wiped cold sweat from her face. She felt her heartbeat gradually slow. She didn't look to her left, though, as they went. She kept her eyes ahead, aware of the trees but not looking at them.

Later that day they came to a small domed sanctuary of Jad, a low fence surrounding it. The merchants wanted to stop and pray, so did two of her guards. Jelena didn't go in. Not that day. She remained outside with the other guard.

Later, she would go inside that sanctuary and see what was on the dome—an old mosaic of the Jaddite god, shown gaunt, dark-bearded, dark-eyed, in the eastern fashion. It was powerful, mysterious, but he wasn't her god. Tesserae sometimes fell in there, the mosaic had been done long ago. She did wonder, at times, who had made it. The clerics didn't know. It was too old, placed overhead too far back in time. Things were always being lost, including knowledge.

That first day she and the guard strolled a little farther along the quiet road. It was a pleasant afternoon, leaves changing colour, not falling yet, a sharp brightness in the air. She remembered these things after.

Just beyond the sanctuary they came to a village, not walled or anything of the sort. It was just a hamlet, a place where charcoal burners, foragers, hunters, those who farmed the small plots she could see south of the road, could live together for protection, comfort, the warmth of being with other people. And be close to a sanctuary and a burial ground.

A dog came out to them. You needed to fear those generally, but this one was gentle, a golden colour, cautiously curious. Jelena extended a hand, despite the guard's quick warning, and the dog licked her fingers, then butted its head against her legs.

"You've made a friend," called a woman, smiling from a doorway.

"Seems that way," Jelena replied, smiling in return.

"I have soup heating, if the two of you are hungry," the woman said.

"That would be wonderful," Jelena said.

She never left that village for the rest of her days, which were long, despite all the violence that came into the world and did not pass them by, even there.

One night a very tall man with hard eyes and a sword wound came riding, because by then the hamlet was known to have a healer. She let him in to her house, quietly, because he was being hunted by the Asharites and his being there put them all at risk.

In her treatment room she cleaned and dressed his wound by lantern light. They spoke little. He thanked her, wouldn't stay. He knew he brought danger. He paid her and left in the dark.

He returned many times, always at night, always quietly, always hunted, injured again, or with an injured man, always going back to war, to his lifelong rebellion, when he left her. Some nights he did stay, however, lying with Jelena for comfort, in shared desire and need, for the shelter that she gave and took, the shelter that she was, all her days.

Shelter can be hard to find. A place can become our home for reasons we do not understand. We build the memories that turn into what we are, then what we were, as we look back. We live in the light that comes to us.

CHAPTER XVII

Brunetto was with me for most of the ride from the place where Teobaldo Monticola died. He has been with me for many of the rides and sea voyages of my life, though this is not the story of those journeys. It is my part in a tale of people and events long ago, when I was young and touched lives brighter than my own.

I have had a friend in him all these years. He knows, I think, how much I value that. I think of the morning we met, when I almost died by an arrow ordered by Adria's father, as I stood in the doorway of the building where I lived.

On the ride east that year I made him leave me where the road branched, several days from Remigio. I was doing something possibly death-seeking, and there was no need, no reason, for him to be with me for that. I gave him one of the two letters Folco had entrusted to me, for the duke in Seressa.

It was better, in any case, that I be alone, I'd decided. No one of any rank—I had a title and office on this mission for Seressa—was ever alone on a journey in Batiara. Arriving before the gates of Remigio by myself would carry a message.

I hoped so, at any rate. She had said she'd kill me if he died.

The grief (and fear) in her, in all of Remigio, would be raw, an open wound. They were unprotected now; the woman, the two children, the city. I was doing something foolish, going there. Brunetto had said so over and again as we rode. And I'd had no good reply. The thought of doing this had just *come* in the courtyard of the retreat. It felt right, but it also didn't feel as though it had been entirely my own decision. It had been given to me. I am not going to be able to explain this any better, even now, years after.

I saw Remigio on a windy morning, the sea beyond, grey and agitated. It sometimes seems to have always been windy in my recollection of those days. I know this is not true, but truth and memory do not easily dance together, as we say in Seressa.

I was, as I'd thought I would be, behind the news of what had happened, though many days ahead of the returning army of Remigio bearing the body of their lord.

They opened the gate for me and I rode through. I was a man alone, no threat, and a guard on the wall remembered me, confirmed I was who I said I was. Seressa shielded and defined me.

I was escorted to the palace. I saw signs of construction halted as we went. Everything would be halted in Remigio now. Except, perhaps, a drumbeat of fear that would surely be growing. The streets were eerily empty for a spring morning. I realized that the sanctuary and clock tower bells were not ringing. I wondered when they'd stopped. I felt the wind blowing from the sea.

They took my horse at the palace gates. I remembered the expansive, handsome room as they opened its door and I entered. I had not changed from my ride; I was dusty and dirty, I didn't know if that would be seen as disrespect, but it hadn't been my choice. I'd have happily gone somewhere to wash and change. There was no formal announcement of my presence as I entered, though they'd obviously been told I was here. A runner from the gates.

"Oh, look," said Ginevra della Valle, "Seressa honours us again."

A different voice from the last time, when everyone had heard her pleasure at seeing me—or her simulation of it. This time there was cold bitterness. I shivered, I remember.

She wasn't sitting on one of the two thrones. She stood in front of them in a long, black, belted gown, her hair coiled under a black lace cap. Near her, a step below, stood Gherardo Monticola, the brother with the twisted hand. The one who had never been a soldier, let alone a commander. Other skills, that one.

There had been forty people or more last time, now there were eight or ten, and as many armed guards. I could feel fear and anger, they weighted the room. It occurred to me that kneeling might be wise.

But I couldn't kneel. I was still a representative of Seressa's duke and council and we were stronger, far more important than Remigio. There were rules for this.

I have been in that situation once or twice since. Your role can limit and control you at risk of your life. It happens. Sometimes it *has* killed people.

I did bow. I came several steps nearer and did so again, to both of them. Straightening, I kept my head as high as I could. *You are Seressa*, I told myself.

They waited. No one spoke, so I had to. I said, carefully, "My sorrow is great, my lady, my lord. I was there, I saw him killed. I saw the man that murdered him also killed. I know they are bringing him home."

"We know it too," said Gherardo Monticola. "Why are you here?" He was brittle, sharp, grieving, angry.

It was a good question, of course. I had had some days to shape my answer. I am a man, I have found, who does better with time to think.

I said, "I have a letter to give you, and—if you allow it—a thought or two to share."

"Why would I want your thoughts?" Ginevra said.

The brother looked back up at her, briefly. No expression, but she did register his glance. She said, to him, "I told this one I'd kill him if Teobaldo died."

"Why him?" Gherardo asked.

"I had reasons," she replied.

I noticed a tall, exceptionally handsome man among the small number here. I knew who this was. I had never met him but his fame was widespread, and the stories about him. This would be Mercati, the artist. He'd been working here on various commissions. They had been building and decorating in Remigio. He was someone else Teobaldo and Folco had been fighting over—and he was wanted in Macera, and by the Patriarch, and Firenta. He was the artist of the day, and remained so for years after. We pursued him, too. Seressa was never going to lag when it came to emblems of status.

He wouldn't stay in Remigio now. Not so much the idea of any danger to him, but this was a man who went where he was paid, and money would become a problem here with no mercenary army led by their lord. Mercati was, I saw, observing us with a predatory attentiveness. We were rabbits in a field, he was a hawk overhead. He would *use* this day, I thought. We weren't a matter of sorrow or concern to this man, we were material for a painting or a sculpture. Our faces, postures, the mood in the room, the morning light from the windows.

Artists, I thought (for the first time but not the last), could be cold people.

Then I forgot about him, because Ginevra said, "I meant what I said to you, Guidanio Cerra. I had a vision of this."

I swallowed. "Had I been able to stop it, my lady, I'd have done so at whatever risk. I did try. I was . . . on the wrong side."

"The wrong side," she repeated bitterly. "That sounds accurate. People die for being on the wrong side, you know."

"My lady, I meant that when—"

"I know what you meant. You say you have a letter."

I wasn't about to die immediately, it seemed. It is hard to explain, but I really had thought, all the way to Remigio, even entering that room, that she might have me killed. Brunetto, trying to dissuade me from going there, had feared the same thing. It wasn't just me.

"I do," I said, and reached into my small purse for it.

"This is from . . . ?" It was Gherardo, deep-voiced, a voice that penetrated a room.

I drew a breath. "It is from Folco d'Acorsi."

Neither of them spoke. Nor did anyone else, of course. I saw the artist lean forward, as if to devour us with watchfulness. I stepped towards the dais and extended the letter in a hand that managed to be steady. Gherardo took it from me. He looked at Ginevra della Valle. She nodded. He opened it.

"You know what this is?" she asked me.

"I do, lady. I am to tell you that copies have gone to every major city-state in Batiara, and to the Patriarch."

"And this letter says?"

Gherardo was reading it. He had walked towards a window to see the words better. But she was looking at me. I remembered Folco dictating this to scribes in the retreat, with the bells still ring-ing. He had had me stand by him as he did, so I would know.

I said, in a very still room, "He declares that he and his father both knew that Teobaldo Monticola never harmed their sister and daughter Vanetta in any way. That she affirmed as much under oath before an altar, and she was also examined. He says he regrets that they did that, and he prays every day for forgiveness. It was decided by their father that it would be a useful thing in their conflicts with the Monticola to have a story of assault spread. When his sister died, there was no one who could refute it, and she had never gone against their father, in any case. Nor did he, though he knows he ought to have done so. It is a mark against his own soul, he declares.

"He then says in the letter that with it he guarantees the inde-pendence of Remigio and the safety of Teobaldo Monticola's widow and children for so long as he, Folco, lives. Any force, from a mer-cenary army to the Patriarch's to a city-state seeking to impose its will upon this city, will fight the army of Acorsi, and he swears this before Jad in sorrow and in memory of a lord dead too soon, and wrongly so."

Everyone knows about this letter now, of course; everyone knew it by the end of that same spring. It was a thunderclap in our world. But this was probably the first time the letter was read by a recipient and its contents spoken aloud.

I'd thought she might weep. She did not. She looked over at her brother-in-law. He nodded his head. Gherardo, I saw, was the one closer to tears.

"It is not enough," said Ginevra della Valle.

Which was not what anyone there, including me, had expected.

I said (I surprised myself), "Nothing will be enough, my lady. The dead cannot be brought back to us. We can try to ease the chaos of their loss."

"The chaos of their loss," she mocked. "How eloquent. And you would know what chaos means, Danino?"

The baby-name. Monticola's favourite for me. Perhaps deserved. I lowered my head. Adria entered my mind suddenly, right then, her death by a blade as well. Knowing I would never see her again in all my days, whenever they ended. I didn't say that, though. Not there. Whatever I might feel, it wasn't the same, and I knew it. Ginevra had lost a husband and this city a shield.

"That mercenary army attacking us could be our own," said Gherardo Monticola.

I looked at him. He was still by the window. "You don't trust their leaders?"

"I trusted their loyalty to my brother. But opportunities beget ambitions."

"But this letter . . . ?"

I date my own beginning as someone who might grow into an understanding of power and the world to that morning. I kept saying things that surprised me. I was *trying*, though. To understand, to affect things the best way. I wanted this to be, if not all right, at least not destruction.

Gherardo turned to Ginevra, his answer was to her, not me.

"This letter might check them."

"And therefore?" she asked. She was very pale.

"And therefore the military leaders, Gaetan especially, might accept a rank and fee to lead our forces. Some might leave, but others should stay, and continue to be our army, so there can be money for the city that way."

"There will likely be time to work that out," I said. "I do not think there will be any warring this year, not after . . ."

"After Sarantium. No. I agree." He looked at me. "It took courage to come here."

I said nothing. We both turned to the woman on the dais.

"It did," she said finally. "You mentioned other things you wanted to say."

Why would I want your thoughts? she'd said a moment ago.

Events can change as they unfold, sometimes quickly. Sometimes even for the good.

I said, "I believe Seressa will support Folco in this matter. We have no claim on Remigio, it is too far south, we don't need your harbour. Our wish will be for your independence, against the assertions of any other power. And for, perhaps, a renegotiated tariff on trade in a sea we keep safe at . . . at our great expense."

"Of course Seressa would speak of money immediately," she said. A hint of colour in her cheeks now.

"In exchange for what?" Gherardo said. "This added tariff?" He walked back, stepped up on the dais again, still below her.

"That is beyond my rank by a long way," I said. "But I am headed home and can carry a proposal from you."

"They will want me to marry a Seressini," Ginevra said. It was blunt, direct, world-weary. "Would you like to marry a widow, Guidanio of Seressa?"

"Don't play with him." Gherardo was not smiling. "None of that happens soon at all."

"No?" she said quietly. "You think not? You think the calculating and the ambitious will not be musing right now about the widow of Teobaldo Monticola, alone in Remigio, with children?"

"You are not alone," he said gravely. "And we have two offers of support already this morning."

She closed her eyes. When she opened them I thought again that I would see tears, but I did not. She said, "But I *am* alone, brother. He will not come back to me."

And I realized that although this was about power, and losses in power's game, it was also something else. There had been a great love here. And it was over now.

THEY DID NOT kill me, of course. I am sitting here and looking back (for many reasons) on my part in an old story. It is twenty-five years after, a night in Seressa, in the great chamber of the ducal palace. We are dealing with events happening now and I am thinking of yesterday. Of that time when it always seems to me there was a wind blowing. I'm thinking about, remembering, Adria, and Monticola, and Folco Cino, and Ginevra della Valle, who died only last year, still in Remigio, her older son ruling there now, commanding their army. They survived. I have survived. He looks like his father did, young Monticola. The other brother favours his mother. Their half-brother died in Sarantium.

On that day long ago, the day when I came to Remigio alone, there had been a knock at my door after dark.

They'd insisted I stay in the palace. Had assigned me a servant, but I'd dismissed him by that hour. I was alone. I'd asked for paper and ink and was at a handsome desk in a handsome room. I was writing down what had happened, and my thoughts, for the duke. Not to send; I would carry them home, but I wanted to set down everything said that morning, including by me. It was possible—entirely so—that I had overreached dangerously in my comments about Seressa offering protection. What was I, *who* was I, to speak for the republic? They knew here that I couldn't do that with any authority, but I had spoken with a formal position, with an office.

I looked up quickly when I heard the knock.

Unless it is a lover being waited for, in my experience, people do not generally welcome visitors at their door after dark. Of course I was afraid. The whole city was afraid. I would be leaving in the morning. I had said and done what I'd come to do. I did not want to be in Remigio when the army returned with the body of their lord. Brunetto had been insistent about that before I sent him home. Whatever people in power said or did, soldiers could have different ideas, and Monticola's men had loved him.

There was no point in *not* answering. It wasn't as if I could stop an assassin by not opening the door, pretending I wasn't there. I stood up, took a quick drink from the wineglass on the desk (very beautiful glass, everything in Remigio seemed to be), and I walked over and opened it.

"Tell me how he died," she said. "Tell me everything that happened."

I was speechless for a moment. She was in a deep blue robe and her hair was down now, late at night. She had probably been preparing for bed herself. I stepped back, wordless, and she came in, brushing past me.

I reminded myself that this was a woman who knew exactly what she was doing, especially with men, that grief would not change that, might even sharpen it. Her needs in a hard world, her children's needs.

I walked to the table and lamp and turned my notes over. She saw that, smiled a little. I took a second glass and poured wine for her. She shook her head and I set it down. I filled my own glass, then decided to set that down, as well.

She sat on the bed. I stood by the fire, which was low by then. I did not add a log, or stoke it.

I told her everything I could remember of that day. The confrontation in the field, coming near to a fight there, in a place they both seemed to remember. Then the bells, and three clerics approaching us with what they knew. Going back with them to the retreat. Praying, what followed.

The deaths that followed.

"I think . . ." I said, "I believe your husband was greatly affected by the thought of his son."

"Of course he was!" She made an impatient gesture. "What could be more obvious? It distracted him, weakened his attention."

"It may also have made him reckless, in anger."

"Grief, not anger," she corrected. "He was stronger when angry. One of those men. I have changed my mind. I will have wine."

I brought her the glass. Her fingers touched mine when she took it. It was deliberate, I knew it was. Had nothing at all to do with desire or interest—it was a stratagem. In some fashion, entirely marginal, done in passing, I was deemed worthy of enlisting as an ally.

I said, "I am an ally to you, my lady. I have no idea what it might mean, you know how small a figure I am. But I will do what I can."

"Why?"

Direct, as was her gaze in the half-light of the room.

I shrugged. "He was good to me. He was unlike anyone I ever met. He should not have died. You have been kind to me."

"You know I had my own reasons. Do not . . ."

"I know you did. I know you do now."

She smiled then. Sipped her wine. She said, "If you survive, Guidanio Cerra, you may grow into someone who matters."

"If you decide not to kill me here?"

She gestured again. "That would be foolish now, perhaps even wasteful."

"Perhaps," I said.

Her mouth crooked upwards again, a very little, but it did. She asked, "Do you really mean us well?"

Looking back, I can *see* myself changing in that time. For good or ill, someone moving through his days. I said, "I do. But I cannot speak for Seressa. I can only—"

"Of course you can't," she said.

After a moment I said, "I really was standing on the wrong side, my lady. Fortune, the chance of things. I heard a sound and I turned. Folco did, too."

"And Teo? What did he do?"

I was remembering. "His eyes were on Folco. Only him."

"Ah," said Ginevra della Valle. "They always were." She sipped from her wine again. "They watched each other, wherever they were. Folco killed his cousin?"

"Yes, my lady. And I know he loved him."

"And that is supposed to comfort me?"

I blinked. "I don't think anything I can say will do that. I am only telling what happened."

She was cradling the glass in both hands now, looking up at me. She said, "Tell me, have you ever comforted a woman, Danio?"

Nothing to do with desire, and I knew it. I was remembering (how could I not remember?) Adria Ripoli, wounded, on a dark stairway in Mylasia as I came down to her. But that sort of comfort wasn't what she meant.

"I have not, my lady. Not in grief. I am sorry." She made me feel very young.

"Perhaps you will one day," she said. "Depending where your life leads you. Kindness can be a good thing. Not always, but sometimes."

"You loved him," I said. I didn't make it a question.

She took longer to answer than I expected. "He sheltered me," she said. "From everything but losing him. So, yes."

She shrugged and stood up. She set the glass down and walked past me towards the door. I followed. She turned there and kissed me, lightly, on the cheek.

"Thank you. Be an ally," she said.

I nodded. It was hard to speak, suddenly.

She looked at me another moment.

"You will never be a bookseller now," she said. "You do know that?"

"I . . . I don't know what will happen when I return to Seressa."

"Of course you don't. But I'm right about this. Also, Danio, you will need to learn how to hide it better when you lie."

"I have not lied, my lady. Not here."

"I know. But still. Remember. Learn. It matters."

I have, in fact. I have learned to hide it better in the years that have run between that night and this one. It is all interwoven, memory, and what we become. We are always the person we were, and we grow into someone very different, if we live long enough. Both things are true.

She went out. I closed the door.

THAT SHOULD HAVE ended the night, ended my memories of that time in Remigio, as I sit here thinking about it in the great chamber of the Council of Twelve in Seressa now, so many years later. We are doing important things here tonight, but there have been delays and my mind has been wandering. There are reasons for that, of course. The woman who came to us here and who just walked out . . .

But on that other night in Remigio when I was young, after Ginevra della Valle kissed me on the cheek and left . . . well, if I were carefully *shaping* this story, guiding it with craft and purpose, my telling of that time would end there, and I'd have left to go home in the morning. But I'm only remembering, and though memory fails and lies, both, I know there was another knock at my door, not long after she left.

Life, the way events actually unfold, is not as precise or as elegantly devised as a storyteller can make it seem. There are moments that find us, like some stray dog on a country road, and they may not carry significance, only truth: that they happened, and we remember them.

I opened the door again. For whatever reason, I was not afraid that second time. I was curious, doubtful, sorrowing, but I no longer feared I would die that night.

The very tall man I had seen observing us all in the throne room stood in the corridor, holding his own lamp.

"I would like to paint you," said Matteo Mercati. "You don't have to fuck me, just sit for me."

"Now?" I said, stupidly.

He laughed. "Are we to talk in the doorway?"

I stood back and he came in. I saw him register the two wineglasses. He looked at me, a brief smile. "I saw her come and I waited. She didn't stay long."

"No," I said.

"You are wondering what this is about," he said. "I told you. I want to paint you, and came to say as much. Also, that you were brave, to come here. Your expression this morning as you entered the room is what I want to capture."

"I see," I said, though I honestly did not. I was dealing with too many things for this to register—or matter.

He walked across the room, a long stride, and picked up Ginevra's glass. "Do you want your wine?" he asked.

Again the assured smile. Such a confident, intelligent man. The pre-eminent painter of our day. Later, I would come to understand that *intelligent* understated the truth.

He didn't wait for my reply. He picked up my glass and walked it over to me. My papers on the desk were still upside down. I was glad of that. He seemed to be someone who noticed everything. *My expression this morning?*

"I'll be leaving in a day or two," he said. "They will not be concerned with art here now, and there will be no money. I prefer to be paid, generally."

I looked at him. "They might ask you to design his tomb."

He nodded. "Eventually. Not soon. All the things you mentioned will need to be worked through. There may be an attack, a siege, their own army might turn on them. Or some military leader who decides he'd like power here. She might have to marry such a man. Many uncertainties."

"Folco promised them protection. He's put it in writing."

"I heard. And if Rhodias offers him one hundred thousand serales a year for five years as the Patriarch's supreme commander, in exchange for letting them claim Remigio and its lovely harbour?"

It remains, to this day, one of the strangest conversations of my life. That he was in my room (*you don't have to fuck me*), the hour of night, that Ginevra had just left . . .

"I don't think he would take that offer. Not if it meant going back on his word. I think that's why it is in writing and being sent everywhere."

He shrugged. "You may know him better. But men change sides, often. I concede Folco is unusual. I've only painted in Acorsi once, and he was away for part of that time. But . . . to be honest, I'd take such an offer if I were him. And I'd make that offer if I were the Patriarch. Not that I'd ever be the Patriarch. Or a mercenary commander." He laughed at his own jest. "Still, this *is* a splendid harbour. Of course, Seressa and others might have something to say if all this comes to pass. It is interesting, isn't it?"

"Not tonight," I said.

His smile faded, then returned. Mercati was such a handsome man, all his life. He died a few years ago, in Rhodias, doing work for the newest Patriarch. All of Batiara mourned him—except, perhaps, some of the other artists. There is more room for them now, I suppose.

"You are judging me," he said that night. "I can hear it, see it. That's all right. I still would like to paint you. Where will I find you?"

"You know where. I'm in Seressa, I serve the council and the duke."

"Perhaps there, then, if you survive. It's a dangerous place, Seressa. I've always found it so. And damp. You do pay, however. There's that. Thank you for the wine."

He set it down and turned to leave, reclaiming the lamp he'd placed on a table.

"Wait," I said. "Why? Why do you want to paint me?"

He was prompt to reply. "You came into the room showing fear, trying not to, dealing with it. I would do your face this morning as that of Lekandros, when he went out to fight Malthias."

Old, old story. Shepherd boy and giant. Our emerging city-states were using it on murals, in statues, to depict themselves resisting tyranny. They were the young Lekandros at the beginning of his own rise to power.

"Someone wants one?" I asked.

"Clever you. Yes, Mylasia has asked, and met my price. They did overthrow their tyrant, after all."

He went out, leaving me with—again—an image of Mylasia where so much of my life began; Adria, the two of us, so young, going down together, out into the world, and apart.

HE NEVER PAINTED ME. Someone else posed for the famous sculpture he made for Mylasia. He did work on a celebrated tomb, but not Monticola's. It was also Mercati who painted Adria on horseback for the Ripoli Chapel in the great sanctuary in Macera.

I've been there, as an envoy on behalf of the Council of Twelve, and more recently as a member of it, after my second marriage gave me stature enough for the duke to arrange for me to be voted to the council. I saw what Mercati did in his rendering of Adria Ripoli. It is a magnificent painting. It looks nothing like her at all.

Both things can be true.

I cannot clearly say why those years when I met her and loved her (and will do so forever, it seems), when I met Folco and Teobaldo and Ginevra, and my own duke, why those years are so intensely within me always, not just tonight in our council chamber.

Perhaps it is true of every life, that times from our youth remain with us, even when the people are gone, even if many, many events have played out between where we are and what we are remembering.

I am so full of memories tonight from that time—when I was being changed, made and remade by those I met.

Folco died the same year Mercati did. His son rules in Acorsi, as Teobaldo's does in Remigio. There is no rancour between the families now. There is even talk that Teobaldo's son will marry Folco's granddaughter. Seressa has no strong views on this, either way; we discussed it and have decided.

Duke Ricci—he had been fully voted to office years before, when Lucino Conti died, after surviving longer than anyone could have expected—represented us at Folco's funeral, when he was interred in the chapel built in the sanctuary in Acorsi. The duke invited me to accompany him, although I was only an emerging merchant and adviser then. I hadn't yet remarried. He knew—he seems to always know so much—how important Folco d'Acorsi had been once in my life, however brief the time had been.

I saw Antenami Sardi there, leader of Firenta since his father's death and his brother's assassination. I remembered him as a fool met on the road to Bischio, then outside Adria's door at an inn. He wasn't a fool any more. Some men can change greatly. I don't think I have; I think I was just unformed, and took shape under guidance, given opportunity.

Sardi is my age, greyer than I am, heavier. We spoke briefly at the funeral, mostly about horses. He actually remembered me from that time in Bischio, which was its own surprise. I told him that I still recalled his magnificent horse and even its name: Fillaro. I have no idea why I remember that. He grew misty-eyed, hearing it.

Sardi had, I learned from the duke on the ride home, travelled with a merchant party to Asharias (which is what Sarantium is called now). There was a confusing story, about the man halting his journey at a sanctuary along the route, staying several days at a hamlet nearby.

It was possible, said the duke, as we rode through a windless autumn day, that the man had matured but remained an eccentric. Still, Firenta was flourishing under his guidance, you needed to give Antenami Sardi credit for that, he said.

As for me, there is no mistaking it, I have done well in our dangerous world and city. Well enough to have those who seek my favour and support, and others who hate me. My second wife dislikes me, but it is mutual and we are good at appearing cordial in public when it is necessary—as it often is here, given my office.

My first wife I came to love a great deal. She gave us a daughter before dying two years later along with our second child. I honour her memory and my love for my daughter is extravagant, and I know it is returned. I have that joy. Not everyone does. That first marriage was also arranged for me, but those can sometimes ripen into caring, and ours did. There was laughter in our house, our bedchamber, a sense that the world was a place worth exploring together. We were young, that makes a difference.

I am judged a too reflective, overly serious man by many. My wives and friends have known otherwise. My first wife enjoyed it, shared a manner with me in private. I was lucky in that. My second, so much better born than I, finds me undignified when I am whimsical or frivolous. Probably she is correct, given my age.

My second marriage is a consequence of the duke wanting me on the council to support him. My second wife's prominent father owed him a great deal of money. My marriage was the price of forgiving the debt. She has never forgiven her father, or me. I can understand that. I am a tradesman's son. My being voted to the Council of Twelve did please her, however, and I have made a great deal of money, and have helped her father, too.

We have no children together. I do not live with love. Not everyone does.

It is strange, how tangled in memory I am tonight. Or perhaps not so strange. The woman who has just walked from this room through the smaller side door, beside the man with whom she will spy for us in Dubrava, reminds me of Adria so much. And I know this woman's father. And I killed her grandfather.

I've only killed two men in my life. Both in Mylasia.

Given this, I suppose it is no wonder that I am sitting at the council table on a spring night and also reliving those years long ago.

What makes one person remind you of another? They didn't look at all alike. This woman was small, delicately formed, more sorrowful when we met than Adria had ever been. She'd been in a Daughters of Jad retreat inland from us, sent there to hide a family shame by her father—who was Erigio Valeri of Mylasia.

She'd borne a child in the retreat; it was taken away at birth. I'd asked, because it might be useful, but they hadn't answered—so I had no idea where the child had gone. We had been sent a report by the Eldest Daughter that they'd received someone again with spirit, intelligence. A woman who might be willing to be of use, in exchange for freedom from life in a retreat. And, of course, a donation from Seressa to them.

We had done this before.

I'd been the man sent by Duke Ricci to talk to her, Brunetto with me. The duke, who knew so much, did *not* know I had killed a Valeri. No one knew that. Riding out to the retreat to meet this woman had begun a circling of time for me, or call it the past cutting into the present like a blade.

She was as she'd been reported to be. Grieving, angry. Unwilling to submit mildly to her family's choice for her life. Her father's choice. I told her what we proposed, what we'd want of her, and went away.

We were back two days after. She agreed to be a spy for Seressa. Said it directly, using the word. We rode with her to the city. She rode wonderfully well, appearing to rediscover the *idea* of joy if not yet the thing itself, riding beside me to Seressa on a good horse.

Perhaps that had been what started me thinking of Adria, who also rejected the choices, the limits the world gave her, who was not allowed to grow up and become what she might have been.

I wanted this woman I didn't know at all, this Leonora Valeri, to have those chances. I had no idea if she would. We were not offering her much, and there was considerable danger. People died as spies. But it was a better life than those walls, she had decided.

And now she has left the chamber, a vivid presence gone. I can see that the duke, too, recognized something in her. His manner when she was here . . .

Even with eyesight fading he registers more than anyone I know. He will leave us soon. He speaks of an isle in the lagoon, conversations with holy men and philosophers, the rituals of prayer. I have promised to visit him when he does that. I am not ready for him to go. Meanwhile, he has set a number of things in motion tonight, and we will see where they lead. He likes to do that. He did it with me twenty-five years ago, and here I am. Here I am.

There is a young artist yet to appear before us tonight, we are waiting for him, there is some delay. It is another scheme, another spy we want to send out—who may perhaps also become an assassin. We always have schemes here in Seressa. No one trusts us.

The lights the servants have set flicker and dance around this great oak table in the night. The chamber is echoing and vast, running into darkness by the walls. It is meant, by its grandeur, to awe. The portraits of the dukes of Seressa look down. They are hard to see just now, set very high up.

It is brighter in my memories. I am not old. I have places I want to see, dreams I may shape and realize. I might find love before I go to the god.

I knew, once, a woman diamond bright, and two men I will not forget. I played a part in a story in a fierce, wild, windblown time. I do have that. I always will. I am here and it is mine, for as near to always as we are allowed.

ACKNOWLEDGMENTS

Some books emerge with a clear origin story, others, including this one, have strands that interweave to produce the beginnings of a novel. One such strand here was reading and thinking about the feud between the Montefeltro and Malatesta families in fifteenth-century Italy (and before). I was engaged by the fact that the great military figures at the apex of the clash (Federico and Sigismondo, who inspired my Folco and Teobaldo) were lords of *small* cities, minor ones. Wealthy enough, due to their large fees as mercenaries, but never truly powerful compared to the city-states they and their armies served.

I began reading into the *condottieri* warfare of that time. There are useful sections in *War in European History*, by Sir Michael Howard. I learned most from *Mercenaries and Their Masters: Warfare in Renaissance Italy*, by Michael Mallett, a classic in that field. I found *Vendetta*, by Hugh Bicheno, focusing on the feud between the two families mentioned, to be very useful, offering some correctives to received wisdom, which had largely treated Montefeltro as good and Malatesta as evil. (The great Piero della Francesca painted both, incidentally.)

Working with this setting again led me to reread a book I'd much admired when researching *Tigana* a long time ago: Lauro Martines's *Power and Imagination: City-States in Renaissance Italy.* Martines also has a much more recent work called *Furies,* which covers a wider period and deals with the terrible collateral damage of European warfare, civilians caught up in the endless fighting: sieges, famines, lawlessness associated with campaigns just about every spring. It is a powerful, compassionate, recommended work.

For the virtually unchecked violence of some of the lords of Italian city-states there is a great deal of evidence. I can say that my "Beast" falls nowhere near the top of the scale, unfortunately. John Addington Symonds, writing stylishly in the nineteenth century, has more than a little of censorious, shocked English attitudes to the Italians, but casts a useful light, nonetheless, in his *Renaissance in Italy: The Age of the Despots.* It may be worth noting that he is of the pro-Federico, anti-Sigismondo party.

On the brighter side of the period, rereading Kate Simon's very accessible *A Renaissance Tapestry* on the Gonzaga of Mantua reminded me of the school there, founded by Vittorino da Feltre, much loved in his time, to which the children of craftsmen *were* sometimes admitted. History as a scaffold for invention.

At the end of the 1980s, we were living and writing for a time between Florence and Siena and one day in Siena stumbled upon one of the victory parades for the district that had won the previous Palio race. It was memorable, and I've been fascinated by that race ever since. Sometimes it takes a long time for an interest to find its way into a novel, but here we are. Several books were useful and allowed me to shape my version of it inspired by elements of the real one. Heywood Williams's *Palio and Ponte* was especially helpful, including mention of a female rider.

A number of historians have thoughtfully (and sometimes dramatically) examined the lives of women in the Renaissance, with a focus—in part because there is more *material*—on some notably independent or courageous aristocrats. Among them, I found much of note in Elizabeth Lev's *The Tigress of Forli*. There is also a strong chapter on the wives of Federico and Sigismondo, and on court women in general, in *The Eagle and The Elephant*, by Maria Grazia Pernis and Laurie Schneider Adams.

Medieval and Renaissance medicine remains an interest, and obviously plays a role in this book. I've mentioned being aided by several texts before, but a new one this time around was Toni Mount's *Medieval Medicine*.

Carole Collier Frick's *Dressing Renaissance Florence* was very interesting, sometimes in unexpected ways. Chiara Frugoni's books on daily life are filled with detail: *Daily Life in a Medieval City* and *Book, Banks, Buttons*.

As always, we may write our books alone but a great many people must be present, before, during, and after, supporting and sustaining the work. I'm grateful to my publishers and editors, Nicole Winstanley and Lara Hinchberger in Toronto, Claire Zion and Rebecca Brewer in New York, and Oliver Johnson in London. It is difficult to convey how much I value their enthusiasm for this novel. Claire read *A Brightness Long Ago* while travelling in Tuscany. She wrote me that she thought she *saw* where Jelena's cottage in the countryside would be.

My agents, John Silbersack, Jonny Geller, and Jerry Kalajian, have all been friends for a long time, as well as trusted colleagues, and I am deeply appreciative. Catherine Marjoribanks, who has copyedited *nine* of my books now, offered her usual blend of precision, humour, and quick, incisive replies to last-minute queries. Lisa Campbell once again helped me chase down articles I was having trouble accessing. A librarian is a splendid resource. Martin Springett, a dear friend, added important details to his map for *Children of Earth and Sky* to clarify the web of towns and cities in the middle parts of Batiara. Deborah Meghnagi and Alec

Lynch continue to monitor and coordinate brightweavings.com, the authorized website on my work.

Finally, as always, my enduring love and deepest gratitude belong to Laura, Sam, Matthew, and to Sybil, my mother.

GUY GAVRIEL KAY is the internationally bestselling author of thirteen previous novels, including *Children of Earth and Sky*, *Under Heaven*, and *River of Stars*. He has been awarded the International Goliardos Prize for his work in the literature of the fantastic and won the World Fantasy Award for *Ysabel* in 2008. In 2014, he was named to the Order of Canada, the country's highest civilian honour. His works have been translated into thirty languages.

The body of *A Brightness Long Ago* has been set in Adobe Garamond. Designed for the Adobe Corporation by Robert Slimbach, the fonts are based on types first cut by Claude Garamond (c.1480–1561). Garamond was a pupil of Geoffrey Tory and is believed to have followed classic Venetian type models, although he did introduce a number of important differences, and it is to him that we owe the letterforms we now know as "old style." Garamond gave his characters a sense of movement and elegance that ultimately won him an international reputation and the patronage of Francis I of France.